I0761748

PRAISE FOR J.T. ELLISON

Last Seen

"My favorite kind of thriller—dark family secrets, high-stakes mystery, and a shocked daughter who will stop at nothing to determine the truth. Wherever J.T. Ellison goes, I want to follow."

—Lisa Gardner, #1 *New York Times* bestselling author of *Still See You Everywhere*

"In *Last Seen*, J.T. Ellison weaves a gripping tale of family secrets, broken trust, and the slippery nature of memory. When Halley James learns her mother was murdered—not killed in an accident—her search for the truth leads to a deceptively perfect town hiding dark secrets. With twists that keep you guessing, this masterfully crafted thriller showcases Ellison at the top of her game."

—Liv Constantine, *New York Times* bestselling author of *The Last Mrs. Parrish*

"Darkly original and bursting with hold-your-breath suspense, *Last Seen* by J.T. Ellison is a haunting deep dive into a harrowing crime, buried memories, and one woman's obsession to discover the truth no matter the consequences. At the top of her game, Ellison's expert storytelling is on full display—*Last Seen* is a must-read for thriller fans."

—Heather Gudenkauf, *New York Times* bestselling author of *The Overnight Guest* and *The Perfect Hosts*

"If someone lies about the things that matter most to you, it's your right, isn't it, to go after the truth? So, bravo to fearless forensic scientist Halley James for daring to peel away the layers of deceit in this dark, twisty, and gripping thriller that grabs you, pulls you in, and keeps you guessing until you reach the final page with your heart pounding in your chest."

—Kate White, *New York Times* bestselling author of *The Last Time She Saw Him*

A Very Bad Thing

"[T]his novel rewards readers who pay close attention to the clues. A fun, fast-paced thriller that keeps secrets until the very last page."

—*Library Journal*

"Once again, J.T. Ellison hits it out of the park. *A Very Bad Thing* is twisting, juicy, suspenseful, and heartfelt—a single-sitting read. I couldn't put it down."

—Meg Gardiner, #1 *New York Times* bestselling author

"*A Very Bad Thing* is a wonderfully smart, twisty psychological thriller infused with dark secrets, high drama, and edgy tension. Wow, what a ride!"

—Jayne Ann Krentz, *New York Times* bestselling author

"J.T. Ellison delivers yet again. *A Very Bad Thing* sizzles from page one. Moving at breakneck speed, Ellison's latest explores the complex relationships between mothers and daughters and delivers twists and turns that make for an irresistible read."

—Lori Roy, Edgar Award–winning author of *Lake County*

"A world-famous author, a devoted daughter, a persistent journalist, and one shocking murder—master storyteller J.T. Ellison has penned another winner to keep us up at night. In *A Very Bad Thing*, Ellison delves into the complex nature of mother-daughter relationships, the price of fame, and the danger of long-held secrets in this addictive, impossible-to-put-down thriller. Loved it!"

—Heather Gudenkauf, *New York Times* bestselling author of *The Overnight Guest*

"J.T. Ellison once again crafts a deliciously suspenseful mystery with the pacing of a top-notch thriller. Just when you think Ellison can't top herself, she does, and *A Very Bad Thing* proves it. Compelling characters, a twisty mystery, and a propulsive story, I savored the book through the very last page."

—Allison Brennan, *New York Times* bestselling author of *You'll Never Find Me*

It's One of Us

"A smart, taut, mind-blowing thriller full of heartbreak and betrayal that moves along at breakneck speed. *It's One of Us* is a force to be reckoned with. I've always been a fan, but Ellison has outdone herself with this one. Readers will be obsessed!"

—Mary Kubica, *New York Times* bestselling author of *Just the Nicest Couple*

"Betrayal, obsession, and familial ties that bind create a tension-filled story with an intriguing theme. Readers will race through the pages to an end they didn't see coming."

—*Library Journal*, starred review

"A heart-stoppingly tense thriller about the price of secrets and the layers behind every marriage."

—Ruth Ware, *New York Times* bestselling author of *The Woman in Cabin 10*

"J.T. Ellison has done the impossible by crafting a riveting domestic thriller full of twists and turns, but also heart and emotion. You'll root for her heroine Olivia Bender every step of the way, as soon as a knock on the door brings shocking news that threatens her marriage and her world. You won't be able to put this novel down!"

—Lisa Scottoline, *New York Times* bestselling author of *Loyalty*

"Expertly explores the intensely complex emotions surrounding infertility, loss, and marriage. Throw in murder, a vivid cast of characters, and shocking secrets, Ellison masterfully mines the human heart in this treasure of a thriller that will keep readers turning the pages long into the night."

—Heather Gudenkauf, *New York Times* bestselling author of *The Overnight Guest*

"J.T. Ellison is one of my favorite authors. I eagerly await everything she writes. And in *It's One of Us* she is at the very top of her formidable game. Don't miss this layered, emotional, and twisting thrill ride."

—Lisa Unger, *New York Times* bestselling author of *Secluded Cabin Sleeps Six*

"Beautifully written and impossible to put down, master storyteller J.T. Ellison will have you spellbound with this deeply layered psychological thriller. Immersive and propulsive, *It's One of Us* keeps you turning pages with an ending you'll never see coming. I loved it!"

—Liv Constantine, bestselling author of *The Last Mrs. Parrish*

"An extremely compelling thriller shot through with twists and turns, a strong emotional pulse, and heartfelt exploration of the pressures of marriage and starting a family. Impressive and gripping."

—Gilly Macmillan, internationally bestselling author of *The Long Weekend*

"Brings all the twists, chills, and thrills I expect from the preternaturally gifted Ellison, and it's also an emotionally resonant read that I can't wait to recommend to my book club. The secrets snarled in the threads of an unraveling marriage and a heroine who wholly won me over put this one on my keeper shelf—you are going to love it!"

—Joshilyn Jackson, *New York Times* bestselling author of *With My Little Eye*

"One of the most compelling psychological suspense stories I've read in years."

—Jacquelyn Mitchard, #1 *New York Times* bestselling author of *The Deep End of the Ocean*

"This gripping, breathless thriller adds an incredibly unique premise and delivers a novel that's also a deeply poignant story about our deepest desire for love, family, and happiness."

—Hannah Mary McKinnon, internationally bestselling author of *Never Coming Home*

"*It's One of Us* is an emotional and thrilling psychological journey through the shadows of the human heart. Just when you think you know what's coming, prepare to gasp with each new revelation. Through multiple fascinating points of view, layers of secrets, lies, love, and loss are revealed. I did not put this book down until the last unexpected and breathless page. Unpredictable, intense, and riveting, J.T. Ellison is at her heart-stopping best."

—Patti Callahan Henry, *New York Times* bestselling author of *Once Upon a Wardrobe*

"The perfect mix of edge-of-your-seat tension, deep emotion, and impeccably developed characters, J.T. Ellison's latest is a masterclass in storytelling. Secrets and lies, love and loss mix flawlessly to create a novel that touches every single emotion. Fans of Lisa Jewell and Ruth Ware will flock to *It's One of Us*, and book clubs won't be able to stop talking about it. Five dazzling stars."

—Kristy Woodson Harvey, *New York Times* bestselling author of *The Wedding Veil*

"An extraordinary, unpredictable, absolutely riveting thriller and a fiercely insightful, emotional journey, this is psychological suspense at its most enthralling and intense."

—Jayne Ann Krentz, *New York Times* bestselling author

"Secrets and lies abound, relationships are tested, and the twists keep coming. Ellison outdid herself, a master storyteller. This is a must read, especially the author's note at the end, which gutted me."

—Kerry Lonsdale, *Wall Street Journal*, *Washington Post*, and Amazon Charts bestselling author

Her Dark Lies

"J.T. Ellison weaves the old and the new, art and history, mystery and love story into one stunning tapestry of a novel. Elegant, propulsive, and utterly unputdownable, *Her Dark Lies* is the work of one of our most talented thriller writers at the very top of her game."

—Lisa Unger, *New York Times* bestselling author of *Confessions on the 7:45*

"I loved *Her Dark Lies*. A great modern gothic. Ellison outdid herself—what an ending!"

—Catherine Coulter, #1 *New York Times* bestselling author of *Vortex*

"Stunning. *Her Dark Lies* is a gorgeously atmospheric thriller, a brilliant contemporary twist on a beloved classic. Beautifully written, psychologically chilling, and gaspingly surprising, J.T. Ellison proves she's our new Daphne du Maurier."

—Hank Phillippi Ryan, *USA Today* bestselling author of *The First to Lie*

"Mesmerizing . . . Fans of Daphne du Maurier's *Rebecca* will want to check out this compulsively readable tale."

—*Publishers Weekly*, starred review

"A compulsive, twisty thriller that is so deftly crafted, you're left wondering who to trust. A highly addictive and deliciously tense read, *Her Dark Lies* is fast paced and full of suspense. This book is a stunner! Readers are going to love it. I'm a forever fan, and I want more."

—Kerry Lonsdale, *Wall Street Journal* and *Washington Post* bestselling author

Good Girls Lie

"[A] high-tension thriller . . . Alternating points of view raise the suspense, blurring the lines between what's true and false."

—*Publishers Weekly*, starred review

"Ellison has created a complex, convoluted plot that mystery fans will savor."

—*Library Journal*

"*Good Girls Lie* is an entertainingly twisted coming-of-age tale, pitting the desire for privacy against the corrosiveness of secrecy and taking an often harrowing look at how wealth and power can lull recipients into believing they're untouchable."

—*BookPage*

Tear Me Apart

"Outstanding . . . Ellison is at the top of her game."

—*Publishers Weekly*, starred review

"A compelling story with a moving message."

—*Booklist*

"Well paced and creative . . . An inventive thriller with a horrifying reveal and a happy ending."

—*Kirkus Reviews*

Lie to Me

"Exceptional . . . Ellison's best work to date."

—*Publishers Weekly*

"Comparisons to *Gone Girl* due to the initial story structure are expected, but Ellison has crafted a much better story that will still echo long after the final page is turned."

—*Associated Press*

"Immensely readable . . . lush."

—*Booklist*

"Fans of Paula Hawkins, A.S.A. Harrison, Mary Kubica, and Karin Slaughter will want to add this to their reading list."

—*Library Journal*

"Wonderful . . . A one-more-chapter, don't-eat-dinner, stay-up-late sensation."

—Lee Child, #1 *New York Times* bestselling author

"Fans of *Gone Girl* will gobble up this thriller about a marriage from hell, which moves at a blazing-fast pace and smoothly negotiates more twists and turns than the back roads of Tennessee. J.T. Ellison will keep you guessing every step of the way to the surprise ending!"

—Lisa Scottoline, *New York Times* bestselling author of *One Perfect Lie*

"A wickedly good thriller about a picture-perfect marriage that is anything but, *Lie to Me* has it all: murder, lies, and betrayal. J.T. Ellison will have readers hanging onto the edge of their seats with her latest cunning tale."

—Mary Kubica, *New York Times* bestselling author of *The Good Girl*

LAST SEEN

ALSO BY J.T. ELLISON

Stand-Alone Novels

A Very Bad Thing

It's One of Us

Her Dark Lies

Good Girls Lie

Tear Me Apart

Lie to Me

No One Knows

Taylor Jackson Series

All the Pretty Girls

14

Judas Kiss

The Cold Room

The Immortals

So Close the Hand of Death

Where All the Dead Lie

Field of Graves

Whiteout (novella)

Blood Sugar Baby (novella)

The Wolves Come at Night

Samantha Owens Series

A Deeper Darkness

Edge of Black

When Shadows Fall

What Lies Behind

A Brit in the FBI Series

Coauthored with Catherine Coulter

The Final Cut

The Lost Key

The End Game

The Devil's Triangle

The Sixth Day

The Last Second

LAST SEEN

J.T. ELLISON

THOMAS & MERCER

This is a work of fiction. Names, characters, organizations, places, events, and incidents are either products of the author's imagination or are used fictitiously. Otherwise, any resemblance to actual persons, living or dead, is purely coincidental.

Published by Thomas & Mercer, Seattle

www.apub.com

EU product safety contact:
Amazon Media EU S. à r.l.
38, avenue John F. Kennedy, L-1855 Luxembourg
amazonpublishing-gpsr@amazon.com

ISBN-13: 9781662520372 (hardcover)
ISBN-13: 9781662520389 (paperback)
ISBN-13: 9781662520365 (digital)

Cover design by Ploy Siripant
Cover image: © Amazing Aerial Premium / Shutterstock;
© ArenaCreative / Adobe Stock; © Michael Pointner / Unsplash

Printed in the United States of America
First edition

For Jameson

PART ONE

We can easily forgive a child who is afraid
of the dark;
the real tragedy of life is when men are
afraid of the light.
—Author Unknown

PROLOGUE

I have never run so fast before.

The woods are thick and impenetrable to the eye, and I stumble through, desperate for a hint of light. Trees reach out with long branches to impede my path. Rocks shift and make me skid. Bushes appear from nowhere, sharp things scratching me open. More than once, my ankle turns, sending searing pain through my body. But I cannot stop. If I stop, I will be dead. Maybe here, under the sky and moon. Maybe there, in the vast darkness.

I have to get away. This is my only chance.

I'm panting, but I must be quiet, breathe through my nose, and pray he can't hear me crashing through the trees. I have a head start, only just, but his footsteps come anyway, their rhythm a corrupt heartbeat. I veer off to the right, then to the left, following no discernible path, trying to throw him off. He is hunting me, I know he is, back there with that look on his face—the twist of his lips, the shine in his dark eyes, the perverse joy in being the cause of my fear.

The trees open into a meadow, and now I can pour on the speed, but my lungs are about to burst. I trip, fall, rolling. Scramble back up. My palms sting; wetness and gravel. I can smell the blood, and other, darker things.

In the deep of night, without much moonglow, the field is not easy to traverse. I stumble again, and again, skin knees, shins, shoulders, but there is darkness at the end of the meadow. A cleaner view. Not light, but infinity. The cliff is ahead. If I can make the cliff . . . then what?

A choice.

I check the bandage wrapped around my chest. It is warm and wet. Blood still seeps from the deep cut. He likes to watch me bleed. Can he follow my path by the scent alone? Am I simply a wounded deer, dragging itself to its inexorable end? He will find me. He will take me back to that hell . . . Panic flows through me anew, and I start off again but can feel the weakness in my legs. My lungs hurt; my body is fighting me. It was not meant to run this far, this fast. But I stay upright, push on, because not to is worse. A fate worse than death, isn't that what they say? If he catches me . . . I don't want to think about that. I don't know how long he's had me captive. Weeks, certainly. Perhaps months? The gentle swell of my belly should tell time better than any watch, but without a calendar, without scans and blood tests, there's no way to know for sure. Long enough to mark me, inside and out. Too long.

The darkness expands, and I realize I'm closing in on the cliffside.

To my left, round twin lights appear, bobbing in the darkness. A car. A car is coming. That means there is a road. There is another escape. I turn and run toward freedom, forgetting all the pains, all the fatigue. There is nothing in me now but hope. A car means a road means a town means help.

The hand on my arm appears from nowhere, yanking me to a halt, almost pulling my shoulder from the socket.

"Where do you think you're going?" he asks, dark amusement in his tone. He isn't even out of breath. As if he's flown here on dark wings, like the demon he is.

Hope vanishes with his closed fist against my jaw. Pain explodes, and I fall to the ground. I try to cry out, but nothing comes. My mouth won't work. Won't open. He covers me with his body, his hand tight against my throat. His weight, his horrible weight, pushing me down to the dirt, hiding me in the long grass.

The car whizzes by, and with it, my last chance.

The woods are silent and hungry, waiting, listening. There is nothing now except the panting of my breath and the singing joy of his black heart. I can hear it pounding above my ear. That, and other things. Arousal, to start. As if he's enjoying this. Of course he is. He's won.

He pulls me to my feet and starts the long, slow march back. I don't help, make him drag me. The pain in my face makes tears flow down my cheeks. I think my jaw is broken and I know my tongue is cut; I'm gurgling blood. I spit and dribble and stay limp until he jerks me upright and in a low, menacing voice explains to me in detail exactly what he's going to do if I don't cooperate. By the third sentence of description, I've found my feet and stiffened my spine.

It's not about what he'll do to me. It's what he'll do to them.

MONDAY

CHAPTER ONE
HALLEY

2017
Washington, DC

"You're fired."

Halley James crosses M Street on her way home from her office in Foggy Bottom, heart pounding. She is in shock. Two words, and her entire world has blown apart.

It is midmorning on a sunny Monday, and the streets are calm. Everyone is already at work, or at school, or in the shops. The lunch rush hasn't started. The few cars behave, not beeping and cursing and rushing. She is alone, marching up the hill, the two words from her boss's mouth replaying with every step.

You're fired you're fired you're fired.

She'd taken special care with her appearance today. Her good-luck suit, her dark, unruly hair wound into a tight bun at the nape of her neck. Her mother's pearls.

A fresh start. A well-earned, long-overdue promotion. And instead, a dead end.

She's not crying, not yet. No doubt the tears are lodged inside, still trying to figure out what the hell just happened. She isn't much of a crier anyway; she is a scientist, too cool and logical to waste time with tears. But she can feel them threatening. They come when she is frustrated, and today qualifies.

She stops at the light on Wisconsin Avenue. Her hands are shaking.

The left looks so strange without her wedding rings. She took them off before her shower this morning and didn't put them back on. The sorrow of that nearly overwhelmed her. But she knows she needs to get accustomed to not seeing the flash of diamonds and platinum, losing the acceptance of others when they immediately know her status as a married woman. Of course, she's spent years as a married woman, and nothing else. A decade of waiting, of trying to be a good wife, of trying to take the next logical step with a man who she found out too late does not want what she does from their life together.

Ten years down the drain. All that's left is two signatures on a long piece of blue-backed paper to officially separate her from him, to divest their lives. So ironic; the very day she was supposed to be starting over, launching her new life as a single woman, this happens.

She hasn't decided when she's going to tell everyone. Well, she'll have to share her new address with Human Resources, obviously, so they can update her file for the official termination package. But her dad, her friends, Theo's family . . . She made this decision to walk away from her marriage, and telling people they've decided to go their separate ways makes it seem too real.

And now, the double whammy. Can she go through the formalities of ending things with Theo if she doesn't have a job?

She doesn't have a *job*.

She's still trying to wrap her head around the one-eighty that just happened. Today was meant to be celebratory. Moving up to lab director was a decade-long ambition. Everyone knew she was about to get the gig. Her boss had been hinting at the bump up for weeks. She'd been counting on the extra money to get her through the separation and divorce. She scored the furnished basement apartment of her friends' town house in Georgetown and was going to propose a short-term lease so she could have a safe place to live while she gets on her feet. It's dark, and it's small, but it is well appointed and, more importantly, missing her husband. She officially left three weeks ago, leaving him with the house in McLean, their dog, Charlie, the art they've collected on various vacations, and the extra room she's been trying to convince him for the past five years would be a great nursery.

She needs this money to house herself, feed herself, start over.

And now . . . a terrifying reversal of fortune.

The light turns green. Yellow. Red again. She is frozen on this corner, unable to move forward, and finding it impossible to go backward.

She ducks into the coffee shop to her left instead. Sits at a blond oak table. Retraces the morning, the week, the month, looking for a word, a sign, that she was about to be blindsided. She can find nothing.

This morning, high on the knowledge she was about to get the promotion she'd been expecting, she'd taken off her rings, determined to become this new person, to open this new chapter. She'd entered the building, swiped her pass, and made her way to the lab, just like always. The sameness of her days is appealing. She loves the lab. Loves her work.

Her admin, Barbara, waved at her. "Ivan is looking for you."

Ivan Howland, her boss, the founder and CEO of their company, the National Investigative Sciences Laboratory, the NISL. Nothing unusual there.

"We have a meeting at ten. He wants me now instead? Why?"

Barbara shrugged. "I don't know, Halley. He's in his office."

So she'd walked the hallway, her block-heeled pumps clacking on the marble. Knocked on his door, like she had a hundred times before. Put on a huge grin.

"Morning!"

He'd looked up—was that fear in his eyes?—and waved her in. "Close the door."

She had. Sat in the leather-and-chrome chair across from his desk. Raised a brow. When he didn't speak, she finally asked, "Everything okay?"

Ivan heaved a huge sigh. "Halley, there's no good way to say this. The investigation into the ransomware attack last month has concluded. Though we've determined this was not a state-sponsored action, simply an international group out to ransom the data, the link that allowed the hackers into the system came from your computer. I'm afraid I have to let you go."

"Excuse me?"

"The board insists. There has to be a head to roll, and you . . . Well, I hate this, I really do. But it's out of my hands. You're fired."

"Ivan. Surely you're joking."

"I wish I was. You're being let go with cause, too, because the board feels this action was in violation of your contract, so unfortunately there will be no severance. HR will be in touch with all the information you need so you can apply for unemployment and COBRA for your insurance. But I'm afraid I have to take your pass, your keys to the lab, any physical notes you've taken on the current work, and you need to leave the premises. Now."

Her entire life unraveling because she clicked on a link in an email? Impossible. This wasn't happening. Recognition dawned. This was an excuse. It wasn't just that phishing email, was it? Last year, she'd reported one of the lab managers for unceasing sexual harassment. Of her, yes, but of the younger women in the lab, too. He'd been the son of one of the board members, thought he could get away with it, that he was untouchable.

"This is retaliation for Kirk Agrant, isn't it."

"Now, Halley. That's long in the past." She noticed he didn't say it wasn't.

"I built this lab with you, Ivan. You're just going to let them throw me out on my ear because of a technicality?"

He took off his glasses and cleaned them. When had he aged so much? He was only twenty years her senior, but today he looked haggard. His beard was streaked with white, his hair thinning. Maybe he was sick. He had the gray pallor of the unwell. Of a man with a destiny curbed by ten men and women in ancillary industries who were pressuring him to take the company public. Halley had been against that, too. Firing her cleared the paths for everyone's goals, no doubt.

He jammed his glasses back on. "It's a bit more than a technicality, Halley. It cost the lab millions to ransom the data they stole and ruined the integrity of multiple cases. We're open to lawsuits now, and the board . . . They need a scalp, and I'm sorry to say they decided on yours. It was a unanimous vote. I hope you understand. I really have no choice here."

A barista comes over. Halley doesn't know this one; she's all of eighteen and fresh as a thorny rose, with her septum piercing and sleeve of tattoos. "Can I get you something?"

"Oh. No. I was just . . ."

"If you're not buying something, I'm afraid you need to leave."

"Right. Of course."

She wanders up Wisconsin, turns left on P Street, crosses Thirty-Third. Her friends' town house is four stories and redbrick Federalist swank, like everything in this neighborhood. What was this morning's elegant freedom is now a bleak set of mossy steps to a basement. Small. Lonely. And completely unaffordable. She can rely on her friends' generosity for a few more days, maybe, but then? Every step she's made in the past few weeks was in anticipation of getting promoted and landing a raise, not losing everything.

It hits her again, hard, and she sags against the door. She is going to have to let this dream go. She has to swallow her pride, move back home with Theo, and try to start again.

She collapses on the sofa. She can't keep on like this anymore. She is being tested. Normally, if there is anything she loves in this life, it's tests. She was always the weird kid who couldn't wait to sit for an exam. It didn't matter if it was a pop quiz in biology or the SATs or the last final for her graduate degree in forensic science or, now, as an adult, the annual boards she takes to keep her license active. Her heart races in anticipation; she sharpens her pencils; the paper appears on her desk—now the link to the test file on the computer—and off she goes. If there are real superpowers, test taking is hers.

This one? She's failing miserably.

She enters the apartment, drops her bag on the floor, sinks onto the sofa, head in her hands. She yanks out the clip, and the dark mass flows over her shoulders.

Okay. Think.

Before she joined NISL, at Ivan Howland's relentless behest, thank you very much, she'd had offers from the FBI, the CIA, Homeland Security, and ATF, mostly thanks to her grad school professors singling her out and putting her on the radar of the organizations so she could do internships with each. She also had an offer to go home to her local police department. Lord knows they were always understaffed and needed as much help as they could get. There was something slightly romantic about the idea, helping police the community she grew up in. Very Mayberry.

But that was ten years ago. When she was twenty-four, she had the arrogance of youth on her side. She had a mission. She would solve crimes with science and might even become famous for it.

Ivan Howland had pounced on her at an American Academy of Forensic Sciences cocktail party just as she was making the decision about where to start her career, pitching a new lab program that he'd just gotten funding for. There was a lot more money in the private sector. They would be the most sophisticated lab in the country, the place where complicated cases would be solved. Cases local law enforcement couldn't afford to solve themselves. They had the funding to stay in front of the caseload, enough to staff a state-of-the-art lab and provide backup to the alphabet agencies.

She jumped at the chance. The freedom of the offer, not to mention the money included, was enticing. And ten years later, as she is about to hit the pinnacle of his promises, a pinnacle he wouldn't have reached without her, he cuts her loose without a second thought.

She supposes there are plenty of cheaper scientists out there now. And plenty more specializing in forensics than when she came out of school. People who won't complain when someone decides to play grab-ass with the interns. Someone who's not stupid enough to click on a link in a phishing email labeled as an internal meeting invite that even the FBI agent who'd investigated said was impeccable.

She has contacts. She has people she can reach out to. Several of the ones she turned down said if she ever changed her mind, to call immediately. She will make a list. Hopefully one or two still have their positions.

And of course, let's not forget the reason she is in a basement apartment in a Georgetown town house instead of driving home to her spacious four-bedroom home in McLean. The six-two, black-haired, blue-eyed ATF agent named Theodore Donovan. Her husband. Her soon-to-be ex-husband.

She loves Theo. She really does. And he loves her. But not quite enough. They've had normal issues over their decade of marriage, but it's been getting harder and harder to be the happy-go-lucky, band-loving, bar-hopping, museum-attending couple they used to be. Their conversations, always so broad-ranging in the beginning, became smaller, more focused. More entrenched. The fights are now singular. Repetitive.

She wants a family. He doesn't.

He claims it's because of his job, that it's too dangerous, that he'd rather not have a child at all than orphan one, but she knows he's just stalling because the idea of a kid terrifies him. She always thought they wanted the same thing. Then, when he said he didn't want kids, she thought she could change his mind. She was wrong.

They've been fighting about it for five years, and now their love is permanently damaged.

Halley is the one who suggested the separation, and he agreed so quickly she knew it was over between them. He didn't fuss, didn't cry or moan, just sighed heavily and said, "You know I will always be here for you." Made her feel worse, but she thinks he's relieved. No more wife glaring at him over dinner, pressuring him to pony up that genetically gorgeous sperm and give her babies.

But now? What is she going to do? The paperwork has been drawn up. They're supposed to meet this evening after work to sign everything. She'll have to get in touch with the lawyers and ask them to hold off. And tell Theo. Will he take her back? Probably. But only if she gives up her dream of children for good. As in, he's "getting a vasectomy, so deal with it" for good.

The tears come at last, hard and deep sobs that shock her with their intensity. She's crying for more than her job, her failed marriage, her childless belly. She's crying for the promise of a life that no longer exists. Nothing can change what's happened over the past ten years. She can't get a do-over. She is thirty-four years old, her eggs are drying up, and her entire world has just crashed down around her ears. She had it all, and now, in a heartbeat, it's gone.

When she is spent, when the tears have stopped, and the reality sets in, she changes clothes, careful to get the seams just right on her pants as she folds them—she won't be able to afford to dry-clean them after every wear anymore—and tackles scrubbing the tiny basement kitchen. It's not dirty, but it gives her something to do. Cleaning is meditative.

Within ten minutes, the kitchen is sparkling, and she has no answers. Now what?

Maybe a walk? Drive across the bridge, sneak into her house, and take the dog for a run? Something, anything, to take her away from this shitty morning. No, she can't chance it with Charlie. Theo might be home, and she just cannot face him right now. She'll just go down to the Potomac, trace the canal path. It's a pretty day with a gruesome interior. Maybe some fresh air will help her think.

Thick dark hair back in a ponytail, sneakers on, she is almost out the door when her phone rings. She sees her dad's smiling face on the screen.

She debates answering. He has a way of sensing when things aren't going right for her. She will have a hard time not just spilling all her woes. But she adores her dad, and he doesn't call during the day very often. He teaches at the private school back home, astronomy and physics, and his classes usually overlap her workday. Something could be wrong. She slides open the phone.

"Dad? Is everything okay?"

"Hey, jellybean. Am I speaking to the new director of the NISL lab?"

"Oh. Well. No."

"You didn't get the promotion?"

Oh boy, this is going to be fun. If your idea of fun is total humiliation. "Not exactly. What's going on?"

He is thankfully easily diverted. "Oh, you know, it's a funny story." His voice sounds strange, thick and syrupy. She hears a beep, then another.

"Dad? What is that noise? It sounds like a heart monitor."

"You, my darling jellybean, are too smart for your own good. Here's a little monkey wrench for you. I took a tumble down the front stairs of Old East and broke my femur."

"You did *what*? Oh my God, Dad. Are you okay?"

"I'm fine. Well, as fine as I can be while still being embarrassed as heck. It's a beautiful day, the quad was full. Everyone saw. And the ambulance . . ." He clicks his tongue. "Anyway, I'm here at the hospital, and I'm a little stoned, they put something in my IV. The not-great news is it's a compound fracture, so they have to put a rod in to stabilize it. I'm going into surgery within the hour."

That explains the weird note in his voice. She's already turning around and heading back into the depths of the apartment. The universe has quite a sense of humor. "I'm on my way." She looks at her watch. Marchburg is a three-hour drive, give or take the traffic. "I'll be there by dinner."

"Honey, you don't have to come home. I just wanted to let you know."

"Dad, you're going to need help, and I'm free for a few days. Good job waiting until finals were over. I commend your impeccable timing."

"But finals aren't over," he laments, and she laughs.

"The school will figure it out. You are responsible for feeling better, stat. I'll see you tonight. I'd say break a leg about the surgery, but . . ."

He gives a hyena giggle that she suspects means whatever pain meds they've given him are kicking in.

"Seriously, behave for the doctors, and I'll be there when you wake up. I love you."

"I love you more, jellybean. Drive carefully."

CHAPTER TWO

Having something to do energizes her. She texts her friends to let them know she is heading home for a few days. She debates calling Theo now to warn him to cancel their appointment at the lawyer's office, decides she'll do it from the road, then packs her Jeep full of everything she's brought from the house in McLean. It all fits in one suitcase and an overnight bag. She is a scientist, not a fashion plate. She wears the same thing almost every day, utilizing a few nice pieces instead of a hundred low-cost ones. It certainly makes packing simpler.

She feels a deep pang for Charlie, who certainly doesn't understand why she's not there for walkies in the morning and evening, but this path involves sacrifice from them all.

Crossing Key Bridge, she glances to her left at the marble monuments, the bridges, the Kennedy Center, all the parts of the city she's grown to love in her years here. DC feels like home now. She did undergrad and grad school at George Washington, got her PhD here, married here, lived here happily for several years before things went south. She supposes a trip back to her childhood hometown is appropriate as she's being forced to make huge life decisions. But the sense of loss she feels leaving the city is palpable. That this is not how things are supposed to go. That everything is changing. That you can't unring a bell, and no matter what, nothing is going to be the same again.

Her phone rings as she gets on the GW Parkway toward 66 West. Theo.

"Is it true?"

Uh-oh. "Is what true?"

"Halley. They sent out a press release."

"What? Oh my God."

She pulls over on the shoulder. They wouldn't. But apparently, they would. She opens her browser and enters the NISL website. The front page has a PR alert.

> NISL Statement Regarding the Confirmed Cyberattack in January
>
> Following a lengthy investigation into the cybersecurity event earlier this year, the National Investigative Sciences Laboratory is pleased to announce that all of our systems are back online, with zero impact on our customers. Investigations revealed the attack came through an email phishing link and was contained almost immediately. No personal data was accessed. More importantly, the integrity of our myriad ongoing cases was not compromised. Our goal from the beginning was to coordinate with all of our partners to make sure they, too, were not compromised, and we have succeeded.
>
> In less auspicious news, Dr. Halley James has left the company. We are sad to see her go and wish her all the best in her new endeavors. Dr. Felip Ayers will be taking over as lab director. Dr. Ayers—

She stops reading. She feels sick. "How *dare* they."

"Well, that answers that. I thought, with all the *changes* you've been making recently, you decided to go in another new direction. But they let you go? Because you clicked on a meeting invite?"

All the *changes*. This new edge to his voice almost breaks her in two.

"Apparently so. Please, Theo. Not now. Okay? My dad took a spill and is heading into surgery. I'm on my way to Marchburg."

"I'm sorry to hear that." He probably is; he and her dad have always gotten along. Then again, her dad could get along with anyone. His voice sharpens. "But Halley, running away is not going to solve things."

She wills her blood pressure not to rise at his imperious tone and pulls the Jeep back onto the road. "A, I am not running away. Ivan screwed me. I will have to get a lawyer, because they're trying to fire me with cause, which means no severance. It's just an excuse to get back at me for filing the harassment claim against Kirk. His dad should have been forced off the board when his creepy son was dismissed. Ivan clearly said this was a 'board' decision. It's retaliation, and they're not allowed to do that."

Just saying it aloud makes her feel more in control. They can't do this—she has a contract, she has rights, and now that she has a tiny bit of altitude, she's thinking more clearly.

"B, my dad needs me. The timing is . . . good."

"Were you even going to tell me? I know things have been rough lately, but I don't even merit a call?"

She avoids the answer. "I apologize. Things have happened very fast. I planned to call on my way to Marchburg. Speaking of, I won't be available to sign the paperwork today."

"Gathered that," he says. "I'll call them."

A silence stretches between them. She wants to cry on his shoulder, have him comfort her, tell her it will all be okay. That they can start over, that he will support her decision to fight back. That he will change his mind about a family.

But it won't be okay. None of this is okay. "*You* are doing this to us," he'd said when she left, and those words still linger between them.

"I'll let you know how Dad is," she says finally. "Kiss Charlie for me."

She hangs up before he can hear the crack in her voice, the crack in her resolve.

Maybe she is running away after all.

The three-hour drive to Marchburg goes by quickly. She distracts herself rocking out to the Pixies and R.E.M. and Nine Inch Nails. If there's anything DC has given her, it's a love of music; the concert venues are absolutely fantastic, and all the coolest bands come through. She especially loves old-school progressive and punk, though she'll go in for most anything that has a beat. As if her car knows her mission, the Violent Femmes start banging out "Gone Daddy Gone."

She feels bad for her dad, but this is surely a blip. A broken leg sucks, but he's strong, in good shape, and she has no doubt he'll be up and moving around in no time. It will be good to see him, and see home. She hasn't been back in months.

The drive is as pretty as always. Thick copses of evergreen commingle with maples and oaks. A red-tailed hawk soars above the EXIT sign. The sun is setting as she winds her way up the last switchback before the top of the mountain, and the town comes into view. Home.

Marchburg is a small town that could double as an ancient Scottish castle fortress if it were on another continent, sequestered behind a redbrick wall. The streets form an X, with the Chilhowie-brick Jacobean-style architecture of the school taking center stage. The town itself relies on the private girls' prep school where her dad teaches—the Goode School—being in session for its lifeblood. Inverse to a beach town that grows in population during the summer months, Marchburg swells to three times its normal population when the girls come to school in the fall and deflates again when they leave in the late spring. The influx of their money—their parents' money—keeps the shops and restaurants in business through the leaner months. The sleepy mountain town has been her home since she was little; they moved here from Nashville after the car accident that took her mother's and sister's lives when she was six. It's been her and her dad ever since.

Being the daughter of a professor wasn't terrible. The girls of Goode had treated her as an unofficial mascot for most of her younger life. When she was fifteen and less sensitive to her own insecurities and desired a more traditional education model rather than continuing to be homeschooled, she enrolled as a day student instead of taking the bus down the mountain to the school in Jasper, one town over.

She didn't fit in with the girls at Goode, especially being both a townie and the daughter of a teacher, not to mention a motherless waif, but she was more interested in the classes than fitting in. Then she left for college, where, from day one, she was a superstar. There has always been something very right about her time in DC. Until now, until today, the city has been good to her—her father has commented more than once that she's blossomed under its careful tutelage. She found a career, a husband, a life. Happiness. Everything he always wanted for her.

Now, the machinations that give it the nickname "the Swamp" have betrayed her in the worst way possible. The bastards screwed her.

She decides not to tell her dad what's going on for the time being. He needs to focus on getting well, not have his energies diverted by her drama.

As she passes the brick walls and tall black wrought iron gate that lead onto Goode's campus, she smiles. All hail the nostalgia. Despite not being an "it" girl, she enjoyed her time there, traipsing around in the quad, sitting on the very steps her father tumbled down. There was something safe about the red bricks and the black gate, something apart from the rest of town. Once you got off the hill, Marchburg looked more like every other small town in the South. But by the school, it was a fairyland. Granted, a student was murdered several years ago in the arboretum, but that was situational. An obsession gone wrong. They've increased security tenfold since then, and the new administration runs a very tight ship.

She goes straight to the hospital, driving down Front Street as the streetlights flicker in welcome. The sidewalks are wide, the antebellum houses standing at attention. Some are still family homes; many are high-end offices for doctors or lawyers. It feels wrong to see small parking lots in place of the wide lawns of her youth. The trees are bigger now, forming a canopy over the street, and she turns left into the hospital parking lot with a sigh of relief.

It's not a big place; for more serious situations, there is medical life flight or ambulance transport to Charlottesville. But there's a solid orthopedics department here, mostly because the sporty girls of Goode tend to break themselves.

She parks in the small lot just as the dark of night settles in with finality. Crossing the asphalt toward the well-lit building, she hears the soft hoots of an owl—once, twice, thrice. There are legends about owls and the portents they bring. But to Halley, it is as natural as breathing. If anything, it feels almost as if the creatures of Marchburg are welcoming her home.

Inside, she approaches the main desk. A dark-haired woman in blue scrubs with a stethoscope around her neck looks up. "Hi, can I help you?" And then recognition dawns on her face. "Holy cow, Halley James! Haven't seen you in years. Your dad said you'd be coming home to visit."

The wonders of living in a small town. Kathryn Star was aptly named—the center of the girls' basketball team at Jasper High; she was an All-American athlete and smart, to boot. She'd lived on their street, and Halley had always liked it when she came over to babysit. It's a little strange seeing her as a woman—an adult peer.

"Hi, Kater. Haven't seen you in a while, either. How's everything?" The nickname—Kater-Tater—came from who knew where, one of the older girl's friends, surely, but had stuck.

"Good, good." Kater gestures at her scrubs, grinning. "Haven't heard that nickname in a long while. I moved back last year to take care of my grandma and got lucky, there was an opening here and I slotted in." She raises one eyebrow and taps her left ring finger. "You're still married, aren't you?"

"Oh, that's . . . it's . . . complicated." *What is it, Halley? Are you, or aren't you?*

"Isn't it always? Just thought I'd mention Aaron is back in Marchburg, too. I could give him a call, we could go get a drink. Unless it feels weird to go out drinking with your old babysitter and your summer lifeguard-at-the-pool crush?"

Halley feels her cheeks flush. Aaron Edwards was ridiculously hot, and she'd crushed hard on him during the summers at the pool, though he had no idea she was alive. Compared to Theo, Aaron had placed a very distant second. Aaron was sweet. Theo was sweet—and a dangerous man. Not a danger to her, but to criminals. Something ridiculously appealing to the younger Halley. From the moment they met, she'd been lost.

"Stop. Seriously. Aaron was not my crush."

"Oh yes, he was."

"I'm here for my dad," Halley says, cheeks still heated.

"Fine. Be a spoilsport. Dr. James is in room 141. They just brought him up from recovery. He's a little loopy still, but he's awake. He did well. The fracture was pretty bad, and there was an ACL tear, too, but they called in Dr. Phillips, and he fixed him up."

"Oh, good." Halley feels her worry slip a notch. Dr. Phillips is one of the best orthos in the state. He was the team doctor for the University of Virginia football and basketball teams. Getting him to oversee her dad's case is lucky.

"I'll talk to you soon, all right? Great to see you." Halley waves and heads down the hall to the right, following the signs to 141. Most of the rooms are empty, though there are a few with beeping monitors and the hushed scent of illness emanating from the half-closed doors. The hospital is an eerie place, even with the lights blazing. She'd seen a horror movie once that took place largely in Georgetown and the hospital there. It always freaked her out. She avoided the *Exorcist* steps, as they were known, as much as possible after that. So many of her college friends liked to hang out there, drink beer and dare each other to do dumb things, but Halley had never been a fan. Even in broad daylight, it felt wrong. She wasn't usually superstitious, but that spot gave her the willies. Tonight, Marchburg General does the same.

She enters her dad's room, horrified to see his leg suspended in midair, encased in bandages, and an external fixation device that looks like a metal halo drilled into the skin from his ankle to just below his knee.

"Ouch," she says, and her dad opens his eyes.

"Halley!" He smiles wide, though she can tell it costs him.

"Hi, Dad." She crosses the room and kisses him on the forehead. He is pale, and she knows he has to be in pain. "Hurts, huh?"

"I'm not going dancing anytime soon." He shifts a bit, and she pushes the starchy pillow deeper under his shoulder blades so he can sit up a bit more. "Thank you. You didn't have to come."

She points at his leg. "Au contraire, mon frère. You're going to need some help. It's no big deal. I'm happy to be here. I needed a few days off. Can I get you anything? There's a kitchen down the hall. I bet it's stocked to the hilt with ginger ale and Jell-O and crackers."

"Be still my beating heart. Crackers."

"Done. Be right back."

She hurries down the hall and raids the family pantry. She gets graham crackers and saltines, two miniature cans of ginger ale. The hall is hushed; visiting hours are nearly over.

When she steps into the room, he blinks slowly at her, like a wise old owl. She sets the loot on the wheeled tray perched next to the bed, careful to avoid his IV. "You look beat. I should let you get some rest. I'll head to the house. When will they spring you?"

"Not right away. Hopefully by the end of the week. But if you're going to the house now, could you do me a favor?"

"Anything."

"There's an insurance letter on my desk. The school changed providers, and I never put the card in my wallet. It will have the new card and all the relevant details for the hospital to bill my new insurance. Great timing, huh? The deductibles just went up." He laughs lightly, and his eyes are heavy. He's slipping into the drugs, and that's probably for the best.

"I'll get it. Anything else you want from home?"

But he's asleep.

She watches for a moment, heart sighing silently, arranges things on the tray to make them easier for him to reach, then winds her way back to the front desk. It's manned by an unfamiliar young nurse now; Kater has been sucked back into her work.

In her Jeep, Halley gives in to the shakes for a few minutes. Seeing her dad hurt, weak and pale, the metal circling his leg and piercing the skin, was a lot. She's never been leery of blood—she wouldn't last five minutes in a lab if she were—but seeing him in pain is too much.

Blowing out a steadying breath, she turns over the engine and heads back into the night.

CHAPTER THREE

The house Halley grew up in looks exactly the same, and there's something so comforting about pulling into the drive. Her headlights catch the rosebush they planted to remember her mother when they moved in; it now tops the six-foot trellis with cheerful aplomb. They are Scots roses, a varietal of salmon and yellow with fuchsia edges that reminds her of sunshine and fire. It's too early for it to fully bloom, but in a month, there will be hundreds of tiny buds ready to spring out.

The house itself is a two-story redbrick colonial revival with a classic structure and symmetry, very similar to the rest of the houses on the street. Two chimneys, three dormers, and memories a mile long. Built at the turn of the last century in conjunction with the expansion of the Goode School, they are stalwart reminders of times past. Many of her dad's fellow teachers live on this little street, an intellectual enclave that often sees classes conducted in drawing rooms and dinners afterward in the kitchens. She grabs the mail from the box, then her bags, and walks up the steps.

Her keys jingle in her hand as she juggles everything, and the lock on the red door gives way with ease.

It smells like woodsmoke and Aqua Velva and red wine and dust. It smells like home.

But there's something odd about this place now. Everything feels different. Precarious. Her career has hit a massive speed bump, her marriage is all but over, and she's standing in her dad's foyer, wondering what it might be like to just move home. She's lived away since she was eighteen, coming back for holidays and breaks only. DC has become her place, not sleepy little Marchburg. Could she be happy here, after all she's seen, all she's experienced? Can you ever really come home? She is a grown woman now. Those simple days of safety and comfort are long gone. And that's what home means, much more than any sort of structure. It's where you feel safe in the dark.

A plaintive meow and thudding from the stairs. After her wedding, when she and Theo moved into the house in McLean, her dad, lonely, had adopted a Siamese cat from the shelter. The kitten was barely weaned, crying for attention, and it was love at first sight for them both. They were meant for one another. Her dad named him Ailuros—Greek for *cat*—and they are inseparable. He's now a fifteen-pound monster with a sweet disposition and an opinion on everything.

"Ailuros, my darling boy, where are you?" She maneuvers into the living room, dropping her bags by the entrance to the kitchen.

Ailuros skids into the foyer, and she kneels down to give him some love. He yowls and purrs and prances around like the little king he is, and then runs into the kitchen and meows again. His bowl is mostly full—he's a free feeder—but he likes some tuna fish in the evening. She makes him his treat, changes his water, and scratches his ears again. "Sweet boy," she says as he happily sticks his face in the tuna.

Her dad is going to be asleep for a while; she has time to pour a glass of wine and decompress. Maybe a bath, too, wash off this horrible day. But wine first.

She finds a bottle that looks interesting—her dad is an amateur oenophile and actually once taught an elective class on wine tasting for one of the nearby colleges. Those were fun nights, the bohemian older students from Jasper coming up the mountain in a small chartered bus so no one would drink too much and drive home down the mountain. Off the mountain. They seemed mystical to her, loud and vibrant and bursting with confidence, and sometimes it's hard for her to reckon that she's now a decade older than they were when they sat on the floor of the living room, rapturous, listening to her father explain varietals, terroirs, food pairings. "Wine is an art," he would say, twirling his glass so the ruby liquid sparkled and sang. "Respect it, and it will always surprise you."

There are several open bottles on the glass-topped bar to choose from; she reaches below for a cabernet glass and gives herself a healthy pour of a Super Tuscan, her salivary glands activating at the luscious plummy scent. The first sip is like drinking liquid gold. The second makes her think moving back home could have its benefits.

Her dad's office is on the exact opposite side of the house. All the first-floor rooms are a mirror image—off the gracious entry to the right is the sitting room with the oriental rug and the gold-and-glass bar cart, and to the left, his office. She enters, smiling indulgently. It is messy, the oak-paneled bookshelves stuffed full of books, stacked haphazardly every which way. It smells of ancient ideas and pipe smoke; though he quit years earlier, there's no way to get that smell out of the books completely. A state-of-the-art Celestron telescope stands in one corner, a large antique globe in a wooden stand in the other, and his desk, a rough-hewn slab of oak, is square in the middle on top of a worn kilim rug.

The desk. Just a glance tells her it might take more than a second to find the insurance paperwork. Her dad is a vertical filer. He knows where every piece of paper he needs is based on the place in the stack. It gives her hives; Halley is a dedicated folder lover and labeler. She found him an antique filing cabinet a few years back, a Christmas gift she thought he'd love, but as far as she knows, he took one short stab at the filing system she built for him, then abandoned it.

His mind is anything but messy, though. It doesn't surprise her, considering how diligent he is about everything else. The man can read Greek and Latin and navigate by the stars—taught her to, as well—but putting a piece of paper in a file folder eludes him.

She takes a sip of her wine and sits at the desk. Ailuros jumps into her lap, his bulk a pleasant weight. The brown leather chair creaks in a friendly greeting. It is as old as she is, has burst at the seams and been stitched back together like a well-loved baseball glove.

She starts with the pile on her left, flipping through the pages. Bills. Papers he's grading. Papers he hasn't gotten to. A stack of pristine note cards with his name embossed along the top edge—a gift? She doesn't recognize them. More bills. Comics cut from the paper—he mails her ones he thinks she'll enjoy. Tax returns.

There is nothing from the insurance company.

She moves over a stack. Then another. Fifteen minutes later, she's touched every piece of paper on the desk, and none of them hold an insurance card.

It's not like him to mistake where something is. Then again, he was on a morphine pump—God knows if his brain was functioning.

She goes through it all again, then eyes the filing cabinet. Surely not, but it's worth a try.

"Sorry, buddy," she says, dumping the cat on the floor. He leaps back into the leather chair with an indignant *mirp* and settles into the warm spot.

The filing cabinet, too, is devoid of insurance papers, though she sees he has halfheartedly attempted to put a few things in order. Mostly it's her childhood information—immunizations, the homeschooling records, an entire file full of report cards from Goode.

Halley is a joy to have in class, she has such a bright future, A, A, A, blah blah blah.

Little did they know adult Halley would click on a link in an email and ruin her life. Three, two, one . . . go.

She doesn't linger on these moments of her past. She has a mission now. Find the insurance card.

She pours out the rest of the wine, careful not to dump the last bit in her glass, and sorts the mail. Not there.

She goes room by room through the downstairs, ferrying the flotsam and jetsam of her dad's life back to their proper homes. The teacup in the bathroom back to the kitchen; the jacket with the patched elbows from the living room sofa to his closet. There's paperwork on his bedside table—another stack of papers he's grading, and some odds and ends, but nothing insurance related. The cat's plaid blanket is nestled at the foot of the bed. She looks under it, just to be sure. Nothing.

She's getting frustrated, and convinced that perhaps he's losing it entirely, when she sees a piece of paper sticking out of his top dresser drawer.

Halley used to know the details of every drawer in his dresser. Not that she snooped, not at all; she was in charge of folding the laundry and putting everything away. T-shirts and undershirts in the top left and right, boxers in the middle, slacks and jeans folded in thirds in the bottom, and the small middle drawer with the silver knob for socks.

Once, hanging up his freshly ironed long-sleeve work shirts, she'd discovered a stack of *Playboys* in the back of the closet under his winter ski clothes. She'd flipped the pages with a growing sense of awe, then unease, put them back, and never looked again.

Seeing her father as a man was . . . odd. He was her *dad*. He was funny and goofy and smart, and hers. He never dated when she was growing up, not for lack of trying by the women around Marchburg, both married and single. A handsome, solid, and eligible widower with a smart daughter? He was a popular choice. She asked him about it once when she was about ten and one of her friends asked why she didn't have a mother. She reported the conversation like the little blue jay she was and asked. He just shook his head. "I've had my marriage. And I have you, and work, and the stars. That's all I need, jellybean."

Those magazines told her maybe he needed more but was happily sacrificing himself for her so there wasn't any more upheaval. She loved him even more that day.

Now, wondering where else she should look without totally invading his privacy, she steels herself and opens the dresser drawer. Papers and magazine articles, a thick heavy book on Magellan and his exploits circumnavigating the globe. She hasn't seen this book since she was a kid. Smiling, she takes it out, memories of her dad reading it as a bedtime story crowding in. She flips the softened pages. Inside, holding his place, is a yellowed manila envelope.

It is old. It was sealed at one point, but the gummy flap is no longer stuck, and her brows twitch closer as she debates opening it. Watermarked, the edges bent, it is clearly not the new insurance card, and not her business, either. But something makes her sit down on the bed and unwind from two circular tabs the red string that holds it closed.

The papers inside are varied. Newspaper articles, something from the Tennessee Department of Correction, blue-backed papers from a law office she's never heard of. She sees her mother's face staring up from the clipping, but the last name doesn't match. As she reads the rest of the headline, horror spreads through her body, chilling her blood.

Susannah Elizabeth Handon, 35, Found Murdered

16-Year-Old Daughter Held for Questioning

CHAPTER FOUR

Halley reads the article, her mind practically shaking with the information.

Her mother, Susannah, was murdered?

Her half sister, Catriona, was held for questioning in the murder?

Her sister murdered her mother?

What. The. Hell?

She can't understand what she's reading. It has to be a mistake. The two of them died in a car accident when she was six. Twenty-eight years ago. She barely remembers them, only snatches, bits and pieces, flashes of memories. She remembers a funeral, people crying, and shoes that pinched her toes. Remembers her dad holding her hand so tightly she had to beg him to let her go. Remembers whispers. And then they moved to Marchburg, a fresh start, and the accident became a dark dream. She didn't want to think about their deaths. Still doesn't. She can't remember any of it anyway. What's the point in trying to look back?

A headache starts in her temple. A throbbing that presages a migraine. She's had them all her life, ever since the accident that took her mother's and sister's lives and left her unmarked except for a small scar, a streak of white in her hair, and lingering headaches. And they are such an annoyance. But she doesn't care right now.

She skims the rest of the papers in the envelope, realizing they are all pieces of a story she has never heard. A story her father has kept from her.

Her mother was murdered. And her half sister did it.

This isn't possible, and yet there is no mistaking either of them in the photos. Halley's sense of dislocation deepens. She is a carbon copy of her mother. And realizing she is only a year younger now than her mom was when she died—*no, Halley, murdered*—sends shock waves through her. It might as well be her in the photos. She is the echo that never stopped reverberating.

But her dad . . . He lied to her. Why would he lie to her?

The fissure that cracks her heart apart is so intense she has to gasp for breath. Her father *lied* to her.

Why would he do that?

The name isn't exact; it should read Susannah Elizabeth James, not Handon, which was her maiden name. But there's no question this is her mother; the same elegant, bold face stares from the single photo on the fireplace. The one that looks so much like Halley.

Her mom was divorced when she met and married Quentin James. Catriona—they called her Cat because Halley couldn't pronounce her half sister's full name—was ten when Halley came along. Old enough to see a new little sister as an inconvenience, surely. But was it more? Cat hadn't taken to Halley, and she could remember the anger, the yelling, the arguments, though only the shape of them, not the real words or topics. Everything is blurred by time. The memories of her mother and her sister are foggy at best, and end abruptly after the accident.

"Cat is perfectly nicknamed," her dad once told Halley when she was crying, having been yelled at for some random transgression. "She hisses and hisses, but it's just fear driving her. You'll be best friends one day. Just watch."

He was firmly convinced, told her that all the time. Halley took his word for it; Cat hated her, but maybe when they were older, it wouldn't be so bad.

Was it something more? Did Halley break something in her sister, and she eventually took it out on their mother? Was having a miniature version of her mother couched as an imperious, beloved girl-child too much for her? Cat looked like her own father. Was she jealous of Halley's resemblance to her mom? Was it something more, something deeper?

Halley could be twisting these memories; she isn't sure of anything anymore.

Why are you blaming yourself? You were six. You were not responsible for any of this.

Halley's heart is pounding, her head throbbing, and she closes her eyes, taking deep breaths. This day is too damn much. From work to her dad to Theo to this bombshell news? It's like a very bad dream. Maybe she'll wake up and none of it will be true.

Her vision is going fuzzy. She finds her purse and puts a tab of ergotamine under her tongue. She must arrest the migraine before it gets too bad and she's flat on her back in the dark for the rest of the night.

As the bittersweet taste fills her mouth, she combs the rest of the papers, feeling a new emotion she's never experienced before. It is grief, but deeper, harsher. Her mother wasn't taken from her by chance. She was stolen by the flaxen-haired girl who flits in and out of Halley's memory like a bright ghost.

How is this even possible?

She has to talk to her dad. Now.

She isn't supposed to drive when she's having an episode, but there is nothing that will stop her right now. She shoves all the papers back into the envelope and hurries to the Jeep, her new truth clutched in her hand. She is careless on the drive back to the hospital, squinting against the haloed lights of oncoming cars, running the yellow light at the end of the street in her rush to get confirmation. She blows past the front desk and runs down the hall, skidding to a stop at her dad's room.

He is asleep; of course he is. He's been through hell today—a painful fall, an even more painful surgery. She's being selfish waking him, but there's no way she isn't going to. She has to find out the truth. She watches him for a moment, heart pounding wildly, breath catching.

"Dad? Daddy? Wake up."

He makes an inarticulate noise. She reaches down and shakes his shoulder, and his eyes open, blank as the night sky. The drugs have their hold on him. It takes him a minute to focus.

"Halley? You're here?"

"I'm here, Dad. I talked to you earlier, remember?"

He closes his eyes and swallows. Seeing how uncomfortable he is dampens her needs for a moment.

"Are you thirsty?" She picks up the Styrofoam pitcher and pours him a glass of water, places the straw in his mouth, and waits for him to suck it down.

"What time is it?" he finally asks. She glances at the clock to the left of his wall-mounted television and winces.

"Almost midnight. Sorry, but I have to talk to you. It's about Mom."

"Tomorrow, honey."

"No, Dad. Now. Wake up."

He struggles to keep his eyes open, but nods. "What?"

"I found the papers about her murder. Mom's *murder. Why* didn't you tell me?"

The fear that flashes over his face takes her breath away. He is instantly awake.

"Shit," he mutters, another rarity. Her dad doesn't cuss in front of her, ever.

"What is it? Dad, you're scaring me."

"Oh, Halley." He sighs, heavily, looking away, anywhere but at her. "This is not the time."

Halley tries to keep her voice even. "My mother was murdered by my sister. And you hid this from me. There's never going to be a good time. Might as well do it when one of us is numb to the pain."

"It's a very long story."

"Give me the highlights. Let's start with why you lied?"

"To protect you, obviously. Your sister is . . . dangerous. Very dangerous."

"Is she not in jail?"

"Not anymore, no. And she wasn't in jail, proper, ever, but a juvenile psychiatric facility. The courts found that she was not fully competent to be tried as an adult, and they kept her in the juvie system until she turned eighteen and was released. I moved us here to keep you safe."

"You moved us to Marchburg to protect me? She didn't know where we were?"

"No, she didn't. I changed our names, dropped Handon in favor of your grandmother's maiden name, James, and have done as much as possible to keep you off her radar."

This does not jibe with anything she knows. Dangerous sisters. Name changes. Murdered mothers.

"Why?" Halley's voice is a whisper. "Why did you have to protect me?"

"Like I said, honey, this is a very long, complicated story. I'm sorry you had to find out this way. It wasn't smart of me to hide it from you, but I didn't want to scare you. Catriona is not someone you want in your life."

"Why did she kill Mom?"

He shifts uncomfortably, and the monitor beeps as he settles back down. A nurse sticks her head in, then rattles inside with a cart. "It's time to check your vitals, sir. Ma'am, you should wait outside."

"I'm fine right here."

"Suit yourself."

When the nurse starts making some very uncomfortable chitchat with her dad about the state of his bowels and bladder, Halley changes her mind and steps out into the hall. He has a catheter; she hadn't noticed it earlier. This is going to be a much more difficult recovery than she thought. She hasn't even started thinking about what happens when he goes home. He's going to need a lot of care, for weeks to come. Probably more than she can provide . . . Of course, she has all the time in the world to play nurse. Maybe even a way to explain to the people in her life why she left her beloved job. Her father needed her.

But on top of all that, this crazy news? There's no way in hell she's not going to look up her sister's record and find out where she is. The initial shock is wearing off, and she's starting to realize what a huge issue this is. She has to reframe her entire life. Always a cheated destiny, not growing up with a mother, only to learn that it wasn't simply fate or chance that took her away but another person's soulless action? A person with whom you share blood? It's incomprehensible.

You're being very rational, Hal. Hold it together a little longer.

Is this why she was also so interested in criminology and forensics? Has she somehow subsumed the truth this whole time? Surely she knew about it when it happened, right? Even though she was little, six is old enough for impressions. Even though she barely remembers the two women themselves, has only a few pictures and some old videotapes that are God knows where, had she overheard her father, or a police officer, or something? Was there a crime scene? She needs the whole story.

But when she goes back into her dad's room, the nurse puts a finger to her lips and points at the morphine drip. "He's going to be out for a while. I gave him a good strong dose, he was hurting. You really should go home. Visiting hours start at seven."

Chastised, Halley gives her dad one last glance, then sets off for home. There will be no more answers from him tonight. But there are other places for her to find information about this shocking news.

Her childhood home belongs to a stranger now. Everything is familiar, yet she is newly unmade, and there is no way she can recapture the nostalgic glow she had before.

Ailuros twines around her legs, begging. She picks him up, and the head rush of pain from bending over nearly topples her.

Her head is still pounding, so she adds an Excedrin into the mix. She shouldn't have had all that wine. Usually it's white wine that sets her off, not red, but every once in a while . . .

She sits with the cat in her lap and breathes and tries not to think until the pain lessens. It's impossible to shut off the tap.

My mother was murdered. Stabbed to death. By Cat.

My dad betrayed me. He lied to me. Why?

My life is over. Nothing is real.

Why did I believe what he told me? Why did I never look back?

Finally, though the grief is still just as intense, her headache starts to ease. She does some jaw exercises to help it stay away. She got lucky—sometimes she is blinded by the pain and has to lock herself away in a dark room until it passes. She's gotten better about stopping them before they get started. The medications are better now, too.

Her instinct, as she has been trained to think, always, is to research the situation, get as many angles of the story as she can. Her laptop sits in her bag, but when she opens it, she realizes the battery is empty. She goes to plug it in but can't find the cord. She searches everywhere until her mind latches on to the plug behind the small built-in desk in the basement kitchen. She put the laptop in her bag and didn't grab the cord.

Idiot.

Her dad is a total Luddite, preferring his books to a screen if at all possible, but he has an old Apple iMac up in the pseudo-office in the small room next to her bedroom. When she was in school, it was her mini library/office; it has bookshelves and a sofa for reading, and a small desk for the computer. It's probably going to need a software update to even get started; she hasn't used it since Christmas.

The last thing she needs is to look at a screen, but she can't help herself.

She puts on her sunglasses to help with the blue-light glare and boots up the computer, dusting it off as the machine whirs to life. She taps a pencil impatiently against the keyboard. It has bite marks in it—she's always had a terrible habit of gnawing on her pencils like a squirrel trapped inside a house. There is something comforting about it, though, and before she knows it, the pencil is between her teeth and she is going down the rabbit hole, kicking herself all the while. She never even thought to question her father's version of events, never tried to look up the accident. She took his word that she had a black spot in her memory because she had a head injury, and now she feels like a fool.

In her defense, the information is not easily found. News from 1989 is still being digitized. There are a few newspaper articles, and that's it. She wonders if her father was able to bury this information, but that gives him more power than she's comfortable imagining. She's seen the obituaries; they are in the box with the videotapes and some old dried flowers from the funeral. They say "Died in a tragic accident." Now she realizes they must have been fake.

Shit.

She is going to need to go deeper, so she pulls out the old National Archives login that she has from her college days and gets a little further. There are actual court records in that system, and she turns on the printer and sends everything. Once she has a small stack of paper, as much as she can find, she takes it all downstairs, lights a fire, gets a Diet Coke—the caffeine will help keep the headache at bay—and starts piecing together the truth from twenty-eight years earlier.

The more she reads, the more concerned she becomes. Her father isn't kidding.

Catriona Handon is dangerous.

And according to the FBI database, which holds a missing persons report, she hasn't been seen since 2002.

Fifteen years. She's been gone for fifteen years.

Where is she?

CHAPTER FIVE

Come here.

Come closer. Closer.

Do you see it? That small hunk of weathered stone, just there?

It glistens, the edge damp with only a trace of wetness. Dew? It is still humid, but last night's rains were too long ago to leave behind moisture. Perhaps . . . tears? Hmm. That is an interesting thought.

Now, take a step back and watch as the stone takes shape. Another step, and another. You can see that gentle arch now, can't you? Look at the contours of the stone. They are covered in moss, the rest still hidden, tangled in the lushness of the overgrowth. Is that what you think it is?

Pull back a bit more and focus. See how the stone reveals itself? I'm proud of your close attention. Yes. You were right. It is a headstone. This is a grave. A lonely, simple grave, given over to the ravages of deciduous and coniferous intimacy. Lost—hidden?—in a forest. Forgotten. Untended. So very solitary. But what difference does that make? Its isolation is simply a construct of time and loss; time has no more meaning to this object, and the loss is unattainable, irrelevant to you. Isn't it?

Come closer, again. Run your hands along the weathered granite. The face of the stone is blank, with no name or dates carved on its surface. Without the telltale shape of a headstone, you might miss that this is a grave. Now a few more steps back. Yes, that's right. You can almost see it from this perspective, but take one more step back, and one more. There. Perfect. The stone stands alone, a bulwark in the late summer grass. Odd, you think?

Why would a grave be here? Who, you might wonder, has died, and been hidden here, at the edge of the forest?

These are excellent questions. If you are very good, if you behave, I will tell you everything you need to know. But for now, if you look to your right—no, not quite that far, back a bit—yes, there you go. See? At the edge of the cliff? Yes, that is a person, standing alone. A young woman, I believe, with dark curly hair.

Is she screaming? Shhh, listen closely. Oh, it's so hard to hear over the crashing of the waves. But if we are silent as the grave behind us, we might hear—yes! A thin wail rises above the ruckus . . . She is! Screaming, crying, thrashing in the spindrift, pulling at her hair.

Did she discover the grave?

Did she discover the truth?

Should you approach? Oh, no, no, I don't think that's wise. She seems quite distraught. Offers of help might be misconstrued. She is deranged, can't you tell? A stranger interfering could end badly. Just imagine yourself in her place.

You are standing on the edge of a cliff. Something has upset you terribly. A storm is building, the sky graying around the edges. An intense wind blows you off your feet, shrieking past in a gale. Sounds blur. Waves crash. The scream is deep, from your core, building, rising. You tear at your hair, forcing your voice into the world, but the wind whisks it away. No one can hear you. No one can help you.

If you go over that sharp edge, whether wind or madness at your back, no one will know.

Except us. It's our little secret.

Now. Leave the screaming woman and the lonely grave and your questions for later. We have a job to do. A story to tell. You must pay close attention. Do not worry about the things you've seen, what you've heard, or that unsettled feeling in your core.

Let us glance back at the grave once more, take it all in, then leave this scene.

I will take care of you. I won't let anything bad happen.

Why would I lie? I have nothing to hide from you.

Are you hiding something from me?

CHAPTER SIX

CATRIONA

Brockville Artist Colony
Literature Workshop
2002

The members of the fiction retreat have gathered in a posh, elegant cabin in the woods in a small town called Brockville. The cabin is an A-frame, with a stone fireplace, chinked wood walls, and a granite-countered kitchen in the back of the room. A fire crackles in the grate; the couches are comfortable; a tea-and-coffee service is set up on the sideboard, along with various delectable and healthy snacks.

No one is eating. Or drinking, for that matter. We're just sitting in a circle, staring at everything but each other, nervous and tense, not sure what to expect. What to think.

The fire is making the room overwarm. The shoulder months in Tennessee are finicky—hot one day, cold the next. Today is quite chilly; fog has wrapped the valley in its damp embrace. It is easy to lose your way in these morning fogs, so the retreat has yellow lighting along the paths so we—the writers—can find the way from our cabins to the main space.

The walk over should have been inspiring. The fields were covered in dew. There was nickering from the barns, the horses still inside, keeping to their dreams, and the song of swallows haunted the air. It was custom-made atmosphere. I don't know if anyone really noticed, but they should have.

We six are the elite. The chosen ones. Each of us harbors a story and reason why we want to pursue a creative path. We've shared that reason—and a thousand-word writing sample—with the board of the lauded Brockville Writers' Retreat, and six lucky writers have been plucked from a field of thousands. And now here we are, five women and one man, in the "writing cabin," absolutely shitting our pants with nerves.

And then there's me. Catriona Handon. Cat, to my friends. I am the youngest one here, and possibly more anxious than the rest, because last night, when the lottery was held at our lavish welcome dinner, I was picked to be the first to read a story to the group.

There is nothing more nauseating than the first time you present your writing to a workshop. To do so at the famed Brockville Retreat, known for launching the careers of three National Book Award winners and two Pulitzers, not to mention a bevy of regional awards, film adaptations, and millions of books sold?

No pressure or anything.

We wait. The fog meanders outside the windows. I occupy my time thinking about our new world.

Brockville itself is a fascinating place. I did a good bit of research before I came, and I have to admit, the town is just as alluring as the retreat. I walked it yesterday when I arrived, wandering the paths by the lake, watching the happy people, gawking at the houses that look like Frank Lloyd Wright designed each one. The restaurants and the general store and the bookstore, dead center, all accessible, friendly. People with gentle smiles on their faces, buzzing around in golf carts.

I could live here. Stay until my bones grow weary and turn to dust. It is as beautiful as it is remote. To be lost in such a place, a small self-sustaining town in the middle of the forest, wouldn't be the worst.

Brockville is broken into equally sized and spaced hamlets, geometric and linear, each with a theme that matches its role in the town's ecosystem. The founder—Miles Brockton, the world-famous leader of biophilic living—built the town to self-sustain off the land. According to the literature, he was charmed by a trip to the Cotswolds; the hamlets' names and shapes have a decidedly British overtone.

Avalon is the arts hamlet, housing the bookstore, the Inn, the labyrinth, a lake, boutique stores for art and clothing, and the famed artists' colony, including the world-famous Brockville Writers' Retreat.

Canter is focused on wellness. Everything from the doctor, midwife, and pharmacy to the gym and elderly care home can be found in its environs.

Glaston is the farm, and so it is home to three restaurants, two coffee shops, the bakery, the florist, and a wildly popular pizza parlor with an old-school Italian wood-fired brick oven, a handcrafted piece imported from Naples.

The final hamlet, Somer, is more practical. Its theme is education, and everything from the schools to the small sheriff's department can be found on its streets. Somer is also the home of the real estate and construction firm that brings people to Brockville and helps them design and build their housing.

And what houses they are. All architectural masterpieces ranging from the modern glass-and-steel chalets I love the most to classic Craftsmans with welcoming porches and wreaths on the doors, to a mixed-use section of town houses that are as cleverly appointed as they are slightly more affordable, to a few modern French château-inspired homes with brick-and-grass courtyards. Everything is built to spec; nothing can be erected without unanimous board approval. These fabulous homes are scattered throughout the hamlets, and the neighbors are friendly and welcoming. Sidewalks are wide; lighting is generous; the branded golf carts whizz by with alarming regularity. Its gregarious camaraderie can be intense. Everyone knows everyone. That is by design. There are no strangers within the town walls; outsiders are welcome to come look, but are treated with great caution.

In the center of it all, the town square holds the post office, an ice cream shop, a general store, and a park surrounding the lake, with many benches and a meandering path perfect for walking. If you veer off it to the northwest, you'll find yourself in Avalon and the entrance to the labyrinth. To the northeast is Canter. Glaston is southwest, and Somer southeast.

It is beautifully planned. A charming little town in the middle of the woods, with every amenity imaginable, but also compact, specific. There is no competition among the businesses—every storefront is singular. There is one mechanic. One doctor. One school. One vet. One gym. Only the restaurants are in multiples, and that is to satisfy the tastes and level of celebration needed; they are all owned and run by the Brocktons themselves.

The people of Brockville choose this way of life for a reason. They seek this elegant isolation. Everything they need, and nothing they don't. It is very much like a medieval Norman English village of old, with every aspect of life centered on the castle, and the town surrounding, its support. Even much of the food is grown on site: the animals responsibly raised on the farm, the wine made from grapes grown on the hill that rises behind Glaston. They have a light footprint; what they can't produce is sourced from small, ethically run farms and established community co-ops. Local and organic, that's their motto.

The people who live here are, for all intents and purposes, self-sufficient. There is little reason to leave. People rarely do. Oh, they travel, of course, and sometimes a run to a store outside the town is necessary—though usually done in concert with other families, in case someone else might need something too esoteric—or generic—to be provided.

And as you can imagine, it costs money to live in Brockville. Money, and approval. No one gets in that the board doesn't meet, background check, consent to, and otherwise vet. The idea that they'd let me live here is folly. The people of Brockville are curated just as carefully as the town's amenities.

Which of course means everyone wants in. But people don't move away once they've gotten in. They stay until they die.

Who knows. Maybe I'll get an in because of the retreat.

I look at the people around me. Every one of them has a gift that's brought them to this place, to this moment. Who will be the best among us? Someone will rise to the top. That is the way of all groups. Dogs. We are all just dogs in a literary milieu. We will spend the first few days nipping at each other's flanks until we find our places in the lineup.

I want to be the best. I can admit that desire. But I have the least experience. The fewest writing credits. I am the youngest by several years. The rest of the group is eyeing me like I'm going to be the first one voted off the island.

Not if I can help it. This isn't *Survivor*; this is a literary workshop. I have to allow my inner narcissist free rein to get through this. I'm not a natural extrovert, but I can turn it on when I want or need to. I want to right now. Very badly. I want to wow them, awe them with my prose, delight them with my talent. I'm as nervous as I've ever been, at least since I was sixteen, and—

"Hello!" The door to the cabin swings open, and a hearty, happy voice assails us. "Welcome to the first day of your retreat! I'm Tammy Boone, and I'll be your teacher."

Well, well, well. Tammy Boone. There are murmurs of appreciation—part of the excitement is not knowing who will be teaching the retreat. It's always someone who graduated from the Brockville Retreat and made it big, though, and Tammy Boone is one of the more successful grads of the program.

Tammy shakes the humidity from the curls of her hair, which spring riotously from her head, like Medusa fresh from the spring. A Gorgon leader is fitting; when she looks at me, I feel I've turned to stone.

“Her new book is being adapted into a movie,” the girl on my right whispers in awe.

The holy grail—adaptation. Ironic if you consider the writer is judged on the success of the actual book, not how well it shows on the screen. What the viewers see and what the reader experiences are often completely different.

Tammy lets the news sink in that she’s ours for the next few weeks, then she starts moving through the cabin in concentric circles. We have to crane our necks to follow her movements.

“Our goal at BWR is to hone your skills as a writer, as an artist, as a creative. I want you to stretch yourselves. I want you to let it all hang out. There’s no reason in the world to hold back now. You’ve all been selected because you are very talented, and you are ready to level up your craft. Our goal is to help you achieve your dreams. Unlock that path to publication, to a *career*. Help you go from curious writer to successful author.

“I’d like to go over some rules for workshop. Be on time, or the door is locked, and you miss out on a whole morning of lessons. My time is valuable, I don’t like it when people are late. Do you understand?”

Six heads nod in unison.

“Show respect for your fellow workshop attendees. And try to keep the funny business out of it. Intimate relationships are frowned upon. They’re a distraction.” She looks at each of us, letting the implication sink in. We nod. No screwing around. Got it.

“Good.” She plops into the center chair facing the fire, big as a throne, and I laugh to myself. Like there will be any dog more important than the leader herself.

“Now, I understand you drew lots last night, and our first reader is Catriona Armstrong. Catriona? Take it away.”

Come out, come out, wherever you are.

I start to stand, and Tammy gives a conspiratorial chuckle. “Oh, no, dear, you can stay right where you are. Just speak up so everyone can hear you.”

Fabulous. I sit back down. Swallow. Lick my lips. And begin.

> Eleanor Glynn was in a rush the moment her life was altered forever.

I look up to the expectant faces of my fellow authors and our powerhouse teacher, who gives me a smile and nod. God, why did I have to be picked to go first? I do so much better seeing how the rest of the room works rather than setting the tone. I start again.

> She was always in a rush, always buzzing from one place to the next, one moment to another. She wasn't good about taking her time, being thorough, unless she was in front of a judge, and a client needed her focus.
>
> She had things to do. Places to be. People to see. She'd been like this since birth, in a hurry: a hurry to grow up, to get through school, to live her life.
>
> Now, the life she hurried into was about to fall apart.
>
> It was a good life. She was happy, or at least, until today, she thought she was. She had a good job, one that meant she could afford to live in one of the tonier suburbs of Nashville in a spacious home with a three-car garage and a weekly housekeeper to handle the heavy stuff. She had a handsome husband whom she adored. A solid education, three weeks of vacation, usually spent trekking across the world, and an adorable Muppet-faced dog. No kids, not for lack of trying, but they would come. She was still young. Thirty was the new twenty.

Her hands were full—briefcase, groceries, keys, a bottle of wine. She juggled everything from the car and scrambled up the stairs to the front door. Three garages, and they still parked the cars in the driveway. All the neighbors did, too, their Porsches and BMWs and Suburbans all on envious display.

Greg's Jag wasn't in the drive, though, which was a relief. She'd left early so she could beat him home. They were celebrating their anniversary tonight, seven years together, five married. They'd met in law school and had been inseparable from the moment their eyes locked in. Eleanor was sure they'd be together forever.

She managed to get the key in the lock and the door open without dropping anything. She used her hip to knock it closed behind her, then stumbled into the kitchen, dropping first the briefcase, then the bag of steak, potatoes, and asparagus, then the wine onto the counter.

"Whew," she said, grinning at the feat. Clumsiness came with the constant hurrying; she was relieved to have it all settled in one piece. She turned on the oven, washed the potatoes and put them on the rack, then went to the bedroom. She'd already been to the gym for a quick workout and needed a shower, needed to shave, get her hair dried and tamed into submission. She had an hour to make herself presentable and have the meal ready. Plenty of time, and that was saying something for a woman who never had enough of it.

In the bedroom, tossing off her shoes and

wrenching herself out of her jacket, she realized water was running in the shower. She closed her eyes and shook her head, blew out a heavy, rueful breath. She'd been gone since seven, and in her rush, must have forgotten to turn it off. Great. She added "Call the water company" to her mental to-do list; they would be kind enough to treat this as a running toilet and comp the bill. At least, the last time she'd left the water on, they had.

Then she heard a small moan and froze.

She placed a hand on the knob, listening. Another, slightly louder moan, which sounded for all the world like a woman saying, "Oh, Greg!"

Eleanor slammed open the bathroom door. It took her a moment to register fully what she was seeing: Her naked husband's eyes jammed shut, his body thrusting frantically at a female shape bent forward at the waist, a hand braced against the glass.

"What the actual fuck?" she yelled, yanking open the shower door.

The look on Greg's face almost—almost—made her laugh. Shock and horror and recognition and shame, all rolled into one.

"Ellie? Ellie, what are you—"

She was out of there before the remainder of the sentence escaped his lips. "What are you doing home?" he was saying.

She didn't let the heartbreak start then. She was too fired up, fury taking root in her soul. She thought briefly about getting the gun from its locked safe in the garage, but it was too far away.

She marched back into the kitchen and went

to the knife block.

Note: Ellie has a small issue with anger. Overwhelming anger. Anger that drives people to do horrific things, like murdering people.

The knife shone in her hand, the ten-inch French-honed blade singing a siren song. It felt right in her hand. Trusted. Good.

Greg came running out of the bedroom as she turned to go back in. He saw the knife and started backing up.

"Ellie, no. No!"

The knife slashed. It caught his forearm, and bright blood spewed across the bedroom door. She slashed again, and again, and he went down hard, her name on his lips, a whispered groan. "Ellie. No. Ellie. Don't."

She was tired of being told "Don't."

The girl was in the bathroom, cowering. Ellie had no remorse or hesitation, her knife an extension of her arm. The tip entered the flesh of the girl's throat, and she ripped it to the left. The girl fell, the meaty scent of her blood a noted juxtaposition to the floral bodywash she'd always coveted.

Back in the kitchen, Ellie found herself standing over the sink, rinsing her hands. The knife shone clean on the counter beside her. The smell of bleach was at odds with the drink of death. She could hear Greg dying in the hall. Tiny gurgles—

"Oh my God, are you kidding me?"

I look up, shocked at being interrupted. It's the blonde who took an immediate dislike to me at dinner last night, the one who made sure everyone in the group knew she had a short story published in an obscure regional literary magazine three years earlier. Whatever her name is . . . Oh, lovely. I realize the entire group is staring at me with distaste etched on their faces.

Tammy's face is twisted in distaste, too, but I don't think it's about my work. She's already on her feet, furious. "We do not interrupt our fellow creatives when they are reading. If that happens again, you will be asked to leave the retreat. Am I clear?"

Abashed nods from the group. The blonde tosses her hair. "I thought this was a literary retreat. Not some slasher-film class."

"Literature takes all forms, across all genres. As do we. Catriona, I apologize. Please, continue."

"If there's more blood, I must excuse myself," the blonde says.

"There's not," I reply. I don't really care what she thinks, but she interrupted me at a crucial point in the story. I put my head down and continue reading.

> The fantasy ended. The fugue lifted. The knife's blade was clean. Greg was not dead, but calling for her to stop, to listen.
>
> She would not.
>
> And she would not ruin her life over Greg Phillips and some idiotic bimbo. They weren't worth her freedom, only worthy of her *disdain*.

I put some emphasis on the last word and look up, giving Blondie a small smirk, then continue.

> She put the knife back in the block unused and hurried out of the house, out of her perfect life, and drove back to the office. It was only then, ensconced in the plush leather of her office couch, that she allowed herself to grieve.
>
> Greg showed up an hour later, calm, collected,

with comb tracks in his thinning hair. How had she never noticed that before? He'd be bald by forty, and she hadn't even realized he was receding.

He looked tired. Exhausted, really. And hangdog sad. How had she ever found him attractive? He wasn't cute, not anymore. He would never be again.

"Get out," she said, and she meant it.

"Babe, we need to talk."

"How dare you call me *babe*? I just caught you balls deep in another woman, in my shower, on our anniversary, and you want to call me *babe*?"

"Ellie. Eleanor, I'm sorry. I never wanted this to happen."

"I suppose you're going to tell me it was a onetime thing, that you'll never see her again."

His chest puffed a bit. "Actually, no. It isn't. We're in love. I was going to tell you tomorrow. I didn't want to ruin our anniversary."

Ellie's jaw hit the floor, then she gathered herself. "That is the stupidest logic I've ever heard."

"I'm sorry you had to find out this way. It was never my intention to disrespect you."

"Really? Screwing another woman in my house is a show of respect? God, Greg. How long has this been going on?"

"A year."

"Who the fuck is she?"

"She works for the Randalls."

The face clicked then. "You're fucking the Randalls' nanny? What is she, all of nineteen? Oh, Greg. How tacky can you be?"

"She loves me! She treats me like a king. She isn't too busy for me. You schedule our life, Ellie. From dinner to conversations to sex, it's all on your calendar. We aren't spontaneous anymore. You've suffocated me with—"

"Oh, shut up and leave. I don't care about your speech. I want a divorce. And be prepared. I am going to ruin you." Ellie pointed to the door, and Greg stared at her a moment, as if he were cooking up some really great insult, but changed his mind and left.

She thought about crying but decided that was going to get her exactly nowhere. Instead, she sent a note to one of her colleagues to ask for a good divorce lawyer. Her firm handled compliance litigation, nothing family related, and she wanted the best.

And then she opened the bottom drawer of her desk and pulled out a bottle of scotch. She poured a hefty glass, shot it down, choking and sputtering a bit—she wasn't a hard-liquor drinker, kept this for when the partners showed up after hours. She poured another and sipped at it. It tasted like gasoline, but she didn't care. It was going to bring oblivion, and that was all she craved at the moment.

A heartbeat. That's all it took to go from the happiest woman in the world to the unhappiest.

She couldn't believe it.

TUESDAY

CHAPTER SEVEN
HALLEY

Halley wakes with a start. The cat is heavy on her hip, snoring. She has a migraine hangover, a strange echo of pain lingering in her temple that makes her head feel hollow. It takes her a second of dislocation to put it all together. She is home, in her childhood bedroom, in Marchburg. Her mother was murdered.

Murdered.

It's so fantastical a thought her mind pushes it away.

She doesn't have many memories of her mom. They're more sensory details now. A soft voice reading a bedtime story. The way her arms felt around Halley's little body, encompassing and warm. The scent of Chanel No. 5 brings back the winter she took Halley sledding and she tripped over an exposed root and fell down the hill, sliding on her back. They'd laughed and laughed. The funeral, rain making the back of her neck cold.

There are a few videotapes, moments she memorized as a little girl but put away as she got older because she could see how much pain it caused her dad. She doesn't know where they are. Her dad made everything disappear except for the photograph of her on the mantel. Her mother is leaning forward, trying to take the camera from him, her eyes sparkling and her smile wide. Halley looks so much like her mother now it's painful to look at the photo at all.

Halley knocked it off the mantel once playing Arthur pulling Excalibur from the stone, and the glass cracked. They tried to change the frame, but by then the photo paper was fused to the glass and began to peel apart, so they left it. The crack goes right through her chest. It's like her heart was broken, too.

Her mother is dead, and her sister is missing.

Still alive, a stubborn little voice says. Missing, but there is no body.

Fifteen years, though. That's a long time. She could be anywhere. She could be in a lake, or a field, or the woods. She could live three streets over and Halley wouldn't know.

Her next thought is of her dad. Anger spikes through her. She hasn't ever felt this way toward him. They are pals. Friends. He's her best friend. He's always been her favorite sounding board. Even after she married Theo, he was her first call when things went right—or wrong. *Except yesterday. You didn't call him to tell him the truth, now did you?*

But now she knows he's a different person than she thought. He's a liar.

She rolls over and sees the time—visiting hours started an hour ago.

She jumps in the shower, winds her wet hair into a bun. There are plenty of groceries, but she's still nauseated from the headache and cooking is too much trouble. She fills Ailuros's bowl, then pours herself some cereal and peels a banana, scarfs them down while the coffee is brewing.

She decants the coffee into her favorite battered thermos, adds cream and sugar for extra energy, and jams on her sunglasses—her eyes are still sensitive to the light. She drives the Jeep to the hospital, her tote bag with the explosive details she's learned on the seat next to her, a rattlesnake coiled and waiting to strike.

Her dad looks worse today than yesterday. Asleep, his mouth slack, she can see the bruises coming up along his cheeks and forehead. He will be loopy from the drugs when he wakes. She backs out of the room, and the nurse on duty intercepts her.

"Good morning. You must be Halley."

"I am."

"Like the comet," the nurse says. "I'm Tonia. The physical therapists were in to see him, so I gave him a shot from his pump. OT will come later today. You might want to be around for that."

"OT?"

"Occupational therapy. They'll talk about whether he can go home or if he needs inpatient rehab. Do you have stairs?"

"Oh yeah."

"Well, they may decide to try IPR for a week, until he can get around without issue."

"How long will he have the device on his leg?"

"Awhile. Six to eight weeks. But don't worry, he's not going anywhere until we get him loaded up with medicine. He needs IV antibiotics and painkillers. He'll probably be here for a week, maybe ten days, before you'll have to decide about taking him home or going to rehab."

A small part of Halley breathes a sigh of relief. "I feel bad to say it, but good. I don't know that I can handle him like this. He looks so . . . hurt."

"He is hurt. That was a bad fall. But he was chattering away this morning, telling me how he named you after Halley's Comet."

"Tell me he skipped the rest?"

"Nope." She grins. "Halley for the comet, Leia for the princess in *Star Wars*. It's funny, you look a little like Carrie Fisher."

"I look like my mother," she says, feeling that new spark of rage surge up in her body. She grew up with the inside-joke names and a face that belonged to a woman who is practically a stranger. That is how much Halley remembers of her mom.

The nurse must sense the change in her emotions, because she pats her on the arm.

"Don't worry. The drugs can make people gregarious. It can also make them very distraught. So if he starts hallucinating, don't be too shocked. It happens on these high doses of intravenous morphine. We'll get him weaned off as quickly as possible. Any other questions?"

Halley shakes her head. "I'm sure I'll have plenty the second you walk away. This is the first time we've had any sort of major hospitalizations, outside of me knocking out a tooth when I was eight."

"Well, he adores you, so you being here is going to get him right as rain in no time."

Yeah. He adores me so much he lied about how my mother died.

She doesn't say that aloud.

He's still out cold, so Halley busies herself with a group text with her friends back in DC. After running out of their town house like her hair was on fire yesterday, she owes them a little explanation. She met Stephanie and Arlo back in the days when she and Theo were an unshakable unit, and they did all the things two couples with lots in common did. They are worried about her, about how quickly she left, but there was a party last night at the Corcoran, and everyone's dragging around feeling sick. Happily, it seems they did not find out about her fall from grace at work.

Which makes her wonder, albeit briefly, how Theo heard so quickly. Why was he on the website to see the press release, anyway? She'd been so shocked she hadn't asked.

She assures Stephanie and Arlo things are fine with her, and that her dad is going to be okay soon. She doesn't confide in them about anything else, not yet. This feels too big to share with anyone until she has a better idea of what's actually going on.

Anyway, how do you tell a group text that your sister murdered your mother?

She does call Theo for the promised check-in, and is relieved when his voicemail comes on. She leaves a dutiful message and tells him she'll be in touch when she knows more. That should suffice for a few days. She can't deal with all this at once.

Then she stews. Frets. Probes her black-hole memory banks, frustrating herself that she can't find the answers there.

Her dad comes to an hour later. He stares at her blankly before saying "You're real, aren't you?"

"Um . . . yes? As real as I can be."

He huffs out a relieved breath, eyes drifting to the ceiling. "I thought you were a ghost."

"Well, that's not disturbing at all."

"I dreamed of you, Halley. You were alone, and you were crying. I did everything I could to find you, but it was dark, so dark. I've never seen such darkness. Thick and alive, like the deepest reaches of space."

A chill parades down her spine. She can imagine it too well, and it's creepy.

"Heads up, Dad, you're on some pretty heavy-duty drugs, so chances are your thoughts and dreams are going to be messed up for a while."

He nods and looks at her searchingly. His voice is soft, and he seems more with it. "I'm sorry I didn't tell you about your mother. You shouldn't have found out like this. Though what were you doing in my dresser?"

"Looking for the insurance card. Hate to say it, and this is not an 'I told you so,' but your infallible vertical filing system failed. There's nothing from the insurance company."

"You were looking at home. Of course there isn't. In my office, at school."

"Oh." She sits back. Why she hadn't thought of searching his work desk, who knows. "You neglected to tell me which desk, I think. I assumed home."

"Sorry."

“I’m sorry, too. I promise I wasn’t snooping. I’d just looked everywhere else and thought maybe you’d left it in your pants pocket. The envelope was in the Galileo book, I was flipping pages and it fell out. I looked . . . Well, that part, I was snooping. But Dad . . . Why didn’t you tell me? I can’t believe you’ve been hiding this from me.”

There is a long pause. “I didn’t want you scared, looking over your shoulder your whole life.”

“Scared of what?”

“Your sister. The situation. The whole thing.”

“The whole thing. Can you back up a little, though? I’m trying very hard not to lose it over here, and you’re not helping.”

“Raise my head, will you?”

She presses the button on the hospital bed, and he grimaces as everything shifts. She lets him gather his thoughts and push down the pain. She presses a pillow deeper under his neck and gives him a drink.

“Thank you. Cat . . . Hell, where do I even start?”

Halley takes a seat in the brown pleather chair by his bed. It squeaks at her presence.

“How about at the beginning? Since the ending is so confused for me now, maybe there’s more you haven’t shared. You met Mom, you got married, she already had a kid . . .”

“All right. The beginning. Yes. Susannah had a daughter named Catriona from her first marriage, yes. Obviously. Which was wonderful for me. I’d always wanted a big family, and Catriona was a shortcut. A head start. And Susannah and I were happy. At least, I thought we were happy. Marriage isn’t always as obvious as it seems.”

“No kidding.”

“Catriona was a handful, but she was only nine when we married. Plenty of time to grow out of it. Then you came along, and she pulled away. She was distant with us, distant with your mom. Susannah loved her so much. She made excuses. She protected her. But . . . How do I say this? Catriona had a mean streak. She would put the cat in your crib, then yank on its tail so it would scratch you. She’d pull your hair.

Pushed you around. She was physical with you, really rough. Gave you a black eye once. Said you two were boxing.

"She was very jealous and, turns out, at a really difficult age for a bad divorce and remarriage. Her behavior was getting more and more aggressive, so we took her to doctors. They said she was having issues adjusting because of an impulse disorder and put her on a stimulant medication. And it helped. Tremendously. Until it didn't. They call it borderline personality disorder now, and they're more careful with the medications. She was diagnosed in 1986, right before the comet."

Halley's Comet was the through line of Halley's young life. It is her first memory, the four of them at the planetarium, her dad shivering in excitement. She was three, and she can remember almost all of that night—the darkened sky, the tail of the comet, her sister holding her hand and saying in awe, "You were named after that. Cool." Her mother, laughing and kissing her dad as if he was the one to discover it through his telescope in the living room. As if he named it himself.

Three years later, her mother and sister were dead, and her memories become flaky.

"A year before she . . . it happened, things went bad again. It was like a light switch. She wouldn't take the medicine willingly, said it made her feel weird. She was depressed, then she was manic, then mean, then crying. They tried all kinds of different treatments. She finally admitted she was hearing voices. It was getting worse and worse, and we were afraid for you, and for ourselves. At that point, she was beyond our abilities as parents. We thought you were in danger."

He blows out a breath, and Halley feels for him. He is struggling for control. She should tell him they can talk later, but she has to know. This is too big to wait any longer.

"I'm not proud of this, Halley. But the doctors recommended a place in the Blue Ridge, and we agreed. It was a summer program that, in addition to intensive psychological work and medications, takes kids out into the wilderness, teaches them self-reliance, teamwork, all of it. She came back worse than ever. We didn't have a choice then. I didn't think camping with other troubled kids was going to help, but your mom . . . She had such a soft spot for Catriona. Even they couldn't handle her. So we arranged for a facility, inpatient treatment, for an extended period. She needed long-term psychiatric care.

"Catriona found out what we were planning. She had a huge fight with your mom. She went after you, tried to take you from the house. And your mom stopped her. Sometime during that fight, Catriona stabbed her. Then it was all over."

Halley thinks there's probably about nine million other facets of this story he's leaving out.

"You were there?"

"No. I was at work. You called me. You told me what happened. You'd been out cold, and when you came to, you speed-dialed the office."

Halley searches her memory and comes up blank.

"How is it that I don't remember any of this?"

"You had a bad bump on the head from the tussle. That scar on your temple?"

Halley's hand goes to the spot.

"You said it was from the accident. From the glass."

"It was Catriona's doing. Not sure how, exactly, but you had a good cut and a huge lump. A bad concussion. Enough to knock you out. We think . . . Well, she clearly thought you were dead, too."

"My migraines don't come from the accident, but from Cat hitting me in the head?"

"Most likely, yes."

"Is that why I don't remember?"

"It's not uncommon, actually. The doctors said you might remember what happened, you might not. Such extreme trauma leaves a mark."

She touches the streak of white in her hair, running right from the spot where the wound was all those years ago. She used to try dyeing it, because it was so distinctive, but the dye wouldn't stay in more than a wash or two. Once or twice, she took scissors to it and cut the white lock away, but it grew back quickly, faster than the rest of her hair. Like it had claimed her. She'd finally learned to accept it wasn't something she could hide, so she told strangers it was a genetic mark of heterochromia. As an adult, she grew to love it. It was something special, something that set her apart. She would make sure it was visible, always.

Now? She has to reframe everything down to her bones.

"So she gave me this?"

Her dad nods. "Yes. Whether you blocked it out or the concussion wiped it, I don't know. The doctors and I discussed it, and they thought it would be better if you didn't remember. That we try to give you a different path to cling to. So when you woke up in the hospital and asked where Mom was, I told you she'd been in an accident. *You* were the one who thought it was a car accident. I think one of the shows we were watching—*Rescue 911*?—had a car accident that week. I didn't say it wasn't, and suddenly, that was the story. A car accident. Both your mom and your sister were killed, and you were hurt but survived."

Halley stalks from the chair, all patience gone. The window looks out onto a courtyard covered in boxwoods and a huge sandpit with large boulders and rakes.

"That's one hell of a lie, Dad."

"Yeah. But the doctors said it was good for you, that a transference of the trauma was how your brain was going to process what it had been through. So we went with that. You cried, you were devastated, but you didn't remember what really happened, that day or afterwards. It was a blessing, honey." He reaches out a hand, and she waits a few beats before grabbing hold with her own.

"A blessing?"

"You healed. You were sad, and you missed your mom like crazy, but you weren't permanently damaged. Do you remember it at all, even now?"

"I don't. I remember a car accident, the flash of lights, the crunch of the car, the sirens . . . What happened to the car, if it wasn't in an accident?"

He looks abashed. "I sold it."

"And you faked an obituary?" She doesn't bother trying to keep the accusatory tone from her voice.

"Yes. It seemed better to keep you focused on the future."

"And what happened to Cat?"

"She . . ." He breaks off. There are tears in his eyes and thickness in his throat. She gives him a moment to compose himself, desperately searching her memory for something, anything, that jogs a recollection of this event. There is nothing but the sense that things are wrong—her mom is gone, and her sister, too. The car-accident narrative is so permanently imprinted on her mind she's having a hard time believing this of her father. That he, of all people, could be capable of such deceit. That she was so easily misled.

Who conflates a car crash on a television show with the stabbing death of their mother? Is that even possible? Is he lying to her even now?

Oh, she is so pissed at him for making her doubt him at all.

Her dad clears his throat. "Cat ran away from the house after your mom . . . She had a boyfriend we didn't like, snotty kid, and she took off with him. The police found her at the bus station a few days later. She'd been . . . mistreated. He'd hurt her, pretty badly, and left her there. Left her alone. They arrested her, she pled guilty to stabbing your mom, and they locked her away. I moved us to Marchburg as soon as I could. I couldn't risk her getting out and coming after you, too."

"Why would she come after me?"

"Halley. Honey. She tried to kill you, too."

Halley sits with the words, trying, and failing, to comprehend what her father has said.

"She tried to kill you, too."

Halley had been there. She'd witnessed all of this. She'd been attacked. She'd survived and was the one who'd called for help. How was this even possible? She has no memories of it at all.

"I can't believe you lied to me. Kept this from me."

"I should have told you sooner. I'm so sorry, jellybean. I guess I hoped you'd never figure it out."

"Did you know that she's missing? Cat?"

"Missing?" He tries to sit up, and Halley puts a hand on his shoulder.

"Yeah. For fifteen years now. I don't know any more than that. There's a very vague missing persons report."

"That's . . . strange."

"It is."

They sit, not speaking, listening to the sounds of the hospital, the beeps and whirs and whooshes and overhead pages. Finally, Halley sighs deeply. "You knew already, didn't you? That she had a life. That she went missing. If she was so much of a threat, of course you did."

His silence gives her the answer.

"God, Dad. You know, I've had a lot of guilt over the years about that accident. That I made it and they didn't. I mean, I had to go to therapy. Did everyone know about the murder but me?"

He turns his face away from hers. "Better a little guilt than remembering. God, Halley. What I came home to, no one should ever have to see."

CHAPTER EIGHT

Halley forces herself to spend the rest of the morning at the hospital, talking to doctors and nurses and therapists, listening with half an ear to the plan for her dad over the next few weeks, trying, and failing, to wrap her head around the story her father shared.

Her mind veers away whenever she tries to think about the reality of her mother's death. The crash is always there; it always has been. It's a sudden thing, the pain, the blackness, the sirens. A sense of panic. There is nothing else.

She's never remembered any details, only fragments. Now she knows why. She knows there are neural pathways that are rebuilt after trauma. She knows people can rewire themselves to not feel pain when thinking about painful situations. Was she able to manipulate her own brain to protect herself from the emotional upheaval the truth would bring? According to her dad, she hadn't told him she saw her mother murdered, only that she woke up to find her dead. So maybe Halley was unconscious when the act occurred. With any luck, she will never access that memory. She doesn't want to relive it. She heard the agony in her dad's voice when he said no one should have to see what he did.

But.

"She tried to kill you, too."

She can't leave it alone now. There is a rabbit hole for her to go down. There will be crime scene photos, maybe even video. Definitely drawings. Evidence collected. Blood-spatter analysis. All the things she's been trained to examine, divining truth from the heavens with an analyst's eye. There have been a lot of changes in forensics since 1989, too.

And there will be an autopsy report.

God, can she even? Her own mother's autopsy?

She had considered, for a moment, becoming a forensic pathologist. A noble and interesting occupation, for sure, gleaning answers from the dead. But it was not her path. She made the decision not to go on to med school her sophomore year, after her pathology class spent a week in the DC morgue. It was oddly too static for her taste. Halley knew then she wanted to solve the crimes through the science of the case, not by determining cause of death. Her talent lies in the detailed aftermath, not in the biological truth. She needs to be removed from the situation to see the evidence presented clearly. She'd moved away from evidence collection to run the lab itself, but there was a time, early on, when that was her total jam. The bloodier, the better. She had a discerning eye, could always find the truth, then use the lab to back it up.

You're removed from this situation, for sure. God, Cat tried to kill me, too?

If there was a trial, there would be transcripts. But if Cat pled guilty, there might have been just an arraignment and sentencing. No matter; there will be legal and forensic documents. Her mother's murder, and the fallout, will be findable.

Will Halley be able to analyze her own mother's crime scene with any sort of impartiality? Read the horrific details about the murder and not come apart at the seams?

Impossible to predict, her empirical mind provides. *It could be fascinating. It could leave such deep scars you'll never recover. The chances of the latter are high. But you might get answers. You might remember.*

And then, the light bulb: *Is this why you are obsessed with forensics? Because your first traumatic event, the moment that shaped your life forever, was a murder scene?*

Why had her father not *said* something?

Her head gives a familiar throb, and Halley decides she needs to take a break. It's lunchtime, and her dad has had another decent dose of morphine. He is out cold for the next hour, at least. She decides to head to campus and retrieve the insurance information.

Campus is still bustling with fresh-faced girls taking their finals. At first glance, with long straight locks parted down the middle, they are only distinguishable by their hair color. They wear their Goode School uniforms like pajamas in the way only teen girls can manage, slouching and unkempt—their blazers and skirts, white shirts and ties coupled with Birkenstocks and white crew socks. They wander the quad, strolling on the grass between the elaborate redbrick paths calling like blue jays, laughing and strutting. The bells start to ring; the enormous white bell tower above Main Hall shakes with the effort, and they scatter like quail flushed by pointers.

Halley shakes her head with wonder. Was she ever that young? Obviously, then, she'd been incredibly naive, immature, and introverted. She now wonders if that was trauma related. Did her father homeschool her so long for her sake, or for his? She will have to readjust every memory, every conversation. The trust that's always lain thick between them is broken.

Of course, she finds the insurance letter and card on her dad's desk, right where he said they would be. If she'd thought to come here first, she would still be in the dark. She wouldn't know the truth.

Ford Westhaven, the young dean of the Goode School, spots Halley descending the brick stairs of Old East—the same stairs her father fell down—and makes a beeline to her. She is totally pulled together in a chignon, suit, hose, and pumps. Halley has never seen the woman with a single hair out of place. She is elegant and smart, the perfect combination for running this institution. She took over for her mother, Jude, after the murder. The PR nearly ruined them.

"My dear Halley." She is enveloped in an effervescent Chanel No. 5 hug. The scent triggers a memory of her mother getting dressed for a faculty dinner. Long blue satin. Beaded bodice. Red lipstick. White carpet. All disjointed, unframed.

Interesting. She usually avoided the dean because Ford wore the same perfume as her mother. Now, she wants to linger and see if more memories fight their way to the surface.

"How is your father? I've been worried sick."

"He's doing okay, Dean. It was a bad break. They put in a rod and stabilizers, and he's probably in the hospital for a week or so, minimum. But he's in good spirits."

It's not really a lie. Had Halley not discovered the article, he *would* be in good spirits. Now, everything is complicated, blurred. All the lines of her life have been plucked like the strings of a poorly tuned harp, the twang resonating and making your skin crawl in its wrongness.

"Well, Quentin has my support. Anything he needs, don't hesitate to ask. We've scheduled the rest of his finals for him, and I'll act as TA and grade them myself."

"I'm sure he will appreciate that, Dean. I'll let him know and get word to you, okay?"

"Do that, my dear. And how are you? You seem . . . distracted."

How am I? Peachy keen, lady.

"Yeah, I suppose I am. There's a lot going on. I have a couple of weeks' vacation saved up, so I can take care of him while he gets back on his feet."

The dean looks enchanted by this. It's something Halley always remembers, Ford's enthusiasm for the success of her students. Most go on to Ivy League schools and make news in a variety of ways, from headlining companies to marrying well. Halley had chosen a different path, of course. She wasn't like the other girls. Now she understands just how different she actually is. A small part of her heart thaws—her father made one hell of a hard decision, but look what he helped her avoid. To be the daughter of a murdered mother in this world? Would she have the strength and verve she does now? Or would she have collapsed under the weight of the world's piteous empathy? She might not have fit in here, but if they'd known the truth? Girls can be incredibly cruel in their lack of concern.

"Give your old dean a hint what you're up to?"

Halley's glad to have her attention pulled back. She's hardly going to admit defeat at this moment, in front of the woman who was so kind to her growing up. "I work in forensic science. A high-end lab where we run samples that are sometimes decades old and degraded, that other labs aren't sophisticated enough to handle. We also do very specialized government work from time to time. Second opinions on high-profile cases, that sort of thing."

Dean Westhaven is nothing if not a diplomat. This is definitely not a typical career path for a Goode girl, but her enthusiasm is not deterred in the slightest. "But how exciting! To have your finger on the pulse of such things. Quentin must be very proud. Though, however did you convince him not to add you to the astronomy faculty?"

They share a genuine laugh this time; her dad's passion for the stars is well known and much respected.

"Speaking of my dad . . ." Halley waves the envelope in her hand. "The hospital needs this. I better get back. It was lovely to see you, Dean."

"Oh, call me Ford. You're not a student any longer."

"Ford. Have a great day. I'll have Dad circle back about finals."

She walks the bumpy Chilhowie path back to Main. She could have gone from the interior of Old East—the buildings are all connected by white wood-and-glass enclosed walkways called trolleys so the girls of Goode aren't forced outdoors in inclement weather—but she left the Jeep parked in the gracious circular drive in front of Main, and this is the quickest path. She stands by the Jeep and stares at her alma mater, admiring the symmetry of the redbrick entrance, the wide stairs and double doors leading to the grand foyer, blowing out a breath. You never feel quite so ancient as when you visit your former high school.

The exchange with her old dean was nice—almost too nice. She's going to be seeing shadows everywhere now, she knows. Second-guessing everything. Because everything seems different. Will she spend the rest of her life wondering who knew about her real past, and who helped her dad hide it? Surely the dean is aware of some of it. Her dad's been spinning the car-accident narrative for a long time. Was he lying to his employer as well? How did he change their names? She knows her birth certificate says James on it, not Handon.

God, every thought brings a hundred more questions. Halley feels very alone right now. Who can she ever tell? And without facts, she's just reacting.

It's normal to react, Hal. You've had a terrible shock, and it's okay to be upset.

See, all that therapy did help.

But she needs to do research, more research than she was able to do last night. She needs to get deep into the files on her sister, and that, she knows, could be very difficult. If she was charged as an adult, no problem, but as a juvenile, those files could be sealed.

As much as she hates to admit it, she needs Theo.

CHAPTER NINE

Exhausted after an afternoon of watching her dad alternately sleep and grimace in pain, and dealing with the hospital and insurance company, Halley picks up a pizza, changes into her pj's, and collapses in the living room. She eats, but her heart isn't in it. She's just watching the clock, waiting for Theo to wrap up his workday before she reaches out to ask for a huge favor. He hasn't called her back, which means he is probably out in the field, serving warrants or some other fun thing. He's been training a junior agent so has a lot of scut work teaching the newbie the ropes. Or maybe he hasn't called back because she's walked out—again, technically—and he's coming to grips with that.

She has rehearsed what she's going to say, how this is a professional ask and she will be in his debt for life, et cetera, but the moment Theo's face comes up on the screen, and his deep voice greets her with a confused "Hals, you okay?" the floodgates open.

It takes a solid five minutes for her weeping to stop, and by the last hiccupy tear, Theo has heard the whole sordid story. He gives a lot of nonjudgmental comfort, which makes her feel gooey and warm inside, and Halley realizes she might be a little more broken up about leaving him than she's been letting on. She hates seeing her marriage collapse. They used to be so good together, as friends and as lovers. But she can't help it; she wants a child more than anything. And he's been crystal clear that it won't be on his watch. That makes everything impossible.

She hardens her heart again, protecting it, shielding it. She left for a reason. She will not be drawn back into this man's web just because he's giving her a shoulder to cry on.

"This is a professional ask," she says, and Theo nods, his own face shuttering.

"Understood. Can you tell me more? I need details if I'm going to dig into the databases for you."

Halley gives him everything she's found thus far and can hear him typing in the background.

Finally, the words she's been hoping for and yet dreading come. "Yeah, your mom is in the system. I have her autopsy here. Do you want to hear the details?"

"No. But go ahead. I think I have to."

"It was a straightforward stabbing, with six wounds, midsternum and thoracic. Cause of death was exsanguination due to multiple stab wounds. It's been closed since 1989, since your sister admitted guilt and was incarcerated. She was in the Davidson County Juvenile Detention Center, then Central State Hospital from 1989 to 1991. She was released on her eighteenth birthday."

"And then?"

"She met the requirements for parole and exited the system in 1993."

"So she murdered a woman and only spent two years behind bars? And two more on parole? That seems . . . lenient. Then where did she go?"

"Unknown. There's nothing in the files. There was a psych consult, but I don't have the transcript here."

"My dad mentioned Cat was psychotic. Hearing voices. But she was diagnosed with borderline personality, not bipolar or schizophrenia."

"You've got to think about the time frame. There were many incorrect diagnoses in the eighties and nineties. They didn't know what they didn't know, especially for juvenile patients. They just thought everyone had ADD and put them on meds. That she went to Central

State—they had a juvenile psychiatric program. Must have been something happening with her mental health."

"Fair. So here's something else odd," Halley says. "I found a missing persons report dated 2002. From Boston."

"I see it. Do you need me to pull the details?"

"Could you? Especially who submitted it?"

"Of course. And I'll have a look at the rest of the case file, too, see if there's anything relevant. Can I get back with you later?"

"Um—"

"It's just that . . . Charlie misses you. He'll want to see your face. But I have to get out of here before someone questions why I'm at my desk and gives me another case to manage."

"Of course. Take your time. It's been fifteen years. Another couple of days isn't going to matter."

"Sage thinking," Theo says. "You hang in there."

And then she's alone again.

It gets dark at night in the mountains. The winds blow hard through the trees. Shadows grow where there were once empty spaces. And this late spring night is chilly, so the fire's backdraft keeps pushing smoke into the room. It smells like rain. She's set up the iMac on the kitchen table, spread out all her notes and files. Her little room upstairs isn't big enough for all this.

Theo FaceTimes her at 9:00 p.m., and she answers the call with trepidation. Until yesterday, they haven't spoken much since she left, and she hasn't seen him in person, either.

He has a nice face to look at. Square jaw, beard scruff, thick hair that has been recently shorn into a much more professional look than when she first met him. They'd slammed into one another at the 9:30 Club, literally slammed, dancing to the Black Rebel Motorcycle Club. It was her first show back in her last year of grad school, and she'd practically fallen into the arms of this huge man with a thick shock of shaggy black hair and vivid blue eyes. Her first thought: musician—which he was, a bassist, lapsed—but he was just there to enjoy the show. They hung out all the rest of the night, avoiding the sticky spots, playing six degrees of separation, the DC version—do you know X, no but I know Y knows her, and she knows Z, hell, Z is my roommate—and things took their natural course from there. He was a year older and had just gotten started at ATF as a junior agent. Luckily, he was stationed in DC. And his GS-7 salary meant they were able to have some fun. They dated their way through the shows, and she saved each ticket in a special envelope, knowing that this might be an important relationship that she would want markers for. She had every ticket from every show she'd ever seen in a scrapbook on the shelf in her empty room in DC. Music is her passion, almost as important to her as evidence collection. They both took levels of excellence and precision that many people didn't have the patience for.

"Hey—" She bites back the *babe* that normally follows. She has to keep this professional, or she'll fall right back into his arms and spend the rest of her life seething with resentment. That won't be good for either of them.

"Hey," Theo says, then clicks his tongue. "Charlie, c'mere, boy."

The blue-eyed husky traces onto the screen. Seeing her face, he turns in happy circles, baying hello.

"Hi to you, too, Charlie."

"You okay, Halley? You look tired."

"I am. It's been a rough twenty-four hours. Are you okay?"

He smiles, a quick flash of white in his tanned face, and she sees a deep scratch on his cheek. He gestures to it. "It's nothing. A fifty-cal kicked back on me. I'll tell you all about it later. Let's worry about you first."

Interested in the commotion, the cat leaps onto the desk and sticks his nose in her ear. "That cat has gotten even bigger since I saw him last."

"I don't disagree. I think he has some Maine coon in him, but Dad's clearly been indulging him." She tries stuffing him into her lap, only manages to get half of him, so he has his paws on the keyboard like he's typing. "Ailuros likes to be seen. Hope you don't mind."

"It's good to see *you*," he says softly.

This is why it's taken her so long to leave. Because he gets that look in his eyes. It would be so much easier if he'd cheated on her or beat her. Wasted their money on booze or gambling. Anything else but this tearing apart of her soul because they can't agree on the most basic covenant of their marriage. His reasoning—his job is too dangerous, he doesn't want to orphan a kid like his dad orphaned him—has never felt completely right to her. Like he's hiding something, holding back the whole truth.

Maybe it's just that some dreams are harder to give up than others.

Keep it business, Halley. Don't do this to yourself, and don't do it to him. You settled this mess when you left. He isn't going to change his mind.

"Don't. Please. Not now. I don't want to fight. Were you able to get anything?"

He shifts in his leather desk chair, which makes a familiar squeak of protest. Charlie flops on his fleece bed on the other side of the office; she can see his tail wagging. It is surreal to be a voyeur into her own home. *Not your home anymore, Halley.*

Theo taps his hand on a file. "I was. How much do you want?"

"I want it all."

"There's autopsy photos and crime scene stuff. I don't know—"

"I've seen my fair share of those over the years."

"This is different. It's your mom. I'm not saying you aren't professional as hell, but it's . . . it's not pretty, Hal."

"I expect it's pretty horrible. But how else am I going to figure this out? I need to repopulate my memory. I can't explain the dislocation I'm feeling right now. Everything I've thought and believed about myself is gone. I'm a stranger."

"You're you, Halley. That will never change. You're just filling in some blanks, that's all."

"Seeing the crime scene photos will do that, I think. Don't you? It could trigger some memories. I don't have anything accurate from that day."

"Maybe." He sighs. "I've pulled together a package for you, including the postmortem report and some of the notes."

"The murder book?" Halley asks hopefully.

"I can't get the murder book. You'll need to go begging to the Nashville police for that. There's quite a bit of information in the postmortem report, though. I'll email what I have here, and FedEx the rest. You'll have the hard copies in the morning."

She hears the whoosh that indicates an email has been sent, and opens her inbox, waiting impatiently for the message to come through. A ding, and it's there.

"Thank you, Theo. I owe you one."

He touches his forehead, his chin, his heart. Glances to the side at the dog. She hears the song in the background shift to the Smiths. She recognizes he needs to say something and is holding himself back. A small buzz starts in her chest. Is he going to change his mind? Is he going to tell her what she's been dying to hear for years?

"What is it?"

"Will you take some advice from me?"

Maybe not. She keeps the disappointment out of her voice. "Of course."

"This is a very difficult situation, and I know you are probably closing off your true feelings in order to investigate. There's a reason why people are recused from their loved ones' cases. You don't have a clear head, no matter how much you think you do. Especially now, with everything happening at work, and . . . with us."

"I am aware of this, Theo."

"I'm just saying, don't let your emotions betray you. They're going to get in your way, and you're going to jump to conclusions, and they might not be correct. Keep an open mind. This is a delicate moment for you, and on top of it, finding out about your mom in this uncontrolled way? It may seem like it happened a long time ago, but as you regain the memories that I am willing to bet my life are right there, just below the surface, you could be destabilized. Promise me you'll call me immediately if you start feeling like there's no end to the madness, okay?"

She is caught off guard by the gentleness in his tone. All they've done recently is argue, and it's been anything but gentle. "Thank you for that offer. It's very kind."

"I mean it. We're still married. You're still my wife, even if this is just a temporary reprieve. I don't like you disappearing from my life like this."

"You know how to fix that."

"Shit, Halley. You're being unreasonable. You never used to be unreasonable." The edge is back, and with it, her heart shutters.

"I think it's better if we stop this, Theo."

"So now you want a divorce? Is that what you're saying?"

"Now is not the time," she says. "We can talk about it when I—"

"When you what? Why is it you get to make all the decisions here? Why do I not get a say?"

She can feel the flush rising on her chest. "You are the one causing this, not me."

"That's entirely unfair. I've explained why this isn't the right path for me, why I think it's not good for us."

"Right. The last time you *explained* your feelings, you made it pretty clear it was your way or nothing."

"Because you gave me no other option. It's always been what you want. You've never even tried to understand . . . Damn it. This isn't some DNA in a test tube for you to puzzle out. There isn't a right or wrong answer." The dog whines.

"That's not enough for me. I want a family. I always have. And you've made it clear you don't. We want fundamentally different things from our lives. So there's really not much more to this."

"You can't leave me. I won't let you."

"You don't get to make that choice, Theo."

Silence. He is frozen on the screen. The moment is so deep and pervasive she wonders if the call has dropped.

Finally, he shifts and heaves in a deep breath, and the spell is broken. He runs his thumbs across his eyes.

"Maybe you're right. Maybe we can't figure this out."

"Can we just . . . table this for a few days? I need time. Everything has changed for me. I haven't processed the news about my past, and I doubt I will until I can find my sister, or at least figure out what happened to her."

He nods. "I think you're throwing away something great, but hey, you do you."

"Thank you."

They sit in another uncomfortable silence, looking at everything but each other. God, she did not want things to go like this. Finally, she pulls them back to the reason for the call.

"My dad says Cat's dangerous. That's why he moved us away. That she tried to kill me, too."

Theo spits out a humorless laugh. "He's not wrong, Halley. You'll read it in the detective's notes, but when she was arrested, Catriona said she just snapped. 'Consumed by a black rage,' that's the quote. She was a volatile individual. Whether her mental illness drove her to kill, or another, deeper issue, who knows. But if you come up dry in your search, I'd look into therapists in the area. These diseases can't be turned on and off like a spigot. She functioned in society from 1993 to 2002, and I'd bet cash money she had professional help doing so."

"That's a great idea. Thank you, Theo. I appreciate your help. Did you eat?" God, the caring is so ingrained in her.

"Um, yeah. Grabbed pizza."

"Funny. So did I."

"Do you want me to stay on here while you open the email?"

She glances over at the email icon. "Yes and no. I think . . . no. I might not look at it tonight anyway."

"Don't lie to me, Halley James. You're going to be deep in it all night."

"Maybe. I have a lot of thinking to do. But I promise I'll call and wake you up if I get too messed up. Seriously. Promise."

"I love you," he says, and she freezes. He hasn't said those three words in a very long time.

"That's . . . nice to hear. It's been a while."

He doesn't flinch but stares deep into her eyes through the screen. "I just wanted you to know that. Before you go off on this understandably huge tangent in your life, I just want you to know you have me in your corner. No matter what. I still think we can find a way through all of this, together. So yeah, pressing pause. You do what you need to, take care of your dad, investigate your past, and when you're done, come home. Charlie and I will be waiting. We'll tackle the lab situation. And we'll talk."

When his face is no longer on her screen, she is surprised to feel bereft by its absence.

It's just the day, she thinks. *It's just you're feeling off balance, and he is a steadying presence. Nothing has really changed.*

Keep telling yourself that.

CHAPTER TEN

In the kitchen, pouring a glass of water, Halley has a moment of sheer dislocation—everything is different, and now she has to go chasing demons from the past. She is hooked, though. She'd be hooked if this were a sample case being taught in one of her old classes or a case coming through the lab. That it's her mother and sister? There is no way she can look away.

She sees another email, from Ivan. It's sent from his personal account, not the lab. She debates opening it, but her curiosity gets the better of her.

> Dear Halley,
>
> I'm sorry everything happened the way it did yesterday. I had no choice. The press release was not appropriate. You have my full support if you plan to file suit against the company for wrongful termination. I will be on your side, I promise. I think you have a case.
>
> IH

A wave of relief flows through her. Well, that's . . . helpful. She wonders if Ivan, too, is being pushed out of the very lab he built, if there is more going on there than she's aware of, but the lure of her mother's murder is stronger right now. She'll deal with DC once she's solved this conundrum to her satisfaction.

Bolstered, she opens Theo's email and downloads the attachment. She writes him back three separate emails, varying degrees of "Thank you for your help, your concern, your love," then finally decides there is nothing to say that she hasn't already. She deletes the drafts and opens the document instead. The computer whirs for a while, then images begin to fill the screen.

The text is dry. Formal. Familiar. She's read plenty of autopsy reports before.

She sees her mother's name. Her weight. The body is that of a well-nourished adult female. The body is sixty-five inches and one hundred fifteen pounds and appears to be the stated age of thirty-five.

The body.

Her mother was elegant, well proportioned, lithe. A skier, a dancer, a runner. She had great legs, calves the shape of hearts, tight tendons in her ankles—two traits Halley has also inherited. She wasn't an athlete like her mom, though. She's softer. Rounder. More lush, as Theo calls it.

> Three gaping stab wounds are present on the midsternum, measuring 2.5 inches in length, 2 inches in length, and 3 inches in length, with clean, regular margins. External contusions to the knees and elbows are present. A patch of hair is missing from the skull.
>
> Perforation left ventricle . . .
>
> Pericardial sac 600 ml of clotted blood . . .
>
> Previous injury to the abdomen, healing hematoma 13 cm . . .
>
> Murder . . .

New words come. A shriek. Halley shuts her eyes and listens to the memory.

"How could you do this to me?"

"Cat, honey, I love you."

She opens her eyes and scans the rest of the report. It is basic, straightforward, and the most painful thing she's ever experienced.

Cat stabbed Susannah three times in the chest. Halley thinks about how hard that is to do—was her mom down on the ground? Standing? Did the first wound happen standing, and the last two when she was down?

She tries to visualize it from the drawing, the almost childlike outline of a body with three lines designating the three stab wounds. It's too bare bones. She needs to get back to the screaming, shrieking voice. That's how she'll know the truth about what happened. She has to access the memories of that day.

She can imagine a million things, and none of them will be accurate until she sees the actual crime scene photos, reads the analysis, and puts herself back in the scenario. Maybe then things will become clear.

Halley scrolls through everything Theo sent, but nothing else shakes free. Her head is starting to hurt again, and a glance at the clock shows it's past midnight. She needs to rest.

Using the ancient poker they found at the annual swap meet when she was eight, she smacks the embers of the fire so they'll die out and goes to bed. Ailuros is already there, on his back, waiting for her to rub his belly.

She does, frustrated. How can she remember the swap meet as if it happened yesterday, and not remember seeing her sister kill their mother?

Growing up, she was enamored of the seasonality of her home, but now, the April winds are too loud, the air too cold. The darkness too dark. The cat jumps from the bed and startles her from a light doze. She tries to get back to sleep but is thwarted by her own brain. It's hammering away on the reality of her new circumstance, trying to comprehend what it all means while her heart concurrently breaks. She tosses and turns, staring at the ceiling of her childhood room, painted black and plastered with pinpoint glow-in-the-dark star stickers and thin strips of barely visible green tape. A representation of the stars and constellations that she knows as intimately as the back of her hand and, oddly enough, exactly mimics the sky outside right now. There is Arcturus, and Betelgeuse, and Pollux. Sirius, and Canis Major. Hydra. The Big Dipper. Orion.

She maps the night skies and listens to the trees whispering their secrets. How is she supposed to move forward with her life, her plans, when the entire past has been a lie?

Her scientific brain chimes in. *It's not really a lie. Your mom is dead regardless.* That philosophical conundrum makes her sit up in the bed and wrap her arms around her knees, like she used to when she'd had a nightmare. There will be no sleeping tonight.

She has a proper argument with herself, just to pass the time.

Mom's been gone all this time—does it matter how she left this earth?

God, yes. Of course it matters.

She was taken away. That's a fact. She dies in either scenario.

But my sister didn't die. I've loved Cat my whole life, mourned her for twenty-eight years, missing the very idea of her, and now? How do I love someone who's done such a horrible thing? How do I turn off the emotions, harden my heart toward her, go from love to hate?

How could Cat have done *such a thing? What drove her to murder the one person who had openly adored her? Yes, they fought; yes, there were tensions in the house because of the new stepfamily and the usual teenage brattiness. But when push came to shove, Susannah would die for Cat.*

Did die for Cat.

It's this last thought that drives Halley from the bed and back downstairs to the computer. She takes a seat. Ailuros is nowhere to be seen, and she realizes she misses him. "Kitty? Where are you?"

He ignores her.

Halley searched on Google for her sister earlier and found the article and the missing persons report, but nothing more. She decides to try a few new parameters, and this time scores an article that was written about Catriona in a long-form magazine, actually only a few years ago. Not wanting to wait until she can get to the library in the morning and read it for free, she pays the subscription fee to access the article, heart in her throat. It's not so much about her sister, she realizes, reading, but about the failures and successes of the juvenile justice system in general. It is unsatisfying, especially because it is so open ended, discussing the need for forgiveness and understanding for juvenile criminals, how there need to be massive reforms, and doesn't detail Cat's crimes at all, other than identifying her as a success story of the system. A success.

But it does leave Halley with one tantalizing piece of information.

While Cat was in juvie, her sister applied to and was accepted into Harvard.

Did they know her sister went to jail for murder? And let her in anyway? Was she part of some sort of rehabilitation program? Did she graduate?

Halley starts digging. This is quantifiable information. If Cat got out of the system in 1993, there's a time frame to look at. Harvard's archives are accessible, and while the Facebook alumni pages are private, some of the members of the groups are listed. She goes through them one by one.

It is nearing dawn when she finds a name that rings a bell.

Tyler Armstrong. Class of 1995.

Tyler Armstrong.

Where has she seen this name?

She scrambles back to the missing persons notice. Scans it. The narrative is brief. No names are listed. Just a phone number to call if there is information.

It's too late—too early—to call the number, so she plugs it into the reverse directory and comes up blank. But the area code is 6-1-7—that's Boston.

It's not out of the realm of reason that her sister had friends in Boston, especially if she went to Harvard. She probably lived there, maybe after graduating.

She searches "Boston Missing Persons" plus "Catriona James," and there's a hit. A long-out-of-date WordPress mommy blog has a very serious entry about a friend of a friend's ex-wife going missing. The friend of a friend is named Tyler.

Halley is going mad trying to put together the pieces. She tries looking him up on Facebook, but there are about forty Tyler Armstrongs. It's not a unique name. But when she puts in "Harvard" plus "Tyler Armstrong," she sees an entry. The face is unfamiliar, but the city he's from is not. Nashville, Tennessee, is listed as his hometown.

Her hometown, too. But her memories of Nashville are so fuzzy, she can barely recall her life there.

She's going at this wrong. Maybe she needs to put herself back in the setting. Over the years, she hasn't thought much about her childhood in Nashville. It's a fun connection—it seems like everyone she's ever met knows someone who lives in Nashville. But Halley hasn't been back. Plus, she was so little. Losing her mom and Cat was so traumatic. She remembers the feelings of pain and loss, but nothing detailed.

She closes her eyes and thinks about their house. Goes for sensory details. It was on a quiet tree-lined street in an area called Belle Meade. It was a cottage, white brick, near the golf course, with a grassy backyard and a gray patio. There was a yellow plastic slide. She fudges in a sliding glass door—there was a door from the backyard to the living room, but it could easily have been something else—and enters. Inside . . . Her room is pink. Back to the living room. The carpet soft under her bare feet. There is a thick slab of dark wood above the fireplace, and she turns—blackness slams her mind. It's unrelenting obsidian, like staring at an empty chalkboard. There is nothing else.

Interesting.

Wondering if she should look into some sort of memory regression therapy, she moves her child self outside the cottage.

She can remember a spring day, with forsythia blooming. Halley was in first grade at the church school down the street from their house. Cat, a decade older and infinitely cooler, went to West End School. She had her driver's license and was newly in charge of dropping off and picking up Halley. She remembers there were arguments about it, but Cat showed up every day, on time. It wasn't until she picked up her friend, too . . . Damn, what was that girl's name?

She gets up and stretches, her poor brain feeling as strained as if she'd just taken the hardest final of her life.

She runs in place for a few minutes. Pretty girl. Buck teeth. Buck teeth . . . They called her Bucktooth . . . Tracy, that was her name. She had a bunch of siblings, and she was nice to Halley because her brother was a friend of Cat's. And his name was . . . "Tyler!" she shouts triumphantly. "I will be damned."

Tracy and Tyler Armstrong grew up on the same street as Halley and Cat.

She gives her left shoulder a little punch, a "Well done, you," then grabs an old, half-used spiral-bound notebook from the junk drawer. She needs to start keeping track of all this information, and this is how she's been trained to think. Exploration of the smallest details, from start to finish, documented.

It doesn't hurt that she has a very good memory, not quite photographic but remarkable enough that she rarely has to write things down. That's also something she needs to explore, because if her memory is so clear from the time they get to Marchburg on but so vague about the most traumatic event of her life, then something is wrong. It's almost like it was interfered with, the way she blanks out every time she thinks back to the accident. The murder, now.

She glances at the clock. It's almost six. The sun is up. Despite the lack of sleep, she feels jazzed and decides to start the coffee and launch herself into the day. She can nap later, after the FedEx comes and she's visited her dad in the hospital. She has the distinct feeling he might know more than he's letting on.

Then she needs to call the mystery number on the missing persons report, and Harvard and the Boston police department, and track down Tyler Armstrong.

Leave this to the professionals, Halley, her mind says.

Shut up, she tells it.

CHAPTER ELEVEN

CATRIONA

Brockville Artist Colony
Literature Workshop
2002

I look up to see every person in the critique group staring at me, and not in a good way. I shuffle the typed pages into a neat stack.

"Um, that's the end of the story."

The assignment was to write something autobiographical, and admittedly, I've gotten a bit carried away, especially imagining the gruesome deaths of my fictional husband and the nanny. But all in all, I thought it was a solid short story—one of my better ones. Though by the rude interruption and the shocked looks, I have clearly unnerved my fellow students.

I fight back a smile. I'm not entirely surprised. I have that effect on people.

After a few beats, there is a smattering of applause. Tammy Boone gives me an approving glance. "It's quite visceral, Catriona. Very nice. I felt Ellie's reaction was well captured, and I like how you pulled us out of her fantasy of killing her husband into the sad reality she was faced with. And I apologize for the interruption just as we were finding out that her imagination had run amok." She turns to the group, to the jury, pushing her oversize glasses up her nose. "Does anyone else have notes for Catriona?"

The jerk blonde—damn, what is her name? I'm usually better with names—chimes in. "I was very pulled out of the story by the aside, when you say Ellie has a small issue with anger. Clearly. Furthermore, it felt redundant, as you so vividly portray her fury. I think you could lose that without impinging upon the integrity of the story."

Impinging upon the integrity of the story? *Screw you, lady.*

There are murmurs of assent from the circle of writers, which infuriates me. Tammy purses her lips. She seems to think that I'm vulnerable and am hurt by the group's reaction. I'm not. I can't be. I don't have access to those kinds of emotions. I want approval as much as the next person, sure, but the disapproval doesn't cost me as it might you.

"I don't know that I agree, Brenda."

(Brenda! That's it. In my defense, she doesn't look like a Brenda. She looks like a Farrah, or a Courtney, or a Sloane. It's the hair, of course. She probably spends more time with her hot rollers than her typewriter.)

Tammy continues. "I think that sort of experimentation in the narrative allows a whole new storytelling mechanism. Think of it as a voiceover. I was particularly reminded of the television show *My So-Called Life*, with Claire Danes. Have you seen it? It has that sort of autobiographical voiceover that gives the viewer more information about the character's internal life. Let's not discount this as an effective technique to understand Ellie's rage. I imagine there's more of that to come, and it could be quite interesting to the story."

"But it's a cheat," Brenda continues. We took an immediate dislike to one another last night. The whole evening had been colored by her condescension and aggressive need to show how smart she was. I simply do not respond to that sort of fire hydrant marking. I'm incapable. God, she's still talking. "Not only a cheat, but it's also a tell. The rule is, we shouldn't tell, we should show. Inserting this sort of aside isn't showing. It's telling." She sits back in her chair, quite pleased with herself.

Tammy turns to me. "Catriona? Do you have a response?"

I have several responses, most of which include colloquial phrases designed specifically to inflame and irritate. I've been trained not to say the first thing that pops into my mind, as it is generally something not socially acceptable. I'm very much like my character Ellie in that regard. Full of rage. The kind of rage that leads one to murder. I just do a better job of hiding it.

Instead, I shake my head. I am acutely aware that the long hair I normally use to hide my face when I'm trying to seem embarrassed is gone. I stupidly cut it off to chin level before I came here, and it sucks. It was a wonderful mask, and without it, I feel exposed.

Tammy shifts in her chair, and the spell is broken. "All right. More thoughts? Anyone?"

And they're off, a round-robin of negative opinions. The more people speak, the more shell-shocked I am. It is quite clear that instead of being the solid story I thought it was, I have just laid a gigantic egg on the most important stage of my life. I have to tune out their "constructive" comments, not making eye contact, just stare out the window at the impenetrable screen of dark-green trees, my anger building to a peak, until finally, Tammy calls time. That was excruciating. But I'm proud of myself for taking it, not reacting. And I promise myself I will not slink into anyone's cabin tonight. Make myself swear it.

But I might watch . . .

No, you will not!

"All right, folks. I think perhaps now is a good time to break for the morning. Great work, everyone. Tomorrow, I want to hear from *you*, Brenda. Since you were the first to jump in with a critique of Catriona's work, you win that honor. I'm sure we will all be dazzled by your words." The slightly accusatory note in Tammy's voice makes me inwardly gloat. Brenda was overtly harsh, has been since the moment we touched hands in greeting.

She's just jealous that you've got more talent than she does.

Stop. Please. Not now.

I have also been trained to turn off the voice in my head, the one that lures with false promises and seduces with honeyed words. And sometimes tells me to do things that I know aren't right. My demon. It has taken years of therapy, years of mind-body integrations, biofeedback, meditation, medication, to learn how to tell the voice to fuck off and leave me alone.

I gave in once. And it almost cost me everything. That will never, ever happen again.

Tammy puts a hand on my arm as she passes, following the rest of the fiction class filing toward the cabin door. I stop myself from yanking my arm away; I do not like being touched.

You're a frigid bitch.

That voice is not my demon's, but my husband's. Ex-husband, now. The papers came the day before I left for the retreat. I shoved them in my bag and am planning to sign them tonight. A private celebration of a marriage that has run its course, and then some.

"What's your plan for the rest of the day, Catriona?"

What is the right response here? *Drink some hemlock because I'm so mortified?* A bit over the top.

Instead, I sigh as if summoning what tiny bit of dignity I have left. I am very good at acting. I have to be.

"Oh, well, I thought I'd take a walk? Then maybe work on this scene some more. Maybe take away a bit of the visceralness. It's too much, I see that now. People recoiled when the knife came out. Not exactly what I was going for."

"Don't do that," Tammy says. "It's a very strong opening. I'm very interested to see where you take this. You know we chose you because your work has an edge. As a matter of fact, from what I've seen of your other poems and stories, this one feels almost tame. Let it all go. Don't hold back. You can allow your natural darkness into your work. It's part of your voice and will become your signature style, if you let it. I'd be happy to do a one-on-one tomorrow after class, if you'd like."

I immediately nod. I don't need the class's approval, but the teacher's? She can be of great use, and I am more than happy to take advantage of her interest. "I would like that. I'm missing something here, and I'm not sure what. Maybe I need to change the point of view?"

"We can talk about that tomorrow. First person could be very effective. It would allow us to get deeper into your character's actions, her thoughts. Think on it, and maybe rewrite a few paragraphs, just to see how it feels."

It's going to feel like you were holding the knife as it slashed him open, and it will feel so good.

Shut. Up.

"I'll do that, Tammy. Thank you. And please, call me Cat."

She smiles at this invitation to familiarity. "Okay. Cat? Don't let this lot upset you. They're all just trying to get my attention. I'll tell you a little secret. I've seen parts of Brenda's story, and predictably, it is excellent writing, but lacking soul. The execution is there, but there's none of the passion and wildness that I see in your work. She has, and will continue to, spend her career writing small. These retreats are an excellent way to cull the writers trying to get noticed who are in love with their own prose. Brenda has been doing this for a long time, and she hasn't had any real success yet. You're young. You're supremely talented. You're going to get pushback, so you might as well learn this lesson now: Be above it all. Don't let them get to you. You will succeed where they fail."

This can't be real. Tammy Boone likes my work. Loves my work.

Don't be an idiot. They pay her to say these things. She gives all of the students the same line.

Shut. Up.

Tammy has a benevolent smile. I've seen them before, from people who are genuinely good inside. There was a therapist, once, when I was young, who had that same shining light inside her. She probably saved my life. And now, in a similar vein, Tammy Boone is glowing like an angel and offering me a leg up.

"Um . . . thank you?"

"You're welcome. So buck up. I guarantee we are going to see it all again tomorrow. This is what the first few days are like. You are a gladiator in the arena, and you are still standing." She gives a symbolic thumbs-up. "Okay?"

Fine. She likes you. Smile pretty for her.

I am desperate to escape now, feeling the claustrophobia build, just me and Tammy Boone—*and me! Don't forget me!*—talking about writing like this is any other day. Being encouraged like this is too much. I am absolutely going to take a pill the second I get back to the cabin. The psychotropics help dim the demon's voice. They ruin the creative voice, as well, but I'd rather write shitty fiction than indulge the monster in my head. I can't believe I've let him in while I'm here, of all places, of all times. Where I've gone to escape. Where I've gone to relax. To connect with my creativity, and finally, finally, write the book I've always dreamed of writing. I am here for two months, and damn it, I'm going to make this work if it kills me. I have so much to see. So much to do. I've been trying to get here for a long, long time.

The Brockville Writers' Retreat almost guarantees a publishing contract when the query letter mentions a successful graduation. If you have to query at all—it's well known that the retreat leaders often pass the favorites along directly to their own publishing teams. The deal announcements in the publishing trades read "a graduate of the Brockville Writers' Retreat" as if the writer earned a double PhD in astrophysics and mythology from Harvard. I'm not going to screw this up, damn it. There is too much at stake.

I've wanted to be an artist since I could pick up a crayon and scribble on the thick art paper in my kindergarten class. A writer since I started making the dot above my *i* a cheery little open circle. At first, the voices were plentiful, and I drew them on the page, skilled drawings for one so young. Then came the words, a torrent of imagination. My childish stories had many points of view, enough that they put me into the gifted-and-talented program at school. I thrived under the individualized attention of the teachers, but it was always a struggle to keep my mind under control. The voices, the characters, the points of view—they were all living in my head.

As I got older, many of those internal characters peeled off. My mind became inscrutable, even to me. It was cacophony, chaos, impossible. I stopped showing people my art, because the darkness of those bleak lines freaked people out. I remember once seeing Munch's *The Scream* and feeling at ease. This was me. I was *The Scream* personified.

And then there was the horrible time when I lost my mother, which I never talk about.

After that, I had professional psychological help. A million meds, a million conversations. And eventually, I was left numbed and with only one extraneous voice. I hate him. He loves me in too many unhealthy ways to count. And we are stuck with one another.

I am twenty-nine years old, about to be divorced, having an early midlife crisis. I've cut my hair and run away to the Blue Ridge Mountains, to a small town in the middle of nowhere, to a retreat that might or might not help me get where I need my career to be, and I am already screwing it up. I don't want to be on the radar; that woman, Brenda, sensed it and called me out at every chance. This kind of attention makes me uncomfortable. As if some people can see inside my mind, see the scrolling black circles that live there. As if they, too, can hear the voice.

My demon loves every minute of discord. He feeds on it. Stress makes it worse.

You know it, baby. Come to Papa.

I need my meds.

I leave the writing cabin and hurry toward mine. I will suck down a pill, drown the bastard out, take a walk, do my assignment, and all will be well. It has to be. I have nothing left.

WEDNESDAY

CHAPTER TWELVE

HALLEY

At 6:30 a.m., the FedEx truck rumbles into the drive. Halley, hair dripping and already fully caffeinated, signs for the package, then retreats to the kitchen and sets it on the table, trying to get up the courage to open the envelope. It is thick. Theo must have gotten some photos. It was bad enough reading the autopsy report. Will she be able to handle seeing her mother's body cut open, reduced to the machine that houses the soul?

Part of her wants to walk away from this. Like her dad says, it's a dangerous road, memory. But what sort of scientist would she be if she shied away when things got difficult?

This is your family.

That's not enough of a deterrent. Her incessant curiosity is usually a help. Usually. Now, it's going to get her in trouble. She can feel it like a breeze coming through the window.

The envelope opens. The pages spill out. Theo has been thorough. He's contacted the Nashville homicide people and gotten more than he'd promised.

Crime scene photos, the autopsy report, notes from the detectives.

Her mother's long white arm, trailing off the stainless steel autopsy table.

Halley feels the pressure building inside her. This was a mistake. A terrible mistake.

She shovels the pages back into the envelope, her throat closing with tears. Who is she kidding? There is no way she can look at this dispassionately. This is her *mom*. She might not remember her well, but there are still moments, sensory details, that give her a sense of who this woman was. The scraps and fragments of a missing life. Warm fuzzies. The scent of Oil of Olay. The shine of a diamond stud—the same diamond studs that Halley wears religiously. A Christmas morning with footie pajamas. Susannah chasing her around with the camcorder.

The hurt of a pulled pigtail. A bruise on her arm being prodded. Whispers, whispers—*"what a nasty little thing you are"*—and nightmares after.

That wall of black. Red spots on the white living room rug.

Are these memories? Are they hers?

Her breath is coming short, and in her hurry, two pictures have dropped to the floor. She tries not to look as she picks them up but catches a glimpse of one: it's of the living room. Her old living room. Different from what she imagined, remembered, but the same.

A sharp pain constricts her chest, but she lets herself remember it, the room coming to life in her mind.

A white rug, and finger paint everywhere. Her mother is going to be so angry. She has to clean it up. But she can't reach the paper towels on the counter. She drags a stool and climbs up. Rips them off. Hurries back to the living room. There is something big lying on the floor. She can't look. She must clean up the paint.

She wipes and wipes and wipes, and it smears, going deeper into the rug's pile. She whimpers in frustration. Fear. Tears. It smells strange. Her head hurts so bad.

Voices. There are voices. The female voice shrieks. She can't make out the words.

She looks at the mantel. The photo of the family has paint on it. The fireplace is red. The doorbell rings, and rings, and rings again . . .

And then she's back in her kitchen, her hair making her neck cold, shivering with some sort of recall chills. She feels ill. Her arm hurts. A bruise has formed on the soft underside, just above her wrist. Did she do that to herself? Ailuros is staring at her with crossed blue eyes, his tail fluffed out in fear. She must have screamed, made some noise of distress.

"Sorry, baby. Come here."

He allows himself to be comforted, then strolls off, indignant.

She needs to talk to her dad. She needs more answers. She needs to understand what's happening to her.

Halley has never been anxious, not like some of her friends. But she recognizes this feeling in herself as more than discomfort, but a frantic desperation to know. To understand.

Is this what it feels like to lose your mind? A rush of emotions and sensations and mysterious memories? All crowing, shouting, fighting to be heard, seen, experienced. What was it Theo said about the madness closing in? How did he know this would happen? She is seeing spots.

God, Halley. Breathe.

She drags in some air, wills her heart rate to slow. She is working herself up, and for what? Nothing she does now will change what happened. Knowing won't undo the act. Her mother will forever be gone, a ghost in the machine. She can never get her back.

She can't help it, though. She has to know. *Why* was Cat dangerous? What was wrong with her mind that made her lash out at her little sister?

Before Halley leaves for the hospital, she tries the number on the missing persons report. It rings and rings, but no one answers, and there's no voicemail. She tries it again, thinking maybe she put in the wrong digit somewhere. Same thing.

Frustrated, she puts the envelope and pictures into her backpack and heads to the Jeep. She cranks some Nirvana and drives to the hospital. As she pulls into the parking lot, her cell rings.

"Theo? Good morning."

"Hey. Did you sleep?"

"Hardly call it that. I dozed a bit. I'm already at the hospital. The package came."

"Did you look at it?"

"I started. You were right, it was too much, so I've put it away. I found out some stuff about Cat, though. She went to Harvard after she got out. I'm going to make some calls after I talk to Dad, see if I can't nail down some more details."

"And do what with them?" he asks, the inquisitorial tone making her pause.

"Well, if she's missing, maybe I can find her."

There is a deep pause on the other side of the phone. "You want to go searching for a woman who's been gone for fifteen years, who, let me remind you, murdered your mother and tried to kill you, too? Isn't that a bit . . ."

"A bit what?"

He sighs. "A bit foolhardy. You have no resources. No training—no real-world experience." At her indignant sigh: "Hal, I know you're a trained forensic scientist, and good at it. That's not what I mean. Everyone is saying your sister is dangerous. I think maybe you need to take a step back, think rationally about this. Let law enforcement know what you've discovered. See if they'll agree to look into it."

She can't help it; she sees red. "I *am* acting more than rationally. This is my world being blown up here, Theo. I think, under the circumstances, I deserve a damn award for how rational I'm being."

"Okay, I'm sorry. I didn't mean to upset you. I'm worried about you. I want to help. What can I do to help?"

"Find out who filed the missing persons report. I want to talk to whoever it was. There's a Boston phone number on it. I called it but it rang off the hook."

Silence. She can imagine him with his head down, running his thumb and forefinger along his eyebrows as he does when he's thinking. "Give me the number. I'll make some calls, see what I can find out. But Halley, you have to promise me you're going to be careful. Some secrets should stay buried."

A knock against the side of the Jeep makes Halley jerk. Kater is standing by the window, grinning.

"I gotta go. I need to talk to my dad. Thanks, Theo. I promise I'll be careful."

She hangs up before he can reply, just in case. Last night's kindnesses from him feel far away.

She rolls down the window. Nurses scurry past into the building. A chilly breeze ruffles her hair, which is still damp.

Kater immediately looks concerned. "You okay? Your face is all red. What were you doing, sitting here holding your breath?"

"Something like that. How are you?"

"I'm fine. Seriously, are you okay? You seem . . . off."

"Oh, you know. Stress about Dad, and stuff."

"Stuff?"

This is a friend, someone she can trust. And she doesn't want to be alone with this right now.

"I just found out my mom didn't die in a car accident like I always thought."

"Oh, Halley, I am so sorry. How did she die?"

"Murder. She was murdered."

Kater's face goes white. "Jeez. That's . . . By who? Not your dad?"

"Oh, God, no. Actually, it was my sister. Who I also thought was dead. Apparently it's been 'hide the truth from Halley' all these years."

"Your dad didn't tell you? Why?"

Damn good question. "He thought I was in danger. Which . . . Well, none of it matters now. I found out, and I need to track down my sister. She went missing fifteen years ago, supposedly."

Halley gets out of the Jeep, and they walk toward the ER entrance, their feet grinding the loose gravel.

"Do you know from where?"

"No, but I'll figure it out. I have some leads to follow. My husband is checking some stuff, too."

"Ooh. Tell me about this husband? Is he the hottie you always dreamed of?"

She thinks back to his declaration of love last night. "Sort of. Yeah. He's hot. Tall. Works for ATF." She smiles despite herself. "We're having some issues. He's worried about me."

They hit the doors, which zoom apart with a pneumatic hiss. Kater pulls her still-wet hair into a bun. "Listen, I hate to run, I want to talk more, but I'm totally late for my shift. You should come out with us tonight. Just some folks from town. No pressure."

"I don't know if I'd be great company, Kater. There's a lot going on."

"It's Marchburg, Halley. How much could possibly be going on?" She winks, and it eases the tension.

Halley laughs. "True. All right. I'll try. Where should I meet you?"

"Taco Joe's. We're getting some beers and tacos."

"We?"

"You, me, Aaron, a few other people from town. You should know most everyone."

"Are you trying to set me up? Because I really do have a husband."

"You're not wearing a ring . . . so . . . maybe?" Kater's pretty face shines when she smiles. "I gotta run. See you at seven."

A night out sounds fun if she could let herself get loose. A few other people from town—Halley didn't go to the high school in Jasper like the rest of this crowd. She wonders if she really will know people, but it doesn't matter. She needs food; it will be nice not to have to cook. And she has to admit she's curious about how Aaron has turned out. They'd had a couple of near misses, but he was four years older and a little bit of a player. Cute. Lacrosse captain, lifeguard at the pool. Always had a girlfriend but wasn't ever in trouble. Wholesome. She often wondered about him when she left but was always too embarrassed to ask. He helped teach her to drive in the pool parking lot the summer before she got her license. Kissed her softly by the lifeguard stand under the fireworks.

Getting together with friends feels like a betrayal of her mother's ghost. She is consumed with the need to see this right, to find her sister and confront her, find out why she's taken away the one thing Halley can't ever replace. Her anger is bubbling below the surface, and she's trying hard to keep it in check.

Her sister is probably dead, and that's the second slap-in-the-face injustice of all this. But she has to know. Has to find out more. Has to find out why.

Her dad's got color in his face today, and they've helped him bathe—his skin is pink from a fresh shave, and his hair is damp, curling around his ears.

And there is a woman in his room, standing by his bed, holding his hand. He is gazing at her with a goofy smile. She is not a nurse.

"Um . . . hello?"

They startle and drop their hands. The woman turns, and Halley recognizes her former English teacher at Goode. "Mrs. Patterson?" she asks, incredulous. Her dad clears his throat.

"Halley. Hi," she says with a blushing smile. She is pretty, with cornflower blue eyes and blond ringlets framing her heart-shaped face, her hair pulled high on her head. She's wearing a blue button-down, the same color as her eyes, and khaki slacks. There is a glint from her left hand, and Halley's jaw drops.

"Something you want to tell me, Dad?" Halley asks archly. She can't decide whether to be happy or furious.

"Halley. You rushed off the phone and came down here before I had a chance to say anything. I . . . I didn't . . . I wanted to tell you in person. Anne and I have been seeing each other for a while now, and . . ." He is sputtering, and Halley squares her shoulders and decides to be pissed later.

"You're allowed to have a girlfriend. And a wife. Mrs. Patterson—"

"Anne. Please," she adds softly.

"You and Anne make a lovely couple."

She isn't kidding; she actually means it. The idea that her dad hasn't been alone this whole time brings her a surprising amount of joy—and relief. He won't be alone if she leaves to investigate Cat's disappearance.

Now that is a selfish thought, Halley James.

Her dad also blows out a relieved breath. "I didn't think you'd mind. Anne's been, well, we've been timing her visits so I could break this to you gently, and you caught us off guard. With everything that's happening, it felt like a lot to pile on."

"Seriously, Dad, Anne, this is great. I'm very happy for you. When's the wedding?"

"Oh, we don't know. Especially now." Anne gestures toward his leg. "Quentin was hoping we'd do it this summer sometime, but I'd like him to be comfortable and healed. We don't need anything big. We just didn't want you to be shocked or dismayed."

"I am far from dismayed. This is the happiest news. I'm thrilled for you both. Congratulations."

Anne opens her arms for a hug, and Halley gladly steps into them. The emotions coursing through her are positive ones, for the most part. Her mom's been gone for a long time. This joy is overdue. Halley admires the ring, a stately, classic round affair in a Tiffany setting, then gives her dad a hug, too. This is a good thing; she knows it deep in her soul.

"If it's okay with you, Anne could move into the house now and help me get back on my feet."

Anne's almost vibrating with excitement. "I absolutely could. School's out next week and I don't have plans. But now that you're home, Halley, I can postpone for a while. I don't want to intrude."

Halley avoids the invisible fist pump, feeling only a tiny bit guilty at her internal reaction. This is the freedom she needs. No responsibilities for a few days so she can really dig into this situation with her sister. "Not intruding at all. I think that's a wonderful idea. If you're here to take care of Dad, and Ailuros . . ."

Anne's eyes are shining. "I am. They are both safe with me."

"I'll be up and around in no time," Quentin bellows, and both women look at him and shake their heads in unison, sharing a sideways glance. He won't be up and around, not for a few weeks at least, but with this surprise, now Halley has nothing to stop her from finding out what happened to her sister.

They catch up a bit—Halley always liked Anne Patterson—and when her dad starts yawning, Anne checks her watch. "Why don't I let you two chat for a bit? I have some errands to run."

She kisses Quentin on the forehead and pats Halley's arm. "Want to have dinner tonight? I'll cook. Lasagna still your favorite?"

"I was supposed to go out with some friends, but I can totally reschedule."

"Oh, don't do that. I'm sure you have loads of folks to catch up with. We'll do it another time."

When Anne's gone, Halley looks at her dad with an arched brow.

He laughs, that nervous-hyena thing the drugs are pressing him into. "I know. I should have told you we were dating."

"Ya think?" Halley grows serious. "We need to talk for a minute. I'm very happy for you, but I'm really upset with you, too. What else are you keeping from me? These are some pretty big life changes to take in all at once. Finding out about Mom, then Cat, now Anne? If there's more, you better hit me now."

"There's not. I swear."

"I need to talk about it. It's too much. I'm starting to remember things."

He immediately grows wary. "What are you remembering?"

"Snatches. Words. Flashes, images. Nothing that makes sense. I'm trying to fill in the blanks, but there's nothing to work with. I need you to fill them in for me."

"You should let this go, Halley. I know you're a curious woman, and I know this seems like a grand mystery for you to solve. But it's not. Chances are Catriona isn't alive. And that would be a relief, to be honest. She had dark thoughts, and I wouldn't be surprised if she hurt herself, ended her own life. When I say she was troubled, I am not kidding. There are things in this world best left alone."

"I can't. This is too big to ignore, Dad." She fills him in on what she's discovered, noticing with interest how he withdraws from her. She's not the only one experiencing pain at these revelations. "It's not fair that you won't talk to me. I understand that you're hurting, but this is huge."

He takes her hand. "I know this week is throwing you for a loop. If there's any way I can counsel you to not get involved, I will."

"Dad. She murdered my mother."

She watches his face for more, but his lids are heavy. This is exhausting him. As much as she wants to hear more, she needs to leave it alone for now.

"I hear you. I promise. I won't take this too far. But if she is alive, and she is dangerous, finding out where she is won't be a bad thing."

"I love you, Halley. I don't want to lose you, too. Please, let this lie."

She squeezes his hand. "Don't worry about me. I can handle myself."

CHAPTER THIRTEEN

Halley stops for a sandwich at her favorite little café right down the street from Goode. The owner, a self-styled hippie named Sunshine, makes Halley a tuna melt and slides a Diet Coke across the tin counter, and in between bites, Halley deflects pointed questions about life, her marriage, and her dad. When she's finished, Sunshine, who's no dummy and can tell Halley's avoiding talking to her, puts a bag of snickerdoodles on the counter with the check, and Halley gives her a grateful hug before she leaves. Snickerdoodles are her favorite.

She leaves the Jeep parked on Main Street and heads through the massive gates to the Goode School library. A bonus of being an alum—you are always welcomed back to campus and are free to avail yourself of its amenities. The gym, the pool, the library, the bookstore. All are places Halley has frequented over the years postgraduation. The library at Goode, funded by the massive alumni endowment, rivals that of any major college. It also has state-of-the-art computers and subscriptions to all the major news services and magazines. Combined with Halley's own database accesses, she is pretty sure she can find Tyler Armstrong.

She checks her email, sees a message from Theo.

> H—the missing persons report was filed by a woman named Alison Everlane. The phone number belongs to her, but it's a private listing for a landline, and might not have voicemail. No idea if it's hers or what.

Everlane was a student at Harvard at the same time as your sister. She works for a nonprofit in DC now. Here's their number. That's all I've got for now.

BE CAREFUL! Theo x

Theo x? What the hell is going on? Her husband has never signed anything with a kiss.

She pulls a ton of phone numbers, wanders outside to the quad, finds an unoccupied bench, eats a cookie, and starts making calls.

First up is the Boston Police Department. After identifying herself as the sister of a missing person, she is transferred to the district that covers Harvard's campuses. A few more transfers get her to a detective named Rafael Cohen, who is wary but willing to talk.

Halley explains who she is, her connection to Cat, and the information she's found on the missing persons report.

She glosses over the "Why now?" she hears in his tone, not wanting to go into the family dynamics, just sticks with the parts of the truth he needs. She and her dad had moved away, and they lost touch, and she just found out Cat was missing. After taking down all of Halley's information, Detective Cohen looks it up and confirms Alison Everlane filed the report, but there's nothing else he can give her. He reminds her that adults go missing all the time. She agrees and promises to call him back if she discovers anything. She doesn't know if he's holding back or if he's not taking her seriously, but either way, he feels like a dead end for the time being.

Her next call is another try at the number on the flyer that Theo says belongs to Alison. She's surprised when, this time, the phone is answered within two bleats of the ringer.

"Hello? Who is this?"

"Um, hi. My name is Halley James. I think you know my sister, Catriona Handon?"

There is a huge, gusty sigh. "Oh, boy. After all this time. They found her, then?"

Bingo.

"No, actually. This is sort of a weird story, but I didn't know Cat was missing. I didn't know she was alive at all. I thought she died when I was six, along with my mother."

"Really? How could that be?"

"Long story. Can you tell me about her going missing?"

There is a long pause. "She never told me she had a sister. How do I know you're not some reporter faking this to get a story?"

What the heck?

"I'm not a reporter. I swear it. I am her sister. For the rest, I guess we're going to have to trust one another," Halley says lightly. "Did she tell you about our mom?"

"That she died when Cat was sixteen? Yes. A terrible car accident. It was tragic, how she was left to fend for herself."

"Fend for herself?"

"She had to finish high school and get into college, and she was all alone. What sort of father leaves a grieving daughter? She said her dad bolted. He was her stepdad, and he never liked her."

Halley makes a note of this. *Cat lies.*

Alison jumps in again. "So why is it she never mentioned you? She didn't live with you?"

"I'm ten years younger. I was only six when our mom died. It was a second marriage. I was the bonus baby."

"Okay." Alison sounds doubtful, but Halley plows on.

"I don't know what all Cat has told you, or didn't, but can we jump ahead to her going missing? You filed a report in 2002. How long had she been gone?"

"Months. She went away to a writers' retreat and never came home. The retreat wouldn't confirm or deny that she showed up. There was nothing after that. And believe me, her husband was not happy."

"Tyler Armstrong? That was her husband?"

"Ex. They were divorcing. She took the papers with her to sign, but disappeared before she did. Tyler was so furious. He's tried to get her declared dead a few times. But the court wouldn't agree. I think they finally did grant him the divorce, though. Took like seven years or something."

"So you know him?"

"Did. He was a piece of work. God's gift to the financial world. He was cheating on her, and she caught him. It wasn't going to be a messy divorce. They both wanted out. Cat was excited to start a new life. I actually thought she'd already signed the papers. We had a little party before she left to celebrate. That's the last time I ever saw her."

Things are coming together, at least a little bit.

"Did the police ever look at him? An interrupted divorce feels like motive to me."

"You sound like a cop." Her tone is wary now.

Go careful, Halley. She's the only thread you have.

"I'm not a cop. I'm not a reporter. I'm a confused little sister who just found out about all of this, and I need to know what happened to her."

The tenor has changed, though. "I really don't know more than that."

"I understand. It's just that we seem to be living in two different worlds—mine where she died when she was sixteen, and hers where I don't exist. I'm baffled by this, and I'd like to get to the bottom of it."

"You'll have to talk to the police, then. They never seemed to think Tyler hurt her."

"Do you?"

There is such a long pause that Halley thinks she might have dropped the call. "Hello? Are you still there?"

"I am. I don't *think* so. He's a blowhard, but not a murderer. And she was several states away. I got the sense that he was as surprised as I was when she never came back."

"Several states away . . . Do you know where, exactly?"

"Tennessee. It was this really important artist-colony writing retreat. Cat was thrilled to get in. She applied religiously the entire time I knew her, every year, and then she finally got accepted. Thought she'd become a world-famous writer. She might have, she was pretty good. I read a few of her stories. They were great. A little dark, but well written. Not like her, actually. Cat was such a bubble of joy. She lit up a room."

Halley is having serious cognitive dissonance. This woman talks so lovingly about a monster. Clearly, she doesn't know the truth. Should she tell her? That her bubble-of-joy friend went to jail for murdering her mother?

She decides to hold off. She needs this information, needs this connection.

"Do you remember what the retreat was called? Or where it was?"

"Yes, Brockville. It is somewhere in the mountains."

Halley writes this down and circles the name of the idyllic-sounding little town three times. *Brockville.*

"Let me ask you a strange question. Was my sister in therapy?"

"God, yes. We all were. Prozac nation."

"Do you happen to know her therapist's name?"

"Sure. Jana Chowdhury. I think she's still practicing. Used to work at school, actually, then left and opened a private practice to focus on couples work. Still saw individuals. We all went to her."

"We?"

"My husband and I, Cat and Tyler, a few more friends. She's really empathetic, a super couples therapist. She saved a lot of marriages."

"But not Cat's?"

"Hard to save a marriage when you're just going through the motions. The love of Cat's life was her writing, and Tyler knew it. That's why he strayed. He was just trying to get her attention."

"Thank you. You've been really helpful."

"Please let me know if you find out anything. I miss my friend."

Alison's wistful tone makes Halley squirm. She promises to and hangs up, trying, and failing, to put together Cat the adult with Cat the child. Halley does not remember Cat lighting up a room. If anything, she was the opposite. Dark, moody, sharp. Always dragging around, wearing black.

"How dare you go into my closet, you little thief? Give me that."

Halley startles. The memory is clear as day. She's in Cat's bedroom, with a folded sweater in her hands, about to set it on Cat's bed. Cat bursts in the door and rips it from her hand.

"I wasn't in your closet," Halley says. "Mom did laundry."

"Mom sent you to spy on me. Get out!"

Did Mom send me to spy? Halley wonders, but the rest of the memory is gone. She is back on the quad, with the bag of cookies and a notebook by her side.

Strange, how vivid it was. Nothing from her time in Nashville is nearly as alive as that. Her breath is coming short, just as it had when Cat yelled at her. Cat yelled at her a lot.

Your memories are coming back. Be careful.

Halley can't decide whether to call the therapist or the husband and settles on trying Tyler.

The first phone number has a recording that says the number isn't in service. The second is answered by a harried woman. "Westcott and Westcott. Where can I direct your call?"

"Tyler Armstrong, please."

"He's in a meeting. Can I take a message?"

"Um . . . sure. My name is Halley James. Tell him my sister is Catriona." She reels off her number and hangs up. Dials the therapist. The number is also in Boston. The phone goes to voicemail, and the soft tones of a woman with a gentle accent make Halley take a deep breath. She sounds very calm and competent.

"This is Dr. Chowdhury. If this is an emergency, please dial eight. Otherwise, I will get back with you as soon as I can."

At the beep, Halley leaves a similar message, identifying herself as Catriona's sister and giving a callback number.

She's half tempted to get on a plane and fly north, though she hardly has the resources—or time—to do that. Besides, are the answers there? No, being an armchair detective—a bench-on-the-quad detective?—is the best she can do right now.

You could go to Tennessee. It's an easy drive . . .

She goes back to the computer bank inside the library and looks up the Brockville Writers' Retreat. They have a slick, elegant website, soothing blues and greens and creams. She reads the "About" page. The retreat exists as part of an artists' colony in a small village called Brockville, a sustainable biophilic community created by a man named Miles Brockton. The fellowships, as they're called, are highly competitive. There is a stipend awarded, a cabin provided, and two months of writing programming and workshops with leading authors in a variety of genres. She reads the accolades with a growing sense of astonishment. Graduates of the Brockville Writers' Retreat have won everything from the Pulitzer to the Orange Prize to the National Book Award. Bookers, Edgars, Thrillers, even a Nobel.

Her sister was a good enough writer to get into this elite retreat?

She wonders what sort of writing Cat did. She should have asked Alison if she had any idea where Cat's work might be.

Well, duh. She types "Catriona Armstrong" into the search engine, and up pops a very old website. But there's a 404 error, nothing to see. Makes sense. If she has been missing for so long, who would be making payments on the website and doing updates to keep it in compliance?

But now she has a track to follow. Searching her sister's married name, Halley gets a hit on a website that apparently published one of Cat's poems. The poem is short and downright creepy:

> She raises the knife like a conductor.
> It has a mind of its own, and
> she can't—won't—stop its path.
> For steel to a heart creates a longing
> That will never be fulfilled.

The bio that follows reads:

> Catriona Armstrong has published numerous poems in a variety of regional journals. She is working on her first novel and has recently been accepted into the prestigious Brockville Writers' Retreat.

Halley feels sick. She searches and finds a few more of Cat's poems. All of them feel dark and partially deranged. There are footprints of the girl she used to be all over the internet. These breadcrumbs feel more like a horror film than something that would fit the literary bent of this Brockville Retreat. But Halley doesn't know this world. She doesn't know what kind of novel Cat was working on. What attracted them to her.

There's no phone number for the Brockville Writers' Retreat. Figures. It's that exclusive. She sends an email inquiry to the contact page, asking to speak to someone who would have been in charge in 2002. She reads a bit about the town of Brockville—they're clearly very proud of the community they've created. And bingo, at the bottom of the web page, there is an address. She puts that into her Maps app. It's about a three-hour drive down I-81, then a direct turn east into the Blue Ridge Mountains. She can do that easily. If she leaves early enough in the morning, she might even be able to come home the same day. Assuming there's nothing to be found, of course. If there are threads to follow in Brockville, she could get a cheap motel room. There will be plenty off the highway.

Happy to have a plan, she opens the search bar once more and inputs her sister's name, then clicks on Images. Hundreds pop up, but none that match her remembrances of her sister's face. Page after page after page, and none are the right one.

She tries to remember what Cat looks like. Blond. Pretty. But the features are blurry in her mind. She is an impression only, a spirit of memory.

Halley closes the browsers, logs out, and stands, wiping her hands down the front of her jeans, and has only taken two steps back toward the quad when her phone buzzes. She answers without looking and keeps heading outside.

"Hello?"

A man's voice; rough, abrasive. "I'm looking for Halley James."

"Is this Tyler Armstrong?"

"Yeah. What's this nonsense about you knowing where Cat is?"

She is taken aback by his harshness. "I didn't say I knew where she was. I said I'm her sister."

"She never told me she had a sister."

"Did she tell you anything about her past?"

"Just that her mom died when she was sixteen."

"Didn't you live in Nashville then? Didn't you know her in high school? I remember you picking me up from school once with her." Unsaid: *"How did you not hear about your friend murdering her mother?"*

"Your memory is better than mine. My family moved to Boston at the beginning of my junior year. We met again in college. What is this about?"

"You had a sister named Tracy, though, right? I was in elementary school with her."

He gives a sharp, nonamused laugh. "You're just determined to ruin my day, aren't you? Tracy OD'd four years ago. Thanks for bringing it up."

"Oh. I am so sorry to hear that. Were you close?"

"Not particularly. I was a lot older, and already out of the house, went to boarding school junior and senior year. She got wrapped up with some guy she met at a church lock-in when she was sixteen, and he got her hooked on crack."

Sixteen. Halley was here, safely ensconced in the bosom of Goode, with her dad looking over her shoulder. Not in a bad way, in a welcome way. He kept her from making too many dumb mistakes. Her shyness helped with that, too.

"And you went to Harvard with Cat?"

"Listen, I'm busy as hell. Cat bailed on me fifteen years ago, and personally I think she's dead, though there's no way to prove it. If you know where she is, I would like to hear, so the court can follow up. Otherwise, you're wasting my time."

"I don't know where she is."

"Then good luck to you." He hangs up.

"Asshole," she mutters. "No wonder she divorced you."

Interesting, though, that Cat used the same story Halley's dad did—that her mom died in an accident. Tyler's recall of Cat's past seemed to be as cut and dried as Alison's. Maybe he knew the truth and was covering for Cat? Though he didn't seem like the type to do anyone a favor that didn't benefit him.

That leaves her wondering how big of a story the murder was. You'd think something as salacious as a daughter murdering her mother would be all over the papers. She hasn't been able to find much at all, but 1989 was before the internet became ubiquitous, and Catriona was a juvenile, too, so it was easier to keep things quiet. But if a friend's mother was murdered, wouldn't you at least hear about it? How had Cat managed to convince everyone her mother had died in an accident?

Maybe she was very convincing. Maybe she was charming. More likely she was a cobra, swaying back and forth, hypnotizing her prey.

Before she can take that thought any further, her phone rings again. She recognizes the number—the therapist.

"This is Jana Chowdhury."

"Hi. Thanks for getting back with me."

"I'm very happy to finally talk to you, Halley. Cat told me so much about you."

"She did? That's surprising to hear. She didn't seem to share anything about her past with her friends. Or her husband."

"Hm. Well, therapy is different. Sometimes people need to protect themselves. That said, you know I can't discuss her case with you unless there is news on her whereabouts, or a court order."

"So you know she's missing?"

"Of course I do. It was strange timing. As I told the police."

"Strange timing? I understand you can't discuss what Cat spoke to you about, but can you at least tell me why you say that?"

The doctor hums in assent. "She had nothing but clear air ahead. She was happy. Achieving her dreams. The divorce was finalized. I will never believe she left of her own accord. I believe there was foul play, and I told the police that."

"So you don't think she just ran away to mess with Tyler and get out of the divorce?"

"No, I don't. I think something happened to her in that town."

"Where the retreat is? Brockville?"

"Yes. And Halley, I must tell you this, and it's the last I'll be able to say. I think you should stay away from this. It would be such a shame if something happened to you, too."

CHAPTER FOURTEEN

Halley makes one more call, to the Metro Nashville Police. She explains who she is and why she's calling. She's transferred around until she gets the voicemail of a detective named Mike Cooper.

She leaves a message asking him to call her, then, with the therapist's warning ringing in her ears, gathers her things and heads to the Jeep.

She swings by the hospital to check on her dad. He's in jovial spirits, helped along by the morphine, no doubt, and she doesn't share what she's learned. Until she has a better grip on all of this—and who are we kidding, she is having some trust issues—she doesn't want to get into it again. As far as he's concerned, he could never talk about the murder again and be perfectly happy.

Can she? Is it even possible to put all of this aside?

No. No way. Not now. She has to find out more about Cat's disappearance. About the place where she disappeared. She'd applied to the retreat regularly. Why? Was it that special of a place? Was it going to launch the literary career she so desired and start her life over?

She realizes her dad's been prattling along and she hasn't heard a word. It doesn't matter; he's too high to have an actual two-way conversation. He talks and laughs and makes no sense until he gets another dose from the pump and passes out again. She is not going to get anything more from him today. And honestly, what else can he really give her? He's not going to get into the details. Not the ones she needs, at least.

A physical therapist with a handful of resistance bands and a Fourth of July–colored belt stops her on the way out to share that they will be getting him up and using some crutches tomorrow so he doesn't waste away, then hurries off before Halley can ask any questions.

She needs to change before dinner, so she heads to the house. She's feeling oddly isolated. In DC, there's always someone around: the ebb and flow of the city, the lab, the short commute, the dog, her walks, the gym, the neighbors, all keeping her in constant motion. Things are quieter here. Too quiet. And maybe she doesn't want to admit that she is unsettled by the relentless calls for her to leave this situation alone. Because how can she heed them? This is her life, her memories. Who are these strangers to tell her what she should and shouldn't do when it comes to something so very personal?

Theo isn't a stranger. Damning herself for the constant urge to reach out, to pretend all is normal, she dials his number, but it goes straight to voicemail. It's the end of the day in DC, always a frantic moment at his job. He rose through the ranks quickly, and when he's at the office, anything that happens late in the day falls on his desk. She hangs up without leaving a message, realizing that she really is disappointed not to have reached him. She has so much to share. She wants to share it with him.

She swings the Jeep into the drive, gathers the mail and a package, and hurries inside, waiting for the familiar thuds from the staircase that herald the cat making a beeline for his dinner. The house is oddly silent.

"Ailuros? Where are you, lazy cat?"

Nothing.

Odd. He's always been a greeter, comes right to the door when someone comes home. She drops her bags and takes a look around. Upstairs, in all his favorite spots, then downstairs. Opens the door to the backyard—did he get out somehow? Nothing. She calls for him again, getting worried now. Back in the living room, she hears a thump, and a tiny meow.

It's coming from the middle of the house. The basement.

The door is latched, like always; it's an original, old door and doesn't fit well in its frame. It used to rattle and bother them—bother her; when she was little, she thought ghosts lived in the space and would get spooked every time the door rattled and shook—so her dad screwed a latch onto it to hold it in place. She undoes it and opens the door, and the cat streaks past.

"How did you get down there?" She follows him to the kitchen, where he is already wolfing his food. She looks at her watch—she left before seven, and it's after four now. She hasn't been in the basement since she arrived in Marchburg; all that's down there is the laundry and all the holiday decorations, old luggage, some other odds and ends. And she certainly didn't sleepwalk. So how in the world did Ailuros get locked in?

She pets his back and croons, and he gives her a furious look and stalks to his box, where she hears him scratching around. The reality hits her.

Someone locked him in the basement.

Someone was in the house.

"Oh, now you're being silly," she says out loud to dispel the concern.

They don't have a security system—it's Marchburg, nothing bad happens here—but she's sure she locked the front door when she left. No one could have gotten in.

But the cat was locked in the basement somehow . . . She needs to go down the stairs into the darkness, and that's not at all appealing. But she has to be responsible and see what sort of mess the cat made. If he was locked in all day, he probably peed somewhere.

The steps are solid maple, built a century earlier, to withstand all manner of activity. They have a runner to cushion chilly feet. Her dad converted the string light bulb to a switch. She flicks it, and the stairwell lights up. Bright. Cheery. Photos of her and her dad on the walls, both of them aging as she goes down. There's never been anything to fear in the basement before, outside of the specters from her youth. At the bottom step, darkness stretches into the corners, but the flick of another switch illuminates the space. The musty scent greets her, but it's not unusual; it's hard not to have a little must in a Virginia basement.

The space looks as familiar and homely as always. It's organized, with her dad's shirts hanging up above the washer and dryer, the color-coded boxes for their holiday ornamentation stacked against the far wall. There are two chairs—one thick with fur, clearly where the cat spent his day. She doesn't see any wet spots anywhere.

A fluke. She must have knocked the door loose and it swung open. She was buzzing around like a bumblebee in a jar this morning.

She runs up the stairs two at a time for a little exercise, then flicks off the light and latches the door well.

"Sorry, buddy. What a good boy you are," she calls to the cat, making him an extra-large helping of tuna in apology, then heads upstairs to change. She must steel herself to see all the people she's escaped from. All the people who never escaped.

Taco Joe's smells divine, and Halley's mouth waters as she enters the eclectic space. She hasn't been here in ages. And despite its being old, with its wood-topped tables sticky and soft from many coats of polyurethane shellac, and loud, with its combination of Mexican and American rock, and its admittedly questionable commercialized decor from years of Cinco de Mayo celebrations past, the place has the best queso she's ever tasted. It's a popular choice.

Kater sees her enter and waves her over. There are a few people she recognizes, and standing relaxed against the bar as if he wants to be seen is Aaron, wearing a baseball cap with a large *M* on the front—his dad owns the tractor-supply company in Jasper; it's their logo. He smiles widely at her, and she can't help but put a mental image of Theo right next to him. Nope. Aaron doesn't stand a chance. He's cute, but Theo eclipses him in every way. It's like comparing a man to a boy. Not that Aaron isn't a man; he's just more like a greyhound, and Theo is built.

She likes built. He makes her feel delicate. Safe. She's not that small, is really normal height, five-seven in her sneakers. He's big enough she has to tilt her head up to look into his eyes, and he can lift her with ease. *Come on, Halley. You're leaving the man. Give it up already.*

She flows into the group, hugging, chatting, catching up, eating queso and drinking a spicy jalapeño margarita, until Kater takes her aside and says, "Okay, I want to hear it all."

"All?" The tequila is making her feel a little loose.

"The whole story about your sister and your mom. Did you find out anything today?"

"Oh, I found out a lot. My sister was married to a real jerk. Once he heard I didn't know where she was, he couldn't have cared less about the situation. Talked to a friend of hers, too, who did the missing persons report. She assumes there was foul play, but she didn't think the husband was involved. And then I talked to a therapist who used to see her in Boston. She couldn't tell me anything, but she did warn me to stay away."

"Which you absolutely should. We don't need you showing up on *Forensic Files*."

"You watch that?"

"Girl. I am obsessed."

And they're off, talking about the goriest and bloodiest and strangest cases that they know of, until Halley goes for another margarita and sees a man across the room staring at her. He has dark hair and dark eyes, and she feels like she should know who he is. He's not being subtle about looking at her, and with everything going on, that makes her uncomfortable.

She turns her back on him and shifts to the side but can still feel his eyes on her. She glances over her shoulder, and he's gone.

"Did you see that guy in the corner?" she asks Kater, who shakes her head.

"You know him?"

"No. I've never seen him before. I gotta pee, will you go with me? Just in case he's lurking?"

"Sure."

She doesn't know why the stranger made her so uncomfortable, but with Kater by her side, it all seems fine again. She's a fun girl, always has been. Smart and protective. Halley used to love spending time with her when they were younger. She tells a naughty joke, and Halley forgets about the stranger. Forgets about most everything troubling her.

When they rejoin the group, she switches to water and has a couple of tacos, enough to stop her head from swimming. She chats with Aaron for a little while, and a few other friends, then finally decides to call it a night. She still feels bad about Ailuros and wants to make it up to him with some extra snuggles.

"Going so soon?"

The deep, sardonic voice is attached to the stranger who was staring at her, and he's blocking her way out.

"Yeah. Long day. Excuse me."

"You don't remember me, do you?"

Halley looks closer, but no, she doesn't. He seems to enjoy her gaze, doesn't shy away or allow his eyes to drift, just drills her with his own stare. His hair looks freshly cut, and his eyes are so dark they could be black. They aren't brown, though; she thinks they're a dark blue. He has a three-day scruff of dark beard that some women would find sexy. He wears jeans that look well broken in and a black T-shirt that shows off sinewy muscles. She sees a black leather jacket on the stool behind him, notices he's also wearing black biker boots. He's older, midforties. He's familiar in an uncomfortable way, but she doesn't ever recall meeting him. She shakes her head.

"I'm sure we've never met. What did you say your name is?"

"I didn't. You have a good night, Halley." He turns and strides away, disappearing through the throng. The bell on the door lets out a merry jingle, and he's gone.

"Who was that?" Aaron is standing next to her now, a look of distaste on his face.

"I don't know."

"Well, he certainly seemed to know you. Do I need to beat him up?"

This is said without irony, though the stranger looks like he would be a feral fighter, no holds barred. Maybe a knife tucked into the jeans pocket.

"No, no, it's fine."

"You're heading out? Why don't I walk you to your car."

"That's nice of you, Aaron. Thanks." She waves at Kater, who is playing pool in the back. Kater blows her a kiss and shouts, "I'll see you tomorrow!"

Halley picks up her bag and immediately realizes something is wrong. It's lighter than when she came in. She rips it open and gasps aloud.

The file on her mother is missing.

CHAPTER FIFTEEN

Halley practically turns over the stools looking for the file, knowing somewhere deep she isn't going to find it. It didn't just fall out of her bag or get picked up and thrown away as bar litter. Someone took it.

And that someone must have been the dark-haired stranger. The one who thought she'd know him.

"Could you have left it in your car?" Aaron asks.

"No. I brought it in. It's not something I'd leave behind. Too sensitive."

"It had to be that guy," Aaron says. "He was lurking around you all night."

"Was he? I didn't notice. I saw him once across the bar, then he spoke to me, but that was it. Damn it. Why would he take the file?"

Kater joins them. "I thought you were taking off. What's wrong?"

"I had a file on my mom's murder in my bag, but now it's gone."

"And that creepy guy was talking to her," Aaron adds. "I think he took it."

"Yeah, he was interesting looking, if you like your men dangerous as hell. He asked me about you, but I made it clear you were not his type, and that you were married. Told him to buzz off. Maybe it's in your Jeep?" Kater is loose with alcohol and not entirely able to focus. Any other time, Halley would find this hilarious. The responsible girl getting a load on. Right now, she just feels annoyed.

"It's not, it was in my bag. It weighs a ton."

"Why don't we go out and take a look."

"Yeah. Okay." She digs into her bag and realizes the Jeep keys are gone, too. Says a very bad word.

"My wallet is here, and everything else, but my keys and the file are missing."

"Should we call the police?" Kater asks.

"Absolutely," Aaron says.

Kater is leaning against the bar now. "I'm hammered. You should probably do it, Halley, not me."

"Let's see if my Jeep is still here first."

They troop outside into the soft mountain air. The lot is dark, down a staircase behind the bar, and half-full. She is relieved to see her Jeep right where she left it. She scans the parking lot. No sign of the stranger. But he could be hiding anywhere. She hates this. One tiny bit of news and everything has changed. She's never been scared like this before. Not in Marchburg.

Kater stage-whispers to Aaron, "Look in the back seat, make sure he's not stashed there waiting to abduct her."

Aaron approaches the Jeep carefully. "No one. But look."

He opens the passenger door, and Halley sees the file sitting upside down on the floorboard, looking for all the world like it toppled right out of her bag. Aaron reaches down and picks up a shiny object from the gravel. "These your keys?"

Halley heaves a sigh of relief. "My God, I am losing my mind. I was in a hurry, I must have dropped them when I got out. Gosh, now I'm starting to think I'm crazy. I wouldn't have left the file here, it must have fallen out of my bag. Thanks for finding them, you guys. I'm just being absent minded, I guess."

"You want me to go home with you?" Kater asks.

"No, no, that's fine. I'm sure it was my mistake."

Aaron looks less than convinced, but they get her into the Jeep, and she waves as she drives off.

Halley berates herself all the way home. She can't afford to be careless like this anymore. She's seeing ghosts everywhere. She really thought she had the file and the keys when she went into Joe's, but maybe she was mistaken. And that sense of dislocation is the worst feeling of all.

The house looks almost menacing tonight, and she wishes she'd taken Kater up on the offer of spending the night. Though it feels ridiculous to be a grown woman and ask your old babysitter to stay over because you're being spooky.

Still, she makes a point of locking and bolting the front door, and double-checks the back door is locked, too. Everything secure, she makes a cup of chamomile tea and lets Ailuros climb in her lap. She has no choice; she needs to go through her mom's file. Even though Occam's razor says it just spilled out of her bag as she hurried in to Taco Joe's, for her to do that and drop her keys, too? It feels off.

But she is admittedly distracted. Anything is possible.

She steels herself, then pulls everything out of the file and stacks it according to category. Crime scene photos, autopsy photos, reports. Three stacks. Answers in all, and more questions, too.

She takes a deep breath and starts with the crime scene. The first few photos are of the exterior of the house and get progressively closer, like a camera is zooming in. The front door with the big wreath, the hallway, shoes lined up under the foyer table. A pink backpack.

The living room, the white carpet, the fingerprints. Her mother's body lying so still, eyes open and staring, a trickle of tear coming down her face.

I'm sorry, Mama. I'll clean it up. I didn't mean to make a mess.

Scrubbing and scrubbing the floor but it only gets worse. Small footprints leading from the kitchen to the living room—she is barefoot, and cold.

Wake up, Mama. Wake up.

Then darkness, that slate slamming across her mind.

Halley sips the tea. These flashbacks are starting to be unnerving. And how they end, so abruptly . . . Will that wall ever come down?

She flips through the stack slowly, processing, but remembers nothing more. The photos are horrifying, and she feels her heart ripping apart as she sees her mother's body, but there is also a strange remove, as if she is looking through a veil. The echoes.

She remembers waking up in the hospital, a woman's voice saying "You're going to be okay"—one of the nurses? Then her dad crying by her bedside. There's not much after that until Marchburg, standing outside the elementary school in Jasper, the sense of panic she felt looking at all the kids streaming inside, and a warm, gentle hand on her shoulder. Her dad's voice saying "You don't have to, jellybean. Let's go home."

All these memories, ricocheting off the one moment she doesn't remember, a moment she didn't realize she had no recall of. Her ability to remember has always been unassailable, and now? She's starting to doubt everything.

Everything, and everyone.

CHAPTER SIXTEEN

Theo FaceTimes as she's going to bed. She debates not answering, texting back that she needs some space, but she also wants to tell him about the weirdness that's happened, the stranger, leaving the file in the car, how her memories—or whatever they are—seem to be coming back in flashes. How disconcerting it is not being able to remember everything. How right he was about the sense of madness chasing her.

She swipes open her phone.

"You called earlier?"

"Uh, force of habit," she lies. "I admit, I'm still getting used to us not being . . . us."

"I'm not thrilled with that, either."

"Can we just . . . not? I've had a very long day."

"All right. What made your day so long?"

She tells him. All of it, while silently cursing herself for using him as a crutch when she knows things are over. It's not fair to either of them. And yet . . .

"I don't like this, Halley. You need to stop. The universe is telling you to back off."

"The universe?" That makes her smile. "When did you get all mystic on me?"

"When plot point after plot point started piling up. Seriously, this story is worthy of a novel. Or one of your shows."

He says "your shows" in a tone that implies daytime television, but in truth they are all crime related. It sparks a memory, though.

Her mom used to call them "my shows." She would tape the afternoon soap operas—*Days of Our Lives*, *Another World*, *Santa Barbara*—and, after she kissed Halley good night, would go to her bedroom to watch her shows. On days Halley was sick, her mom stayed home from work, and they'd snuggle together in her room and watch them live.

She hasn't thought of that in years. These memories, stealing in on cats' feet, will unhinge her if she doesn't find a way to order them. Make them behave.

"Hey, where'd you go?" Theo asks softly.

Halley shakes her head. "Sorry. Everything seems to remind me of something I haven't thought about in years. A novel, huh? Would you read it if I wrote it?"

"Of course. I'd read anything you wrote. I didn't take you for a novelist, though."

"Oh, trust me, I'm about as likely to write a book as I am to get on a roller coaster. But apparently, my sister did. She was a poet and was planning to write a novel at this retreat in Tennessee. I just wonder what she was using as inspiration. The poetry I was able to find online was really dark."

His forehead creases in concern. "You aren't going to let this go, are you?"

"Theo, it's my past. My mother. My sister. I can't just pretend everything is okay. Nothing is the same. Every memory I have is . . . not real."

"That's not true. *All* of your memories are real. What was the first thing I said to you when we met?"

"'*Ma'am, I think you dropped your scarf.*'" She says it in as deep a voice as she can muster, and it makes him laugh.

"God, do I sound like that?"

"Yours is deeper. You could stand in for James Earl Jones."

"Yeah, whatever. Now you're being silly. I'm serious, though. Your memories are fine, Halley. You had a traumatic event that you've blocked out. That's all."

"Maybe." She plays with the ends of her hair. "Dad's getting married, by the way. Another thing he neglected to tell me." She hears the sarcasm, and so does Theo.

"That's kind of big news. Are you pissed at your dad for getting remarried?"

"No. Not at all. It just feels like he's keeping an awful lot from me these days."

"He had a pretty bad trauma, too, Hals. His wife was killed. His stepdaughter jailed. He was afraid for you. He did what he thought was best. I don't know that I'd do it any differently if I was faced with the same situation. Maybe it was better that you didn't remember? Those kinds of events can submarine a person. You were so little . . . I don't know. See, this is why having kids is impossible. There are no good results. Whatever decision you make, they get pissed at you in the end."

"And . . . we're back."

He sighs. "I just think that maybe you try to do the remembering in a safer environment. Like with a therapist or something."

"I'll think about it." She yawns. "I'm beat. Talk tomorrow? Maybe you can tell me about you for a change. I'm getting bored of me." The words slip out before she even thinks about them. *Shit.* She needs to get a handle on this. They are separated. They are not *they* anymore. But Theo looks happier than she's seen him in weeks at the ask.

"You could never be boring. I got nothing right now anyway. Just doing my thing. There's an interesting case brewing in Texas, though. I'm heading there in the morning. Some alleged terrorists left behind some matériel in a house in Dallas. Yours truly gets to bring the newbie along to catalog and identify."

"That's good, right? I mean, not that there are terrorists in Dallas, but if he's being allowed on field assignments, he's almost done training. You'll be free again."

"Right."

"Charlie?"

"Will be staying next door overnight." Their neighbor works from home and has a cocker spaniel whom Charlie adores. The two are BFFs. "Can you sleep, do you think?"

"I've had two margaritas. I will be dead to the world in five minutes." She pauses. "Theo? Things are admittedly complicated right now. But I really appreciate you supporting me through all of this. I know it's been a lot."

"Car bombs are a lot. This is nothing. It's dealable. We'll figure it out. Just promise me you won't be reckless. I don't like this idea of you getting in the middle of this."

"Promise. Give Charlie a kiss for me."

"Just Charlie?"

"You too." And she clicks off before he can respond. Before she chucks it all and drives straight back to McLean, to his arms, to his bed. God, this is not going how it's supposed to go. All they did before she moved out was fight. Snarl and spit and slam doors. This gentle, concerned Theo is more like the guy she dated and married, and she likes him. Maybe leaving has made him see her side of things, finally.

It doesn't matter. Chemistry was never their issue. There is so much water under their proverbial bridge that a few kind words aren't going to fix a thing.

Still, the house feels lonely without his handsome face on the screen. She straightens up, gathers up the cat and her phone, checks all the doors again, and wanders up the stairs. She's asleep within moments of her head hitting the pillow.

The dream is new, a memory unleashed. She is walking down her old street in Nashville. Birds chirp. Cars whoosh past. A man on a bicycle rings his bell as he goes by. She is holding something, something soft. A stuffed animal, a rabbit. Her best friend. His name is Elvis. He goes with her everywhere. He is clutched tightly in her arms as she walks up the street. She's not supposed to leave the yard, but Elvis saw a beautiful rose on a neighbor's bush and wanted a closer look. The rose is pink, just the same color as his nose. It has so many petals, and they shimmer in the sunlight. She looks around, up the street, down the street, sees no one, so breaks the rose from its stem and cradles it in her hand. She scoots back to the house, to her yard, and goes inside to the kitchen. Presents Elvis with his prize.

There are voices in the living room—Mom and Cat, having another argument. She ignores them, finds a small bowl, fills it with water, sets the rose in it. It is so beautiful. She will take it to her mom when they stop fighting, and it will make her feel better. Loved. She doesn't get enough love. The rose flickers prettily in the bowl, and she sets Elvis on the counter so he can see. But Elvis is covered in something. His sweet pink nose is bleeding. She tries to wipe it away, but he comes alive, hopping across the counter, spilling the rose water and knocking over the bowl and leaving a trail of blood behind him. She hurries after him, only to realize his throat is cut. Gouts of blood pour from his small body, and she is covered in it, she is crying, there is no more fighting but silence, dark silence, deeper than anything she's ever heard. She runs after him and trips, falling. And the scream comes from her very soul, louder and louder and louder—

Halley comes awake sitting bolt upright, the scream dying in her throat. Ailuros is nowhere to be seen; she must have scared him away.

Her chest is heaving. She flips on the light. *My God, what was that?*

Elvis, she thinks, remembering the soft velveteen rabbit. Cat had done something to Elvis. Was it real blood? Or had she scrawled on him in red lipstick? A slash across his plush little throat. A threat against her? She'd cried and cried and cried, and her mom had promised to buy her another. But she didn't want another, she wanted her Elvis. So her mom tried to wash him, and his fur tinged red so he was pink, not gray, and that bloody leer from his throat never went away. Who would do that to their sister's favorite toy? The bosom buddy Halley insisted sit at the kitchen table and have his own plate of food at dinnertime?

She hated me. Cat hated me.

Halley realizes she is crying, that her heart hurts. Theo is right. Maybe she's better off not remembering. She wipes her face and lies back down, but sleep will not come again.

She is motionless and quiet, breath shallow, forcing her mind to that spot of darkness within and getting nowhere.

When the first rays of dawn turn the light in the window milky, she gets up and moves downstairs woodenly. She makes coffee, going through the motions, still not fully awake.

The dream—the memory—is so vivid still. She doesn't want to think about it, but her mind is compelled to reach back, to look, to see. The rabbit with its throat cut; her tripping in the living room—how much of this is metaphor, and how much of it is real? What had she tripped over? Her mother's body? And there it is, bright in her mind, the photo she stared at last night playing out in Technicolor, her mother with red stains spreading across her chest and her eyes open, the tears, her mouth moving. What is she saying? She's telling Halley something.

Halley closes her eyes and strains to access the memory; what is it? That thin whisper, so light, almost impossible to hear. One syllable. She says it again and again. These are her mother's last words.

"Run. Run. Run."

Blackness.

Chills course through her body. Halley opens her eyes. Her heart is pounding. The mug is clenched in her hands, empty. She is in the kitchen of her home in Marchburg. The file on her mother's murder is spread across the kitchen table, photos a jumbled mess, everything out of order, the stacks disturbed as if she'd stirred them with her hands like shuffling a large deck of cards. And the doorbell is ringing.

She sets the mug on the table and hurries to the door. Glances out the sidelight at a female face she doesn't recognize.

"Don't open the door for strangers," her dad used to say. But she is a grown-up. The woman on the step is older, midfifties, dark hair streaked with gray in a perfect, shiny bob and kind brown eyes ringed in dark smudges. She looks very tired.

Halley opens the door, and the woman smiles politely. She has large, straight teeth.

"Good morning. I'm Jana Chowdhury. We spoke yesterday. May I come in?"

CHAPTER SEVENTEEN

Halley offers some coffee, which the doctor accepts gratefully. They sit at the table. She moves the photos and notes out of the way, stacks them all up. The doctor looks at them curiously, and Halley puts a possessive hand on top. The wind whips up outside, and she feels the air start to loosen around them.

The therapist takes a deep sip of her coffee. "Mm, this is excellent. There's a storm coming. I didn't know if I'd make it before the heavens opened."

"They steal up on you here sometimes. You came all the way from Boston?" Halley's voice is rough, her throat raw from the screaming.

"No. I'm in DC now. Moved my practice there several years ago. I do mostly couples work, but individual psychotherapy as well."

She thinks of Theo, and wonders if maybe they need to talk to Chowdhury. *Focus, Halley. Cat.*

"And how did you get my address?"

"From Cat, naturally."

This is a shocking bit of news. Her dad's plan hadn't worked at all. Cat did know where they were. Why had she never reached out? Or, conversely, come after them? If she was so dangerous, why had she never tried to hurt them?

"I'm very confused," Halley says. "Care to enlighten me?"

The doctor glances at the file again, raising her brow in query as if she knows exactly what it is and wants a quick peek. Halley slides it out of reach possessively.

A little sigh. "You need to leave your sister's situation alone."

"I thought you couldn't talk about her."

"I can't. Not specifics. I'm making a judgment call here. I did a little checking on you. You're a smart girl. Top of your class in undergrad at GW, graduated your master's with honors. PhD by twenty-six, making a name in the forensics industry. On a path to run NISL. Until you left your company out of the blue Monday." That eyebrow again, an open invitation to share. It probably works wonders with her patients. For Halley, having a stranger digging makes her uncomfortable.

"How do you know all of this? Are you some sort of private investigator?"

"Not at all. Cat thought you had a bright future, and you do. I'd like to help you keep it that way. Here."

She hands Halley an envelope. It is worn, and thin. "I didn't want to say anything on the phone. Your sister said if you ever got in touch, to give you this."

"What is it?"

"A letter, I believe."

"And you've been holding on to this for fifteen years?"

The therapist nods. "Your sister was a complicated woman. You've obviously found out a little bit about her past?"

"A little bit? She murdered our mother!"

"And she went to jail for that admission. Granted, it was a juvenile psychiatric facility, but she didn't have an easy time of it. They rarely do."

"An easy time . . . Dr. Chowdhury, forgive me for being obtuse, but when you go to jail, is it supposed to be cushy? She murdered a woman, the one who brought her into this world. Some would say matricide is a worse crime than killing a stranger."

The doctor crosses her legs. She is the epitome of a cool customer.

"Interesting that you point that out. Matricide is horrible, and very, very rare for young women. And of course her sentence was supposed to be punishment. But recidivism is dramatically reduced if a juvenile can get the proper support. Counseling, medication, tools to handle their rage. When the environment they're put into simply exacerbates the problem and creates an even deeper risk-reward system . . ." Chowdhury takes a sip of her coffee. "I see you aren't buying any of this, are you?"

"I don't see that letting people get away with murder is a good thing."

The way Chowdhury looks at her makes Halley feel quite prim. No, not prim. Naive. She has a sad, knowing smile, like Halley is a recalcitrant child. "You have a highly developed moral compass. That's good. Whoever you choose to work for next will be lucky to have you."

Halley feels the anger that's been simmering since Ivan called her into his office and blew up her life bubbling up to the surface. Who the hell is this woman? "Doctor, forgive me, but you could have mailed me that letter. Why are you here if you can't tell me anything worthwhile about my sister's disappearance?"

Chowdhury smiles, unperturbed by Halley's aggression. "Cat was one of my favorite patients. She was complicated, without a doubt, but incredibly self-aware. Driven. Smart. Talented. Not unlike yourself. When she went missing, I was very upset. We'd made so much progress. And now . . . It's been so long, I'd almost given up hope. But when you reached out, I admit, a spark relit. You were there, of course, in her defining moment. It was a very powerful psychological event."

Well, that's not weird.

"I may have been there, but I don't remember anything. And every time I try to think about it, there's an immediate blackout. Like, jet black in my brain."

"Is there? That's interesting."

"But what does it mean?"

"Well, before I offer my opinion, would you tell me how it makes you feel? This darkness?"

"Panicky. Fearful. Frozen. But safe, too. As if whatever is on the other side of it is dangerous, but as anxious as I am, I know nothing will hurt me if I don't look."

Chowdhury has leaned forward at this description.

"Do you sense a difference in your surroundings? Do you lose time?"

Halley shakes her head.

"In many instances of dissociative identity disorders, there is a place the psyche retreats to that feels safe, and another iteration of the personality emerges to defend the subject. Have any of your friends or family ever said you speak or act differently when you're frightened?"

"No. Never."

"Hm. Well, it could just be you're protecting yourself from a traumatic experience. The brain is a delicate and powerful place. You may not be ready to drop the wall and see what's on the other side."

"Not surprising. My father told me my sister tried to kill me, too. I don't know that I'd like to remember that. Did she tell you that? Is that why I am the chosen one here?"

Chowdhury searches Halley's face with those dark, kind eyes. She is used to being challenged, uses silence as her armor. It works; Halley is uncomfortable enough to speak again.

"I just want to know what happened. Why she killed our mother. Why she disappeared. If she's dead, then I can start putting the pieces back together."

"I understand that urge. But you shouldn't. You need to stay away from this. It's bigger than you could possibly imagine. There is danger. Leave it to the professionals. Let them go searching again. Cat suffered a real trauma. Trauma leaves marks. You needn't get caught up in the fray."

"I suffered a real trauma, too. My mother was murdered in front of me, and I can't remember it." Halley's voice is rising. She needs to stay calm, not lose her temper and chase the doctor away.

Chowdhury taps a finger on her knee. "Where do your memories of the event end?"

A breath. "I'm not sure. Bits and pieces are coming back. But I didn't even know it happened at all until two days ago. I call that a trauma. Don't you?"

The doctor finishes her coffee. "Some are worse than others," she says lightly. "I'd highly recommend you speak with someone about this loss, Halley. You need help processing this information. It's a lot."

"Thanks. I'll look into that."

"Good. I have to get back. Thank you for seeing me."

"You drove down from DC, and now you're going back? What if I have more questions? I need to get a handle on who my sister was."

"I've given you all I can. And delivered the letter, which has been burning a hole in my safe for a very long time."

"Dr. Chowdhury, why *didn't* you just mail it? If you knew where I was?"

"Cat didn't know what you remembered, and what you didn't. She specifically said that unless you came to me directly asking questions, I was not to share it."

"Well, here I am, asking questions. And you aren't being very forthcoming."

"Then let me be clear. Your sister was stubborn, too. Desperate to confront her demons, always looking for the path back to the darkness that she felt made her. I didn't think she should go to Brockville, and my intuition was correct. I'm going to say the same thing to you as I did to her. Some things should be left in the past. Powerful people do terrible things to keep their secrets."

"So there are powerful people in Brockville keeping secrets?"

A flare of something in those dark eyes. "I didn't say that."

"I think you just did. Did you tell the police searching for Cat the same thing? Did you warn them off, too?" She is getting frustrated by the enigmatic therapist. "You know more about this than you're saying. Do you know where my sister is?"

The doctor shakes her head. "I don't. I wish I did. And I shared as much as I legally could with the police when she went missing. I told them to look at Brockville."

"Did you show them this letter? What if there's something in here that will give a clue as to where she is?"

"If I thought that was the case, I would have given it to them. It won't. This was written well before she went missing. This was her way of making amends."

"But—"

"Thank you for the coffee, Halley. It was nice meeting you."

Without another word, Chowdhury gets up from the table and heads to the door. Halley has no choice but to follow her.

The rain has started, thrumming hard onto the pavement. A bolt of lightning crashes, and thunder rumbles quickly on its heels.

"You should be very careful going down the mountain, Dr. Chowdhury. The roads get slick. Are you sure you don't want to wait?"

"I'll be fine. Thank you, Halley." She gets behind the wheel of a white rental sedan, closes the door, and pulls out of the driveway.

"Shit," Halley says. She is thoroughly unsettled. Strangers paying attention to her life, knowing more about her past than she does? Not good.

She needs to take a look at this letter.

It's on top of the file, and Halley breathes a tiny sigh of . . . not relief, exactly, but recognition. She has a lot more information than she did when she first found out about her mother's murder. It's not like she's trying to solve an actual case; the criminal act was committed, and Cat copped a plea and went to jail for it. This is more an enlightenment, learning the truth. Something in these pages could give her an idea of where her sister is. Maybe even why she killed their mother.

Halley realizes the *why* is the most important part. Accident? Purposeful? It's so unthinkable, and yet it happened. Halley needs to be in Cat's mind twenty-eight years ago. Needs to hear her sister's thoughts.

And then what, Halley? What are you going to do? Forgive her? Hate her more? Go search for her?

She realizes that's exactly what she wants to do. Find her sister. And ask her why she would do such a thing. Demand answers. Get retribution.

Get revenge.

A word that sparks her soul into flames. She is so furious she is practically levitating. Yes, she wants revenge. Her sister ruined her life.

She sits, and the cat leaps into her lap, making happy biscuits on her thigh.

"You couldn't care less, could you?" she says to him, and he settles in with a heavy purr. It takes a little of the edge off, but not much.

The envelope has been sealed for a long time. She has to use her dad's letter opener to get into it. Inside are four pages of script, almost elegant in their precision and consistency. Like calligraphy, but printed, the letters perfectly formed, so exact it looks like a computer printed the pages. But they are done in blue ink, and the words are nonsensical.

> Dear Halley,
> I need to apologize for taking our mother away from you, and for how terrible I was to you as a child.
>
> You cannot possibly understand what has happened, but I want to try and explain. Her death is my fault. You are too young to comprehend how difficult it was for me when you came into our lives. You were perfect. You were sunny and smart and joy. I am darkness and rain, a thundercloud. I knew I would always be in your shadow, and that was infuriating for a teenage girl to realize. My illness is no excuse, but there were many voices in my head, many paths I was forced to follow. Your father was right to send me away, but the chain reaction of that decision changed

everything. I sought comfort from the wrong people. And I destroyed everything.

I have spent my life trying to rectify this terrible event. To do penance. I have stayed away from you and your father. I made a life for myself far away. I healed. Dr. Chowdhury helped me understand what happened and gave me the tools to start over. One of them is making true and heartfelt apologies to the ones I've wronged. The wounds I created for you, and your father, are the worst of my transgressions. I am humbly and truly sorry. I only ask that you know that everything I've done since our mother's death, I've done for you.

I hope you've been able to live a good life. That you are not haunted by the loss of our mother. That you are happy. It is all I want for you, happiness.

I do not believe we will ever meet again. Actually, I hope we do not. But know if I can, I will do everything in my power to right the wrong against you.

You are forever in my heart and prayers.

Cat

Halley smooths the letter and puts it back into the envelope. This tells her nothing. Platitudes and excuses.

Everything I've done, I've done for you.

What in the hell? Who says such a thing?

Halley's temper rises, and she has to force herself not to rip the letter to shreds and scream.

There is no way a letter of apology can resolve her animosity toward her sister. If anything, she realizes it's made her even more determined to find her and demand real answers.

The doctor's visit has only increased her curiosity instead of satisfied it.

She thinks about the map she pulled up yesterday. To get to Brockville from Boston, you drive right past the turnoff to Marchburg. Her sister was that close. Granted, Halley lived in the dorms at GW in 2002, but still.

She looks at her watch. It's not even eight. If she leaves in the next half hour, hour even, she can be in Brockville by lunch.

It feels like the next logical step. It feels like the only choice she has. Granted, she could try to get to Nashville, try to find their old house, try to get inside . . . But what's that going to do besides perhaps unlock a moment in time?

Finding her sister could unlock everything else.

She will talk to the people at the writing retreat directly. Find out what happened to her sister when she went to Brockville. Surely, if there are answers to be had, they'll be where Cat was last seen.

CHAPTER EIGHTEEN

CATRIONA

Brockville Artist Colony
Literature Workshop
2002

As I wander the beautiful, fragrant path, drowning out my demon's cackle with the birdsong and splashing river, I can't help but spiral a bit. My divorce was agreed to with somewhat undue haste because neither of us could wait to get out of the marriage. We were not compatible, especially when he, like my fictional Greg, started sticking it to the neighbor's babysitter. The girl was in college, but still, Tyler was flirting with the half-your-age-plus-seven line.

It feels like years ago, but it's only been two days since my best friend, Alison, came over to celebrate the impending official split. "You start your marriage with a party, you should end it with one, too." That's what Alison said when she showed up at my front door with two bottles of wine and an insouciant grin. We drank, and we talked, and finally, when we were hammered enough, Alison asked me what was next.

"Writing."

"No, I mean, what are you really going to do now?" Alison was slumped back in her chair with her glass of Chablis. We were beyond drunk, and I was kicking myself. I know better than to have more than two glasses of wine. It doesn't mix well with my meds. I am going to wake up feeling sick, with a headache and nausea, and I had a very long drive from Boston to Tennessee. Getting drunk on top of the convoluted thoughts brought about by the ending of this failed chapter of my life was maybe not the smartest thing to do. I can still taste the sour wine in my mouth.

But then, high on wine and girl power, I'd answered emphatically, sloshing some of the wine out of the glass into my lap. "I'm not kidding. I've been applying to Brockville for a long time. I was accepted a few years ago but couldn't pull the trigger. This time? I am going to drop everything and go. Find a way to make it through, deal with the rest later." I shot back the last of my wine and declared, with all the seriousness I could muster, "Writing is my future."

"I didn't know you got in before. Why didn't you go?"

I was weak. Scared. Not ready to face my fate. *Don't scare her, idiot.* "Tyler forbade it. He didn't want to spend the money."

Alison had squinted one eye at me. "I mean, it's not that I disapprove of you shaking things up. But you're making a lot of changes all at once. Divorce is a moment of reflection. I get cutting your hair. I even get wanting to change jobs. But to sell all your stuff so you can afford to run off to the forest and write a book? With no source of income other than some alimony, which runs out in . . ."

"Five years or a new marriage."

"Right." Alison took a swig of the wine. "What does Dr. Chowdhury say?"

Ah, the good doctor. One of the bright points in my life, truth be told. The only person who knows everything about me. And I mean everything. "It took a bit of convincing, but she thinks it's good for me to have agency here, to make decisions about my life that only affect *me* for a change. I've never been able to do that. I met Tyler practically the first day I moved here, and I haven't been without him since. I need to find myself, and that's why I'm following this dream at last."

I hooked myself onto him the moment I realized he wasn't bright enough to see me for who I really was. That he didn't even put *me* together with his past.

The acting got boring, in the end. And I let slip, just a tiny bit, who I really was, and he ran right between the legs of the first young thing he could find. It's fine. He wasn't much of a challenge, and I don't like to be bored. Ten years is a long time to be bored.

"Well"—Alison finished the last of her wine and tipped the empty glass toward me in a final toast—"I am thrilled for you, and I hope you won't forget us little people when you're some rich and famous author."

"Hardly," I replied, knocking my glass against hers. "I mean, that's not going to happen—"

"No, no, don't you dare. Agency, remember? Visualization. You only put into the world what you want to have happen. Say it after me: 'I'm going to be famous and successful in my chosen career.'"

"I'm going to be famous and successful in my chosen career."

"'I will not talk down to myself.'"

"Ali—"

"Say it."

"I will not talk down to myself."

"'I will live a wonderful life, full of joy and happiness.'"

"Who's the therapist now?" At Alison's glare, I shook my head. "Fine. I will live a wonderful life, full of joy and happiness."

Alison stood, wobbly as a colt, and she threw her arms around me. "I'm holding you to that, Armstrong."

"Handon," I said. "I'm taking back my maiden name."

Alison grinned. "Good for you! Fuck him. Fuck Tyler!"

"Yeah, fuck him."

I poured Alison into a cab, then went back up to the loft. Even though I was bored and wanted it, divorce was sad, no matter how you cut it. I'd been promised joy, promised happiness, but all I'd gotten was a richly oppressive sorrow, something new for me. Maybe a little rage thrown in for good measure.

The honest truth? While our marriage ended because I checked out, Tyler thinks he left me. He thought I didn't know he'd found another woman. That didn't matter to me in the least. What pained me was the argument at the end of it all. The hurtful things he said—because as much as I didn't feel them the way another woman might, they hurt me in their way. That he wanted to be with someone who wasn't always detached. Someone who wanted to make love all the time, who wasn't dulled into a stupor by medication, unable to accept or receive pleasure. It had become a thing, I learned during our last blowout fight. Somehow, my inability to get off was the end for him.

I could. I can. Just not with him.

I had no choice, really; I had to start over. Tyler had always laughed at my dreams. I will take great pleasure in showing him that he's wrong.

Getting into the retreat after all this time was providence and reminds me again and again that I deserve this and I need to believe in my creative abilities. I've always been a writer. Now I'm going to try to make it a profession.

And perhaps take care of a few other loose ends along the way. If I'm lucky.

I'm so lost in thought that I don't see the small root pushing its way up through the cement, and catch my toe, stumbling forward. I windmill my arms to gain my balance and end up sprawled on the pavement. My knee is on fire, and when I pull up my jeans, I realize it's bleeding. Damn.

"Whatever, asshole," I say aloud, clambering to my feet. "I'm going to be famous and successful in my chosen career." The birds chirp their agreement. That part of my life is over. I'm shedding Tyler like an ill-fitting dress. Had I ever loved him? I must have, to agree to marry him, right? If love is something someone like me can experience, then yes, I think I did. He was safety. A handsome, safe place to land when I struck out on my own after college, a seemingly nice guy who wanted the same things I did—no kids, travel, culture. At the beginning, he loved that I wasn't clingy, or needy. Turned out, he did want kids, he preferred football to the symphony, and his idea of travel was taking the Staten Island Ferry to work on Wall Street. Plus, he started to see my emotional independence as a detriment. Apparently he did want someone to fawn all over him.

I couldn't be honest with him. Not about everything. Not about who I really am. He knew a version of me, the one I curate for people, the person I molded myself into being to fit into society. To be on guard all the time with the person who shares everything in your life is exhausting.

Little by little, the marriage chipped away. My world shrank, until I started to realize nothing was going to change.

Well, that isn't true any longer, is it? The second I sign the papers and put them in the mail, the business of the divorce will be complete, and I will be free. I will start fresh, rise up from the ashes, become the writer I was always meant to be. After years of applications, I'm here, in the writing program at Brockville, fulfilling my dearest dream.

Yeah, you really are something. Shrinking away from it after the first opportunity to shine.

I can't argue when he tells the truth. I hadn't shone. I maybe glowed for a second, a heartbeat, but that nascent flame had been extinguished immediately because that blond bitch tried to get on top first.

Why did I let Brenda, of all people, get to me? I allowed a stranger to size me up and judge me unworthy. I am just as worthy as Brenda, just as capable of creative excellence. Probably more so.

So why didn't I stand up for myself? Why had I let the whole class drag on my story?

You know why.

"Shut. Up."

I'm talking to empty air. And the trip down memory lane has cost me; I've lost track of where I am. I stop and turn in circles. The path along the river winds serpentine through Brockville, the only nongeometric thing I've seen so far. The sky is a shimmery cobalt and the trees a vibrant viridian. The water reflects them both, and it is disorienting. The cabin is that way, right?

All these trees. It's beautiful, but it's sinister, too. I haven't slept well since I got here. Too quiet. Too gentle. I'm used to Boston, to the sirens and bustle and the constancy of the noise. The sense that I'm never really alone, that a knock on the wall will produce one in return. Probably with a curse word to boot.

Brockville is lovely, but it's isolated. To hear the wind moving the treetops, the hoots of an owl, makes me uncomfortable. The forest has eyes everywhere. I feel like I'm under constant surveillance. Who knew the depths of nature could be so overwhelming? That such pervasive silence would allow my soul to be noisy?

Grow up. A breeze won't hurt you.

I grit my teeth and get my bearings—I don't think I've passed the path to the cabins yet, so I must still be on the appropriate route. I continue walking the river footpath, now examining my purpose, my goals. Reminding myself that I am here for a reason, notably to break out of my old construct, to become someone new. To be a writer, I need to let go of the shackles on my own ego, allow the voice in my head to shift into something entertaining and exciting. Something real. I can't be uneasy with it any longer. Tammy is right. I need to let go. Dig deep and allow myself to have some kind of authenticity on the page. It's the one place I *can* be myself and no one will be the wiser. The one place I can unleash the horror and pain and cataclysmic thinking that have come to be my normal.

I see now how trite the story is. Fantasizing a husband's death when he is caught cheating? Come on. There's nothing new there. Nothing fresh. I could be the best writer in the world, and without a better concept, I will go nowhere.

That's my girl. Spiral out.

Tension fills my body, the urge to lash out strong. I take a deep breath. I say the words like an exorcism. "I will not talk down to myself. I will live a wonderful life, full of joy and happiness."

I feel like an idiot, wandering the path back to the cabin bolstering myself like this, but Brenda's snide remarks really have me rattled. The woman isn't wrong, my demon isn't wrong, and that is the problem. There's no fixing it, either. I need to toss out this story, start fresh. I began writing it soon after I discovered Tyler's indiscretion, my fantasy life rushing in to overtake reality. It was a good exercise, allowed me to take out some frustration, but that's it.

I need a new story. One worthy of Brockville.

You know the one you want to tell. It would sell a million. Can you imagine—

"Oh, fuck *off*, won't you?"

"Excuse me?" a rich baritone of amusement calls from the riverbank. I freeze, searching, but see no one. I thought I was alone on the path, but clearly I'm not. My heart is staggering, it's beating so hard. I hate being startled. I unclench my fists and heave in a breath.

"Um, sorry? I was talking to myself."

"I promise you haven't done enough wrong to warrant that vehemence."

The man who belongs to the voice comes into view, climbing up the bank. I wouldn't have tried it in a million years—the bank is steep and muddy; it rained last night—but he comes up as easily as a deer.

He is handsome. Ridiculously handsome. His jaw could cut glass, his dark hair is thick and wavy, and his eyes are the color of the sky after storm clouds depart, a clear, startling deep blue. He wears a green plaid shirt. He is the sky and the trees and the water. He belongs in this space as perfectly as the rest of the scene.

He looks just like . . .

My heart thumps hard, once, then again, in familiarity, before I realize of course I've never seen him before. He's younger. Bigger. And now that I look closer, not an exact replica. Everyone has a doppelgänger, isn't that what they say? But there's no question that he lives here. That he is a part of the Brockville town proper. I did mention it's not just a writing retreat. There's a whole village here. A self-sustaining village tucked in a mountain valley, full of extremely wealthy pioneers trying to live a sustainable life away from the prying eyes of the world. The wilderness. The wonderfully helpful wilderness.

"Noah," he says, pointing at his chest. Grinning. Even teeth, nicely shaped, not too overwhelming, normal. As normal as a beautiful man rising from the depths can be.

"Cat. I'm here for the writing retreat."

"Nice to meet you. You seem to be in need of a Band-Aid."

I glance down, and sure enough, blood is soaking through my jeans.

He holds out a string of fish. "Could I interest you in some dinner and a patching-up?"

"You go around catching fish and offering them to strangers regularly?"

He laughs. It is a good laugh, deep and throaty. My stomach clenches—I haven't made a man laugh in a long time. Haven't been smiled at like this in a long time, either. That smile, though. God. It's like *he* has come back to life and has taken this man's body for his own.

The man I've sworn to never think of again.

But why did you really want to come to Brockville, Cat? Don't lie . . .

Shut the fuck up right now.

"No, I don't, in general. But as the fish is fresh, it seemed rude not to."

"I appreciate the offer, but I need to keep going." I gesture to the path. "My first story just crashed and burned. I have to come up with a better one. I was thinking while I walked. Tripped. I need to change."

"You must be pretty good if you got into the retreat." He somehow manages to lean on his fishing pole, crossing his arms and nodding. "Have you published yet?"

"Some poetry, but not anything else. Yet. I'm here to learn how to be a better writer so I can."

"Well, Cat the writer. If you ever decide you want some trout, I'll teach you how to make an amandine that will make your friends cry."

"You're a chef?"

"I am."

Things start to click. I know exactly who this is. The youngest Brockton. The outlier.

I soften my voice, make it friendlier. He could be an asset. "I assume I have you to thank for the ridiculously luscious basket of muffins at my door this morning?"

"You do. I mean, not me, my pâtissier made everything. I'm just the boss. I run the restaurants for Brockville."

"You're the farm-to-table guru?"

"That's my brother. I just cook what he provides. And if you're not going to join me, I will sadly have to see you along the river path another time." He shakes the fish, and their scales glisten in the sun. "These guys need to get prepped."

"It was nice meeting you, Noah."

He looks so deep into my eyes that I nearly have a panic attack. We've talked for less than five minutes, but it's like he knows my soul, knows my thoughts, and wants me to speak them aloud. And that would be dangerous. For both of us.

"Likewise, Cat."

With a final heart-melting smile, he's off, whistling as he saunters back the way I came. I almost turn and run after him, but that won't do. I need to focus. I have goals, important goals, and getting involved with cute chefs is definitely not part of the program.

I'm impressed, the voice says. *He's just your type, isn't he? He looks so much like that wonderful young man you used to know. Imagine all the fun we could—*

"Stop!" My shriek startles a blue jay, which flaps past my head with a squawk.

Why are you pretending? Why are you lying to yourself?

"Leave. Me. Alone!"

I dive off the main path into a side gravel entrance that leads into woods, swiping at my face, at my eyes, which have traitorously begun to leak in an approximation of crying that is simply my frustration having a laugh. I don't cry like you do. And I don't want to think about him. Never again.

I'm making so much noise it takes me a moment to realize someone is following me.

Someone is following me into the forest.

THURSDAY

CHAPTER NINETEEN

HALLEY

Halley's dad is happy to see her. His room is fragrant, filled with get-well balloons and cards and flowers, and he's sitting up in the bed, fresh from a shower and shave. His face is pink from exertion. "Ave, filia. The docs were just in. They're going to spring me on Monday."

"Salve, Pater. So soon? Aren't you the star pupil!" She gives him a hug. She needs that comforting touch regardless of how upset she is. And if he's greeting her in Latin, he really is getting better.

"Yeah. They said it's healing great, and they started me on some crutches at PT this morning, which were a piece of cake, so I'm going to be able to come home instead of going to an inpatient rehab facility." He gestures to the corner, where his shiny new crutches lean against the wheelchair he's been bound to since the accident.

"Oh, Dad, that's great news. Everyone heals better at home. But the stairs might be a challenge."

"Definitely. I'll probably sleep on the foldout in the living room for the first little bit. Anne can make it all cozy."

"My rugged 'let's sleep on the ground instead of a tent so we can see the stars' father, looking for *cozy*. Lord, what has happened?"

"Ha ha. They've dialed back the drugs, too. I'm telling you, Hals, I was dreaming some really weird stuff." He is effervescent this morning; the happy professor is back. She's glad to see it, though she knows she's about to upset him. She approaches with caution.

"Since you're doing so great, I'm going to head out of town for a day or two."

He sighs. "Yeah, I suppose you need to get back to work. Anne can handle things. She and that beast of mine are best friends, he won't mind her taking care of him. It was great of you to come, jellybean. I really appreciate it."

"I'm not going back to DC just yet. Listen. I've been doing some research about Cat."

His eyes narrow and his lips compress, as if the word causes him pain.

"I know. But hear me out. I spoke with some of the people who knew her. A friend. Her ex-husband. And her therapist." She shudders a little at the idea of the letter in her backpack. Should she show him? Or will that really set him off?

"Halley, you must stop. You can't open this chapter of our lives. You can't."

"Well, I have. It's not fair to expect me to simply learn this news and go about my life as if nothing has changed. Everything has changed. And I'm going to finish this. I'm going to find her. At least find out what happened to her. The last place she was supposed to be is just a few hours south of here. I'm going to take a quick run down there and see what they have to say."

His demeanor shifts immediately. *Unhappy* isn't a strong enough term. He is furious.

"Absolutely not. I forbid you to go."

She was afraid he was going to react like this. She goes for the logical response.

"I understand your concern, but you can't forbid me to do anything, Dad. I'm an adult. This has to happen. I have to know why she did it, and to do that, I have to find out where she is. Whether she's alive or not. I just wanted you to tell Anne to stop by and give Ailuros his tuna. I filled up his bowls, and he's all set for the day. Seriously, you don't need to worry. I'll be back tomorrow, Saturday at the latest."

She's never seen him so fired up. He never yells, but he does now. "You have no business getting involved. Hire a private investigator if you're that hell bent on finding that monster. I'll pay for it." He struggles in the bed as if he will get up and physically stop her, and she shakes her head and presses his shoulders back down to the thin, crackly mattress. Whoever designed hospital beds didn't have snuggly rest in mind.

"Relax. Okay? I won't take any chances. It's a writers' retreat in a sweet little town that has a huge farm on its land. It looks like a really nice place. I just want to talk to them. It will be a quick in and out. I want to get the lay of the land, see what she saw. It might help me figure out where she is."

"Then call them and ask them for pictures."

"You're funny."

"And how does Theo feel about this?"

She blows out a breath. "We're on a break."

"You don't get breaks from your husband, Halley. What the hell is going on? Is that why you were so available to come running?"

"You're my dad. You got hurt. Of course I was going to come running. That's not fair."

"And work is cool with you skipping out?"

"I have some . . . Oh, hell, might as well. I got fired, okay? I've lost my job, my world's been turned upside down, and then I find out you've been lying to me my whole life. Now I have one tiny chance at finding out the truth about my past, and you're telling me not to. I'm sorry. That doesn't work for me."

"You got fired?"

She plops into an infuriated pile in his side chair. "Yes. The board is blaming me for a ransomware attack. I believe it's in retaliation for a sexual harassment incident. I am going to have to sue them, and things with Theo have been really rough. Okay? This is just something I need to do, because if I sit here another minute, I'm going to go mad."

His face twists with hurt.

"I don't mean you. I mean I have nothing to lose right now."

"You. You could lose yourself. And that would kill me, Halley. For God's sake, please. Don't do this."

"It's going to be fine. Promise. I love you, Dad. I'll see you in a couple of days. I'll bring you back some homegrown zucchini."

The joke falls flat. He's so mad his voice is shaking.

"I've never known you to act foolishly, Halley Leia James. But that's what you're doing. You are flaunting my concerns—my very valid concerns, and I bet your husband's as well—and putting yourself, and your family, at risk. I will not stand for it."

All three names, huh? Her temper is starting to flare now, too. But she's not going to engage. She has every right to her own story, and finding Cat is integral to learning the truth.

"We'll see. I'll be back before you get released. Promise."

She blows him a kiss and leaves the room before he goes apoplectic. He's broken her trust, and now he doesn't have a say in what she does. She stifles a pang at his anguished roar—"Halley, please"—and closes the door to his room.

Out at the nurses' station, she looks for Kater, but she must be in a room. She asks the nurse on duty if she's seen her.

"No, actually. She hasn't come in yet this morning. She's late."

"We were at Joe's last night. Playing pool."

The nurse—her name badge says "Triss"—smiles conspiratorially and stage-whispers, "Might be the margarita flu."

"It might," Halley agrees. "We let loose."

"She usually calls, though. She's very responsible."

"I'll swing by her place on my way out of town, see if I can roust her. Have a good day. Don't let my dad give you any hell. He's pretty fired up right now."

"I won't. He's a good guy. You should listen to him."

Halley frowns. "You were eavesdropping?"

"Not on purpose, y'all were shouting. He's been pretty stoned, Halley. He talks to us like we're you sometimes. He's mentioned your mom. How she died. I'm really sorry. That must be hard."

Halley shoves her hands into her jeans pockets, protecting, withdrawing. She's not ready to discuss her mom with strangers. "Thanks. I'm not sure how I feel yet. What else has he said?"

"Nothing much, just that he's worried about you. Like, really worried."

"I can take care of myself."

The nurse smiles. "Of course you can. But he's your dad. He only wants what's best for you."

"I'll take it under advisement." Halley flees before the nurse can push it further. She's getting really tired of everyone trying to protect her. No one can possibly understand how this feels. The terror, the flashbacks, the sorrow. She's losing everything, and it's too much.

Leaving the hospital, she's tempted to call Theo but reminds herself they are separated, and besides, he's on a plane to Texas and will be out of touch until the case is wrapped. Being married to someone who gets sent off at a moment's notice to any number of dangerous places and situations has always been hard for her to swallow. It was something they talked about in the beginning, before she took the job at NISL, the stable job, instead of one of the alphabet agencies, because she knew their relationship wouldn't stand the constant fractures of never having a regular schedule. Never knowing if the other will be home for dinner? What state, or country, they're in at any given time? She has friends who were in these situations—med school and military, two different agencies with separate deployments—and the strain on their relationships was palpable, and eventually, broke them. If a long-term situation is going to work, eventually, someone has to give up and hold down the fort. Usually the woman, since she's in charge of birthing and raising the kids. And Halley made those decisions happily, not expecting him to give up his career to raise a family. Of course, then it all backfired on her. A few missed dinners seems like nothing in comparison to what she did for him.

There it is, that spark of anger at the situation. *Don't forget why you left, Halley. It was about more than the babies. It was about everything you gave up for him, too.*

The Jeep is a good road trip car. She puts on some music as she winds down the mountain. It's not a complicated drive. Over to I-81, then straight down to the Tennessee border, turn east when she hits Bristol. Brockville is an hour off the highway, in a valley not unlike the one she's driving into now at the base of her own mountain.

She has to pass Kater's house to get to the highway; it's right at the crossroads. West, you head into Jasper. East, the highway. The rain is letting up as she reaches the drive. It used to be Kater's grandmother's place; she left it to Kater, who moved in after she passed. It's a sweet little cedar shake saltbox with flower boxes in the windows and black shutters. A white picket fence. She parks the Jeep, walks to the front door, rings the bell.

No answer.

She walks to the back through a tidy garden, pink azaleas in bloom, grateful for the flagstone path. It's muddy out here after the storm. Kater's car is in the carport, and Halley shakes her head in rueful amusement. She can't imagine Kater being so hungover that she couldn't get up and go to work, but clearly she's still zonked out. She glances in the car as she passes, just to be safe. Nothing.

The back door has a glass-panel inset with a curtain over the bottom half, so she has to get on tiptoes to look over it. It opens into the kitchen, and there's a mess. Kater's purse is on the table.

Halley pulls out her phone and calls. Hears the phone ring, ring, ring. It's in the purse; the brown leather is shimmying on the table.

She waits for Kater to come, bleary eyed, to the table to retrieve it, but nothing. There is no movement.

She puts her hand on the knob, and it turns easily. She steps into the silent kitchen.

"Kater?" she calls loudly. "You in here?" Nothing. She moves farther into the house. "Kater?"

The living room has an open book on the couch and an afghan wadded up. A half-full glass of water sits on the side table.

Halley gets the strange sense that she's walked into a scene interrupted. It seems Kater came home, threw her stuff on the table, grabbed some water, and curled up on the couch to read. A normal night, probably. Says she wasn't too drunk to drive home and settle in with a book, so that's good. But something feels off.

She calls down the hallway. All the doors are closed. This is a small house: kitchen, living room, two bedrooms that face the front driveway, and a bath at the end of the hallway. She opens the first door. Nothing. The second. This is Kater's bedroom, and it looks like a bomb went off. No Kater.

The bathroom door is shut, but she can hear water running. Halley feels a chill, but knocks. "Kater?" No reply. She tries the knob. The door opens. The water in the sink is turned on. Kater's neon-pink toothbrush lies in the sink, the water rushing over it frantically. The small bathroom is empty.

Halley carefully turns off the water. Now she's really starting to freak out. Something is very wrong. Her analytical, forensically trained brain says, "*Photograph and catalog.*" She doesn't have a camera, and her notebook is in the car.

The second voice says, "*Call the police.*"

So she does. She backs out of the house, stopping at the kitchen door to look closely at the lock. There are scratches in the paint by the brass plate. Someone forced the lock. Heart pounding, she calls 9-1-1.

A soft southern voice answers the call. "Nine-one-one, what's your emergency?"

"My name is Halley James. I need someone to come out to 6542 Travis Lane. My friend Katie Star didn't show up for work this morning. I'm at her house now. All of her things are here, her purse, her phone, and her car is in the drive, but she's not home. Water was running in the bathroom sink, there are scratches in the paint by the back door like someone jimmied the lock. Something is wrong."

"I'll send the chief right now. Halley James? You remember me? Jessie McGraw? I gave you a tour of the department when you interviewed."

"I do remember, Jessie. Hi. It's been a while."

"You think something happened to Kater?"

The nickname instead of a formal query: this is the joy of a small town. "She missed her shift this morning, so I stopped by. We were out together last night. Everything here feels . . . off. Water was running in the bathroom. Even if she got distracted and went for a run, would she have left the back door unlocked?"

"I don't know, hon. Chief's on his way. You stick close and keep your eyes open. Want to stay on with me until he gets there?"

"No, I'm okay. Thanks, Jessie."

"You ever think about joining the force? I know there's an opening."

Halley cringes. Does everyone know she got fired? But no, there's no way. Jessie's just making conversation.

"Yeah? I will take it under advisement."

"We'd love to have you. Smart young thing like you could really rattle some of the good old boys' cages around here, you know?"

Despite her concern for Kater, Halley is amused. "You know these calls are recorded, don't you?"

"Oh, what's Baird Early gonna do, fire me for telling the truth? Besides, I turned it off after you said you were okay. No one here in the room but me."

They chat for a bit about the crime in the area, mostly petty stuff, and Halley gets the sense this is the most excitement Jessie has seen in months.

She hears the faint wail of a siren. "Sounds like the chief is nearly here."

"All right. You take care, now, you hear? Think about it. Marchburg could use a bright light like yourself."

"Thanks, Jessie." She flips her phone closed as the Marchburg police chief pulls into the drive, his tricked-out black-and-white Ford Expedition effectively blocking her in. Baird Early is a large square-faced man in a tan uniform and a green trooper's hat. Everything about him is slow—his walk, his speech—but his mind is as sharp and intense, the finest of any law enforcement individual she's ever met. He is a transplant from Richmond who followed his wife to town when she came home to care for her ailing father. *Like you have,* Halley thinks. Only Mrs. Chief Early got it in her head that it would be a good idea to stick around, and now they are never going to leave.

And they say you can never come home again.

"Chief. Thank you for coming so quickly."

"Hello, Miss James," he drawls. "It's good to see you. Sorry to hear about your daddy. Glad he's gonna be okay."

"Thank you. And you can drop the good old boy with me, Chief. I know better."

He laughs. "You never do miss a trick, do you, Sass?" He called her *sassy pants* when she was younger, and won't give it up. "You say Miss Star is missin'? Why would you think that?"

"There was a stranger at Joe's last night. He creeped me out. I've never seen him around, but there was something about him that felt familiar. He asked her about me, but she told him to take a hike. He had a motorcycle, I don't know what kind. Are there cameras at Joe's?"

"Nope. But there's a security camera pointing toward that lot from the feedstore across the way. They put it in last year, someone was stealing the bags of grain from the stack out front. I'll have a look. So this stranger, he was paying attention to you and Kater? Did you get his name?"

"No. Kater chased him off. God, you don't think he was pissed and took it out on her?"

"Any idea why he would do that?"

"Maybe. Some men don't like to be told no. Chief . . ."

"What?"

"Do you know anything about my mother's death?"

He scratches his thigh, the thick fabric bunching beneath his big hand. "Car accident, wasn't it?"

There is something in his tone, or maybe how he's looking over her shoulder instead of at her face, that makes Halley take a step back.

"You know the truth. Dad told you about my sister. When? Recently? Or when we moved here?"

He holds up both hands. "It was after I became chief of police. Listen. Your dad was only trying to protect you. He just told me to look out for your sister in case she made a move on you, and I have. She's never shown up here as far as I know."

Halley breathes in deeply through her nose, trying to contain the fury. "I can't believe you didn't tell me. I can't believe he didn't. It's completely unfair. How am I supposed to trust any of you?"

"An excellent question, but not one for this moment. Right now, we need to worry about Kater."

"Fine. Yes. But we're not done with this discussion, Chief."

Early's relief is palpable. "Yes. Absolutely. Let's go inside. Tell me everything you touched. I'm gonna have to print you for exclusion."

"Of course." She leads him through her steps, from front door to carport to back porch and door, inside, all the way to the bath. "I turned off the water with my knuckle. That's it. I stepped out, checked the lock, saw the scratches, and called you immediately."

He lumbers around the place, harrumphing. "You think she was interrupted brushing her teeth?"

"I do. I think the stranger followed her here. The question is why."

"You're asking questions about your mom's case. Could be you rattled someone's cage. Tell me what this guy looks like again?"

Halley gives the best description she can of the stranger, and the chief gnaws on a toothpick, looking for all the world like the country bumpkin he pretends to be to disarm people into saying and doing more than they'd like. He gets more confessions than anyone she's ever seen.

He wanders outside, doing three perimeters before stopping at the edge of the long grass where Kater's yard meets the meadow. He calls her over. "Get the camera from the back of my cruiser, wouldja?" He tosses her the keys.

"You found something?"

At his implacable look, she hurries to the cruiser, bringing back a Nikon D7200 DSLR camera. She takes off the lens cap and hands it over. He shoots toward the toe of his right boot with an audible click. Then farther, toward the drive. She cranes her neck, but his bulk is blocking the way.

"What is it?"

He glances over his shoulder at her, his face set. "Blood."

CHAPTER TWENTY

Youth is wasted on the young, don't you think?

Just look at her. Ferrying tools, following orders, glowing, she's absolutely glowing. Brimming with excitement. Concern, worry, yes. But inside, she's feeling the titillation, the thrill of being a part of something dark and sinister. Something bigger than herself. She doesn't even know what it means yet, this arousal, but she will.

I admit to a twinge of it myself. She's not going to back down. She's going to try and find out the truth. What will it cost her?

We shall see.

I never thought I'd need to come here, to watch her, to follow. But the chief said it perfectly. She rattled the bars of my cage. Couldn't leave well enough alone, started asking questions, making calls, pulling files, and I had to visit her in person. See the woman she's grown into.

And somehow, someway, a new, deeper connection has been formed. One much stronger than the previous one we had.

I admit, my feelings are hurt. How can she not know? How can she not remember?

Not to pat myself on the back, but I do tend to leave an impression. The photos were remarkable. Considering the limitations of the equipment, the composition was stellar. I was sorry to leave them behind.

Of course, I have most of the file, every bit of blood and bone. Collecting crime scene photos is a hobby of mine. I probably have some of the finest memorabilia from the greats of any collector. They are such inspiring decor.

And when looking isn't enough, there is a whole world to experience.

These connections . . . I never know what will cause them. A look? A smile? The sound of a voice, the fit of her jeans? Something. Anything.

Now I have no choice. And there will be consequences. Memories are best when cloudy and unformed. When one seeks clarity, they become troublesome.

What do you think? Should I spook her a little more? You'd think locking the cat in the basement would have been enough to alarm her, then taking the keys and the file, facing her directly, but even though a woman grown, a woman of great intelligence and charm, she's too young to be appropriately suspicious yet. She's too young to be afraid of every bump in the night. To realize death is coming for her, as he comes for all of us. The more you have to live for, the more afraid you are of dying. At this age? You still think you're invincible. That nothing bad happens outside of your dreams.

Come to me, curious bee. Let me show you how the real world works. I'm doing you a favor by teaching this lesson.

What?

For God's sake, shut up already.

CHAPTER TWENTY-ONE

HALLEY

"Is it Kater's blood?" Halley asks, trying to tamp down the panic.

"Excellent question. You and I both know that until it's tested, there's no saying for sure. Could be someone nicked a deer and it ran through here. Can't jump to conclusions." But as he's saying this, he's fingering his shoulder mike. "Dispatch, get the K-9 down to Miss Star's place. And send Meredith out to the feedstore, get their security video from last night."

A disembodied voice replies, "Roger that, Chief."

Halley, feeling sick to her stomach now, carefully follows the blood trail to the street, where it disappears. The chief crosses the street, looking around, triangulating. "Nothing here. Trail stops at the gravel shoulder. Maybe the dog will find something more."

"Should I . . . search the woods or something?"

"Dog will be here in a minute. You stay put."

She shifts around, glancing at her watch, thinking. Leaving for Brockville seems like a distant memory already. She knows this is how the world works, that it can shift on a dime, that there is nothing sacred, but she didn't realize this would be happening to and around her this week. Maybe her eagerness to right the wrongs and help crack crimes is misplaced. This doesn't feel good. Not at all. She's just grateful Early is taking this seriously. And that she stopped by. If Kater was taken by the stranger—heck, by anyone—they will at least have a jump on finding her. The first twenty-four hours are vital.

Another Expedition pulls up a few moments later, and the K-9 officer and his dog leap out. He is a gorgeous red German shepherd named Hermes with a bright-yellow harness and a badge. Halley met them on her last ride-along, and Hermes is a brilliant worker.

It takes only a few minutes to set him up with the scent. Halley watches the dog snuffle around eagerly, baying, following the trail of blood, then working the road up and down. He returns to a single spot again and again, moves a few yards east, then back. That's as far as he goes.

"That's it, Chief."

"Vehicle," Early replies grimly. "Taken and transported. Bleeding."

"Yeah," the K-9 officer concurs. "We'll give it another go, just in case."

The K-9 handler, nameplate "D. Carlin," moves the dog around the house's perimeter, emerging from the backyard shaking his head. "We've got nothing else, Chief."

"All right. Hey, Sass, think you can sit down with the sketch artist and help with a look at the stranger? I don't want to jump to conclusions—you don't live here anymore, so it could just be someone you haven't met before—but having a visual sure would help."

Halley is relieved to have something to contribute. "Of course. Yes, he might be someone from town, but Kater and Aaron didn't recognize him, either."

"Aaron Edwards. He was there?"

"And a whole bunch of people. But Aaron was upset when the stranger talked to me."

"Run me through everything he said. Was he interested in Kater? Hanging around her?"

"Not that I saw. He said he thought I might recognize him. But I didn't, and he left before he gave me his name. He knew mine, though."

"You're sure he had a motorcycle?"

"Well . . . no. He was wearing biker gear, and right after he left Joe's, I heard a bike start up. But he could have gotten into a car."

"I suppose he could have strapped her to his bike, but that would be hard, especially if she was unconscious."

Halley has been trying to play it cool, professional, as if she's investigating this case, following procedures, gathering the evidence and providing insights. But at this mental image—her friend bloody and unconscious, being strapped to the back of a motorcycle by that horrible creep—it's all too much. She feels the tears start. She swallows them down and swipes at her eyes. The chief notices, though.

"Hey. It's okay. She's your friend. I know what you're doing, depersonalizing so you can help, but this is different."

"How am I supposed to feel?"

"Scared. Upset. But do it later, yeah? I need to get a team out here—no, Miss James, you do not count, you're a civilian—and start searching. Get this information out on the wires so folks can start searching. Give me your prints, and your current info, then go back up the mountain or wherever you were headed. I'll be in touch if I find anything."

"You should let me help. I can help. I can—"

"Halley. No. You're involved in this now. You're a witness. I can't have you on this case. You hear?"

She dips her head. "Yes, Chief."

By the time Halley finishes at the police station, the sun is dipping gracefully behind the edge of the forest and the entire town is abuzz with the news of Kater's disappearance. The sketch artist did a pretty good job with her description of the stranger, and an unidentified partial fingerprint was found on her mother's file. Chances are it's Theo's, or maybe Aaron's, but just in case, they are putting it into the system.

She can't leave for Brockville now. At least not tonight. She's as rattled as everyone else. Plus, the chief was pretty clear that she needed to stick around. No sense pissing off Early. He's one of the good ones, and she wants to keep him on her side. She checks on her dad, who is relieved she's still in Marchburg, then heads to the house. Ailuros deigns to speak to her, but only after she gives him a snack. Spoiled rotten, that cat.

Anne calls, then comes over and makes lasagna, and while it should be comforting to have someone take care of her, Halley can't settle. They sit at the table together awkwardly, two women who love the same man finding their bearings, drinking wine, and making small talk about her dad, town, the latest from school, and, eventually, Kater's disappearance. Anne is not tuned in to the crime world, and Halley gives her a rundown of what happened at the scene, and what steps will happen next. Finally, they've exhausted all the chitchat, and Anne clears the table, sits back down, and with a sigh says, "Ask me. I can tell you're about to burst."

"Did you know?" Halley asks. "Did you know about my mom?"

Anne's curly blond hair is tamed in a thick braid today. She has a habit of playing with it, and she immediately reaches for it as she starts talking. "He didn't tell me the whole story, no. He said she died in a terrible accident, and that it rocked him to the core. He loved your mom. A lot. I think she was the love of his life, to be honest. I admit, I was upset when he shared the truth yesterday. I can understand why you were, as well. But Halley, you need to know that everything—everything—he's done your whole life has been to protect you."

"Everyone keeps saying that. I don't know that I agree. Changing our names and running away? I understand that everyone thinks Cat is dangerous—"

"Not *thinks*, Halley. She's a killer. And by all accounts, an unstable one."

"So I've talked to some people who say otherwise. It seems like once she got out of jail or juvie or whatever you want to call it, she straightened out her life. She went to school. Got married—though it ended in divorce. She has friends. They're sick with worry over her disappearance. Does that sound like a killer to you?"

"I understand how your emotions can be clouded here. And I admire you for the attitude that one horrible action doesn't define a person. That's an incredibly mature and hopeful reaction. But the woman you're describing is a sociopath who killed your mother and tried to kill you, too. She doesn't deserve an ounce of loyalty, sister or no."

"I can't let this go, Anne. I have to know what happened to her."

"Even if it puts all you hold dear in danger?"

"I think it's the other way around. I think not knowing, not having any concrete proof that Cat's alive or dead, is much more dangerous. She could pop up anywhere, anytime, if I don't figure this out now. I'm interested in resolving the danger."

Anne shakes her head sadly. "Your dad said you wouldn't be persuaded. That when you get an idea in your head, you can't ever let up. But Halley, you need to realize that this isn't only about you and your feelings. Your dad's packed a lot away to keep you happy and safe. You're tearing him apart, too. And we don't know if it's tied, but another woman is missing. Or worse. This has gotten bigger than your desires, Halley. We can't have something happen to you, too. It would break your dad. And that would break me."

"Heard, Anne. Loud and clear." Halley stands. "I'll help you clean up."

"I'll take care of it. I know you're anxious, Halley. This is a lot to handle. Your whole life has been upended."

"Yeah. Well. I guess. I'm more worried about Kater right now."

"Do you think her disappearance has anything to do with you finding out about your sister and your mom? The timing, that strange man last night—"

Halley's cell phone rings, and she digs it out of her pocket. At the number on the screen, her heart drops. "It's the chief," she tells Anne, then answers.

Early's voice is sharp and tense. "Halley, I have some bad news. We've found Miss Star's remains. I need you to come to the station immediately."

"Wait. What? She's dead?" A gasp from the teacher, her eyes wide, mirroring Halley's.

"I'm sending a car for you, Halley. Are you alone?"

"No. Mrs. Peterson—sorry, Anne—is here."

"Good. Stay right there, and we'll be by to get you in a few."

"Am I under arrest or something?"

"Stay put," he says and hangs up.

"Oh, God," she says, stumbling to Anne, accepting the hug, her entire being shifting. Is this her fault? Has she caused her friend's death?

Anne lets her go and sits down hard at the table. "They found Kater's body?"

"Yes."

"Was she murdered?"

"I don't know. He didn't say." Halley is in shock. She stares out the window into the black darkness, empty. She recognizes the sensations of disbelief and confusion. They were just together. Just talking. How could Kater be gone? How could she be dead?

Only a few moments later, the doorbell rings. Anne's startled expression brings Halley back to reality.

"Listen to me. Tell Dad what's going on. Tell him Kater's body was found, and that they are bringing me to the police station. I don't know if I'm a suspect somehow, which would be absolutely absurd, but just in case, I am going to say nothing until I make sure I'm not being arrested. I'll call if he needs to get a lawyer down there to be with me. Okay? Do you understand?"

"I do. That's very smart, Halley. This situation feels precarious."

Banging on the door now. "Miss James? It's Officer Meredith. I need you to come with me."

"I don't know what's going on, but please, go as soon as I leave. He'll know what to do."

Anne nods, and Halley grabs her backpack with the notebook and her phone. She opens it and texts Theo. Just in case, he needs to know.

> Friend here was killed, chief bringing me in. No idea if it's for questioning or security. I'll be in touch if I can.

She confirms the message sends, then stows the phone in her pocket and opens the door. Officer Meredith—midthirties, former Marine, reddish-blond hair cut in a bristling flattop, powder blue eyes, the whole menacing-meathead act derailed by a smattering of freckles across his nose—looks downright relieved to see her.

"Come with me," he says. She picks up her bag and follows him to the cruiser. The neighbors are out and watching, of course; Meredith was yelling at the door. She keeps her back straight and her eyes forward, ignoring them all. Then he steps around her to the front passenger door and yanks it open, and she lets out the breath she's been holding. Not under arrest, it seems, at least not yet. Not that she's done anything that would warrant being put into custody.

She climbs in, buckles her belt, and seconds later Meredith has the truck in gear and is pulling out of the drive.

She wants to ask what's happening, but she also wants to be careful, so she doesn't say a word, just waits quietly, timing her breaths with the siren, watching the town pass by in a blur as he flies to the station.

Less than five minutes later, he has her out of the truck, tucked into his side, and hustles up the back steps. He doesn't relax his grip on her until the door swings closed behind them. He visibly relaxes and lets her go.

"Glad you're okay," he says gruffly. "Chief's waiting on us. Let's go."

CHAPTER TWENTY-TWO

Meredith marches Halley through the halls into the chief's inner sanctum. She takes a seat on the hard metal chair facing Early, and Meredith closes the door and leans against the frame with his arms folded across his chest.

Early dwarfs his government-issue desk. He is clearly upset; his face is red, and he is on the phone with someone, his tone clipped and angry.

"I don't care. Figure it out," he says, then slams the phone into its cradle. He takes a deep breath and rubs a big hand over his face.

"Halley," he says finally.

"Do I need a lawyer?" she blurts out.

Early blinks in surprise, then shakes his head. "No. That's not what this is about. I'm so sorry to tell you this. There's really no doubt that Kater was murdered. We have a lot of investigating to do, but we found her body off the highway about five miles north of here."

"How? How was she killed?"

"She was stabbed."

Halley tries not to let the emotion of that blunt statement overtake her. An awful lot of stabbing in the past few days.

"Suspects?" she manages.

"Not you, so you can relax. But we have a lot of people we need to talk to. There have to be fifty-odd people who came in and out of Joe's last night while Kater was there. We need to track down her folks—"

"They moved to Boca Raton last year," Halley says inanely, because of course the chief knows this; everyone does. It's a small town, and they made a big fuss about retiring to warmer weather.

"We have the Boca PD reaching out to them right now. But I want to show you some footage from the feedstore, if you wouldn't mind. Tell me if you see anyone who looks familiar—as in, might be the stranger who talked to you." He swivels the screen of his desktop. Grainy black-and-white footage, snowy with interference.

"What time did you leave?" he asks.

"Probably around eight forty-five, nine o'clock? No later than nine fifteen. I didn't look at the clock, but I know I was home and settled before the local news started." He moves the time bar to 8:40 and hits play. They sit in silence, watching the creeping darkness of the parking lot. She can feel Meredith behind her, watching over her shoulder.

At 8:55 p.m., someone rounds the building and enters the parking lot. They make a beeline to her Jeep. The dome light flashes for a heartbeat, then the door is closed and they're moving away. There is no sound, but in her mind, Halley hears the motorcycle vroom to life.

"That has to be him," she says. "Right build, right time. Is there a better shot of his face?"

"No, but we might be able to ask for some help enhancing this video." Early pauses the video, runs it back. They watch again. It's really too grainy to see anything for sure. "What's he doing with your Jeep?"

"I think he took my mother's file from my bag, and my car keys. He must have thrown the file into the front seat and then dropped the keys so it would seem like I did it in a rush. I know for sure I had the file in my bag when I went in, and I would never not lock my Jeep." As she says it, there's another flash of light. The passenger door of her Jeep is opened again, the dome light shining for the briefest of seconds.

"Who's that?" Early says. He squints at the screen. "It's a woman. That you?"

"No, it's not me," Halley replies. "I was with Aaron and Kater. Whoever that is, she's alone."

The door is closed again, and there is darkness, but seconds later, another moment of light, as if a flashlight reflected off the Jeep's door or a lighter was lit. At that exact moment, the woman glances over her shoulder, and Halley feels the chill shoot through her body. She is a stranger, and there is a look of madness, or desperation, on her face. It's hard to tell how old she is exactly, but she's definitely older than Halley. Maybe in her forties?

"Who is that?" she asks.

"I don't know."

"Will you play it back? Can you go slow?"

Early fiddles with the mouse, and the screen goes black, then grainy again. He hits play. "Half speed's the best I can do."

The flash of light. The hair. The shape of her face. Then her face, looking over her shoulder, as if startled. Determined. Frightened.

Early hits pause, and Halley shakes her head.

"I have no idea who that is."

"You sure that isn't your sister, back from the dead?"

"I don't think so."

"When did you see your sister last?"

Halley meets Early's eyes. "When I was six years old. Probably right after she murdered my mother. And tried to kill me."

"Halley, you're absolutely sure this isn't her? Twenty-eight years is a long time. People change."

"I am . . . ninety percent sure? I can give the sketch artist a description of her, just like I did with the man. I don't know, maybe with age progression . . . but I really don't think it's her."

Now that she's been reminded, Cat's face comes to her easily. Blond curls, cherub lips, clear china blue eyes. Innocent. Charming. Lovely, when she wasn't furious and dyeing her hair black and lining her eyes with kohl and sowing hate with her family. Her natural coloring was the opposite of Halley's; with her dark hair and eyes, Halley was a twin to their mother. Cat took after her deadbeat father, something she never stopped crowing about. A man who disappeared into the fabric of the universe after the divorce and never even sent a birthday card or called. Her attachment to a practical ghost was epic.

No, the younger version of Cat, though, that's what Halley is remembering now. There's exactly zero chance anyone would look at that innocent girl and think she was capable of murder. But truth is truth.

"Run, Halley. Run."

Not now. She shakes off the echoes of her past. Who was this person, and why was she here at this particular moment in time? Maybe it was someone Halley contacted who decided to get in touch. Maybe it was Alison Everlane, playing some twisted little game. The age is about right.

"I think we should assume that's another stranger, Chief. Then the question becomes, Who is she and what was she doing in my car? Is she *with* this guy who was at Joe's? Or is she after him for something? Maybe a jealous ex, thinking he's been slinking around with someone else?"

"I have no idea. We did get that partial, and it's still running in the system. Maybe it's female, not male. Let's see what else we can find." Early hits play again, and five minutes later, Halley sees herself on the video, with Aaron and Kater by her side. They find her keys, chat for a bit. Then she's off. When her taillights leave the lot, the video time stamp says 9:03 p.m.

The chief is talking, and Halley is trying to focus, but her mind is going a thousand miles an hour. Someone is paying attention in the most horrible way. She doesn't like how that feels.

"What now?" she asks.

"Not enough to work with on the male, but the female—I'm going to call a friend in the BCI, see if their techs can help enhance this video so we can get a better look at them both. We need to know who we're dealing with. And hit your Jeep, of course."

"That seems eminently reasonable. Can I go now?"

Early shuts down the computer. He's looking everywhere but at her: the paneled walls, the map of the city, the American flag in the corner, the photos of him shaking hands with President Bush and President Obama when they came through town for fundraising events. Finally, his eyes land somewhere above her forehead, but at least they're trained in her direction.

"There's another reason I wanted you here. We found a note with Kater's body. On her body. Shoot, Halley, there isn't a good way to say it. It mentions you by name."

A cascade of fear flows through her, so intense that the hair on her arms stands up. Her heart thunders, and she shuts her eyes for a moment, practicing her square breathing, which is designed to tamp down the adrenaline rush that comes with the fight-or-flight response everyone has when faced with danger. She's been trained for this. You can't walk into a bloody crime scene and not have your prehensile tail curl. To know someone's evil is directed at you?

"May I see it?" she asks finally.

Early shoots a glance at Meredith, then back at Halley. He opens his top drawer and pulls out a photo. Lays it on the desk gingerly.

Halley tries to process what she's seeing, but it takes a moment. There is blood. So much blood.

The white carpet painted red. Mama will be so mad.

Gotta get it out gotta get it clean.

"Run."

"Run, Halley Bear."

Her mom called her Halley Bear. She hasn't thought of that nickname in years. *Focus!*

She trains her eyes on the photo, prepared this time for its horrors.

The knife juts from what must be Kater's sternum. She recognizes the fabric of the shirt she'd worn to Joe's, a blue-and-white swirl that merged into a peony on the back. The paper is pinned between the knife and her friend's body. Ripped out of a spiral notebook—same size and color paper as the one she's been using. But no, that's a bridge too far. Surely. The notebook's been with her since she picked it up off the desk.

It's the words scrawled in thick black marker that make her want to crawl in a hole and never come out. They're all capped and followed with a lopsided smiley face.

YOU'RE NEXT HALLEY BEAR

CHAPTER TWENTY-THREE

Time has no real meaning anymore. Halley goes straight home from the station in a state of suspended animation, a drumbeat of thoughts propelling her. *Kater is dead. You're next. Kater is dead. You're next.*

It took a lot of convincing for Early to let her leave at all. He wants to put her in protective custody, but that feels like making herself a sitting duck. She wants to move, to be free to fight this battle head on instead of hiding behind the police.

What she really wants is to get the hell out of Marchburg. And in the morning, once she makes sure her father is going to be safe, that is exactly what she's going to do. She refuses to sit back and wait for a stranger to visit her and shove a knife into her chest.

But she isn't going to be empty handed.

Deep in the recesses of her father's closet, there is a weapon, and after giving Ailuros a quick snuggle, she heads there. A personal-protection Smith & Wesson .38 Special snub-nose revolver is up in a box on the back shelf (something she discovered around the same time as the *Playboys*), and she lifts it from its hiding place with appropriate care. It smells of gun oil; her dad has kept it cleaned and in good shape. There is no sense in having a weapon if you don't treat it properly; he always told her that growing up.

Halley knows how to shoot. Using the ubiquitous southern hunting rifles of friends in town, they used to go deep into the woods and take target practice. Her dad would set up cans in a row along a fence post or rock outcropping, and she would take aim, pulling the trigger, hitting can after can with metallic pings and whoops of excitement. She loved those outings. He'd offered to teach her to hunt properly—he grew up in the rolling hills of rural Tennessee and was more than familiar with the pastime—but she refused. She couldn't see her way clear to take a life for sport. If it was their only source of sustenance, that was one thing, but they had a Piggly Wiggly right down the street, and there was no reason to go through the hassle of killing and dressing their own meat.

But the shooting itself . . . that was something she enjoyed. It took concentration and practice, two things she excelled at. And being married to an ATF agent meant there were guns around all the time. She and Theo often spent Saturday afternoons at the range.

When she was younger, her dad claimed he didn't have a gun in the house. But she'd found this one years ago and kept that from him. She felt better knowing he had one, truth be told, especially when she moved to DC. She has her own contingent of self-defense weapons in her bag—pepper spray, a shrill whistle, and a pocketknife—plus plenty of self-defense classes over the years, but that doesn't feel like nearly enough now. This hunk of metal? It brings her confidence.

She doesn't have a concealed carry permit, but the laws in Virginia allow open carry, so she isn't terribly concerned. Granted, she will be transporting a weapon across state lines, and that might get her in trouble, but she isn't about to make a move without that gun stashed in the main compartment of her purse for easy access.

She loads the chambers, gives the barrel a spin, clicks it into place, and sights down on her dad's favorite sweater.

"Come at me now, bitch."

Despite her desire to get on the road early, Halley sleeps later than she wanted. She needed the rest; she feels sharper than she has in days. She takes care of the cat, gives him a good brushing, downs her coffee, and is heading out the door when Theo calls.

"Are you okay? What's happening?"

Halley fills him in, leaving out only the part about the note with her name on it. If she tells him that, he'll be on a plane to Virginia before she can blink, and going AWOL isn't taken lightly, no matter the service you're in. She takes heart from the knowledge that he would throw everything away for her and leaves it there.

"You think someone is after you in Marchburg?"

"Don't think. Know. There's no question in my mind. Which is why I'm getting the hell out of Dodge."

"Where are you going to go? Back home?"

"Brockville."

"Um, may I remind you that your sister went missing from that place?"

"I know. That's why I have to go there, Theo. I have to find out what happened. I just have a gut sense that it holds the answers."

"Can you wait until this weekend? I'll be home Sunday, I can go with you."

"I appreciate that, but I don't want to stick around here. And honestly? I need to do this now. Before anyone else is hurt. Before anyone else is killed because of me. I can't let Kater's death be in vain. And I can't just sit here waiting for them to come for me. A moving target is a lot harder to hit. You know that."

"Yeah, but . . . Please, Halley. Wait for me, at least. It's just a couple of days."

"I'll be back in DC by then. Promise. I'm going to Brockville, then straight home."

"At least take someone with you from town. Don't you have an old boyfriend or two hanging around who can help protect you?"

"I sure do. His name is Smith Wesson. And he's the best protector I could have."

She can tell he's fighting back a frustrated laugh. "Seriously, Theo, you know I can handle myself. Now that I have my guard up, no one's going to sneak in and surprise me. And if they do? Pow."

"Pow. Shit, Halley. Be careful."

"You know I will. I can't just sit here, Theo. You know that. And I've been trained to do this. I'm going to hunt down Cat and find out why she killed my mother. I know there are answers out there."

"Just . . . be careful. I love you, girl." But this time he hangs up before she can hesitate or respond, protecting himself.

She stares at the black screen of her phone. So he loves her. Again. Twice in one week.

Months of nothing but arguing over her desire to have kids, then him pulling away, avoiding her, avoiding the conversation, or blowing up at her with the strain. Months of her heart shriveling up every time he kissed her good night on the forehead instead of the mouth, then him not coming home until well after she was asleep, then just not bothering at all, sleeping on the couch in his office. She finally gets sick of their impasse and leaves, and *now* he's all sorts of regretful? What did he think was going to happen?

It took her leaving for real to wake him up, apparently. She can't decide if this is good or not. If he wants a second chance and will be open to her wishes, or if he just misses having her around to walk the dog.

Do not get distracted, Halley. Get out while you can.

She tops up the cat's food and is cautious locking up and getting to the Jeep. There is black fingerprint dust on the passenger door, the hood. A crime scene tech has been here, silent as the grave. She hopes whoever it is, they're long gone. If she's not careful, Early will sic Meredith on her and she'll never get out of here.

At the hospital, Anne is sitting with her dad, and she has to admit that gives her some relief. There's security here, at least at the entrances, and she wants them all on their toes.

Her father doesn't fight with her this time. If anything, he seems relieved that she's leaving. Kater's death has spooked everyone. They chat for a while, and she arranges times when she will call, and safe words, everything she can think of that will make him feel better about her heading out. Finally, he nods.

"Just be careful, jellybean. I'd never forgive myself if something happened to you."

"Anne, you'll keep an eye on him, right?"

"You know I will."

"Good. I'll be in touch. Don't worry about me. I can handle myself."

She kisses and hugs them both goodbye, and at the desk ignores the frantic wave of the nurse on duty, who she knows just wants to question her about Kater. She can't do this right now. She has a mission.

In the hospital parking lot, Halley checks the Jeep up and down for anything that might be suspicious, like a tracker, and finds it clean. Watching over her shoulder for anyone following, she drives down the mountain, eyes blurring with tears when she drives past the crime scene tape strung across Kater's driveway. One of Early's officers is going to report seeing her Jeep, she has no doubt about that, but hopefully the chief will leave her be. She needs to do this. She knows the retreat will have all the answers. Knows it deep in her soul.

The drive goes smoothly. She is certain no one is following her. She pats her purse grimly, comforted by the hard metal. No surprise will be a match for this.

She listens to her playlists and thinks it's a hoot when R.E.M. comes on. She sings the lyrics and, in a perverse joke, inserts her own. "Don't go back to Brockville . . ."

Her phone rings as she crosses into Tennessee, the car's speaker kicking in when she answers.

"Halley James? This is Detective Mike Cooper, Metro Nashville. You called about a case from 1989?"

"Yes, I did. My mother's murder. I was hoping to talk to the detective who worked the case."

"He's no longer with us, I'm afraid. I see some of the file was shared already?"

"Yes, the crime scene documents. I'm looking for something else, specifically. My sister was the perpetrator. She was caught and pled guilty to the crime. I was hoping for transcripts from her interviews with the detectives. She's missing. I'm trying to find her, filling in the blanks."

"I understand. I took a quick look myself. The case has been archived. They're working to get all the old cases online, digitize everything. You'll need to fill out a formal request from records, all that. You have an email? I can send you a link to the form. Afraid that's all I can do right now."

"I'd appreciate that." She rattles off the address, and he repeats it back.

"I'll get this to you right away. There is one other thing. You said she's missing—there's a missing persons report on file."

"From Boston, yes."

"No, from Brockville, Tennessee. Dated June of 2002. Filed by a woman named Tammy Boone."

This is news. Someone else missed Cat.

"That's a huge help, thank you. I'm actually on my way to Brockville now. I'll see if she's around to talk."

"Sorry I couldn't be of more help."

"I understand. Thanks for the assist, Detective."

So much for that. The wheels of justice continue turning. Even when a sixteen-year-old pleads guilty to murder, the case files are put in a box labeled "Closed" and left to gather dust on a shelf.

The sun is just starting to descend when she takes the exit off the highway and points the Jeep east. She winds up a mountain that reminds her of Marchburg, switchbacks and steep drops and rocks and trees, then crests the hill and starts down. She does this five times, driving into the darkening sky, until, as she starts the last descent, she sees the great stone entrance, flanked by a well-tended sign with looping scrolls around the letters.

Welcome to Brockville!

PART TWO

There is a pleasure in the pathless woods,
There is a rapture on the lonely shore,
There is society where none intrudes,
By the deep Sea, and music in its roar:
I love not Man the less, but Nature more.

—George Gordon Byron,
Childe Harold's Pilgrimage,
canto IV, verse 178

FRIDAY

CHAPTER TWENTY-FOUR

The last of the sun breaks through the trees, shining its meager light on a woman's bare legs. She is not moving. Asleep? Dead? We do not know yet. But welcome. Welcome at last to our little town.

This land she lies upon was cleared two decades earlier to accommodate the town of Brockville, but the dense forest still surrounds it on all four sides, and this is where she's managed to disappear. It is thick with trees and wildlife, and she is vulnerable. Or was. Maybe she is still. Don't be distracted by something so banal.

Instead, let's look down the mountain toward the valley below. This declivity is man made, though you wouldn't know it without the town's history in your hand. Oh, you have one? A beautiful brochure, isn't it? The village nestles by the river on the western edge, which is used for irrigation and fishing, and a retention pond has been built in the very center with a large fountain delineating it as the town square. This overlays an expansive geothermal heating and cooling system for the homes, and a solar farm on the eastern slope provides energy to the whole town. Who knows what might be hidden inside.

Yes, our little town has grown into quite the showstopper. People don't move away once they've gotten in. They stay until they die.

That's been happening a bit more lately. Recall our woman on the mountain. We'll get back to her shortly, but while this place is meant to be nirvana, there are always cracks. Perfection can't exist, not when there are men to destroy it.

So how did this utopia come into being? Settle in, and I'll tell you a story.

Brockville is named for the Brockton family. At the head of the board's twenty-foot reclaimed barnwood table, you will find a man named Miles Brockton. Yes, that Miles Brockton. You don't know who he is? Wow. Thought everyone did.

Miles is famous—infamous really—and not just for his biophilic-planning expertise. Yes, people come here from around the world to learn how to create their own villages. But it's more than the practical; they want to rub elbows with the man who is known as a modern-day Thoreau.

Why am I telling you this? You thought you'd already read it all? You have no idea what you've missed. You need to understand where we are now. We need to go into the darker recesses of this little town off the map, where people don't leave unless they die, where women go missing and no one seems to notice, where Miles gets richer and richer and richer. Ironic for a man who has eschewed the societal norms, who defies convention, who publicly celebrates and privately vilifies the bourgeois who populate his own world.

What do I know about Miles that isn't in the literature?

That's an excellent question. You're paying attention. Bravo. It's an interesting story. Yes, of course you have time.

Miles had a normal life until he started butting heads with his father. Yes, that old saw. The prodigal son, the controlling father. A story repeated over time immemorial. The son rebels, eschews his father's wishes, and either fails or succeeds. Our Miles succeeded. He had no choice. He simply couldn't handle his father's incessant demands for him (especially when he found out there was a dirty little secret the family had been hiding). He soon saw his father not only as a nuisance but as a hypocrite, as well. That was the end for them.

Always beguiled by stories of isolation and self-exile, Miles left and spent the next several years off the grid. He graduated college, sold all his belongings, drove west . . . and disappeared.

This was 1960. It wasn't typical for people to tune out yet. Always a man ahead of his time, our Miles.

His parents were terribly upset; they'd been hard on him growing up and regretted that. He had a sister, MaryEmily, but they weren't close until he was gone and she realized how much she missed him. It was MaryEmily who convinced their parents to look for Miles. After a few years of nothing—no proof of life or death—she grew despondent, and, convinced at last something was awry, they hired a private investigative firm.

There were sightings. In New Mexico and California. In Washington State and Montana. The PI managed to map out a trail that crisscrossed much of the western US and Alaska, with dips into Mexico and Canada, and then to the wilderness of Maine, and then . . . nothing.

Two years later, it was widely assumed the wild frontier had killed Miles dead. A bear. Starvation. Exposure. Something nefarious. He'd been gone for five years at this point. MaryEmily graduated from Sweet Briar and married, had a child of her own. Her parents passed, one after the other, barely a year separating them. She didn't learn the secret. Not until much later.

Three years: Articles were written.

Five years: A book.

Seven: A movie made.

Miles Brockton was the great American mystery. He was Schrödinger's cat, living in a state of suspended animation, neither here nor gone. Dead or alive, he'd vanished.

And just when MaryEmily's heart had grown tissue over the scar of her brother's loss, he appeared. Walked out of the Maine wilderness healthy and well.

It was the land that sustained him, he claimed. He'd come to the forest, and it had sheltered him. He'd eaten only what he could catch or grow, and it had nourished him. He forgave his father his foibles, but it was too late to tell him so.

That last caused some emotional upheaval, as you can imagine.

The feelings were too much, so to the land he decided to return. But this time, he had people. Followers. Acolytes. Disciples.

He was thirty-one when he marched back into the wilderness with nineteen hearty young souls, excited to create a new world.

He returned five years later, alone but for a barely breathing infant son wrapped in his coat, raving, raging with fever and nonsensical stories.

It was a virus that got them, he claimed. In the wilderness, without proper medical care and subzero temperatures, things fell apart quickly. Not many people were like Miles. He'd seen the abyss, gazed into it, and laughed. But it killed lesser people.

That failure was enough to turn people away from his cause. You might wonder if anyone ever thought to charge him with some form of negligent homicide, but they didn't. Apparently, you aren't fully responsible for other people's stupidity.

But our Miles was not deterred. He wanted to go off grid again. He wanted people to be with him in this desire. And this time, he didn't want to lose his flock. Once was a tragedy. Twice? A disaster, and someone might take umbrage.

So using his own ingenious skills for living in the wild, Miles Brockton took that Columbia-educated mind and put it to work on creating a real self-sustaining community. He scouted a spot in the Blue Ridge Mountains on the border of Tennessee and Virginia that fit all his needs. The cold could kill; the heat, too, but the nearness of a few bigger cities meant no one had to die. It would take money, of course, to buy the land, and not surprisingly, he had very little of it: his parents had left a small inheritance, but much of it had been lost on the years of MaryEmily's relentless private investigations.

So Miles got creative and got sponsors. Investors. Venture capital. After all, he was living proof the land would give what they needed.

He traveled the world learning more sustainable ways of living off the land, and two years later, when he was ready to try again, when memories were dampened, the money appeared. A lawyer, too, attached to his hip, who claimed that Miles had rights to his own story and was due royalties from both the successful book and movie ventures. And a judge agreed.

Important people love this sort of story. The Buffetts and Templetons and Soroses of the late seventies ate this shit up.

Suddenly, Miles had plenty of income, and he put it to good use. He bought up the ten thousand acres of deserted valley in the Blue Ridge he'd found and created an oasis in the woods. The building of Brockville, so aptly named, was as environmentally friendly as he could manage. As few trees felled as possible, the contours of the land defining the contours of the town. The state forced utilities on him in the early nineties, when it was clear that he would generate a wealth of tax income for them. So he leaned in and decided to define it as a conservation resort town. A biophilic dream. And a decidedly lucrative one. Seems his second foray into the woods also cured him of his desire to be poor. Live off the land, yes, but do it from the lap of luxury.

During all this, he married Sonia Whitley, the young widow of his dear friend and first investor, Carl Whitley. Carl's death was so perfectly timed. No whispers there. At least none to Miles's face.

They had a passel of children, and they all worked the land alongside him, learning how to live without access to modern amenities, stores. Hearty boys with strong backs and malleable minds to help a man, feral, free-range children who were educated by the earth and sun in the old ways, and a wife who wanted nothing more than to raise her family well.

And the people came. They flocked to Miles's side. People who wanted to escape the real world and live in this utopia of their own creation fought for a coveted spot. His investors were the first families of Brockville, of course. They wanted to escape their lives, too, and Miles always had been a visionary.

That was forty years ago.

Now, Miles is staring down the barrel of his last years, and Brockville is a modern mecca to the world of biophilia. Now, people come to Miles for instruction. No one remembers those failed ventures, not in the face of this level of success. No one remembers the nineteen people he lost. Any sort of history can be rewritten. In the face of glory, Miles's own past was remade, a phoenix from the ashes. Brockville is everything he always dreamed of. He is sharing the earth's bounty with the followers of sustainable living, and his people are happy. So very happy.

He disappears on occasion, still. Overwhelmed by the people who want and need him, he hauls his aging body into the woods to live in the silence. And it is his sons who make Brockville run. His sons who carry on the legacy of independent spirit.

And other legacies. Darker legacies. But let's not talk about that yet.

Their mother, well, she wasn't as enamored of the Brockton family ethos as she should have been. It's a badly kept secret. Before she died, Sonia didn't need much vodka to share that she thought her husband was a bit of a maniac. Who goes into the wilderness alone and doesn't come out a little off? No one can blame him. All geniuses are mad. They have to be. They are the Cassandras, and with such foresight comes a sense of dislocation from reality.

Is this why the woman in the first frame is alone in the forest, possibly dead? Is this one of Miles's people, lost in the Maine tundra to a virus? Or is she one of the women who clamor to attend the artists' colony, to come paint and draw and write on the grounds of the Brockville Retreat?

Hmm. Neither? Both? Could she perhaps be someone who has stuck her nose in too deeply, who thought to take advantage of the town's unique mentality? Or someone who happened along at exactly the wrong time?

Let me get my shovel, and then we'll find out.

CHAPTER TWENTY-FIVE

HALLEY

Halley feels like she's entered Oz. There are no yellow brick roads or dead witches with striped socks and ruby slippers or Lollipop Guilds to welcome her, sure, but from the moment she crosses into Brockville, the sense that she's gone somewhere *different* is pervasive. She weaves her way through the woods, carefully following the posted ten-miles-per-hour speed limit, though the traffic-calming bumps are placed perfectly to impede the ability to go any faster without launching the Jeep into the air. She's glad it's not totally dark; the woods are as close and imposing as her own at home, and she imagines this place is pretty spooky in the dead of night.

And then she's in the town center, facing a well-lit lake, a fountain shooting to the sky. The last of the sun shimmers on the water's glassy surface. A charming path meanders around the water. Dogs play off their leashes; children run screaming around the most intricate playground she's ever seen.

It's like a modern Mayberry, but sophisticated, swanky. The buildings probably win awards for their architectural elegance; it's hard to balance chic and homey, but the white walls and black windows and cedar accents do just that.

People smile and wave from their electric golf carts. Plenty are walking; the wide sidewalks are full. A woman jogs with a high-end double stroller, two identical babies inside goggling at the world. There's a bookseller to her left, with a crowd; they must be having an event. The sign above the building she's facing says **General Store**. It's more cedar and black, like the bookstore, with carved posts and gaslights flanking glass double doors. Cottage-style houses with large porches and no visible garages line the streets, flanking the amenities, and people on the porches watch the scene benevolently, happy and content. Every door is a different color: deep blues, pinks, black, purple, and sunshine yellow. Some are glass, and she can see right into the living rooms. This is the heart of the little town, she can tell. What a reception for a stranger.

She finds a place to park—free, happily—and plays a quick game of Eeney, Meeney, Miney, Mo among the storefronts and settles on the General Store to make her first inquiries. The bookseller will be next if she strikes out here.

The store is in a glammed-up cabin. Fairy lights string across the street above her. It's a rustic ski chalet in Aspen on the outside, but the moment you step in from the stone-and-cedar porch, it's clear this is the grocery store. There's a state-of-the-art cooler with drinks and snacks, tables and chairs, and shelves advertising gluten-free and keto food. Bespoke farm-to-table meats and cheese line the cases, plus ready-to-heat-and-eat packages, all made "right here in Brockville." Racks of fresh vegetables receive audible thunderstorms before they are sprayed with water. Barrels advertise the local honey, and floor-to-ceiling wooden racks showcase a bottle waterfall of the local wines.

A few people browse for their evening meals. And there are four teenagers behind the register, smiling happily at her.

She approaches with her own smile. Kids are easier.

"Hi!" they say in unison, four pure, innocent voices offering succor to the weary traveler.

"Hi there," Halley replies. "I was wondering if you could direct me to the writers' retreat."

Four comically confused faces.

"The Brockville Writers' Retreat?" she repeats, as if the formal name will make a difference.

The fourth kid on the right says, "No, we know what you mean. It's just not in session now."

"Oh." Good job, Halley. You didn't think to see if it was a regular thing.

The third kid chimes in. "But one of the instructors, Tammy Boone, lives here in town. Maybe you could talk to her. I don't know if they take in-person applications."

Kid Two shakes her perfect blond head. "No, it's really exclusive."

Kid One: "But Tammy likes to eat around this time, so if you want to talk to her, you could find her at the Rustic Crust. Noah had a special tonight, so most everyone is there."

Kid Four: "That's a great idea, One."

Did Halley just hear that right? Did Four really call that kid One? Or is she tired and hearing things? Not to mention—Tammy Boone. That's the person the cop in Nashville said filed a report on her sister. Bingo.

"Thanks, Cody." The girl dimples at him, and he blushes a deep red.

Halley has to get this right. "Your name is . . . ?"

"Jenna Whon. Nice to meet you. You are?"

Ah. So she'd misheard slightly. Still, that was funny. "I'm Halley. Halley James."

The moment it's out of her mouth, she mentally kicks herself. *Way to be incognito, idiot.* Too late now. "So where is this restaurant?"

They must have it practiced, because each kid hands her a piece of literature, one after the other. Town brochure. Real estate listings. A brochure for the Inn at Brockville—it's late enough she might consider staying there instead of going back out to the highway motels. Then One plops her sheet down on the counter, and Halley takes in a detailed map of the area.

"We're here." One draws a small *X* in pencil. "The Rustic Crust is here, in Glaston. I'd drive your Jeep if it were me. They have parking." She draws the lines with exaggerated care so there's no missing the path Halley is supposed to take.

She knows what car I'm in, Halley thinks. Are there cameras? Were they watching out the window? She realizes it's just her and these four teenagers in the building now; the other folks who were shopping have disappeared. Maybe out the back? Weird.

"Left, then right at the sign to Glaston, you'll pass the farm, and then all the restaurants are in a row. That's where everyone is right now," One says, almost as if she read Halley's mind. "Dinner service starts at seven. Noah's making a lobster pizza tonight, it's the best anyone's ever had. It's a crossover night between Pesche and the Rustic Crust. You can get the pizza at both restaurants. Main Street Eats is the other restaurant, but I'm willing to bet Ms. Boone's at the RC. It's always a special occasion when Noah cross-pollinates."

Four chimes in. "And if you stay at the Inn, in the morning, you can go to the Steep and Brew for your coffee. Or Croissant Moon, but they don't open until ten. You do drink coffee, right? If not, they have a wide assortment of teas. The juice bar next door is to die for. Do you need us to look at the Inn, see if there's a room available?"

Two smiles. Three smiles. Four smiles. One smiles.

They're like perfect little hospitality robots. Wind them up and watch them go. Maybe she was wrong about the Lollipop Guild after all.

"Thanks," Halley says. "That would be great. I'll go check all this out. Appreciate your help."

"You're welcome," they say in unison. One continues alone with another charming smile. "Leave us your phone number, and I'll give you a shout once we know about the Inn."

Halley does and is relieved to get back outside into the cool mountain air. She looks up the name "Tammy Boone," finds the woman's website. There is a smiling photo under the "About Me" section, a glamour shot of a bottle blonde with blue eye shadow and her hand under her chin. Maybe not the most current look, but enough that Halley will be able to identify her.

She consults the map, then turns the Jeep southwest into the hamlet called Glaston. The sun has set now, and she must navigate by the streetlights. She assumes they're solar; a large box attaches to the bases with reflectors on it, and the signs are well lit and easy to follow. Golf carts whizz past in the opposite direction. She sees a stylized sign: **The Farm**. And another two blocks of the black, white, and cedar cottages later, the street opens up into another small-town square. As promised, there are three restaurants in a row. Pesche and the Rustic Crust flank Main Street Eats. Pesche's building is sharper than the other two. She's impressed that the architecture so obviously signals the level of dining experience.

The lights of the restaurants bleed onto the street; they are packed. There are outside tables with heaters, too, also packed.

There's parking on the street, but not a single empty spot, so she follows the signs down a small alley to parking in the back of the restaurants. Walks around to the entrance of the Rustic Crust—the RC, according to the Stepford Quadruplets. A hostess with a wide smile and a bun of blond confection on top of her head greets her. "Hi! We're pretty slammed but I might be able to get you a seat at the bar."

"Thanks. I'm actually looking for someone. Tammy Boone?"

The girl's face falls, just a bit. "Um . . ."

Halley has a moment of realization. Tammy Boone is a minor celebrity. Strangers must come looking for her all the time.

"I'm sorry, that must have sounded weird. You have to protect her privacy, I know." Halley leans in conspiratorially. "I'm a former student, passing through town. I was hoping to give her a hug and tell her what I'm up to. I just got a book deal!"

"Oh! Oh my God, congratulations! That's amazing. I bet she'll be so excited. She's over there, in the corner. Table for eight."

Halley follows the pointed finger and nods her thanks. "Appreciate it."

"I'll get you a chair. We'll shove it in somewhere."

Halley weaves through the happy chaos that is the pizza joint. The delicious smells make her mouth water—she's hungry. Everyone here is so cheerful. Happy. Engaged with their tablemates. There's not a single cell phone or iPad in sight. It's almost weird.

At the corner table for eight, she scans some faces until she finds the one she's looking for. Boone's in the back corner, where she can see the whole room—and be seen, of course. The blond hair is now a more natural mousy brown shot with silver, and she looks to be telling a joke; everyone is laughing uproariously and her face is flushed red with merriment. Or wine. There are jugs of Chianti on the tables, and white candles burn and drip wax down the edges of empty bottles. She approaches and waits for Tammy to notice her.

The hostess trots over with a chair. "Tammy, hey! Mind if we squeeze her in here?" She plops the chair down, and a couple of people shove over. "Congrats again on the deal," the girl says and hurries off.

Tammy looks drunkenly terrified. Halley waves. "Hi. Remember me?"

Tammy is either too drunk to admit she doesn't, or doesn't want to seem rude, because she rearranges her face and pats the chair. "Of course I do. Have a seat."

Halley does. "Hi. Thanks for this."

Tammy stares. "I am sorry, but I can't say that I recall your name. I have so many names in my head, characters and such, and I teach a lot of people."

Halley leans over and says, "Nice to meet you, Ms. Boone. I'm Halley James. I think you might have known my sister. Catriona Handon."

There is a sharp gasp from the writer, who then buries her face in her wine. Halley realizes the redness might be a more permanent feature from excessive alcohol intake rather than current merriment.

"I'm sorry to just appear like this," she says quietly. "I really need to talk to you."

"I don't know if I have anything to say," Boone replies. "Anyway, I'm busy at the moment. Obviously."

It comes out "obvioushly" in a slur, and Halley nods her understanding. "Of course. I didn't mean to interrupt your dinner. Could we talk after you finish eating? It's very important, and I've come a long way."

"So long ago," Tammy says, almost to herself.

"Fifteen years. Please, Ms. Boone."

Boone finishes her wine and pushes back from the table. "Ten minutes. Let's go to the Steep and Brew. It will be quieter."

She gets to her feet, excuses herself from her friends, and gestures for Halley to walk in front of her. They are halfway to the door when a rangy, handsome man with blue eyes and floppy brown hair steps into their path. He's wearing chef's whites. He feels familiar, but Halley has no idea why.

"Tammy! Going so soon? Did you enjoy the pizza?"

The woman's entire demeanor changes. She shifts her body so her bosom is more prominent, and her face turns coquettish. "Noah Brockton, you've outdone yourself, again. No one can make a lobster scream like you."

"Aw, shucks, ma'am," he teases right back. "You heard them screaming all the way from Maine, I bet. Who's your friend?"

Halley looks up to see the man watching her with a raised brow. His eyes are a peculiar shade of blue, very dark, and his stare is direct. "Halley James," she says, sticking out a hand. "I'm visiting town."

"Welcome to Brockville, Halley James."

"Brockville, Brockton . . . Is there a connection?"

"Sort of. My dad was the one who founded Brockville. I take it you haven't read the brochure yet." He laughs, and the joyful freedom of it makes her laugh, too.

"I guess I haven't."

"We should go," Tammy urges. "Great work as always, Noah."

"Merci beaucoup," he says in a beautiful French accent. "Au revoir, Tammy, and friend of Tammy." He has a nice smile, not the feigned happiness of the others she's encountered, but warm and genuine. She can't help but glance back as they leave the restaurant. And is surprised to see him watching her, a look of faint confusion on his face.

CHAPTER TWENTY-SIX

Halley and Tammy walk on the wide, gracious sidewalk past the other restaurants and enter a quiet, coffee-scented space. There is only one barista at this time of night, who smiles winningly. Are they all hopped up on coke or Adderall? Who has this much social energy? She's had a summer job in the business, and she knows the toll it takes. No one here seems remotely affected by the need to smile smile smile.

Halley orders a large Americano and buys a decaf coffee for Boone. There is a display of granola bars—a brand she doesn't recognize—but a quick glance at the label tells her they are homemade here in Brockville, so she takes one. A slice of that decadent lobster pizza would have been welcome, but this is better than nothing. Maybe she'll stop at the pizza joint again after they talk.

Tammy sits heavily with a deep sigh, toying with her glazed ceramic mug. "Your sister," she says, shaking her head. "What do you want to know?"

"I have to admit, ma'am, that I don't know much about what happened here. But you clearly knew Cat."

"I met her briefly. She was only at the retreat for two days before she . . . left."

"Left? She walked out?"

"I think so. I think . . . Well, it's not really my place to think anything. Have you talked to the sheriff yet?"

"No. I will. I want to. But I thought you would be a better resource." Halley sips her coffee, composing her thoughts. "If I'm totally honest, I came looking for information about the writing retreat, because I know my sister was headed here and then went missing. Then the kids at the General Store sent me your way. I think I just got lucky."

Boone snorts. "I'll say. The universe gives you what you want, though, I suppose." She no longer seems happily tipsy, but fidgety and uncomfortable.

"Can you tell me what you know about Cat's disappearance? A detective from Nashville told me you filed a missing persons report."

Tammy gazes into the depths of her pottery mug. "I really don't know if I should talk to you, Halley. The sheriff—"

"Will be my next stop, I promise. You can call him right now and ask him to come over, if you want. I'm not trying to hide anything. I'm just trying to figure out what happened to my sister."

Boone narrows her eyes. "It's been fifteen years. No offense, but why now? Where have you been all this time?"

"Would you believe I just found out that she didn't die when I was a kid like I'd been told?" Halley gives an unamused laugh. "Talk about a story. I grew up believing my mother and my sister were killed in a car accident when I was six. Turns out that wasn't true. My mother was killed, but my sister wasn't. I learned that earlier this week. I'm trying to find out what happened to her, so I can . . . I don't know. Reconnect?"

She holds back the whole truth. She gets the sense that in this state, Tammy Boone isn't going to respond well to learning her former student was a murderer.

Her instincts are rewarded moments later when the woman bursts into tears. "I always knew something bad happened to her, but no one would listen. You have to understand, Brockville is a special place. It operates with its own rules. Cameron—Sheriff Brockton—he did some looking for her, but he was of the opinion she left on her own. Everyone was. But everything she brought with her, she left behind. She even had divorce papers in her bag, but they weren't signed. Who goes off and leaves their divorce papers? Not to mention, we're the Brockville Writers' Retreat. I mean, not to sound snooty, but it's hard to get in. The idea that someone would go through all of that and then walk out at the beginning is unprecedented."

"I can imagine."

"Your sister seemed like a great girl. You remind me of her a bit."

"Oh. Thank you." That is what she's supposed to say, not what she's actually thinking. *I am nothing like her. She is cruel and cold and calculating. A monster. A great girl?* Again, Cat has either snowed everyone around her or changed into a different person. Is that possible? Can you truly change? Turn your life around? Morph evil into good?

Tammy wipes her eyes. "I saw so much possibility in her writing. She had an edge to her writing that I absolutely loved. There was a sense of spectacle to her work. She had *it*. The elusive something that allows a writer to break into the publishing world. I don't see it often. Yes, a Brockville graduate almost always gets a book deal, but it doesn't guarantee a career. I could have helped her, but she disappeared."

"You looked for her?"

"Of course I did. Cat was assigned Adelaide Cottage, the closest to the woods, the farthest from the main writing cabin. Nothing in the retreat is more than a few hundred yards apart, but it manages to feel completely and totally isolated. It's part of the mystique. I left after the morning session and hiked to her cabin. Her breakfast was undisturbed on the porch, the basket still full of treats, muffins and fruit. The door was unlocked. I knocked, scared to death of what I might find.

"It felt like she'd just gone for a walk. The bed was unmade, her suitcase was open. I never thought she'd bailed on the retreat. It can be hard, very hard, to have your work critiqued. Part of my job is to teach writers how to accept this criticism gracefully, to learn what is of worth, what serves the story, and how to execute those revisions, without the rest getting in their head."

"Teach a writer to fish . . ." Halley says, and Tammy hiccups a laugh.

"Exactly. In case she was overwhelmed and upset, I left her a note, encouraging her to return to the cabin, rejoin the workshop. But she didn't. That's when I called Cameron. We hardly need a sheriff, Brockville has no crime. Cameron rides around the village twice a day in his golf cart, waving to the people who live here, and that's all the deterrence anyone needs. He has never drawn his weapon, the only reports he's had to file are about hikers who every once in a while camp in the woods within the borders of their land. He chases them off quickly, and it's done. People do not steal here. They do not break into each other's homes. They might smoke a little weed, have some shrooms from the gardens, but that's hardly a problem for Cameron to deal with. Autonomy means something here. I fought hard to get the sheriff to do more, but he wasn't interested in my thoughts."

"Why do you think that is? Why wouldn't he want to investigate?"

"He was of the opinion that she was an adult. The divorce papers were also rather damning. Cameron felt like she bailed on everyone and went to start her life over somewhere."

"That's . . . an interesting reaction to a possible missing person."

Boone leans forward and speaks quietly. "You didn't hear it from me, but Cameron's lazy. His dad owns all of this, you know. Miles Brockton is a legend around here. The Brockton boys all have a role, but it's Miles who runs the show. If Miles had told Cameron to leave no stone unturned, he would have. But he didn't. It was more the opposite, actually. Miles wouldn't want that sort of bad publicity."

"So the sheriff is the son of the town's founder?"

"Oh, yes. All of Miles's boys work here. Cameron is the sheriff, and you already met Noah, he's the chef and in charge of the restaurants. Stick around a few days and you'll meet Elliot and Chase, too. They run the farm and school respectively. The oldest is trouble, if you ask me. Charms the larks from the trees, but only to eat them. He's sly. Be careful if you ever come across him."

"Cameron? The sheriff?"

She blinks heavily, her face paling. A hand goes up to cover her mouth.

"Are you okay?"

"I shouldn't have said that."

"Oh, seriously, don't worry. I would never share. We're in the cone of silence right now, as far as I'm concerned." She draws an invisible circle around them.

Boone watches her. Halley sits under the gaze, unmoving. She doesn't want to startle her away.

"In that case, I have to tell you, Halley. Cat is not the only person who went missing from Brockville. There was another, a young writer from France. A few years before Cat. I wasn't here then, I heard about it from another teacher."

Halley's heart does a quick rhumba. This is news. "Can you give me the teacher's name? Can I speak with her?"

"Unfortunately, she passed away. But there was a woman in the FBI who came to town looking for that writer. The agency she was represented by asked them to look into it. The circumstances were similar."

"So is that why you think something happened to Cat, instead of her leaving on her own? Because it had happened before, and Cameron didn't really look into her disappearance? He didn't want to make waves and have it get out that women disappeared when they came to Brockville?"

Fear crashes over Boone's features, and her tone changes. "Oh, no. I would never say that. My God, I really have had too much to drink. I'm spreading rumors now. I should get going. I just thought it strange that your sister left when she'd finally gotten what she so wanted, but what do I know?"

My God. That's quite a bombshell.

"Thank you, Ms. Boone," she says, reaching over to pat the woman's hand. "I appreciate all of this. I agree, I can't imagine Cat would just walk away from her lifelong dream." She starts to rise, but Boone shoots her a confused glance and doesn't move, so she sinks back down.

The woman's tone is accusatory. "I thought you said you didn't know anything about her?"

"I don't, not really. I've been talking to her friends. They agree with you that something happened to her, that she wouldn't have just disappeared from the life she'd built."

Boone nods, glances over her shoulder, and leans forward again. The woman is mercurial, and flighty. The drink, maybe. Or being a writer, an artist. "It didn't make sense. She was clearly affected by the critique of her work that day, and believe me, it can be incredibly rough your first time. I've had writers here who fall apart and can't hack it. But she wasn't like that. It was as if she was detached from the criticism. She heard it all, she wanted to change the story and make it better, but she wasn't . . . defeated, I guess is the best term. I've not met a lot of young authors who can handle a room full of critics with such a blasé attitude."

"Any chance you have the story?"

"Hmm . . . I might. The sheriff has all her things, but I bet I have a copy. I would have kept it, in case she ever came back and wanted my help. Do you want it?"

"That would be amazing. Maybe there's a clue there as to her state of mind."

And maybe there's something that will explain what happened.

"It will have to be tomorrow. I need to find it. It will be in my files, but I'm in no condition to go looking."

"Tomorrow is fine. Thank you."

"Are you staying here?"

"The kids at the store were going to check if the Inn had any rooms available."

"Okay. Meet me tomorrow morning at the retreat cabin. Nine." She stands. "Now if you'll excuse me, I have a dinner to get back to."

"Of course. Thank you so much, Ms. Boone."

"You're welcome." She looks at Halley, squinting. "It's so strange. You remind me of her."

"I do? We didn't look anything alike."

"Yes, I know. But you make the memories of her stronger. Interesting." And she's gone, the door tinkling a farewell.

Halley looks at her watch. It's after ten. She's tired. She's hungry. Her butt hurts from sitting too long. She wants to find a quiet spot—alone—and process all she's just learned. She gets in the Jeep and drives back to the General Store.

The kids are still inside, playing a game of cards. They look up guiltily when she enters.

One stands and approaches. No smiles this time. "Unfortunately, the Inn doesn't have room for you this evening. I called around, but none of our short-term rentals are free, either. Sorry about that." She is no longer the chirpy, happy girl from earlier. It's like a darkness descended when the sun went down.

"That's all right. I'll find someplace by the highway. Thank you anyway, Jenna."

"Drive carefully," she says flatly. "And thank you for coming to Brockville."

Halley decides to check for herself if the Inn has room. She looks at the map, then winds through the hamlets, looking for and finding the sign to Avalon. She passes the writing retreat; there's a wooden sign with the name painted on it, lit with small spotlights. She's half tempted to turn in and take a look around, but she needs to find a place to stay. Tomorrow is soon enough.

The parking lot of the Inn is empty of cars. No one's here. Surely there's a room for her. She knocks on the entrance door, then tries it, only to find it locked.

Weird. Maybe it's off season; maybe they just don't open all the rooms until summer. The retreat doesn't run all year, either. Maybe they didn't feel like opening to accommodate a single guest for a night. Maybe they're sending her a message.

With a sigh, she tosses it over. Sleep in the Jeep in one of the parking lots or drive back over the mountain to a hotel near the highway. It's an easy choice. Brockville at night, without the charming lights and ubiquitous golf carts, feels somehow menacing. She's out of here.

She winds her way back out of the hamlet to the main road. She isn't surprised to see a police vehicle sitting at the intersection. But she is shocked when he turns on his light bar as she passes him, and taps his siren, a familiar sharp squawk.

Why is he pulling her over? She's done nothing wrong. That doesn't mean her heart doesn't leap into her throat and try to choke her in its anxiety. A natural reaction to sirens.

She guides the Jeep to the edge of the wide road and puts on her hazard lights. She pulls out her license and registration and sets them on the dash, then puts down her window and makes sure her hands are visible on the steering wheel. A courtesy.

The sheriff swaggers in her rearview. She rolls her eyes and waits.

He stops by the window. He has a Maglite, shines it right into her face. She shields her eyes, catches his face for a heartbeat, and sucks in a breath. He, too, looks so familiar. Like some sort of handsome movie star vampire. Square jaw. Sharp teeth.

His brother, Noah, is a taller and younger version, she realizes. She needs to look up Miles Brockton. Some men really do pass on their genes. The similarities tell her this is probably the case.

"Hey," she exclaims "Ouch. That's bright."

"Halley James? I need you to get out of the car, please."

"Why? Was I speeding?"

"Out. Now." He has a bark on him, she'll give him that.

She doesn't like this. There is no one around, no friendly headlights or walkers or golf carts, just her and the sheriff and the looming woods. The trees seem closer than ever, claustrophobically close.

He wears a tan uniform and sports a thick gold band on his left ring finger. His hands are huge, fingers thick, nails buffed. He is not used to being defied.

"Out. Of. The. Car. Now. *Miss* James."

The sheriff puts a hand on his weapon. Halley gets out of the car.

CHAPTER TWENTY-SEVEN

The sheriff efficiently and not very gently turns Halley around and slaps handcuffs on her. The metal bites into her wrists, and she feels the external claustrophobia settle into her body. She has to breathe squarely so she doesn't start struggling.

He kicks her legs apart.

"What the hell are you doing?"

"It's called a search. You carrying any weapons I need to know about?"

Shit. Shit!

"In my purse. It's registered."

"Oh-ho," he says, expertly, impersonally running his hands down her sides, her legs, her shoulders, her back. The violation is hard to take even though there is nothing lewd in his touch.

"Turn around."

"I told you, there's a personal-protection weapon in my purse. That's all."

He whips her around to face him, finishes his pat-down. He thoroughly searches the car, then her bag, confiscating the gun. Steps back, one meaty hand again resting on his Glock. "What brings you to Brockville with a weapon in your purse. Expecting trouble?"

"I think I should call a lawyer."

"Don't do that. We're just talking."

"No such thing when you're wearing handcuffs."

"Listen to me. I can make your life very difficult."

She doesn't say anything, and he curses under his breath. She decides to gamble.

"My friend was murdered last night. I'm just being cautious."

"Murdered where?"

"Marchburg, Virginia."

"You know it's illegal to transport weapons across state lines that aren't properly secured. I'd think you of all people would know that, Miss James. You're taking an awful big risk right now."

"How do you know so much about me, Sheriff?"

He shuffles his feet again. "Might have gotten a call from your friend Baird Early. He was concerned enough to ask me to keep an eye on you."

Halley relaxes a touch. This is a show.

"And the handcuffs?"

"Weapons trafficking is something we take rather seriously, Miss James."

"As I said, it's for protection. I'm not planning to sell it."

"I'll make that determination. Let's go to my place and have a chat, shall we? You can leave the keys, one of my deputies will bring the car."

"Great. Fine. Take off the handcuffs, though. Please?"

He says nothing, and doesn't make a move toward the handcuff key, just leads her to his truck. It's an Escalade, a huge black beast. He settles her uncomfortably in the back seat, buckles her in, and gets behind the wheel. There is a thick plexiglass-screen cage between them, and she can't hear him talking on the radio, just sees the handset go up to his mouth.

This is outrageous. She has to keep her head and not let her frustration get the better of her here, or she's going to end up in a cell. Maybe she is anyway. Maybe he's actually going to charge her.

She needs a lawyer.

She needs Theo.

A swell of emotion rises, and she fights back the tears. She is not behaving like a grown-ass woman right now. She doesn't need a *man* to come save her. An ATF agent, though? That could help.

Just . . . chill. You've done nothing wrong. Not really. Early probably told him to take you in and keep an eye on you. Interfering is one of his superpowers.

That makes her feel better, and she adjusts herself as comfortably as she can. The ride isn't long. She spots the sign to the hamlet of Somer, and the practicalities of town living start showing themselves. The Montessori school, the mechanic, an architect's office, the hair salon, a huge fire station, and next to it, a state-of-the-art, modern black-and-cedar police station. It looks like something out of a design magazine, elegantly lurching into the hill.

The sheriff pulls in, drives around to the back, and parks in the spot closest to the back door. He hauls her out and marches her inside, still wordless.

The station is spotless. And somewhat deserted. He takes her to a booking station and, thankfully, past it. She breathes another little sigh of relief. There's a glass door to a fully equipped crime lab down the hall, which is surprising considering the size of the place. She would assume any samples they have would go straight to the state lab, but no, they have a whole setup here. The bullpen is full of brand-new desks with monitors and printers that look like they've gotten almost no use. As if the entire station were built for a whole crew of cops but no one ever came but the cleaning people.

They are clearly well funded.

Sound and fury, she thinks. *How much crime can there really be around here to justify this setup?*

The sheriff's office is as pristine as the rest of the station. His desk is free of papers, holding only a sleek black phone, an iMac, and a leather blotter with a gold pen lined up like a smart soldier. He sits her in a chair facing him, finally takes the cuff off her left wrist, and attaches her right to a small ring on the chair she's in. It looks custom made, like it should be in some killer's basement instead of out in the open in the sheriff's office. There's something almost worse about having one hand free and one chained to the chair. He takes his seat, which is slightly higher than hers so he can look down at her, pulls out a brand-new legal notepad from the drawer, and unposts his pen, a clearly expensive masterpiece of black and gold. He looks at it, buffs the edge as if removing a fingerprint, then trains his gaze on her.

Anal-retentive sheriff, she thinks, imagining him on a *Saturday Night Live* skit, and has to bite back the laugh.

She doesn't feel any merriment when he starts to speak.

"You're being held until we clear up some things."

"Then, again . . . I need a lawyer."

He huffs an impatient sigh.

"You know a woman named Chowdhury?"

She shrugs. "Lawyer."

"Stop being an idiot. I'm trying to protect you."

His imperious tone pisses her off. She puts up her chin. She will not be intimidated by this man, even if she's chained like a dog to a stake.

"Prove it. Take off the handcuff."

He moves so quickly she almost flinches, and then she's free. She leaps to her feet and goes to the opposite side of the office. Watching her, he sits behind the desk and picks up the pen again.

"Now. Dr. Chowdhury?"

"She was my sister's therapist in Boston. She came to my house yesterday morning and . . ." *Gave me a letter from my sister, which you're going to find when you dig through my bag again,* but she decides to hold this back for now.

"And?"

"Told me she thought my sister's disappearance from Brockville wasn't taken as seriously as she would have liked. A theme I've now heard from several people."

"Your sister?"

"Yes. Her name is Catriona Handon. People called her Cat. She was a student at the retreat here, studying writing under Tammy Boone, and went missing fifteen years ago. As I understand it, you were well aware of her disappearance. Investigated briefly and found nothing. I was actually going to come talk to you in the morning about the case."

He visibly relaxes. She comes back to the chair, ignoring the metal rings and the handcuffs dangling from the side like props in some bizarre bondage game. He is like an eagle on a branch scanning for a snack; no move she makes goes unnoticed.

Finally, he drops the pen and leans back in the chair. "Hmm. *Missing* is an interesting word."

"You don't think she went missing?"

"Let's stick with Chowdhury. She's the one I'm concerned about now."

"Why?"

"I'm asking the questions here, Miss James. Don't make me regret letting you loose."

She narrows her eyes at him. "Don't make me regret not having counsel present for this chat."

A smile quirks the corner of his mouth so briefly she thinks she imagined it. With a sigh, she says, "I spoke to the doctor for a grand total of thirty minutes, tops. She came to my house uninvited and drove off into the rain. I know nothing more than that. I'm here about my sister, Sheriff. The doctor didn't give me anything concrete to go on."

The sheriff is handsome in an eerie way, and when he furrows his brow, she sees even more echoes of his younger brother, Noah the chef, in his face. There's an openness to Noah, though, a joyfulness that the sheriff is clearly missing.

There is something else about him that feels familiar, but she can't put her finger on it. His eyes, maybe. They are dark and fathomless. Like a snake's.

The eyes. That's it. The sheriff reminds her of the man in the bar, the stranger who talked to her.

"You don't remember me, do you?"

She didn't know then, and still doesn't, why she should have remembered him. But now, looking into another set of dark eyes just as bottomless, and feeling the chill rush through her body, she realizes she's in deeper trouble than she thought. She shouldn't have come here. She shouldn't be talking to him. She should have left this alone. She needs to get out of here, and fast.

But she has to know. Leaving things alone is not her forte. Curiosity killed the cat.

Curiosity killed Cat, her mind provides. *Or at least got her into a lot of trouble. Go careful.*

"You have a lot of brothers, don't you? Are there any pictures of all of you around here?"

"Why?"

"I wanted to see . . . Listen, a stranger came to my hometown, spoke to me, and then my friend was murdered. He looks a bit like you, actually. Chief Early will have the artist rendering that you can see. Maybe you'll know him."

The sheriff's face is hard to decipher. She tries again.

"How much did Early tell you about what was going on? Did he mention Cat?"

Cameron leans back and raises a brow, rocking in his designer chair, but doesn't answer. She knows this tactic, and vows to keep her mouth shut from this moment on. He can't be trusted. This she knows deep in her soul.

He watches her. She doesn't look away.

The staring contest has gone on for a few moments when she hears a voice calling.

"Cameron? Cam? Where the hell are you?"

"Oh, for Christ's sake," the sheriff mutters.

The chef from the pizza place appears in the doorway.

"What do you want, Noah?"

"I hear you arrested the girl."

"The *girl* has a name," Halley says.

"Halley," Noah replies. "I know. Cam. What are you doing?"

"Leave. Noah. This isn't your business."

"The hell it isn't."

"Go back to flouring your pans, little brother. I have real work to do."

"Oh, fuck off, Cam."

So there is no love lost between the Brockton brothers. Interesting.

"Would you shut it?" the sheriff growls. "This is a murder suspect and I'm in the middle of an interrogation."

"A murder suspect?" Halley gasps. "Who am I supposed to have murdered?"

They both turn to look at her, and the sheriff runs a hand across his face as if he's tired, the first bit of humanity she's seen out of him.

"Dr. Jana Chowdhury. She's dead."

CHAPTER TWENTY-EIGHT

Halley forces her jaw closed. Things are going from bad to worse. First Kater, now Chowdhury?

"How? How did she die?"

"Why don't you tell me?"

"I didn't kill her," she says with impatience. "I have exactly zero reasons to want the woman dead. On the contrary, her death hampers my investigation."

"Oh yeah, *your* investigation. Early warned me you'd style yourself as some sort of law enforcement investigator because of your limited background in crime scene forensics. But you don't have a job at all, so I hear. You certainly don't have a badge. You have no protection, you're carrying a weapon illegally, and two women you had contact with in the past forty-eight hours are dead. You tell *me* what I'm supposed to think."

Noah sits heavily in the second chair. "Hey," he says to her, the gentleness in his tone a total contrast to his brother's bluster.

"Why are you here?" she asks him.

"Because you're asking about your sister, and I was the last person to see—"

"Enough!" Cameron roars. "Stop right there. Leave, Noah. I have this covered. Unless you'd like to spend a night in a cell, too?"

Noah hesitates, then meets her eyes. "I'll be waiting right outside." Then, to his brother, "Stop fucking with her, Cameron. Tell her the truth."

Halley is more and more confused. Noah, true to his word, seethes out the door, slamming it behind him.

"You can explain all that to me later," Halley says to the sheriff. "How did Chowdhury die?"

He sits on the edge of his desk, arms crossed.

"Stabbed. Just like your friend. Early found the car pulled to the side of the road and the doctor lying across the seat. She'd been dead for a few hours, ME said."

She covers her mouth with her hand. What in the hell is going on? Kater. Chowdhury. All because Halley started asking questions about her sister? Everyone she's talked to . . .

"Was there a note or anything?"

"Like what was tacked to your friend's chest? No. Nothing like that. Early said it was messy and violent. Less controlled. The doctor fought back."

"You need to call the Boston PD and do a welfare check on a woman named Alison Everlane. She was my sister's best friend, and she was the one who gave me Chowdhury's name."

He assesses her for a moment, then puts a hand on his phone. "You talk to anyone else?"

"Just Cat's ex-husband, Tyler Armstrong."

"What the hell you think you're doing? You planning to be a PI or something?"

"Check on Alison, and I'll explain."

"You have a phone number for her?"

"In my bag."

He nods and leaves for a second, then comes back with her bag, dumps it in her lap. It is missing the gun, but the letter Chowdhury gave her is in there, along with the spiral-bound she'd been taking notes in. A flash in her mind of the notebook paper tacked to Kater's chest . . .

Yes, whoever is behind these deaths must have looked in her notebook. Which means someone was in the house.

The cat, locked in the basement. It wasn't an accident. Whoever it was must have come in that way.

She flips through the pages and reads off the number. He taps on the computer for a few minutes, then dials his phone. The phone rings several times, then goes to voicemail.

He dials another number. This one is answered. The conversation is one sided but she can follow easily.

"This is Sheriff Brockton from Brockville, Tennessee. I need a welfare check on a woman named Alison Everlane, on Massachusetts Avenue in Cambridge. Yes. Right, that's the one. I've tried calling but there's no answer. I don't have a cellular number for her. Great. Yes, of course. My number is 555-423-9009. Appreciate it."

He hangs up and cocks a brow. "Your turn."

"All right. I spent my whole life thinking my mother and sister died together in a car accident when I was six. But earlier this week, I found out my father had lied to me. My mother was murdered. Stabbed to death. By my sister."

"Cat killed your mom?" This comes from the other side of the door. Noah has been eavesdropping.

"Oh, for God's sake . . . get in here," Cameron commands, and Noah opens the door and enters sheepishly. The blurt was so shocking, so familiar, so intimate, that it is Halley's turn to raise a brow.

"Sounds like you know my sister."

Noah looks at Cameron, who throws up his hands in disgust. "Fine. On your head be it."

Noah sits again. He is earnest, and clearly concerned. "We met on the river path. We had a lovely conversation, and she was heading back to her cabin to rework a story. She was cool. I don't know that I can believe what you've just told us."

"But it's true. Sheriff? Look it up. 'Susannah Handon Murder Nashville.' It will all be there."

"I thought her last name was Armstrong," Noah says.

"That's her married name. Her maiden name is Handon. Trust me. I think I'd know."

Cameron taps away, reading the screen, his eyes going wider, then his face collapses. The printer whirs to life, startling her. Noah puts a calming hand on her arm. It's big, and warm, and rough from the kitchens, but in this moment, when all things are confused and bewildering, she takes comfort, and doesn't push it away. She has to say, though, all this touching by strangers is making her jumpy. The Brocktons are handsy men.

Cameron gets the paper off the printer and hands it to Noah, who reads it. Halley can see the headline: it's the same article she looked at. Noah's gone pale as a ghost.

"I know. It's shocking as hell. Believe me, I've had a hard time wrapping my own head around it."

"And now people are dying," Cameron says. "Your friend. Cat's doctor."

"Yes. I told Kater, and I called Dr. Chowdhury to ask for information. I talked to Tammy for a while tonight, too. And, of course, called Alison and Tyler." She calculates, then draws out the letter. "Dr. Chowdhury brought me this. This is why she came to Marchburg after I called her. She couldn't share anything about Cat's treatment, of course, but she's been holding on to this letter for years, just waiting to give it to me."

She hands it to Cameron, who flips through the pages. "Sounds like she got into a program and was working the steps."

"Maybe. Asking for forgiveness is a big part."

Noah is still staring at the article printout.

"She wasn't very nice to me when I was growing up. I'm glad you had a different experience with her. I don't have the best memories."

"Run, Halley Bear. Run."

"That's why you're digging into this now?" the sheriff asks. "Because you've just discovered the truth?"

"Yes. I haven't thought through what's next. And with people dying, it seemed smart to get away from town."

"We'll protect you," Noah says, and Cameron snorts.

"No, we won't. She's going back to Marchburg in the morning. This is not our problem, and I can't take the chance—"

"It most certainly *is* your problem," Halley says. "My sister disappeared from your town, Sheriff. It's high time you do a proper investigation and help me figure out why."

"Oh it is, is it?"

"Yes," Halley answers. "And I'll assist. But I need to find out why people are dying *now*. I have to find out what can of worms I've opened. I want to know who the stranger is, why he pilfered my mom's file. And Cat—"

He puts up a hand. "You can do that back in your hometown, with your police chief. We will put you up tonight and get you on the road in the morning."

"She won't be safe, Cam. She needs a guard. An escort. What are you thinking?"

"I'm thinking this is exactly the kind of drama we don't need here. That's my final word." And to Halley, "You may stay the night at the Inn, or you can stay the night in the jail, I don't care which. And then you are leaving Brockville. For good."

There is no more arguing, she can see that. Noah leaves, frowning. He knows more than he's letting on, for sure. This whole situation is bizarre, and Halley is torn between wanting to figure it out and wanting to get as far away as possible. Someone is trying to either send her a message or taunt her, and for the first time, she admits to herself that she is in way over her head.

There is no question where she is staying—the Inn. She tells him that, and he gives her a curt nod. She follows the sheriff from his office out to the parking lot. The Escalade is waiting. He puts her in the back seat again, but thankfully without the handcuffs this time. The drive to the Inn is quick. Her Jeep sits in the parking lot, and Brockton unlocks it and hands out her overnight bag. She has no idea how the Jeep got there, nor when the sheriff got the keys. She hasn't seen any other law enforcement officials. Magic, maybe. At this point, she doesn't care. She just wants to sleep, though she doubts that will come easily.

The lot is still empty, the windows shuttered, but the sheriff has a key to the front door. Soft lights burn on the desk, the space lined with cedar paneling and well-worn brown leather sofas and chairs set on a plush red-and-brown kilim batik rug, a huge stone fireplace with a reclaimed wood mantel topped by a massive stag's head with more antler points than she's ever seen, its eyes black and knowing, and blackout curtains drawn. That's why it looks dark and closed from the outside. The room is permeated by a scent she recognizes from her time in the dorms at school, a heady incense the kids used to burn in order to cover up when they smoked weed. Nag Champa, it was called. Stylish and strange, this is unlike any hotel she's ever been in before.

A woman comes bustling out from the back. She is dressed in pleated tan slacks and an ivory cable-knit sweater, wearing thick-rimmed glasses. Her graying blond hair is in a bun on the top of her head, and she seems alert and awake considering the hour. "Hello there? Oh, Cameron. Nice to see you. Do we have a visitor?"

"Hi, Emma. Yes, we do. Could you put Miss James up for the night? Didn't want her trying the roads at this late hour."

"Of course. Of course. It's not safe out there at night. We have plenty of rooms."

Except the kids at the General Store said there weren't any available. Were they trying to make her leave town? Showing her how unwelcome she was? Or did the sheriff's command merit a room? And why was it so unsafe?

With a tip of his ridiculous performative hat, the sheriff leaves her to it. "Out of here first thing in the morning, Miss James. Your keys will be waiting for you when you get up."

"Can't I have them now?"

He ignores her, and she realizes that she's in jail regardless of where she stays. Why would he do this? What is the endgame for the sheriff? Her mind is spinning with questions, but she bites her tongue. He's not going to answer her, so why bother?

"I have a meeting in the morning. With Tammy Boone."

"Consider it canceled," he says.

"You can't do that. I have the right to talk to whomever I want."

He smiles, a quirking of the lips. "Of course you do. You can phone her any time you want once you are out of Brockville."

The woman called Emma locks up after the sheriff, then goes behind the desk to a set of cubbyholes. She pauses, looking back over her shoulder at Halley, considering, then pulls down an old-fashioned key attached to a thick crimson tassel. Closer inspection shows each tasseled key to each room is a different color, and the woman confirms Halley's suspicions moments later.

"Let's get you settled in the Red Room. You should feel right at home there."

"Why red?" Halley asks. "If you don't mind my asking. Why not green, or blue, or gold?"

The woman smiles warmly. "Your aura, dear. Red as blood."

CHAPTER TWENTY-NINE

The room is comfortable, albeit painted a vivid vermilion that Halley doesn't think is going to be conducive to sleep. There is a lovely spa bathroom with a claw-foot tub, marble countertops, a toilet room, and towels so fluffy she is tempted to shove one in her bag. She takes a shower, luxuriating despite herself. Her misgivings washed away by homemade lavender soap.

The whole evening parades past in Technicolor—the humiliations, the revelations, the sorrow. Chowdhury seemed like a very nice woman. Halley doesn't want to admit how terrified she is right now, not even to herself.

The sheriff's crack about her not having a job is unnerving. The words stung, yes, but he seems to know a lot more about her than she does of him. Chief Early must really have been running his mouth.

And the spacey woman who runs the Inn. What in the world was that? Saying Halley's aura is red? What the hell does that even mean?

She looks it up online, out of curiosity. Strength, passion, resilience, power. A tendency to live in the moment.

Well, she's sure as hell living in the moment right now.

It's nearly midnight, but she needs to check in before anyone else starts sending messages and gets her arrested again, or worse. She texts her dad, taking comfort in the tiny chirps of connection as each letter appears on the screen. She uses the safe word they'd agreed on: *ailurophile.*

Cat lover.

She calls Alison Everlane's phone, gets voicemail. "Alison, it's Halley James. Just wanted you to be on alert. Someone's hurt the people I've talked with about Cat's disappearance. Please watch your back."

Hurt. As if they can recover.

There is a three-word email from Theo.

> Please check in.

He just will not let her go.

Do you want him to, Halley? Do you want him to just walk away? Or do you want him to keep fighting for you?

It. Doesn't. Matter. We want different things.

In the end, after debating with herself and her powerful, resilient, impetuous aura for five minutes, she calls, reminding herself to keep it light.

Theo answers on the first ring, voice frantic. "Tell me you're okay."

"I'm okay."

He sighs in relief. "It's been hours. I thought something might have happened."

"I ran afoul of the local sheriff. This place is a little odd."

"Do they know anything about your sister?"

"More than they're saying, for sure. I can't seem to get a straight answer out of anyone. I lucked into a conversation with a woman who teaches at the writers' retreat and filed the missing persons report on Cat. She was a little drunk and said a lot of things. I get the sense Cat's disappearance was brushed under the rug."

"Never good."

"No."

"So what's your plan? You said you're heading home tomorrow?"

"I think so. I'm being encouraged to do just that. I'm all tucked up at the Inn, in a bright-red room because that's what my aura dictated, and will be given my Jeep keys in the morning. The sheriff actually put me in cuffs earlier and dragged me to the station. Which is incredibly nice and totally modern. The architecture is beautiful. There's a lot of money here."

"Wait. Back up to the handcuffs."

In another world, another life, she would make a silly comment about the handcuffs, and Theo would respond with something seductive, and they'd have a fun few hours. Now, it just feels wrong. Everything feels wrong and she just wants to collapse.

"He was just trying to scare me, I think."

"Unlawful arrest is a serious issue. And he's holding your keys?"

"Long story. So Baird Early, the chief of police in Marchburg, remember? He called down here and warned them I was coming. Brockton, that's the sheriff here, he's one of the sons of the founder, claims he knows nothing about my sister, and treated me like a suspect for a while. I think it was more a scare tactic, to be honest. I lawyered up, then he backed off and told me what was going on."

"Suspect for what? What's going on?"

She explains about Dr. Chowdhury, dead on the heels of Kater. The stranger in the bar, and the female stranger who followed on the video.

"Halley," he says with dread. "You're in danger."

"I mean, obviously I'm rattling cages. The more I do, the more information I get."

"And people are dying. You could, too."

"Fair point. That was never my intention. But there's something going on here. Why would all of this suddenly happen? I make a few phone calls and people start getting killed? It makes no sense."

"It makes perfect sense. Whoever killed your sister fifteen years ago is hunting *you* now."

"Assuming she was killed . . . I suppose that's possible. What a cheery thought."

"I really want you to get out of there. I want to come get you."

She thinks about that for a minute. To be rescued. To need rescuing. There is some comfort in the idea, and of course, allowing Theo to come might save their marriage. But the cold, hard reality is, things are not good between them, and though he might be trying now, it's awfully late. She's still furious at him, and scared, and this is not a good place to be making decisions. There will be no knight in shining armor to come save her at the end of the day, when things get hard, when she becomes a target. She has to save herself first.

"That's very romantic, Theo. I appreciate it."

His tone shifts, cooling. "I'm serious."

"I know you are. Seriously. I think the sheriff just wants to make sure I'm not going to be making waves. Bad press for their idyllic little town, that sort of thing. I think I have what I need from here anyway. The minute he gives me my keys, I'm gone."

"And why did he take your keys, might I ask?"

"For my safety, he says."

"No. Stop right there. I am on my way."

"May I remind you that you're in Texas? You have responsibilities, and so do I. I'm fine. No one's getting in this room. I took precautions."

"I assume he took your gun, too?"

"Yes."

"So you're under house arrest unarmed, in a strange town that your sister disappeared from. Halley. You're being incredibly reckless. You aren't showing the appropriate amount of concern here. None of this is kosher."

Her confidence begins to lag, and her anger rises. "What would you have me do, Theo? The man has my keys and my weapon, and I'm stashed away in this weird inn for the night. In a few hours, he'll escort me out of town, with admonishments not to come back. Watch."

"I do not like this. Not at all."

She doesn't tell him about the younger brother's concern that she needs an escort, or any of the other strange things. He's tuned up enough already.

"Listen. If you're that worried, get someone from a local agency to come. You absolutely can't leave your post. But I am fine. I swear. I'll be out of here in the morning, and when you get home . . . we can talk. Now is not the time. Okay?"

She can hear him breathing. Weighing the options. He knows she's right, he knows he can't just run off. That he's offered—twice—is something they're going to have to talk about. She knows he means well, but it's stifling. She doesn't need saving.

Finally, he sighs. "You will call if you need help?"

"You know I will. And I'll call the local cops, too. I'm not an idiot, Theo. Now I have to get some sleep. It's been a really, really long day. Talk soon. I promise."

She hangs up before he can protest anymore. She already feels dumb enough for getting in over her head. Having him point it out to her again and again isn't helping. The push-pull of loving him and hating him is wearing on her, too.

She tries to watch TV to distract herself, but every squeak and clank makes her tense. She finally puts on the Golf Channel and is having the nightmare about Elvis, the blood pouring from his fuzzy neck, but she's not totally asleep and knows she's dreaming when she hears a rhythmic knocking. It's coming from outside.

Ping.

Ping.

Ping.

She is fully awake now. Something is hitting her window.

She moves to the frame carefully, lifts the edge of the curtain.

A man is standing below. Noah Brockton. Throwing rocks at the glass.

He sees her looking and waves, miming for her to open the window.

She tries a few times before she can get the old crank to turn. The air meanders in, cool, soft, with a hint of pine and rain. She is surprised to realize it smells like home.

"Can I come up?" he stage-whispers, moving toward the huge oak tree that she's just now noticing has a thick branch that would make climbing to her window a piece of cake.

Halley may be curious and impetuous and looking to rattle cages, but she is not stupid.

"Absolutely not."

For a second, he looks amused. "Then the lobby. It's important."

He jingles something—are those her keys?

He's breaking her out. Now, this is a whole different story.

She holds up a finger and closes the window. Grabs all her things, shoving them into her overnight bag. She pulls on her Vans and is out the door, leaving the TV on for a bit of subterfuge in case the innkeeper is spying for the sheriff. She makes her way quietly down the hallway, down the stairs, into the incense-perfumed lobby. Noah is already inside and waiting, and she stifles a little yelp of surprise. She'd seen the innkeeper lock the door after the sheriff left.

"I have keys," he says quietly, noticing her alarm. "We all do."

"Why?"

He gives her a bemused look. "Because it's our town."

"Oh. Okay. Is this a jailbreak?"

He nods, reaching out a hand for her bag. "I don't like how heavy handed my brother is being. You've done nothing wrong, and no one can blame you for wanting to learn more about your sister's disappearance."

"May I have them?"

Noah frowns. "Yes. If you'll agree to let me make you an omelet and tell you my version of things."

She ignores her stomach's gleeful anticipation of proper food. "I gotta admit, I'd like to book it out of here. Your brother isn't a big fan of mine. I don't know that I want to chance it."

"I don't blame you for feeling that way. And yes, of course, here." He hands her the keys, and her blood pressure drops a notch. "But the offer still stands. I'd really like to talk."

He seems so sincere. *So did Ted Bundy,* she reminds herself.

She flips the keys through her fingers, mentally reminding herself to make sure she has the locks changed in both Marchburg and DC. It would take no effort at all to copy the house keys to all her places. She shudders inwardly. That seems so incredibly devious, but so does killing two women. She does not trust the Brockton brothers. Even though Noah is helping her.

"No chance he gave you my gun?"

"Why are you carrying a gun?"

"I'll take that as a no. Listen, fine, we can talk, but can we get out of here? This place is lovely, but it gives me the creeps."

He looks around as if seeing it for the first time, nodding. He's taller than her, and he looks over her head as if there's something visible only to him. Or through her, maybe.

She glances over her shoulder, but no one's there.

"I get it. It always gave me the creeps, too. There are tunnels out of the basement to other parts of town. Used to freak me out when I was a kid. My brothers would take my things and leave them in the tunnels so I'd have to go down there in the dark to retrieve them, then they'd jump out and scare me."

"Your family ran the Inn?"

"No." He smiles absently, then shakes his head. "Of course, you wouldn't know. This was our house. This was the first building my dad completed. The red room you were in? It was my room growing up."

Halley doesn't want to use the phrase "against my better judgment," but aware and wary, she agrees to move their conversation to the restaurant. A neutral third-party location, as Noah calls it. Plus, he promises they won't be alone; the morning staff are already there prepping for breakfast. They technically aren't alone here, she thinks, until Noah says, "Leave the key for Emma. She'll see it when she comes in the morning."

Deep breaths, Halley.

He notices her discomfort. "I know you want to leave as soon as possible. Follow me? I'll make sure we don't cross paths with Cameron."

"Don't make me regret this, Noah."

He gives her a smile that's so devilishly charming she can't help but smile back. "Anything to piss off my brother."

She gets behind the wheel of the Jeep, blocking out Theo's voice, which is shouting *"Leave, leave now,"* and follows Noah to the restaurant. She's already decided if it's dark she's just going to floor it. But he's true to his word; she sees people moving about inside. It's 4:00 a.m. The first light of dawn is a whisper away. With a sigh, she puts the Jeep in park, palms her pepper spray, and goes inside.

CHAPTER THIRTY

Noah is greeted warmly by the staff and gets her seated in the dining room, away from the window but within easy view of the kitchen. He delivers an espresso, freshly pulled and aromatic enough to make her mouth water, holds up a finger and disappears again, then brings back two plates with an omelet on each. "Lobster and gruyère, with chives and spring onion. If you've ever had one better . . . don't tell me, or it will not be on the house."

He sets the plates on the table with a flourish. They are bone white, and the omelet steams in the center, fragrant and perfect. The freshly chopped chives smell as luscious as a summer day.

"Let me get some salt and pepper. And cream? Or half-and-half?"

"Cream."

"You got it. Be right back."

The second his back is turned, she swaps the plates. Just in case.

"So I—" He looks at the plates, fighting back a grin. "I gave you more lobster. My gain." He sets the salt and pepper in front of her, the cream between them, then takes his seat and digs in, looking up at her between bites. "Eat it while it's hot. It's a waste otherwise."

Halley takes a careful bite and tries not to moan aloud. It is delicious. Buttery and divine.

"Where'd you learn to cook like this?"

"France. They made us chop onions until our hands bled, get up before dawn to bake bread for days on end, and finally allowed us to try our hands at actually cooking something other people might enjoy, starting with the humble omelet. It was a wonderful experience. Do you want some toast? I have a multigrain black bread that would go perfectly, and freshly churned butter." He's off before she can say yes, and back minutes later with a dark loaf of bread and a crock of sun-yellow butter. He rips off a piece and slathers it, hands it to her. It's warm, as if it just came out of the oven, and she can taste the caraway seeds and hearty grains.

"My God," she groans. "You are a magician."

"The basics are the best, in my mind. Take something simple—like an omelet—and perfect it. Only then can you experiment."

"You cook for all the restaurants here in Brockville?"

"Yes. I love it. Kitchens make me happy. I skipped out of high school the day after I turned eighteen and went to the Le Cordon Bleu in Paris to get my formal culinary arts training. I got my Grand Diplôme, which covers both pastry and cuisine, and now I'm a couple months away from sitting my Master Sommelier exam."

"A triple threat."

"It helps. We have five different kitchens, one for each style of restaurant, from the bakery to the pizza place, and each with a different goal in mind. I design the menus and oversee them all, and train their chefs, too, though the majority of my time is spent at Pesche. I want a Michelin star before I'm forty and it's too late."

"That's . . . aggressive. Granted, the restaurant I worked in wasn't going to get a star, but it catered to a decent enough clientele, so I got a chance to see how a good kitchen runs. Yours is in tip-top shape, by all accounts."

"You're in the industry?" The way he lights up, she recognizes a man with a passion that overrides everything—common sense, love, life. She notices he does not wear a wedding ring. Not that it means he's not married; she doesn't have hers on, either, and her marriage is . . . complicated. With the kitchen work, she doubts a ring fits his lifestyle anyway.

"I was a server. That's all. Nothing like what you're doing, and it's not my lifelong love. Just a temporary gig during school. It helped pay the bills. Maybe I'll do it again. I'm suddenly between jobs."

"Between jobs?"

Why did she say that? Now what is she supposed to do? Share her situation with this complete stranger? *I fucked up my life so now I have to start over?* "It's a long story."

He waves it off. "Well, I hope you love it as much as I love my work. Suffice it to say I've put some pressure on myself, but it's worth it, I think. In the long run."

"Why food? I mean, Paris, obviously, but why not architecture or forestry or . . . law enforcement?"

"Good question. With a super-simple answer. My mom used to let me help her make dinner. She was self-taught, and no one made better food, in my opinion."

"And now?" Halley asks, though by the look on his face and the wistful tone in his voice, she can already tell his answer will be a sad one.

"She died a few years ago. Breast cancer. Refused any treatment outside of the holistic. She said if this was what she was meant to die from, then so be it. Better than being eaten by a bear on a three-day camping trip. She got to say goodbye to us all. I wish . . . Well."

His voice breaks and he looks down, and she realizes he's truly marked by this. Though his accomplishments and confidence and extroversion and air of expertise make him seem larger than life, sharing the sorrow of loss makes him more vulnerable. She understands his loss all too well. The past few days have been like losing her mother all over again. She's been trying not to think about Susannah, trying to stay focused on finding Cat, but it's not working. Her mother is everywhere.

"It must have been upsetting to have her refuse treatment like that," she says gently.

He forks in a pile of lobster dripping with cheese. "Yes and no. She wasn't very happy here, in the end. I like to think she's in a better place."

He chews, noticing Halley has stopped eating. "I'm sorry. You lost yours, too."

"Yes. But mine didn't have a chance to say goodbye. The last word I heard from her was *'Run.'*"

His brows draw together.

"You're serious."

"As a heart attack. Cat took her away from me. She went to jail—well, she was housed in a juvenile psychiatric facility. Got out when she was eighteen, went to Harvard, of all places, and studied psychology, got married, divorced, and came here. This is where the trail ends. Apparently, with you. You, who claim you're the last one to talk to her. Fifteen years ago."

She eats the rest of her omelet calmly, allowing him a moment to adjust his memories. He didn't know the truth, and it's the only reason she isn't leaping from the table and getting in the Jeep.

"Still want to tell me what you know?"

He nods. "Think I better. Do you know anything about my dad?"

"Just what I've read online and what Tammy told me. Modern-day Thoreau, started this place to be a kind of new urban utopia, had a bunch of boys who all work here in Brockville to help him. He is world famous."

"All of that is true. He's also a very . . . strange man. Anyone who is perfectly at ease alone in the wilderness for years at a time isn't completely right in the head, you know? By the time I came along—I'm the youngest—he and my mother weren't super close anymore, and I was closest to her. She and Dad had their final falling-out when I was eight, and she moved out of the house and took me with her. We lived in a place of our own, here in Brockville but away from the rest of the family. She took me to Paris when I was twelve and got me hooked on food. She never spoke badly about him, till the day she died, but the strain on their relationship was so clear. She wouldn't tell me what broke them up, either, and trust me, I asked. So I've had the benefit of seeing

Dad from a slightly different perspective than my brothers, all of whom worship him and will do anything he asks."

Halley says nothing, because there's nothing to say. She doesn't want to interrupt him, and he continues.

"Brockville is built around his image, his ethos, his genius. The money was invested in *him*. Not the town, not the people who live here, not the amenities. They came because of him. He is their messiah. You know what I mean?"

"You make it sound like he's a cult leader."

He snickers, sips his coffee, makes a face. "It's cold." He looks over her shoulder, a move she's starting to realize is a way for him to gather his thoughts. "I suppose I do make him out to be someone . . . above others. He's not, of course. He's no different from anyone else who's knocked down walls and stayed at the top of a major operation for years—people revere and respect him. But the way people look up to him and take his word as law does make me uncomfortable. There wasn't a lot of room in his life for a son who didn't want to obey his every command."

"So why are you still here?"

He nods as if he knew that's what she was going to ask. "Because I can't leave. I'm tied here. Every time I try, something draws me back. I've moved away four times, and the moment I start somewhere else, I get pulled back in. Now I think it's just easier to do what I do—innovate the culinary scene in town, draw in people for *my* creations, and stay out of his way."

"That's . . . interesting."

His face sharpens. "Your sister . . . I felt a connection with her. A spark of something."

"Attraction, maybe?"

"Not that. You're much more my type." He says this freely, with a frank smile that belies any underlying agenda, but she blushes, nonetheless. "You're very French. You have that fine-boned Angevin thing going on that all the women in Paris have. Très charmante."

"Thank you, I think."

But he's already moved on. "Cat . . . I felt . . . immediately protective toward her. Like you would a sister, and I never had one of those. It was weird. I sensed she needed . . . something. I wanted to be her friend. I was excited to realize she was going to be in town for a couple of months, that we'd have a chance to get to know one another. I was in a rush, though, to get dinner service started, and offered to make her some food, and then I left her. Alone. You can understand how I feel this horrible responsibility. If I'd talked longer or walked her back to her cabin . . . maybe she'd still be with us."

"It's not your fault."

"You don't know that," he retorts.

"I can tell. I'm a pretty decent judge of character. Or else I wouldn't be sitting here right now."

That's not entirely true. She doesn't trust him, not a bit, but she's intrigued. Maybe a little too intrigued. She's always been a sucker for an interesting life story. Maybe because hers was so sheltered, so different from anyone else she knew. She's wrestled every detail out of her friends. She probably knows more about their upbringings than their siblings.

Noah dips his head closer and speaks quietly. "So here's what I wanted to tell you. Right before Cat and I met on the path, she was talking to someone. Harshly. Told them to fuck off. I don't know who it was, but I can't imagine they took the words lightly, considering her tone. She was royally pissed. And she disappeared right after that."

"So she was walking with someone? Or talking on the phone?"

"I didn't see. Not a person, at least, and she didn't have a phone with her. It was fifteen years ago. Not everyone had one."

"True."

"So I told Cameron all of this. And when Tammy filed the missing persons report, I mentioned it again. He did look for her, Halley. I swear he did. Cat just . . . disappeared into thin air. We don't have cameras or anything around here like you do in the city. It's a very safe place. No crime at all. The people who live here wouldn't stand for it."

"The police station has its own crime lab. Yet you have no crime?"

"Part of the town's charter is to have every possible amenity so our people don't have to leave if they don't want to. We're sometimes socked in by bad weather, too, so we have to be able to provide services. Self-sufficiency is part of this kind of living."

"You grow your own lobsters and make the gruyère here, too?"

He narrows his eyes, then bursts out laughing. "Touché. Obviously not. These babies are deepwater, specially flown in from Maine. And the cheese, too, is imported. But were we not able to get these little luxuries, we would be completely fine. Cut us off from the world and we've got everything we need right here. The land provides. The expertise lives on site. And if there *were* any crimes, Cameron would be able to solve them with the most modern equipment available."

"Seems like a bit of a juxtaposition in your ethos, Noah. You say you're completely self-contained and self-sufficient, yet everything you do revolves around bringing in little delights. And as interesting as I find the fact that you're able to go off grid, none of this is germane to our discussion. Cat."

He leans forward, all amusement gone. "It is germane. And I'll tell you why. We're such a small, close-knit world that if she *were* still here, everyone would know. If she was hurt here, we would know it. There's no privacy in a world like this. Brockville is its own microcosm. Yes, there are doors closed at night, maybe even some get locked. But everyone here has bought into the community with the knowledge that they are going to have a hard time with secret lives. We live in utter isolation. Gossip is the bread and butter of Brockville." He breaks off a piece of the bread and butters it, just to drive the point home. "How do you get an entire town to keep a secret like that?" He pops the bread in his mouth and chews.

"You live in Stepford?"

"Ha ha."

"All right. So you're saying there was no foul play. That she had to have left on her own after having a heated fight with an invisible person. You can understand how I might have a hard time buying into the mythology here, Noah."

"Which is another reason why I wanted to talk to you. I want to invite you to stay."

"Stay here? In Brockville? With your brother just itching to throw his cuffs on me again?"

"I know you want to leave. I don't blame you. But I think you're possibly safer here than you are anywhere else."

"Cat wasn't safe here."

"Cat left here. There is no other logical answer."

A flash of light blinds her, and Halley realizes the sun has risen. The restaurant glows: the silver shining, the tables with their crisp linens and fresh flowers in vases as pristine and charming as one could hope.

"Stay, Halley. This is bigger than an hour's conversation."

She's an idiot for even considering his offer. Staying here would be a disaster. There's something off about Brockville. Part of her wants to stay and keep trying to unravel this mystery, but the rest of her has ten years of being fine-tuned to Theo's station, and she can almost hear him broadcasting *"You got what you came for, time to go."* But why listen to him? It's not as if he has her best interest at heart anymore.

That inner stubbornness is trying to rear its head, the person who wants to do the opposite of what's expected. Who wants to tell her phantom husband *"We're separated for a reason, because you're bossy and demanding and dismissive, and now that I'm gone you want me back and I don't like it."*

No, she can't listen to Theo. But she also doesn't need to get herself in deeper than she already is.

She wipes her mouth with a napkin, and Noah sits back in his chair, arms crossed, openly disappointed. He already knows what she's going to say.

"I appreciate the offer, really, I do. But if there's nothing more to be gained in the search for my sister, if she truly left here and then disappeared, then I need to move along, too. My goal is to find her or find out what happened to her. Full stop."

He nods, clearly crestfallen. She doesn't understand why it means so much to him, other than what he said earlier about her being his type. To be honest, he is hers, too, but she's not here for a hookup. Things are complicated enough without adding another man, another relationship, another need, into the mix. So it's time to quit this place and figure out her next steps. Go back to DC, through Marchburg. Check on her dad. Talk to Chief Early and see if he has any ideas of where she can look next. See if he's discovered a trail to the killer.

Noah stands. "I'll walk you to your car. I have something you'll probably want."

He calls out in French to one of the kitchen staff, who laughs good-naturedly, and gestures toward the door. She precedes him, stopping at the door of the Jeep. He passes her, going to his car, a sleek black BMW convertible, and returns with a shopping bag.

"I abhor guns. We had to hunt growing up, especially before the foothold was fully established here, and I developed an aversion." He hands her the shopping bag and she spies her Smith & Wesson inside. She looks up to see his deep-blue eyes staring at her intently.

"You said—"

"I wanted to talk to you first. I'm sorry. Drive safely, Halley James."

CHAPTER THIRTY-ONE

Touching, isn't it? She cares so much about the person she should despise the most. She has no idea the impact that little investigation will have.

What people don't like to think about is what happens when someone goes missing and no one takes it seriously. Perhaps the person was lost to their family already. Perhaps they never had anyone to start with. Perhaps they were poisoned inside and people were happy to have them gone.

People disappear every day. Hundreds of them every year. And you don't hear about 99 percent of them. Only when it's an adorable young child or a plucky college student are you made aware. And if they are not from a suburban, white world? Good luck ever learning about it. Unless you seek it out, of course. There's usually a family in tears, or a boyfriend praying no one runs luminol over his back seat.

Catriona Handon was able to disappear off the face of the earth from a swank spot in the middle of nowhere. And what, two people give a shit? Three? Of the how many people she came across in her life? How come no one came here looking before now? It's been fifteen years—fifteen years, one month, and eighteen days, to be exact. Why does it take a feisty little sister who—let's not delude ourselves for a moment here—is out for revenge upon the person she now believes ruined her life to start asking all the right questions?

Granted, Cat was a very bad girl, and naughty girls don't engender loyalty. Girls who kill their mommies aren't lauded by society. Did you know that when Harvard found out about her past, they rescinded their invitation to join the class of 1996? She flew up to Boston and insisted on making her case in person, making them look her in the eyes and deny her the privilege they'd extended when they didn't know of the mistakes she'd made, refuting the claims that they weren't aware of the rehabilitation she'd gone through. Turns out they were just covering their asses. She had disclosed her circumstances in her essay, and they'd been happy to invite her to matriculate because recidivism is so much lower among the educated and they thought it was fiction and other nonsense they spewed to justify letting her in. Turns out, the parents of someone else in the entering class did some background checking on their sweet daughter's suitemate-to-be and forced the school to back out of their offer. When faced with a discrimination lawsuit by a legal eagle tied to the juvenile psychiatric facility in Nashville, though, the school happily backed away. The problem student's parents sent her to Yale instead, and Catriona Handon got her second chance at the ivy-and-brick paragon of elite intellectualism, where she excelled.

There's an article about it. You should read it. Quite the little social experiment.

Cat was a smart girl. Always had been. Sometimes too smart for her own good, and certainly leaps and bounds above her parents and her teachers. She was gifted, gifted with intelligence, yes, but also with a preternatural self-awareness that every little thing she did caused trouble somewhere along the line. Maybe it was the voices; maybe it wasn't organic at all, and simply her personality. She was mercurial. Unpredictable.

How could a man not fall in love with that kind of chaos?

But for a woman like that to go missing, for fifteen years, and no one came looking? No one came to Brockville until now? Until sweet, delectable little sister, whom I just want to touch, to skim my hands along her strong shoulders, to count those freckles I bet she hates? Smell her breath and the nape of her neck, discover that silent place every woman has and is different on them all. Little sister is young enough to be impetuous and think she's impervious to harm, but old enough to understand the ways of the world. My heart cannot take much more.

She is perfection.

She must not go.

She must stay.

SATURDAY

CHAPTER THIRTY-TWO

HALLEY

Halley checks the Jeep as if she's about to pilot a Cessna, paranoid but knowing she can't chance it. She walks around the entirety of the car, examining the bumpers and the wheel wells, looking in the back for anything amiss—anyone lurking—then gets in and reloads the pistol. Noah might not like guns, but he was savvy enough about them to have unloaded it before handing her the bag. She checks her purse for the letter from her sister, which is nestled in its spot, and plugs her phone into the car charger. It beeps with a new voicemail.

She can leave now. Go . . . elsewhere and try to figure all of this out. She needs to puzzle out the letter. She should have done that first. Though it seems straightforward, she's convinced whatever message lies inside might hold all the answers.

She puts the Jeep into gear and gives Noah a little wave. He watches her pull out of the parking space, shrugs and shakes his head as if acknowledging that he tried, then returns to the restaurant.

She hits the speaker on her phone to play the message.

"Halley, it's Baird. We got a line on the woman from the feedstore video. She's FBI. Or was, she resigned two years ago. Name is Kade. Donnata Kade. Has a former address near where you are. What the hell she was doing in Marchburg messing with your Jeep is beyond me. Get in touch when you can. I let the sheriff down there know about your visit, and I'll also let him know about Kade."

So a retired FBI agent is poking around all this, now, too? One that lives here in Brockville? Boy, would Halley like to talk to her. She has to admit she is lost. Her sister's disappearance seems more menacing by the hour, and now she doesn't know what to do.

Should she go home to Marchburg? Death and destruction await her there, but she has Early, and Meredith for backup. DC? Patch things up with Theo, or end them for good? Stay here? Brockville in the daylight isn't nearly as forbidding as nighttime. And Noah really did seem like he wanted to help. A second set of eyes on all this wouldn't be a bad thing. Nashville? See if being in the setting would help her remember exactly what happened that fateful day?

Damn it. Nothing feels right, so she turns to the infallible. Her brain says there are answers here. But her gut says to leave Brockville.

So that is what she'll do. She'll figure out whether to turn east or west once she gets to the highway. She can always come back. Maybe she'll have more answers next time. Maybe whoever is playing games with her will be gone.

The sun peeks over her shoulder as she wends her way out of town, shining on her dash, showing all the dust and grime that's built up since she last detailed her car. The trees are vibrant under the morning dew, and this time, as she gets to the big sign on the edge of town, there is no police car waiting for her. By now, there's no way Cameron doesn't know she's pulling a runner. They really are letting her go.

With a huge sigh of relief, she follows the well-maintained road out of the valley, up, up, up the mountain, and five minutes later clears the last switchback. Her ears pop. The sky is close. From this vantage point, she can see the misty blue ridges that make up the titular range spreading into the distance and looks down the valley at the town of Brockville below. It seems so quaint. So unthreatening. She is tempted to stop and admire the scenery, but her desire to leave prevents her.

She has escaped, and she isn't going to stop now.

She keeps the Jeep rolling, is five hundred feet down the back side of the crest of the hill when something catches her eye. It's there, then gone, and she slams on the brakes when her brain processes what it was.

A boy. A young boy, maybe five, six years old. Wrapped in a blanket. On the side of the road.

She skids to a stop, looking over her shoulder, in the rearview. Nothing there.

She puts it in reverse and slowly, slowly, eases backward until she is at the spot where she saw . . . something.

There is a flash of white retreating into the woods. It is low to the ground, and then it is gone, swallowed by the green trees that line the road.

Was it a deer? Did she have Noah's story of his childhood in her head and her mind turned a young fawn into a young boy?

She puts down the passenger-side window and listens. Can't hear anything over the engine. Turns it off.

Her heart, thundering in her chest. The shriek of a hawk. The wind whispering through the branches. A thin cry. A human cry.

"Damn." She gets out of the car. Puts the gun in her waistband. Marches into the tall grass on the side of the road, listening carefully. The sobs are real and coming from the screen of trees fifty feet ahead.

"Little boy? Sweetie, you can come out. I won't hurt you."

The crying stops. She edges closer to the tree line. She can see the corner of the white blanket now. Do people camp around here? Is he homeless? Has he managed to get himself here from Brockville? It would be quite a hike, but if he was scared and desperate, she supposes that it's not out of the question.

A twig snaps, and she halts. There he is. He's even younger than she thought.

"Hi," she says. "Are you lost?"

He shakes his head. He is dirty, as if he's been out in the wilderness for weeks. His cobalt eyes are wide and frightened, the blanket around his thin shoulders grubby and worn. He looks at her briefly, then bursts away, bounding into the forest, and without thinking, she goes after him.

The trees grow closer together; the path is soon obscured. She has to stop after only a few minutes. What works for a small child is not going to work for her. "Stay here. I'll get help," she calls, then hurries back toward the Jeep. Just before she breaks from the trees, she hears a car's engine, there and gone again. Darn it, just missed them.

She has to tell the sheriff about this child.

Halley makes her way to the road carefully but quickly. She will drive back to the town. Tell the sheriff about the kid, then be on her way again.

But as she approaches the Jeep, she sees that her right rear tire is flat.

She says several very bad words and examines the tire. There's a cut in the wall. This is not a nail in the tread; it's a three-inch slice. And worse, her spare is desecrated, too.

This is purposeful. This is sabotage.

Someone doesn't want her leaving Brockville.

She looks around, but no one is visible. A chill hammers through her, and she reaches for the door handle and leaps inside, locking the doors. She will be damned if she's going to stay here and wait for some crazed serial killer to snatch her. She will limp the Jeep back to the interstate even if it means she'll have to buy a new wheel instead of just replacing the tire.

But the Jeep won't turn over. She tries again and again, frantic now, but it just clicks and glugs and revs. It won't roar to life and get her the hell out of here.

Shit. Shit shit shit.

There is no one around. She scans the road, the trees. Puts the pistol in her lap, soothed by the fact that if someone comes at her, she will be able to stop them. Then she grabs her phone and dials 9-1-1.

A familiar greeting, one she seems to be hearing too much lately.

"Nine-one-one, what's your emergency?"

The words come out in a panicked rush. "My name is Halley James and my car has been disabled, and there was a little boy on the side of the road and he's disappeared into the woods. I'm about two miles out of Brockville, Tennessee, heading west. I don't know the area so I can't tell you exactly where I am."

"Okay. Slow down. You're going to be fine. I'll send Sheriff Brockton your way right now. You're west, going toward the highway? Are you in a safe place?"

Sheriff Brockton. Brockville. Even the 9-1-1 dispatch is run out of the town. They really are self-sufficient.

She strokes the gun. "That's correct. I'm locked in the car. It's a Jeep Wrangler, white with black trim. Something's wrong with the engine, and someone slashed my tires." Damn it, there's a quake in her voice. Fear is a powerful thing, and she doesn't remember ever feeling quite so scared before.

Don't lie. You know this feeling. You know it so well.

Red. Everything is so red.

"Run, Halley Bear. Run."

Her mind flashes to the note stabbed to Kater's chest. *You're next.*

Am I next? Is it now? Am I about to die?

She's hyperventilating. The 9-1-1 operator is saying soothing words. The sun is beating down mercilessly. The lost little boy is crying, crying, crying.

Theo's words: *"You can't leave me. I won't let you."*

Noah's words: *"Stay. This is bigger than an hour's conversation."*

The stranger at home: *"You don't remember me, do you?"*

Early's confusion: *"I don't know why Kade was messing with your Jeep."*

Tammy Boone's revelation: *"The circumstances were similar . . ."*

Stop stop stop. "Stop!"

The squawk of the sheriff's siren pulls her from the abyss. She fumbles the gun into her bag, feels an unfamiliar piece of paper inside. She pulls it out and unfolds it. There is one word on it, written in shaky letters: *HELP*.

What the hell is this?

Brockton is almost to her door now. She shoves it back in the bag and puts her hand on the gun. Uses her left to wipe the tears away. She gets out of the Jeep.

Brockton's swagger is gone; the concern on his face is clear.

"Miss James? What's happening?"

She is unmoored and unloads everything. The kid, the Jeep, the tire, her sister, Theo's threat, the stranger, and before she realizes what's happening, he's holding her as she weeps. He's an awkward comforter, patting her shoulders and saying "Now, now. Now, now" over and over, but somehow, it works. She finds herself again; the fear, the pure dismay receding until she is finally able to take a full breath and a step backward. It's the first time a man has willingly touched her in months. She doesn't want to admit how normal it makes her feel.

"Sorry about that," she says, wiping her eyes. "I feel like an idiot." She hears a truck's engine roaring up the road, tenses, but it's a tow truck with *Eddie's Garage* stenciled on the side. She passed that garage last night.

Brockton pats her shoulder again. "For having emotions? Don't. You've had a few shocks this week. Eddie will take the Jeep back to his place and fix the tires for you."

"Something else is wrong, too. With the engine. Someone made sure I couldn't leave."

And left a note asking for help in my bag. For some reason, she holds this back. It feels too ominous to mention. She doesn't know who wrote it, or when it was put there. It could have been any moment from the second she left the jail until now.

The sheriff is speaking; she tunes back in. "We'll figure it out. Now, show me where this little boy was?"

They head back to the tree line. Halley explains seeing the child out of the corner of her eye, then stopping and following him into the woods. "He's so little. So dirty. I can't imagine he's okay out here. Are there people living in these woods? Or was he a lure to get me to leave the vehicle long enough for someone to sabotage it? I heard a car while I was looking for him. It has to have happened then."

Saying it aloud sends shivers down her spine. What if she hadn't been in the woods? What if she had still been in the Jeep? Would she have come face to face with Kater's killer?

Is it the stranger from the bar? Or is someone she knows all too well after her?

The sheriff tries to calm her. "Miss James, this is quite the story. Sure you're not writing mystery novels in your spare time?"

"This is not a joking matter. *You* were the one who wouldn't let me leave last night."

"About that," he starts, but freezes, holding up a finger. She hears the crashing seconds later, impressed that he was so attuned to the woods that he heard it first. He peers into the forest, hand on his weapon, then relaxes. "Deer."

"How do you know?"

"I have eyes," he says, pointing, and sure enough, she sees the soft tan flank of a doe twenty yards away. The doe stares at them for a moment, tail twitching, then puts her head down to the grass and starts cropping it.

"I wasn't holding you hostage, or in custody. I just didn't want you on the switchbacks late at night. In case something happened." He points at the Jeep. "Turns out that was a good thing. If there's a maintenance issue—"

"Oh, come on. I take perfect care of my vehicle. Someone slashed the tires, and I bet you ten bucks when Eddie the mechanic over there gets the hood open, there will be something else damaged, too."

He narrows his eyes. "I don't gamble."

"Is there a car rental in town? You do have all the amenities."

"No, there isn't. Closest one's in Bristol. Let's just see what's up with the Jeep first."

"I don't feel safe in Brockville," she says. "Obviously."

"You're safer in Brockville than out here alone in the woods, looking for phantom children."

"That boy was no phantom. He was as real as you or me."

He squints toward the woods. "Whatever you say. Like you said, having a youngster on their own in these woods is pretty unlikely. Now, let's go back to town. I'll buy you a cup of coffee. Since I know you already had breakfast."

"Oh, we're busted, huh?"

"Noah is . . . impetuous. And you're just as reckless as him, tearing out of here like this without letting me know. People are dying, Miss James. A killer is on the loose. I take that rather seriously."

They're back to the road now. Eddie is hooking the Jeep to his wrecker. He wears a classic mechanic's jumpsuit like he's in a 1950s movie, blue-and-white stripes, with a rag in his hand, grease stains along his thigh, and a white cap on his head. He is good looking in a devil-may-care way, lots of scruff and muscles. "Fan belt's worn straight through. You're lucky you weren't farther away, you'd be stuck with no reception waiting for a stranger to come by. I can fix it, but I'll have to order the part. Your tires, well, that is going to be a few days at least to get the replacements here."

"A few *days*?"

"Yep. You have these fancy Firestone all-terrain tires, and I don't have them in stock. Unless you want to change out the whole set, which will run you a couple thousand, and all I have is more of a performance truck tire rather than rugged off-roaders. Your gas mileage must suck."

She nods. It does. But the bigger tires are cool, so she splurges. Replacing the whole set, though . . . it's not like she has money to spare. She'll have to wait it out.

He continues scolding her. "If you'd broken down before the winter it would have been different, but it's spring now. Everyone's shifted out of the snow tires, so that's what I have ready. As for the belt, well, you'd be better off with the factory-made than a generic replacement on this particular vehicle. Your call, of course."

"Let me guess. A few days for it to come in?"

"Yep."

She's stuck, and they all know it. "Fine. Order the tire, and the belt. I'll figure something out."

He nods. "Yes, ma'am."

"And Eddie? Thank you," she adds, turning on the wattage, and he gives her a shy smile back. She needs to keep as many people on her side as possible.

"Sure thing. I'll be in touch when I have exact times, okay?"

"Thank you. My number—do you have something to write on?"

"Don't need it." He gives her a look, and inside, she squirms. "I'll be able to find you. Town's not that big."

CHAPTER THIRTY-THREE

Halley retrieves her overnight bag and backpack from the Jeep, calculating what she has and what she'll need to supplement for a few days. Surely they have a laundromat in their perfect little town. And as much as she wants to leave, maybe the universe—as Tammy Boone suggested—is giving her a chance to figure out who needs her help.

She joins the sheriff in his Escalade. He's talking to someone on the phone and furtively ends the call when she opens the door.

"I'm sorry. I didn't mean to interrupt."

"It's fine. The Inn will be booked up starting tonight. There's a wedding this weekend, and they're all arriving today, so I was arranging a place for you. It's a little more rustic, but I figured you wouldn't mind."

More rustic than the weird inn. Great.

He reads the question on her face. "We have short-term rentals for folks who come here for vacations and don't want the fancy spa treatment. It comes with a golf cart, so you don't have to be totally isolated if you'd like to get to know the town a bit better. Walking paths to the lake, too." He glances at her overnight bag. "If you need anything, the shops open at ten. They're all grouped on Main Street in Avalon. Near where you came in, the bookstore and the General Store, that area."

"What about the kid?"

He glances at her, then back at the road. "I'm gonna change into some better gear and come back out with a dog, see if I can get farther into the brush."

The relief she feels is immediate and surprising. "Thank you. He seemed . . . terrified."

"I checked with dispatch, but we don't have any reports of anyone missing, no kids missing, nothing. So it really could just be someone playing. That hill there leads right into the back of Somer."

"He didn't look like he was playing, Sheriff. And if he was, he's much too little to be playing alone."

The sheriff grunts in agreement, though she knows he thinks she's lost her mind. Maybe she has. Maybe she was seeing things.

The boy's cries ring in her ears again. His dark eyes, the panic in them. No. He was very, very real.

They are down the mountain now, and the sheriff swings the Escalade back toward Brockville.

"Do we need to talk about who might want you to stay here in Brockville? You mentioned you're having some issues with your husband?"

She taps a finger against her lips. That little outburst really has gotten her into a mess.

"You agree that my car was sabotaged?"

"The tires didn't slit themselves. Your husband pissed off enough to follow you here?"

"He's mad at me, not homicidal."

"You sure about that?"

She sits with this for a moment. Theo, lashing out. Theo, murdering Kater, Chowdhury. Theo, lying about being in Texas. So angry with her for leaving that he'd follow her, handicap her, and then . . . what?

Well, that's terrifying.

"No, I am not sure, but for God's sake, he's my husband. Our issues aren't the kind that are solved at the end of a knife. It's typical career and family stuff. He wouldn't hurt me." *I don't think.*

"He threatened you."

"He was mad. People separate and get divorced all the time without one of them ending up dead."

"He get mad like that a lot?"

"Oh my God, we really are having this conversation. Not really. Usually he's too busy working to care what I'm doing. And seriously, my marriage is off limits here."

"Halley, nothing is off limits in a murder investigation. You know that."

"This isn't murder."

"Yet."

He stops at an intersection, turns on his blinker. The sheriff is measured in all his actions. He pulls into a parking lot, and she realizes the Steep and Brew has a drive-through. He stops in front of the elaborate menu.

"What's your druthers?"

She scans the board. They have everything, not surprising, considering, but she's not feeling fancy. "Iced vanilla latte. Extra shot."

He places the order, gets himself a small coffee, black—shocking—and pulls to the window. He hands hers over, puts his in the cup holder, and they're off again. She notices that he does not pay, nor is he asked to. Perks of owning the town.

"Sorry about the line of questioning. Just making sure we don't have a problem brewing. If your husband knows you're here, he might be trying to send a message."

"He's not afraid to tell me exactly what he thinks. Can we talk about something else?"

"Yup."

"Do you know a woman who lives in Brockville named Donnata Kade?"

His hands tighten on the wheel.

"Yes."

"Where does she live? I'd like to talk to her."

"I don't know if that's such a great idea."

"Why?"

He shoots her a glance. "Kade is . . . Well, she moved here after an emotional breakdown following a pretty intense caseload, and she wasn't totally right in the head. I assume you saw the article on her?"

"No, I haven't. What is it about?"

"Then how do you know that name?" he asks sharply. Halley debates for a minute. Early will certainly tell Brockton what he's found out if they talk. She might as well share.

"I spoke with Chief Early as I was leaving this morning. He was able to identify her from a video feed in Marchburg the night my friend was killed."

"Kade was in Marchburg?"

"Yes. So that's why I'd like to talk to her. To find out why. What's the article about?"

He fights back a little groan. "She was dismissed from the FBI for falsifying information to get an arrest. Had a breakdown when she was let go. She moved here to get away from the fallout. Rented a place over in Avalon from the Esworthys. They own a few homes here, investment properties. Bruce and my dad go way back. They travel a lot, though. Brockville is a second home for them."

"The Esworthys? Why do I know that name?"

"Bruce owns a number of car dealerships around the South. Porsches. Why, are you in the market for something new?"

"My God, you do have a sense of humor. Noah said you did. I didn't believe him."

"Noah talks too much," he says gruffly.

"Noah doesn't talk nearly enough. No Porsches. I'd just like to speak with Donnata Kade."

"She's not around."

Of course she isn't. Because she's in Marchburg. Or other environs.

"She has a phone, I assume?"

"It's a waste of time, Halley. She . . . doesn't live here anymore."

"Would the Esworthys know where she's gone?"

"Doubt it, but their number will be in the book."

"All right. I will look them up in the book. I assume it will be with my golf cart?"

"Don't sass me, girl."

She fights back the retort—*"girl?"*—because he's right; now she's just needling him because she's still pissed off about the handcuffs. *Keep him on your side.* She sips the latte. It is divine. She's starting to wonder if everything Noah Brockton touches turns to gold.

Could Noah have slashed the tires? No. No way. He didn't have that kind of darkness in him.

You never know . . .

"Noah told me you did search for my sister. Thank you."

He is silent for a moment. "Your sister, what she did. Killing your mother, I mean. Why in the world would you *want* to find her? Wouldn't you rather she was out of your life forever?"

You better believe it. But I want answers first.

"I have to admit, that's a good question. I think not knowing is worse than knowing. I had no idea what happened. I still don't have the whole story. And I guess I want to hear from her directly how she could do such a thing. Why she would kill our mother for wanting to send her to a wilderness camp. And if I'm being honest, I want to find out how the people who knew her—loved her, even—didn't know that she was a monster."

The sheriff turns down a narrow lane, cobblestones making the big truck shudder. Halfway down, he stops in front of a charming cottage, like something you'd see in the Cotswolds or a movie set. He turns off the engine. "This is Brooke Cottage. I'll get you settled."

"I'm fine—"

"I'll get you settled."

The place is adorable—gray stone with a pitched roof, two perfectly symmetrical chimneys, a red door with a brass knocker. There is a small zen garden in the front with a cedar bench, evergreen boxwoods in a half-circle labyrinth, and the promised golf cart under its own replica roof attached to the side of the house. It's much too big for one person, but she's hardly going to complain. Privacy is exactly what she needs right now.

The sheriff takes her bag and leads her up the walkway. Inside is as nice as the outside. There is an open floor plan with a stone fireplace and modern kitchen. The floors are stained a deep walnut, there are thick rugs, and the sofa and chairs are lush and inviting. English-country-house decor, bookshelves, wildlife paintings.

"Very nice," she says.

"Bedrooms are through there. There's wood for the fireplaces on the back porch. I'll have some groceries delivered. Have any requests?"

"You don't need to do that. I won't be staying *that* long."

"Consider it my apology for the cuffs yesterday."

She writes up a quick list of basics—coffee, eggs, bread, OJ, apples, peanut butter. Her tastes are simple, especially since there are so many food options close by that she can try.

Admit it. You want to talk to Noah Brockton again. Maybe he'll be willing to talk about the other missing writer.

She wants to ask Brockton directly, but she's enjoying their tenuous détente. She doesn't need him shutting down on her now, especially since he seems to be on her side. She hands him the list. "The book? I'd like to look up the Esworthys' number."

"By the phone, of course." He narrows his eyes. "Listen, Donnata Kade is trouble."

"Then why do you let her live here?"

"'Let.' Like I said, it was temporary. And I don't have control of who people rent to. I don't know what she could possibly do to help you find your sister."

"She's FBI, right?"

"Was."

"Maybe she'll have an idea or two that you and I haven't thought of."

He starts to say something but bites it back. "I'll leave you to it. Call me if you feel uncomfortable about anything. But I promise, no one will bother you here."

Now that they've made sure I can't leave.

She shakes the ice in her latte. "Thanks for the coffee."

They stand in silence for a moment, then he nods once. "I'll leave you to it."

As he's shutting the front door, she calls out, "I do appreciate the assist, Sheriff."

"No worries," he says, and then she's alone.

She digs out her charger and plugs in her phone, then calls the hospital. They route her to her father's room, and he answers the phone, a little breathless.

"Hi. Everything okay?" she asks.

"Yeah. They had me working on the crutches again. Are you okay? Code word?"

"I'm fine."

"Halley . . ."

She laughs. "*Ailurophile.* See? I'm all good, but I'm stuck here in Brockville for a bit. Had some car trouble." She is not about to tell him the truth about the Jeep being disabled. He will lose his marbles. "They've put me up in a sweet little cottage, with its own golf cart so I can go buzzing around town. Should be a couple of days before the Jeep's fixed. The mechanic had to order parts."

"I could have Anne come get you. You said it's only four hours away."

"No, that's all right. It will give me a chance to learn more about Cat." *From the people who saw her last,* but she doesn't add it. "Anyway, I'm fine, and I will continue to check in. This town has a little bit of everything. I won't get bored. Okay?"

"Okay, jellybean." He's quiet for a moment. "Have you heard from Theo?"

"Yes. Why?"

"He might have called."

"Are you kidding me?"

"He's worried about you, honey."

"Little late for that," she fumes.

"He said you moved out. Why didn't you tell me?"

She sighs. "Because. Okay? I told you before, it's complicated. Did he tattle about work, too?"

"The lab? He may have mentioned something . . ."

Great. Thanks a hell of a lot, Theo.

"I don't know what he said, but what *I* told you is the truth. The board fired me in retribution for the sexual harassment complaint I filed. I will deal with it when I figure out what's happening here. I am not in any sort of mood for all the hovering you guys are doing."

"Halley, I am not hovering—"

"No, you just spent your whole life lying to me."

She realizes she is shouting. Damn it, she is done with all of this. She ratchets it back. "Listen. I need some time. I am furious with you, and I am furious with Theo, and I need some space. Please. No more check-ins and code words. I am not a child. I am exactly where I want to be right now."

"You know that's not true. And running away from your responsibilities won't help a thing. You need—"

She does something she has never done in her entire life. She hangs up on her father.

He calls back immediately, and she lets it go to voicemail.

She is tired of pretending she's okay. She is tired of being told what to do. She's gotten herself into this mess, and she will find her way out.

She searches Donnata Kade's name and is met with a long-form article from *East Fifth* magazine, of all places. She thumbs it open, takes a seat at the kitchen table to read and finish her latte. It is full of qualifiers—*allegedly*, *supposedly*, *ostensibly*. But the gist of it is Donnata Kade was a decorated FBI agent until she was removed from the organization following a nervous breakdown brought on by what they call a phantom case. She claimed a powerful, unnamed man was actually a serial killer in league with a cabal of other powerful men who were also killers. Directing them who to kill, and where. It was a fantastical tale without merit, according to the FBI. There was no proof, no evidence, and no way to bring a case against this person, but she wouldn't stop. She neglected all of her other cases, abused her powers as an agent to investigate on her own, until the FBI had no choice but to let her go. She did not go gently, showing up at the homes of leadership and doing all sorts of other crazy things. They had to cite her for harassment, and finally committed her to a psychiatric facility, claiming she suffered from a late-stage schizoaffective disorder. This was fifteen years ago. The same year Cat went missing.

Obviously Kade is out in the world again; she was in Marchburg following the stranger. And possibly disabling Halley's Jeep.

The article ends with a wild supposition—a former coworker "playing devil's advocate" suggested that the former FBI agent was actually killing people in order to make her story hold water, though there was no proof of that, either.

Halley sets down her phone. Wow. Character assassination, or is the woman totally bonkers? No wonder the sheriff discouraged her from reaching out. Kade does sound a bit unhinged.

Having just been let go without real cause, though, Halley finds herself sympathetic to the woman. She understands what it's like to have your entire world, your entire career, yanked away unfairly and without warning.

She finds the phone book—a cognac leather-covered listing of Brockville's residents—and starts thumbing through. The names are alphabetical; Esworthy is listed on the second page. She dials the number and listens to it ring, then voicemail kicks in. It's automated, no personalized greeting. She leaves her cell phone number and asks for them to call her back.

She could go to the Esworthys' cottage herself and knock, see if there's really no one home. A walk might do her good. A nap, maybe? She hasn't slept more than a few hours, and those were fitful.

She is wired, though. Sleep may be impossible. She is on overload—systemic overload.

Her phone buzzes, and she recognizes the number she just called. "Hello?"

"This is Cathy Esworthy. You just left me a message. Sorry I missed you, I was in the garden."

"Thanks for getting back to me. I wanted to ask about your renter Donnata Kade. Have you spoken to her recently, or have a way I can contact her?"

There is silence, then a small sigh. "I'm afraid I don't."

"Maybe your husband—"

A deep voice responds. "We no longer have any contact with Donnata. It was a difficult decision, she was a friend of mine from school, and we tried to help her get back on her feet. But her accusations, her demeanor, were so disruptive, we couldn't let it go on."

"Mr. Esworthy?"

"Yes. You're on speaker. We really don't have any idea where she is now."

Mrs. Esworthy chimes in. "Bruce and I moved here to have a quieter life, and she . . . Well, I'm sorry to say this, but Donnata is severely mentally ill. When she lost her job, we did all we could to get her help, but she wasn't interested in treatment. She was obsessed with her delusions. They were frightening, and to watch her be so consumed . . . We haven't seen her since she moved out."

"You mentioned accusations? Against whom?"

"That's really all we know," Mr. Esworthy says. "And unfortunately, we have to go. We have an appointment in Atlanta."

"Right. Thank you for your time."

She sets the phone back into its cradle. *Thanks for nothing.* Everyone is so tight lipped about Kade. It makes Halley wonder how delusional the woman really was. Where there's smoke, there's fire, right?

She explores the cottage, familiarizing herself with everything. A few minutes into her scrutiny, the doorbell rings. She looks out the peephole to see a kid with grocery bags. Damn, that was quick.

She opens the door, and the kid smiles. "Sheriff Brockton asked me to drop these off."

"How much do I owe you?"

"Oh, nothing. Here you go."

He hands off the bags and is back in his golf cart and buzzing away before she can get her wallet to give him a tip.

She goes back into the house, determined to unpack and figure out her next steps. She pulls out the note, wishing she had a fingerprinting kit, something, anything, so she can do more than just stare at the word *HELP* and wonder what the heck it is about. Who in this supposedly idyllic town needs help? And who would ask her, a total stranger, for it?

She tries to assemble all of the data she's inputted into a coalescent timeline. Cat killed her mother. She came to Brockville. To the retreat. She went missing. Years later, her little sister finds out the truth and follows in her footsteps. She finds that the perfect little town isn't so very perfect after all.

The story. Cat's story.

Oh God, she's forgotten entirely about meeting Tammy Boone.

A quick glance at the clock shows it's five to nine. Assuming the sheriff hasn't canceled her appointment, she can make it if she hurries.

The golf cart fires to life with no issue. She consults the map, figures out the path she needs to take, and buzzes off.

And the monster smiles.

CHAPTER THIRTY-FOUR

Halley has the same sense of dislocation that she had when she arrived in town last night. It is bustling. Cheery. Happy. The day is sunny, clear, azure spring skies with only the faintest hint of chill still left in the mountain air. People in golf carts buzz past, waving and smiling. Many stop to chat with one another or with someone on a porch or in a driveway. Almost all of them wave at her as she passes.

As she makes the turn toward the writers' retreat cabin, a six-seater golf cart full of people approaches. She can hear them chatting, laughing, pointing. Almost as if they're on a tour.

Behind the wheel, she sees a man who looks like an older version of Noah and the sheriff. His shoulders are broad, his thick hair more salt than pepper but still hanging in there. His eyes are dark and have that bottomless edge to them, and his handsome face is lined by years in the sun. He looks like an actor playing the part of town leader. He is almost too perfect in the role.

He sees her and immediately stops the cart with a tiny screech. The people with him peer at her curiously.

"Hallo!" he calls to her, waving. "Are you lost? You look lost."

"Um, no, I'm heading right in there." She points at the sign, and he excuses himself from his group and gets out of the cart. He comes to her, hand extended. Though she assumes he's in his late seventies, he's strong and moves quickly, with no hint of age.

"I'm Miles Brockton. Founder of Brockville. It's a pleasure to meet you. Welcome to our humble town." His hand is huge and envelops hers like a baseball mitt. He smells like marijuana and patchouli and something else, dark and ineffable, like fresh mulch. Is he high? Maybe. But his eyes are clear.

"Halley James," she says. "I have a meeting at the retreat."

"You do? It's not in session right now. You're a writer?"

"I'm talking about writing with Tammy Boone."

"Ah, Tammy. Wonderful lady. Well, if you know where you are, I won't keep you. But please, make sure you stop in at one of the wellness centers when you're done." He eyes her critically. "You need a realignment. Fatigue is hard to combat on a trip, and you will feel like a million dollars afterward."

"Oh, I don't think I need a chiropractor."

His smile is bright white and avuncular. "Not a physical realignment. Your energy is all off. I have a fabulous machine that gives off the exact kind of vibes you need to reset yourself. It's a Tesla coil biocharger, and trust me, you won't recognize yourself afterward." He looks at his watch. She notices it is a simple black face with a single silver hand. It looks ridiculously expensive. "I'll tell you what. Meet me there at ten, that's an hour from now, and I will change your life." He grins, looking even more like a Hollywood movie star, and she understands in that instant how Miles Brockton manages to get so many people to buy into his idea of how life should be led.

The problem is his enthusiasm is contagious; she can't help but smile back. If there's anything she needs right now, it's a life change. And whatever a biocharger is sounds insane, but who cares. She's a scientist. She's naturally curious.

And she is intrigued by this man whom everyone speaks of as a guru. Noah didn't seem to be as enamored of him, but even she can't deny the man has a magnetism. Who has that sort of power over people? Is it power? Is it charm? Is he an emotional vampire, draining the people around him of their essence while growing stronger and more in control? She envisions him in a laboratory cooking up some special sauce to feed to all the people in town so they are happy and compliant, then reminds herself she's gotten very little rest and had a trauma and maybe her imagination is in overdrive.

"All right. I'll see you there."

His smile is even bigger now, and he smacks his big hands together. "Groovy. See you there."

He turns back to his cart and the crowd of people inside. "Now, this is the infamous Brockville Writers' Retreat, and what a treat for you to have just met one of our talented students!" He's off, the cart whirring away, and she feels like a hurricane has just passed through.

She drives up the hill to the cabin. It looks more like a Swiss ski chalet, a beautiful cedar A-frame with smoked glass and a stacked stone chimney, wispy smoke from an already-lit fire rising in the mountain air. It's not that chilly—she is wearing her sweater and jeans from the road yesterday and is comfortable—but she is entranced by the idea of a bunch of creatives sitting around a fire, talking about their work. Then she realizes her sister stood here once, looking at the same view, waiting her turn to go inside, and chills spread across her body.

She mounts the flagstone stairs and knocks on the door. It swings open, and at first glance, the interior is as cozy and elegant as she was expecting.

"Tammy?"

Something smells off, like meat left too long in the sun. She takes three steps in and slips on something red.

Blood. Blood, everywhere.

"Run, Halley Bear. Run!"

"Tammy! Tammy Boone? Are you here?"

Grabbing onto a chair, Halley rights herself, realizing what's happening. She moves carefully around the puddle of blood. It streaks and whorls and eddies over the hardwoods, a dying crimson river. She can easily envision someone staggering from the door to the living space. Ahead there are couches and chairs in an approximation of a circle, and in the largest one, in the head of the circle facing the fire, is the outline of a body.

Sensory overload. There is so much red.

A white rug, and finger paint everywhere. Her mother is going to be so angry. She has to clean it up. But she can't reach the paper towels on the counter. She drags a stool and climbs up. Rips them off. Hurries back to the living room. There is something big lying on the floor. She can't look. She must clean up the paint.

She wipes and wipes and wipes and it smears, going deeper into the rug's pile. She whimpers in frustration. Fear. Tears. It smells strange. Her head hurts so bad.

Voices. There are voices. The female voice shrieks. She can't make out the words.

She looks at the mantel. The photo of the family has paint on it. The fireplace is red.

The doorbell rings, and rings, and rings again . . .

Her head hurts so badly. She needs to answer the door. Needs to make the ringing stop.

But hands hold her down. A woman's voice, soft and urgent in her ear. "Stay down. Don't move. Make him think you're dead."

Halley shakes away the memory. Something new there, that voice she recognizes and yet doesn't. The pressure of hands on her shoulders, a gasp of surprise, or was it relief? This is confusing, too much to interpret. She is on sensory overload, and she must focus.

She turns carefully, eyes trained for anything she might be trampling or otherwise ruining at what is clearly a crime scene. Her worst suspicions are confirmed.

Tammy Boone has collapsed in the leather chair facing the fire as if she sat down to rest for a moment. But she will never be rising again. Her head lolls against the cracked brown leather, and her entire torso is covered in life's blood. Her eyes are slitted, her legs splayed apart.

Halley feels her neck for a pulse, knowing she will find none. She is surprised by the lingering warmth on the woman's skin. Is she being warmed by the fire, or has she expired so recently that the body hasn't even cooled yet? The state of the blood, the laxity of her flesh, tells her this murder is recent. If she had arrived sooner, could she have prevented it?

Stay calm. Focus. Call for help.

HELP. The note. Did it come from Tammy? Did she know she was in the killer's sights?

"Stay down. Don't move. Make him think you're dead."

Her hands are shaking, her fingers clumsy as she dials.

"Nine-one-one, what is your emergency?"

"Please send the sheriff. I'm at the writers' retreat cabin, and there's been a murder."

Cameron Brockton has never seen a murder victim up close and in person, of this Halley is certain. He takes one look at Tammy and bolts for the door. She hears him vomiting off the front step. Interesting. She hasn't moved since she made the phone call, afraid to contaminate the scene more than she already has. She and the woman were alone together, and it gave her a few minutes to think. Time that was wasted, because Halley's adrenaline is surging, and she spent it all forcing herself not to run away. Avoiding the footprints she tracked to the center of the cabin, she makes her way carefully to the front door and looks out.

"You okay?"

"Yes," he says gruffly, wiping his mouth. His skin is the shade of curdled milk. "Are you?"

"I can't say I'm thrilled at the moment, but yes, as far as my stomach, I'm okay. I don't know what the hell is going on, though."

"Let me get some people here." He's stumbling over his words, and Halley takes pity on him.

"Hey. Look at me."

He does, and she looks him straight in the eye. "It's going to be okay. We need to freeze this scene, and I need to be processed. I stepped in her blood when I came in and grabbed onto that chair for support, before I realized what was happening. Do you have any crime scene training?"

"Of course I do," he snaps. "She's a friend. I have a heart, you know."

"I understand how hard this is. Believe me."

"I doubt that," he mutters. "Murder weapon?"

"I didn't see anything. Though that much blood . . . A knife, I'd guess. In keeping with the other murders." Who has these conversations? What has her life become? A fucking horror show, that's what.

"Why is it every person you talk to dies?"

"I am wondering the same thing. You're still alive. So is your brother. You both know the truth. And whoever did it . . . Well, the note in Marchburg said I was next, but I wasn't, was I?"

"How are you so calm?"

Calm? Oh, Sheriff. If you had any idea what a mess the inside of my head is right now.

"I'm not. I haven't been. I'm scared to death right now, but giving in to that invites in whoever this is. It's what they want. They're trying to scare me. It's working, but getting hysterical is not going to solve anything. As for Tammy, I've seen crime scenes before, obviously, for work. I'm trained how to react. I've just never been at the center of it. Maybe that's why? Now, do you have a crime scene tech, or do you need my help? This is a mess, and we're wasting time."

He studies her. "Or you know more than you're letting on."

She holds out her bloody hands. "If you honestly believe I am capable of this, put your cuffs on me again and take me to jail."

Cameron's face goes through an array of emotions, stopping on anger. Tammy's final words about him come back to her. *"The oldest is trouble, if you ask me. Charms the larks from the trees, but only to eat them. He's sly. Be careful if you ever come across him."*

"I didn't do this. But I do need to ask you why you didn't mention that another woman went missing from the Brockville Writers' Retreat and you didn't bother mentioning that my sister created a pattern."

"Where in the hell did you hear that?"

She nods toward Boone. "She told me. And now she's dead, like all the others."

He looks over her shoulder at the body again and runs a hand over his face. "I know it wasn't you."

"How? Am I under surveillance?"

Something moves in his dark eyes, something disturbing. Of course she is.

"If you have eyes on me, surely you have eyes on the cabin."

"I don't. And I'm not watching you, either. It's a small town. People are vigilant."

"Yeah, so vigilant no one's talking about the women who go missing from your small town."

"Quit attacking me. I don't have answers, okay?"

"Well, I met your father a few minutes before I stumbled onto this scene. Maybe he can educate us both. Why don't we go have a chat—" Her words are cut off by the sound of an electric golf cart crunching to a halt in the gravel. Speak of the devil.

"Cameron?" Miles Brockton is furious. That handsome charm is gone, replaced by a black rage. He sees Halley, and his face changes, smoothing out, losing the irate edge, but not before she recognizes something.

In that split second, he looked like the stranger who approached her.

"You really don't remember me."

But it's Miles's voice instead, saying "Oh, no. Oh, no" over and over again, until the sheriff takes his father by the shoulder and leads him away. They talk quietly, and Halley tries not to panic.

The stranger is tied more deeply to Marchburg than she realized.

CHAPTER THIRTY-FIVE

She hasn't lied to the sheriff about her emotional state. She is outwardly calm, but inside, everything is surreal, as if Halley were in a dream, departed from her body and watching from above. The anger and fear fuel something deep inside that shuts off her senses, and she enters some sort of fugue state. It happened when she was fired. It happened when she found out Cat murdered her mother. And it's happening now, again, in front of witnesses. She is present, but not. She watches the scene being processed and enacts her own role in the play—*move over there; what is that? Look down; there is blood on your shoes*—but doesn't feel anything. There are no sensations but horror, playing on a loop.

Does this strange state emanate from the original murder? The head injury she sustained during her mother's death? Is there now a lack of control in her prefrontal cortex? Is she a toddler having an emotional-meltdown tantrum because her brain stopped developing at six when she was lashed with unassailable trauma?

Is she simply in shock, the reality of the situation settling in? Three women dead. Three innocent people who did nothing but lend an ear to a friend and stranger.

Is it because she knows, deep in her heart, she is close to the murderer?

She is responsible for their deaths, just as surely as if she'd held the knife in her own hand.

She watches and waits. The killer is here. He is nearby. If she is careful, sentient, she will catch him out. If she steps wrongly, she will be at the receiving end of his knife.

She wonders now if the motivation behind the murders even matters. What will she do at the end? Try to reason with them? Ask questions and demand answers before she submits to the fateful cut? Of course, it won't be like that. Whoever is doing this is playing a game, a sick and twisted game, and she is the chess piece they most covet. She is the queen, and all the moves are designed to fell her.

The knowledge of this, the understanding of her own futility, is almost a relief. There is an inevitability to this game.

But what if there is a stalemate?

In too many games, there can be no tie. There is always a winner, and there is always a loser. But in this one, perhaps there is a way to come to a draw. She just has to find it.

Noah Brockton arrives on the scene moments after his father, flour in his hair and a wild look in his eyes. He makes straight for Halley. "Are you okay?"

She nods.

"Thank God. Don't move. I need to talk to Cam."

He disappears into the cabin. On his heels, first responders and a contingent of townsfolk. They are bees in a disturbed hive; everyone seems to have a job to do—even the onlookers, standing in a knot at the base of the drive to the cabin, faces ashen and aghast, murmur incessantly. And lo, a slew of deputies appear, who Halley learns are all volunteers with their own specialized skill sets. Like firefighters in a rural area, trained well and on call as necessary.

She waits, but not as long as she should. Tammy's body is being transferred much too soon for Halley's liking. When she worked cases, years earlier, it could take hours before a homicide scene was fully processed and cleared for the victim to be moved. They are less than an hour in here, and she thinks the sheriff is being pressured to make it all disappear.

The sheriff is not interested in her help, nor her opinions. Instead, she is forced to sit by Noah in Miles's golf cart, watching and being watched by the growing crowd, until summoned for processing by one of the sheriff's volunteer strangers. On display to everyone, she is fingerprinted, her shoes confiscated, and, in a horrifying move that brings the sheriff running when she pitches a fit, her bag, containing her laptop, her gun, and her phone, is taken as well. And the note. They're going to see the note.

Knowing another might be in danger pulls her back to herself at last.

"You can't take my bag," she says to the sheriff.

"Come on, Miss James. You know the drill. They will process everything and get it back to you shortly."

"You have to at least let me keep my phone. It never left my bag. None of the contents did."

Just let me get my hand in there. Let me slip out that note.

She can tell he's wavering, but his father is watching, along with much of the rest of town. With a quick glance over his shoulder, he straightens. His tone brooks no arguments.

"This is procedure. Don't make a fuss. I'll return them to you myself."

He ignores her retort—"Procedure my ass"—and disappears back into the cabin. Frustrated, she turns and sees the people of Brockville watching her. Theirs are not friendly faces. As if she did this. As if she were the murderer. Cunning glances her way, openly accusatory looks, the muttering of the crowd. Sweat breaks out on her forehead. Their frustration is growing. All they are missing are pitchforks and lit torches and cries of *"Kill it, burn the monster!"* In the sea of anger, there are faces she's beginning to recognize. The four kids from the General Store are there, whispering behind their hands. The friends Tammy ate with, her round table of compatriots, noses red and cheeks streaked with tears. The people Halley passed on the street as she entered the town; the female jogger with her deluxe side-by-side double stroller and those cherubic blond angels within. It's like the whole cast from a movie being gathered in one place for an announcement. They shuffle and stare and titter. She is exposed and raw.

All she needs now is the news showing up and trying to interview her. That will set Theo off. And her dad. Any reporter worth their salt will ask about her dismissal from the lab, too, and then she's tarnishing their reputation and all that she's built, and it will ruin her chances to sue for her job back, or at least get a proper severance, and Tammy's face, so slack and empty, the flood of crimson . . . Oh, God, this is bad.

She drags in a breath and the scene begins moving again. No one has noticed her freak-out. And she realizes that is what's missing here, so stark in its absence.

There is no media.

This is a completely controlled scene, populated only by Brockvillians, and there is no one to report on the story of a dead body found in this small, isolated, exclusive mountain town.

It feels very odd, and very uncomfortable. Though she hasn't been looking online at the news about Kater's murder, or Dr. Chowdhury's, she knows stories are being done. They must be. Two murders in a small town are catnip to reporters.

But here? There is nothing. No one. No news trucks with satellite dishes, no cameras, no field reporters. Their absence feels almost sinister.

Will the townspeople allow word to get out that one of their brethren has fallen? Or will this be hidden away, become part of the lore of Brockville?

Is that why they've taken her phone and she is being guarded by the founder's son?

Halley is starting to spin out again. She needs to get herself together. Now. Her life depends on it.

With no real recourse, and not wanting to face the sea of fury lining the drive of the writers' retreat any longer, she agrees to be given a ride back to her cottage to change and shower. Noah, pale and serious, follows in his own golf cart. He has become her unofficial bodyguard. Who knows, maybe he is the official one. The way Miles controls his sons is disturbing. She watches them all talking, sees the other two brothers who also worked for the town for the first time. They are uncannily alike, the four of them. All variations on a theme of their father. None of them are the man she met in Marchburg.

So where does the stranger fit into all this? The man who, for the briefest of moments, she saw in Miles Brockton's face?

She isn't sure she wants Noah near her, not sure she wants any of the Brocktons near her, but at the same time, she is strangely grateful for his company. He feels like he's on her side. They have a strange connection, the intimacies of their overnight confessional coupled with . . . something.

When she comes from the shower and sees him slumped in one of the chairs in the cottage's living room, in a position not unlike the one she found Tammy's body in, a streaking thought flies through her mind. *Is he the murderer?*

No, of course not. He would have his hands around her throat by now if he were.

Then another. Why is it only the women she's talked to have died?

And one more. Why has the murderer not tried to kill her yet?

He will, soon enough.

She needs to alert Baird Early about what's happened here. It's time for her to raise the red flags and have someone drag her from the undertow. Because she is sinking; she is drowning. She is afraid. She is no longer in control.

But she needs to keep her head about her. Someone here asked for her help, and she is loath to leave before finding out who.

There is no way to send a text message from the landline, but she can make a call out. There's only one problem. Any 9-1-1 call she makes from here is going straight to the Brockville switchboard. Which means her only chance to reach Early directly is calling the Marchburg police station, and she has to look up the number. She has no way to do that.

She has another option. Make for the kitchen and dial Theo.

He will come running, this she knows. He will send the cavalry. But to what end? Does she need saving? Rescuing? If this killer wanted her dead, she would be.

She makes a pretense of banging around in the kitchen and lifts the receiver. The phone is dead. Was it never hooked up? Or has the line been cut to isolate her further?

Noah has a phone. She can just use his.

Her hair is wet, and she is bone weary, but she takes a seat opposite the chef. He doesn't look up.

"You okay?"

"Bad morning," he replies.

"Yeah. You were friends?"

"I've known her a long time."

"I'm sorry."

They sit in silence for a few moments. Finally, Halley blows out a breath.

"Do you have any pictures of your family on your phone?"

Noah nods. "Of course. Why?"

"I was just curious about them. It's unusual these days for a family to have the kind of proximity yours does. Everyone working for Dad, living where you grew up, that kind of thing. There's usually at least one who goes off to be a monk or something."

He laughs weakly. "I guess that would be me. I left but came back."

"Do you have cousins?"

"Sure. My dad's little sister, MaryEmily, has three kids—two boys and a girl. I think the girl is a doctor, and the boys . . . one is a park ranger, and the other works IT for some company in Silicon Valley. They're all very different from us."

"Did they grow up here, too?"

"Oh, no. We're not close. Dad and MaryEmily had a pretty bad falling-out after he came back from Maine. She was pretty pissed at him for disappearing without word for so long."

"What was he doing in Maine?"

Noah eyes her searchingly. "Why all the questions, Halley?"

"I'm just trying to figure out some stuff."

"Then ask me directly. I have nothing to hide, and after today, I'm not responding well to subterfuge."

"All right. I'm looking for someone. He was in Marchburg, and I think he's involved in all of this, deeply. For a second, when your dad was angry, I recognized something about him. I'm wondering if he's related to you or the family in some way."

"Well, there's only the four of us."

"The cousins, maybe? Any pic of them?"

"That's a stretch. Maybe my aunt has some on her Facebook? I don't know, I haven't seen them in years. But I can't imagine one of my cousins being a killer. They're . . . normal. Probably more so than any of us, considering."

"Maybe your dad had an affair, and—"

"Halley. Stop. Okay? I don't have it in me right now. Can we pivot?"

"All right. Sorry. Pivoting. I need to get in touch with some people. Your brother has my phone. And the house phone here is dead."

"And? You want me to get it back?"

"Well, yes. But in the interim, I was hoping to look up a number?"

He pulls out his phone. "Tell me."

"Chief of Police Baird Early. Marchburg, Virginia." She holds her breath but Noah doesn't hesitate. He searches for a minute.

"Main number okay?"

She nods, and he dials the phone. Puts it on speaker. Halley relaxes a touch. She is not a captive after all.

Early is on the line a minute later, anger simmering in his voice. "Brockton called me, told me what was happening. You okay?"

"He called you?"

"Yeah. Said you had yourself another close call. What exactly is going on, Halley? Where are you now?"

"I'm in a cabin in Brockville. Noah Brockton, the sheriff's brother, is with me. I'm fine. I'm safe."

"Not when there's a murderer on the loose. Brockton tells me you spoke with the victim before her death?"

"Yes. Just like all the rest."

"Halley. You need to come home."

Noah clears his throat. "Sir, I think it's better if she stays here for the time being. We're in an isolated area, and now everyone's on their guard. We can keep her safe. Much safer than if she headed out on the road."

"Which I tried to do before my tires were slashed and my engine tampered with. I want out of here, too, Baird. I need—"

"Then I'll come get you myself," he says with finality.

"I appreciate that. But I was about to say I need to stay here for the time being. I'm close to figuring all of this out, and whoever is killing these women is trying to stop me from learning the truth."

"Plenty of truth to be learned from right here in Marchburg. You'll be safe here."

"Kater wasn't safe. Dr. Chowdhury wasn't safe. I don't think I'll be safe no matter where I am, Baird. The killer is trying to get my attention. He has it."

"So what, you're going to sit there and wait for them to show up? It may not be a him, Halley. We know that now."

"How?"

"How do you think?"

"You have DNA?" She turns away from Noah's searching eyes. She can't bear to watch him deflate with this reality. Noah seems too innocent by half. A chef, looking to create beautiful things, to evoke wonderful emotions. There is no darkness in him. At least not this kind.

"We do. From both scenes. Like the killer was cut during the attack. But here's the part that is going to blow your mind."

"What's that?"

“There’s a match in CODIS.”

“A match? So you know who the killer is?”

“I can’t say that definitively. But I do know who the blood at the scenes belongs to.”

“Who?” she asks, dread building in her gut.

“Your sister.”

CHAPTER THIRTY-SIX

"Whoa whoa whoa. What?" Halley is dumbfounded.

"There were drops of your sister's blood on both bodies. I've already told Brockton to have all the blood at the scene tested. And put into CODIS immediately."

Good luck with that.

"So wait a sec. You're telling me my sister murdered these women?"

"I didn't say that. But the match is to your mother's crime scene. Catriona's blood was in the system, and CODIS popped a hit. There were several, in fact. Multistate hits."

"Several murders? In addition to my mother's? More than the three new ones that we know of?"

"Yes. It seems to be the signature of this killer. You know the limitations of the databases better than most. Without knowing what to look for, it's hard to tie a bunch of extraneous cases together. Now that we have this, yes. The databases are talking."

"How many murders?"

"I can't say for sure. It's still working, Halley."

"Baird. How many so far?"

"Eighteen."

Blood rushes to her head. Eighteen murders, and counting? Across multiple states?

"Run, Halley Bear. Run."

"My God. All stabbed?"

"No. That's the interesting part. Different CODs, different parts of the country. Different ages, different looks. There's no clear victimology yet."

"But my sister's blood is at every scene. Baird. This is fucked up as hell. You can't tell me that she's not responsible."

"It is fucked up, and now you can understand why I want you home, where I can keep an eye on you. I don't know if it's her or what, but you're in real danger, Halley."

The reality hits her, and she has to stiffen her spine simply to not collapse under the weight of it. "I don't think it matters where I am. A traveling serial killer tied to my sister, who might be my sister, has killed the last three people I spoke to about the case? Whoever it is, they're coming for me no matter where I am."

Noah is watching her with horror. She can almost hear his thoughts. *Leave. Leave now and take this curse with you.*

Baird Early is having none of it. "I'm not joking. I will come and get you myself right now."

Four hours, and she can be free of this place. Her mind says, *Don't be an idiot. Let him come get you.* Her heart is still mired in doubt. She is still tied here with inexorable forces.

Noah stands, sighing. "I'll drive you home." He takes the phone. "There's no need for you to come here, Chief. I've got her back. I can bring her home."

"No offense, son. But I don't know you from Adam's house cat."

"No, you don't. I'm Noah Brockton, my father is Miles Brockton, and Halley is a grown woman who can make her own decisions."

She smiles at this. Nice to have someone not treating her like a child.

"Baird, I'm going to stay for the time being, at least until the sheriff clears me to leave. No sense causing more trouble, and he has all my things."

"Halley, I disagree with that decision. It would kill your father if something happened to you."

With that, he's gone, and she feels the weight of his judgment deeply. Staying here is like watching a tidal wave surge toward her, knowing it is too large and she will be knocked off her feet and dragged out to sea. Leaving feels as monumentally scary. Alone, out on the road, anything can happen. Even with escorts, if this killer wants her dead, he—she—is going to find a way.

Stay or go, she is screwed no matter what she does. And if there's a chance of finding the truth?

The only course of action is to figure out who the stranger is, determine if he's the killer, and confront this twisted fate she's been given. Her world has turned as quickly as flipping over an hourglass, the sand drifting in another direction without recourse.

"This is a terrible situation," Noah says. "No one knows exactly what to do. But get your things. I'll take you back to Marchburg."

"My car. My phone. My weapon. I have things here that I need. Running away without them just means I have to come back. I don't know that running is the answer."

"Then what do you propose otherwise?"

"Honestly? I have no idea."

She plops down onto the couch. She is so tired. She won't be able to stay awake much longer. The craziness of the past few days means she's been running on adrenaline, but it, too, is fading in the face of basic biology. If she doesn't sleep, she will collapse.

"Can I ask you something?"

"Anything."

"Tammy told me there was another woman who went missing. Before Cat. What do you know about that?"

He strokes his chin, and she can hear the rasp of his beard. It is short, hip scruff, the barest hint of hair, but defines his ridiculously handsome face.

"So, I wasn't here then. But I did hear that a writer disappeared. It was years before your sister. There's no way they're related."

"Of course there is. It's a pattern. Don't you see? Writers come to Brockville and never leave."

"I'm kind of hoping you never leave." He smiles.

"I'm serious."

"So am I." He scooches closer. "You're fierce. You're gorgeous. You're clearly smart. And you're not taken." He takes her hand, running a finger over where her rings used to be. "Why is that?"

"Another complicated, long story."

"I have time."

He is too close. He is too handsome. He is too much everything. She leans away, and he takes the hint and does the same.

"You were going to show me pictures of your family?" she asks.

"Yeah? Okay." He opens his phone. Scrolls around for a few moments. Turns the screen her way. "Here's my mom."

The woman staring out from the screen is stunningly beautiful but fragile, delicate, a doe-eyed waif who doesn't look sturdy enough to have birthed four strapping boys. She is haunted, possesses the sort of ethereal beauty that makes men want to protect and treasure. To own.

"She's beautiful."

"Yeah, she really was. Cameron looks like her the most, I think."

"You all look like your dad."

"You think? He'd be happy to hear that." He swipes around some more. "Ah. Here we all are. I think I was about fourteen in this picture. Christmas. This was 1995, now that I think about it. We brought back gifts from Paris. My dad was annoyed, felt like everything was too commercial. He wanted everyone to be more connected to the earth. Natural was always better."

She stares at the faces, searching for the one that matches the stranger. She can't find him among the brothers.

Noah closes the phone. "What about you?" he asks.

"What?"

"Do you have pictures of your family?"

"Oh. Obviously not on me. But on my phone? No, not really. Mom died when I was six, well before we had all our pictures in our pockets. There's one family portrait, but I think my dad destroyed pretty much anything else that reminded him of Nashville."

The portrait, on the mantel, covered in a spray of blood.

He sets his phone on the table. "So you haven't been back?"

"To Nashville? No."

"Run, Halley Bear. Run."

"Stay down. Don't move. Make him think you're dead."

Two voices. Not one.

Two voices.

Blackness.

"Where did you go just now?"

She startles and is back in the cabin again. She gets up and pours a glass of water. Drinks it down. Stares out into the charming garden. This place feels so gentle, so warm. She has brought death to their door. If she could just remember. There is something in the memories that will break this case wide open; she can feel it.

She sits again. Despite the sunlight streaming into the room now, the tiny dust motes dancing in its light, darkness is tugging at her. "My memories of my mother's death are jumbled up. Nothing is clear. I keep getting little flashes, but nothing concrete. Like I'm pulled back in time and can't escape, but I can't see clearly now, either. It's frustrating."

"Being there might change that. We're only four hours away."

He's not wrong. She could try Nashville. Talk to the police there again, see if any others who worked the case are alive and willing to talk.

"It's a good idea, but I can't make it four hours right now." She drops her face into her hands. "I am exhausted. This week, these past few days, it's too much. I haven't slept. I have to sleep. Can you stay?"

"Of course. Go lie down. I'll be here."

"The restaurant?"

"Will be fine without me for a while." He pulls her to her feet. "Seriously. Go on. I will stand guard, happily, until you send me away."

She stares into his eyes. He is so different from Theo. Gentler. Kinder. She reaches a hand to his cheek, and he inhales, shocked, but doesn't move away. His skin is soft. Impulsively, she rises on her toes and touches her lips to his.

"Thank you."

She turns for the bedroom, but he catches her hand. "Why did you do that?"

"What?"

"Kiss me." There is something rising between them, she can feel it, and she tries to push it away by pulling her hand from his. The connection is maintained. They don't need to be touching to have this magnetic pull toward one another. She felt it from their first meeting. And by the reaction he's having right now, he did, too.

"I'm tired. I'm scared. I—"

"Come here." His arms go around her; his face bends to hers. His breath is warm. She has not been touched, been desired, in so long. A completely different kind of wave moves through her. One of desertion and fear. Of desperate longing.

His lips claim hers, and the wave crashes over her head.

What are you doing, Halley? What the hell are you doing?

Her hands go to Noah's broad chest. He deepens the kiss. She pulls away, putting some space between them.

"I'm sorry. I can't. This is . . . too much. Too soon."

Noah is breathing heavily. He hesitates—a fraction of a moment when Halley wonders if he's going to stop. Does she really want him to? What if he refuses? What if . . . Then he steps backward. She retreats a few feet away.

"Right. Sorry. Got carried away."

"No, it's fine," she says. It is anything but fine. Raw, elemental desire for a complete stranger, one closely tied to this horrifying situation? One she's known for a day at most?

She isn't using her head.

Noah sits down again. "Go sleep. I'll stand guard. Call me if you need me."

She staggers to the bedroom. It takes her longer than she'd like to admit to fall asleep.

When Halley wakes, the room is dark and cool. Curtains block the windows. She is under the covers. Memories assail her, Noah's lips on hers, and a flash of shame courses through her. She dodged a bullet, for sure. She laughs to herself. *You're an idiot, Halley.*

Her head hurts. She must have been gritting her teeth. A headache has taken hold.

"Hi," a male voice says, and she rolls over to see Noah sitting in the chair by the fireplace. He's abandoned his post in the living room and joined her in the bedroom. Perhaps hoping she'd change her mind? Should she?

No. The moment is past. They are no longer ships lost at sea, but two grown-ups in an untenable situation.

He is reading something on his phone and closes it with a click. "You okay?"

"What time is it?"

"Three in the afternoon. You've been out for a few hours."

She stretches.

"You stayed."

"Of course I did."

"Is there any news?"

"No. All's calm. There's a town meeting tonight—nothing unusual there. Everyone wants answers about what happened to Tammy."

"This is a pretty tight-knit community."

"Yeah. Claustrophobic at times for some, but we take care of one another."

"It's just . . . Doesn't all this isolation get to you? You're cut off from the world. Alone. No news vans showed up when Tammy was killed. Has her murder been reported on at all?"

"Everyone here knows. Cameron is investigating. Who else needs to hear it?"

She sits up. "Sorry. I'm still a little wigged out."

"That's understandable. I am, too."

"Do you know anything about the little boy in the woods? The one I saw when I left town? Your brother said he was going back out with a dog to see if he could locate him, but then Tammy . . . happened."

His brow furrows. "I don't know about that, but I wouldn't worry too much. The kids here are pretty free range. That's part of the attraction. They're safe to wander the streets. It takes a village, right? Everyone looks out for the others."

"You that closely vet the people who live here? How can you be so sure none of them would do something to harm a child? Or a woman?"

"Point taken. But yes. The people who live here—such a thing would be an aberrance. They wouldn't, because everyone would know, and they'd be asked to leave. And prosecuted, obviously."

"You can't know what people do behind closed doors. On their computers. You can't know their darkest hearts. Women are missing, and now a woman has been openly murdered. That will certainly be talked about, yes? How will your town react to that? Will they come for me with pitchforks and torches because I've brought this horror to your doors?"

"How can you think that? This is not your fault."

"But it is," she says, the confession making tears well up. "If I hadn't come here, if I hadn't tried to find my sister, Tammy would be alive."

"Halley," he says softly, coming to the bed. He perches on the side and runs a hand over her hair. His fingers linger over the shock of white. "Don't do that to yourself. Don't take the blame for what a madman has done. If you hadn't come, we wouldn't be here. And I like being here."

He starts to lean in for another kiss. Once, she can attribute to the shock and the pain and the horror of the week, and the need to be comforted. Twice? That's intentional. And damn her, she wants him. She wants him so badly. Wants to forget, for a little while, this madness.

But she can't do that to Theo. She owes it to her husband not to complicate things even more. Not to make reckless decisions that will ruin everything.

"Please," she says, and he stops.

"Bad timing, huh?"

"Yes. Very bad. My head is killing me." She's not lying; it is. She can feel the migraine building. She needs her medicine. But it's in her bag. *Oh, shit.*

Noah sighs heavily. "A shame. You and I could be good together."

She is thirsty and grabs the glass of water she left by the bed to cover up her discomfort. She downs it, using the moment to escape his devastatingly gorgeous eyes.

She's alive, at least. Noah is not the killer. But her head swims, the pain starting to build in her temple. "No, not now," she groans.

"What is it?"

The headache is fast and intense. She's seeing spots, black dancing in the edges.

"I get migraines. One is starting. I need my medicine from my bag. But your brother has it." She shuts her eyes. Vertigo. This is going to be a whopper if she doesn't stop it soon.

"Get my bag, Noah. Please."

She lies back down, fighting the headache, putting the pillow over her head. She needs dark. She needs her pills. She is an idiot for not leaving when she had the chance.

CHAPTER THIRTY-SEVEN

Knocking brings Halley to the surface again. She is alone in the bedroom, and the sun has begun its journey into the horizon. Her head is splitting. The cottage door opens, and two male voices start talking. It's Noah and Cameron. The sheriff must have brought her meds.

She wants the pills but stops at the door when she realizes they are arguing, craning to overhear their words.

"This has gone too far. Does Dad know what's happening?"

"He does, and he is livid. You have to get her out of here. She's a danger to us all."

"I think that's a little—"

"Noah. Do not get attached."

"I'm not."

A smothered, unamused laugh. "Don't lie to me, little brother. You've been mooning over her since she walked into the restaurant."

"Hey, it wasn't me that slashed her tires and disabled her Jeep. She would have been gone, and all this mess with her, if not for that."

"Well, we're dealing with it. The car will be ready in an hour. So do what you need to, but we need to get her out of here."

"She's flat on her back in there with a migraine. Needs her meds. They're in her bag. When she's functioning again, I'll get her out of here. I suggested she go to Nashville. She's stubborn, though. Asked about the little boy she saw."

"I don't know who the hell that could have been. Do you?"

"Of course not. I'm sure it was just some kid from town playing."

"Let's hope so. We can't have a repeat of what happened last time. Here's her bag. Give her the medicine and send her packing. Now, Noah. Dad's orders."

"I will. I promise."

Their conversation moves to Tammy's murder, and Halley backs away from the door, panic and pain filling her. What in the world? These men are giving her whiplash. *"You can't leave; you have to leave."* What is the deal? She is more than happy to leave. It wouldn't take much convincing at all. But every time she tries to go, someone gets in her way. And now it's too late. She can't drive in this state.

She is half tempted to confront them, but the other half, the one with the prehensile tail that recognizes danger deep in the recesses of the brain, says not to. For once, she listens.

She scans the room, looking for what, she doesn't know. And she sees it. Noah's phone. He left his phone by the bed.

She snatches it up and hurries into the bathroom, closing the door as silently as possible. Screens are the worst for a migraine, but there's something she wants to see again. She saw the pattern of the code he used when he opened it yesterday, but in a stroke of luck, it's still unlocked. He must have been reading on his phone, watching over her, when Cameron came to the door.

Maybe they're letting her leave so she doesn't bother reaching out to anyone else? They want her gone because . . . Why? What happened last time? Is that the other writer who went missing? Are Cameron and Noah trying to keep her safe by making her go? Does something dark stalk the streets of Brockville, and they think by sending her away they are saving her? Or do they think if she leaves, the darkness will follow?

This place is too confusing; these men are bewildering. And her curious brain wants to know the why behind it all. She feels the blackness surging; waves of pain building to the point that she thinks her head will burst like a balloon too full of air, then releasing, only to rise again.

"Run, Halley Bear. Run!"

She ignores that voice urging her to leave. It is her mother's; that she knows. She can distinguish now between the two voices, the one that told her to run and the one that told her to be still. To play dead. Why? Why, and who?

She opens the Photos app. She wants to look at that family picture again.

This is a horrible invasion of privacy, and if he finds out, she's pretty much guaranteed that he will disappear from her life. She doesn't know if that outcome is enough of a deterrent. Noah is cool, but he's deeply tied into this horror show.

A moment of weakness shouldn't define the rest of their lives, either of them. She wouldn't hold him to anything. She can't imagine he would, either. It was just a kiss. Heightened emotions driven by a horrible situation and her own circumstances of a broken marriage, a sad garden long unwatered, do not equal lifetime commitments. Just because she needed the finality of finding succor from another doesn't mean there's anything more here.

Guilt is starting to creep in.

Do not think about Theo right now, you idiot. Hold it together.

Her head is swimming, making it hard to focus. Noah's phone is full of impressively high-quality photos of food, not a shock. There are a few selfies with kitchen staff, pictures of the Brockville restaurants full to the brim. Paris. London. Luxembourg. Monaco. A stunning redhead with full lips and adoring eyes, wearing a skimpy white bikini. Several photos of her, and recent ones, too. So he does have someone. Halley is surprised to feel a spike of jealousy.

There are thousands of photos. She has no real idea what she's looking for here, and time is running out. Noah seems like an organized guy. She looks at the albums. There is one labeled *The Farm*; the main photo is the sign to the farm in Glaston, here in Brockville.

These pictures are similar to the others, high-quality portraits of various vegetables and crops. She hastily scrolls, sees nothing of note.

Backs out to the folders list. Clicks Search. There are several options on the screen, groupings, classifications. *Moments*, *People*, *Places*. She taps on *Faces*, slides through the photos, most of unfamiliar people. And then, at the end, unlabeled, she sees him. The stranger.

Is her mind playing tricks on her? She breathes, willing the migraine to ease, then clicks on the face. There is no doubt this is him. The same pooling darkness in his eyes, the same cock to his head, an inquisitorial crow. There are twenty photos. It looks like they're all from the Farm. All from some sort of event. A harvest? Halloween maybe; there are jack-o'-lanterns and pumpkins. She opens one and looks at the date. She's right. October 31, 2010. Seven years ago.

She looks at each photo carefully. The stranger is in two. One is the candid; he's looking at the camera but unaware a photo is being taken. He looks angry, staring at something over the photographer's shoulder. In the second, he is standing with a blond woman, her body mostly in profile. The outline of a pregnancy is clear.

Halley zooms in on the woman's face.

There is no way. This is impossible.

She swipes quickly now, looking for anything to confirm her suspicions. And there, at the end of the photo stream, a shot of the woman again. She is heavily pregnant. She is not smiling.

She is Catriona Handon.

Halley's first thought—well, second, after the unbelievable *What the hell?* that crosses through—is to send the photo to herself. But Noah and Cameron are out in the other room, with her phone. She doesn't need the text to ding and one of them to see this.

So she sends it to Theo, with a text message.

Save this to your phone. I'm going to delete this text.

He writes back, the ding audible. Halley curses under her breath, turns the volume down.

What is this? Who is this?

It's Halley. This is my sister and the man who's killing everyone. Run him. Run facial recognition. Hurry. I have to delete this now. Not my phone.

R u ok?

Do it. Hurry!

Done.

Thank you. I will have my phone back in a few minutes. Be careful what you send. I'm leaving Brockville and going to Nashville. I will be in touch.

She deletes the message. Hauls in a deep breath. Opens the bathroom door.

Noah Brockton stands there.

She puts her hand with his phone behind her back, the other on her heart. Forces a smile. Her head throbs with the effort.

"Oh, wow, you startled me."

"I was about to knock. Everything okay?"

"Yeah. Feeling ill."

She hopes he doesn't notice there was no water running, the shower is dry, the towels undisturbed.

"I have your bag. Are these the pills?"

"Yes."

He pushes the tab out of the blister and she accepts it, shoves it in her mouth. "I need more water."

"Of course."

He grabs her glass and heads to the kitchen. She follows, stopping to set his phone back on the bedside table. She's pulled it off.

Her mind is spinning. She can feel the tablet melting, wills herself to hold it together for a few more minutes. The ergotamine works fast.

Cat. Cat and the stranger. Cat pregnant in 2010. Unmistakably Cat.

The little boy she saw. Could that possibly be Cat's child?

Now you're reaching, her mind says. *That has to be a coincidence. He's younger than seven, isn't he?*

Noah returns with her glass. "Wow, are you okay? You're white. Here, lie down."

She gives in but doesn't go horizontal. Instead, she sits and puts her head in her hands, praying it doesn't explode.

"Sorry. Really bad headache."

"Well, here's some good news. Eddie was able to fix your Jeep sooner than expected. It will be ready for you in an hour. We can go to Nashville, or back to Marchburg. Whatever you want."

"We?"

"I told your sheriff I'd keep an eye on you. I intend to honor that promise."

"Thanks."

God, is she going to throw up? *Work, medicine. Please.*

She hears a small ding. Her phone, in the living room. Theo is texting. She needs to get her hands on that phone.

She breathes, in and out, the pain hitting a remarkable, blinding crescendo, then easing just a touch. She recognizes the sensation; she has crested the wave. She doesn't move. Slowly, so slowly, the pain lessens. She sits up. Still killing her, throbbing, but the medicine is kicking in.

"Is there caffeine?" she manages.

He brings her a Diet Coke. She drinks it and is finally able to open her eyes without the world spinning. Noah is watching her as if she is a bomb that might go off at any second.

"Sorry. They get the better of me sometimes. Thanks for helping."

"Of course. I'm going to keep helping, Halley. What do you want to do now?"

Leave. I want to leave. "Nashville, I think."

"Great. We can stop by my place on the way to get your car. I need to grab a bag."

The pain is echoing now. She rolls her neck with an audible pop, allowing her shoulders to drop. Tension doesn't help.

"Are you sure you want to leave with me, Noah? You have a lot of responsibilities here. There's no telling how long—"

"Do you not want me to go?"

Noah's voice is flat, empty, and she has that odd sensation again that there's a familiarity between the Brockton boys and the stranger. *"You really don't recognize me, do you?"*

"I didn't say that. I just don't want to be responsible for tearing you away from your life so you can protect me. I don't need you to."

"Oh, good to know." Now she's made him angry. "You just swoop into town, act the damsel in distress, and now you're gone? Is that what this is?"

"Noah. Please."

He scrambles off the bed. "Damn it, Cameron was right about you."

"Excuse me?"

"He said you were trouble."

"I am not trouble," she scoffs. "That's insulting. There are circumstances here that are beyond my control. I've tried to leave twice, and you guys wouldn't let me. Now you want me out of here immediately. Dad's orders, right?" The words slip out, and she realizes she's made a terrible mistake.

"You were listening."

"You weren't exactly being quiet."

"Is that why you were hiding in the bathroom with my phone? You don't have a headache at all, do you?" At the look that must cross her face, he shakes his head. "You thought I didn't know? Come on, Halley. I'm not an idiot. Did you get what you were looking for?"

"I can't fake a migraine, Noah. And since we're being honest, why do you have pictures of my sister on your phone?" she retorts. It costs her, but she's feeling stronger.

"What the hell are you talking about?" His genuine confusion takes her anger down a notch. Either he's a good actor, or he really doesn't know.

"Pull up your photos. Go to your albums. There's a set of photos from 2010, I found it from your *Faces* section. You have pictures of the stranger I saw, and my sister. And she's pregnant, Noah. She was here, in Brockville, pregnant, eight *years* after she went missing. How could you lie to me like this? How could you not know? This place where you claim everyone knows everything about each other. You've known she never left all along. I'd wager Cameron does, too, and your dad. That's why you're all messing with me."

"Stay down. Don't move. Make him think you're dead."

A warning from her past? Or some sort of cosmic signal for now? Is she in more danger than she realizes?

The overwhelming emotions are unfurling in her again; she feels them building, feels the blackness of her past growing. A brain is only designed to handle so much at once. Hers is starting to unravel. Add in the migraine, the medicine, the confusion . . . She can't keep this up much longer.

Noah is staring at her with alarm. He unlocks the phone and hands it to her.

"Show me."

Breathing hard to quell the wild dread rising in her, she flicks through until she has the pictures again. Hands it back wordlessly. Watches as his face goes entirely white.

"You look like you've seen a ghost."

"I think I have. Jesus."

He sinks down onto the edge of the bed, swiping, swiping, swiping.

"Who is he, Noah? Who is the man with my sister? And why were you taking pictures of him?"

He is shaking his head and humming nervously. She realizes he's saying "No, no, no" like a scared little boy. His reaction is not helping her concern.

"Noah? Who is it?"

"Ian." His voice holds a note of terror that makes her spine tingle.

"Who is Ian?"

"He's the one we don't speak of."

He says this robotically. He's clearly been deeply shocked by the photos.

She grabs his face and points it toward hers. "Noah. Who is Ian?"

He meets her eyes, and what she sees in them she will never be able to erase. "He's my half brother. He's the oldest. He's the one who survived my father's encampment in Maine. I thought he was dead. Dad said he was dead."

"What? Survived . . . What are you talking about?"

"My dad had a group of followers who went into the woods with him, to live off the land. They all died, taken by a terrible fever. Ian survived. He was a tiny baby, came out with my dad. He was the only one. But he's been dead for years. He died when I was just a kid. My dad . . ."

The words are choked off.

"Your dad?"

"He caught him. He caught him doing things to a neighbor girl. There was a fight. My father hit him. He fell, hit his head, and died. My dad told us. He took responsibility. He killed his son and saved us from that monster. He was wrecked by it. That's when my mother took me away the first time."

Noah is shaking. The trauma of the memory is overwhelming him. She wonders what else the monster he describes did. Fathers don't kill their sons. They don't hide their sons' deaths. They certainly don't hide when women come to town and go missing.

What in the hell is this place?

"Noah. He's alive. You can see proof of that. This is from seven years ago. And those pictures are from Brockville, aren't they?"

"Yes. That's the farm. October 2010. He was just a little older than Cameron."

Watch out for the oldest, Tammy Boone had warned. Not Cameron. *Ian.*

"Who knows about Ian?"

"The people who lived here while he was alive, obviously. But I was eight when he died."

"But he's not dead," she says again. "He was in Marchburg just this week. He confronted me. He said how surprised he was I didn't recognize him. Why should I recognize him, Noah? Why should I know him?"

"I don't know. I swear it."

"Who took these pictures? These are pictures of your dead brother and my dead sister—who took them?"

His eyes are bleak, revulsion and fear and something deeper, a terror she is starting to understand. A terror that has to do with her, somehow.

"I inherited this phone. I swear to you I didn't take those pictures. There's no way I could, I was out of the country in October of 2010. I was in France."

"Then who did? Whose phone is it?"

He swallows, hard. "It was my dad's."

CHAPTER THIRTY-EIGHT

Well, well. At last, you've finally arrived at the truth. My truth. Are you surprised? You shouldn't be. You should have known from the beginning. I left you a trail to follow. I gave you everything you needed to discover who I am.

Not enough for you? Fine. Leave. Go find another story. But if you choose to stay, I'll tell you more.

Ready?

Good.

Let's get to know one another properly, shall we?

Yes, I am the eldest Brockton, the one who survived the wilderness. Oh, I know, you thought that was Cameron. But no. He came soon after we returned. My stepmother was widowed, and my father wasted no time in getting her with child. The sorrows of a man who lost everything were assuaged by the warm body of a lover who seemed not to mind the circumstance of her own husband's untimely death. Did my father kill her husband so he could have her? Did she help him? Without a doubt, though it would be hard to prove. Accidents happen in the mountains. People fall. People disappear.

Cameron and I are only ten months apart, the two of us. His mother called me the vampire child. I needed. I needed so much. At first I was sickly, and then I was voracious. I walked early. I talked early. Instead of the circumstances whence I came stunting my growth, I grew into a functional toddler much faster than anyone expected. My father swore it was the way we lived, natural, hearty, that she was nurturing me so well.

But when she had her own child, I was set aside.

No reason to feel sorry for me. I certainly don't. Feelings are not something I indulge in. I don't experience "feelings" the way you do. I have a strict moral compass, my father gave me that, but feelings? Nothing there. An empty well.

I bet Cat told you that, too. What she is and what I am are very different indeed. She tries so hard to be different. I embrace my shadows. I was made to be this. Why fight it? Indulging is so much nicer.

I have no remorse. I have no fear. Things that terrify you are as normal to me as the sun rising in the morning. I take things as I need or want them. I kill as easily as saying hello. I am darkness, but I am not dark. I am a rather pleasant fellow, actually. How else do you think I've lived for so long among you? People like me. Love me, even. They are drawn to me. Want to please me. They see my father in me, the visionary, the leader, the magnate, and they ascribe those attributes to me as well.

She did. You will, too.

Of all my brothers, I am most like my father. They call me handsome and brooding. They say I can charm the sun from the sky. Maybe that is so. I am my father's envoy to the world. I am the one who leaves and brings back the worthy to live on the land.

And the others. The ones we need to slake our thirst.

You think me mad. I understand. My story is full of contradictions. And I admit, I always wanted to be special. It was hard, with an illustrious, sought-after father, and capable brothers who had a mother who loved them better. I was alone in a household of people, the lone survivor of a fever that wiped out my father's flock. At least, that's the story the world was told. It wasn't entirely true.

Perhaps it was the fever that made me who I am.

Perhaps it was him. Many things happened in that dark time. My father would tell of it sometimes, sharing his truths, his memories. We would sit under the stars with a fire burning, and he would admit his indiscretions. The way they died, one after another. The way he couldn't help himself. He saw himself in me, and to his credit, he did try to curb my urges—our urges—for a time. He found keeping himself busy was the best trick—it allowed him to forget, for a time, what he was. What he'd done. What he needed to become whole.

He built, and built, and built, channeling his shadows into good for others. He evolved.

I couldn't do that. I could never forget how that first girl made me feel.

From the beginning, my appetites were ravenous. I had to have more. Addicts are genetically predisposed that way, correct? The difference between an alcoholic and a social drinker: from that first sip, the alcoholic is lost. They are a bottomless well. There will never be enough to satiate the urges. They will destroy everything for their drug.

In the beginning, that's how it was for me. That first taste, honey sweet, and I was lost.

But you recoil. Interesting.

Then why have you come? Why are you here, if not to discover the truth? You are shackled, just like them. You are stuck in this life, this world, this town, and you will never be free. You might escape, yes. But you will never be without me. I will live in your mind and suckle your soul and drive you utterly mad if you try to leave.

I am the only one with freedom around here. I am the only one who can escape, who can leave you—this—behind. Yes, I come back. The nature of my business draws me home again, and again, and again. It is such a convenient place to hide, when hiding is needed. Out in the world, it is so easy to pretend, to walk among the people as my father does, to make people happy. It is also just as easy to sow discord. To trample dreams, to end existences.

My father gave me such cover with those words to his family. "I killed him. He fell and hit his head. It was by my hand, and I alone will bear the responsibility."

He didn't, obviously. He hid the nasty little secret away, told the townsfolk that I was gone. He didn't tell them I'd struck out on my own.

That he made rules for me to follow and sent me, a feral wolf, out to the lambs.

Oh, he hit me that day. Beat me to within an inch of my life. Then he gave me the tools to leave. He warned me to never come back. That the world he'd built had no room for my kind of darkness.

Ironic, that. What a hypocrite. He was reacting to seeing his own darkness. I am his mirror, and the reflection was terrifying. The shadow earthquake that would cause fissures in his life's work.

He created me, clay shaped in his own image. And then he cast me aside.

Shall I tell you what happened in Maine, that dreaded fever?

He was that fever. He drained the life of every person there. Picked them off one by one. Oh, plenty died on their own—living without resources in the woods is difficult.

But the rest. He sent them into the woods . . . and followed.

Amazing the lies we can tell ourselves. Amazing the lies we tell those around us.

Certainly, he convinced himself he had changed. That he'd slaked his bloodlust. That Brockville would be his salvation.

Never trust the ones who tell you how pure their hearts, how good their intentions. They insist they are servants to the world. There are lies in their words. They say they are servants to the greater good? They are servants to their own urges alone.

Forgive me. I've gotten off track.

When my father forced me to leave, that was the moment. My moment. I died, and I was reborn.

Being cast out of my family, sent into that abyss alone, gave me the freedom to become the monster I am. And when I returned, when the mirror image of his darkest soul appeared, he caved. Of course he did. Brought me back to life, back to the fold. No one could know, naturally. We made a deal. I stayed in the shadows. I brought him his dessert. Bring, still.

What? You want to know where we first met?

In the wilderness camp, of course. The day she came, I was entranced. She was so young. Delectable. Broken, and so frightened. Arguing with those ridiculous voices. She did not belong in the woods, she belonged in a straitjacket. But she was wily, my little kitten cat. Nine lives and then some.

It was her own fault for coming back. I knew better than to hunt at home, yes. Those rules were inviolate. I broke them once and swore to never do it again.

But it was my Cat. I made her. She was mine. She came back to me. Maybe she thought she could end me. What a mistake.

Now, if you'll excuse me, I have work to do.

Oh, stop already. Don't cry. I know it's dark. The darkest, emptiest place you will ever experience. The deprivation of senses will drive you mad if you're not careful. That blackness will overwhelm you and your mind will shatter. It's not a pleasant thing to experience. I should know.

Now, on with the show.

Do try to hold yourself together.

CHAPTER THIRTY-NINE

HALLEY

"We have to leave." Noah bounds from the room, gathering things in his arms. "We have to leave now."

"Is this why Cameron was telling you to get rid of me?" Halley asks. His movement is making her dizzy. "Does he know about Ian?"

"He must. Or at least he suspects. Shit. Seriously, we need to go. I can't stay here. Not knowing he's alive. Not knowing he might be here."

He sounds like a child, panicked by a nightmare. Halley doesn't know how to help him; she is as deeply afraid as she has ever been.

"What did he do to you?"

"You don't want to know. My brother was cruel, and he was mentally ill. My father sent him off to a camp to straighten him out, but it only made him worse. Please, Halley. We need to leave."

Bells are ringing. Her sister was sent to a wilderness camp to work on her behavioral issues, too.

"You really don't remember me, do you?"

Why? Why should she know him?

"Okay, yes. We'll go to Nashville. We'll figure it out from there."

Noah throws her a grateful glance, then stops, halting dead. The meager color in his face drains, and his eyes go wild. He takes three steps back.

"Where do you think you'll get to, little brother? Do you think you can go anywhere without me finding you?"

She whirls, and a man stands between them and the front door of the cottage.

It is the stranger from Marchburg. The man from the pictures. Ian. His words are slow and measured and crawl on her skin like ants on honey. She is nearly frozen in place.

He moves sinuously into the living room. She is reminded of a great snake slithering through the grass. Has he been here all along? When did he get in? How?

Worse, he is holding Halley's gun.

"Come with me," he says to her, pleasantly, as if inviting her for a picnic.

"No!" Noah roars. "Halley, run!"

He surges forward, and Ian pulls the trigger. It is so sudden. Noah collapses as if he's a folding table, straight down in a heap, and stays there.

Before she can react, Ian has her by the arm and is dragging her out of the door. She starts to scream, but he yanks her to a halt and puts a hand over her mouth. The madness in his eyes is enough to rob her of her voice anyway.

"Do that and I might as well just put a bullet in your chest, too."

Better death than whatever horribleness this man is planning for her. She looks over his shoulder at Noah. Blood is spreading beneath him.

"He needs help or he'll bleed out," she manages. "He'll die."

"Like I care. Sniveling little twit. Besides, *you* killed him."

"What are you talking about?"

"Your prints on the gun, my sweet." He waves it in front of her. He's wearing gloves. "Your Jeep found in Nashville. You shot him, you ran.

You disappeared into the fabric of the universe, with law enforcement on your tail."

"No one would believe I could do such a thing. My Jeep is here."

"Not anymore. A little birdie did me a favor."

"This is insane. This isn't happening." She has conjured this fever dream. It is the migraine. None of this is real. Please. Please let it be her imagination.

"Your inner monologue aloud is fascinating." The sarcasm in his voice, the dismissive tone, the ease with which he murdered his brother, without blinking an eye, makes the hair stand up on the back of her neck. His hand is bruising her arm. The pain is very, very real. "It is happening, because I've made it so. You were with every single victim of this little spree. You were unstable. You were upset. Your life was falling apart. You went a little mad, killed a few people, and went on the lam. It's not a stretch at all, considering."

"You're sick. This isn't going to work."

"Really? Watch."

He tightens the grip on her arm and drags her out to the garden shed. There is a plank in the floorboard pulled up, and she sees stairs into the darkness below. Noah said something about tunnels.

"No, no, I won't! Hel—"

Her shouts are cut off. She sees the gun coming at her, then she sees nothing else.

Halley wakes in darkness.

It is velvet and alive, wrapping her in a claustrophobic embrace so intense she has to fight back a scream. She feels her face; she is not wearing a blindfold. She can't see her hands.

She looks everywhere, sees nothing.

The migraines sometimes strip her of sight, but she feels only the echo of that previous pain. No, there is a lump on the side of her head, crusted blood in her hair. She remembers the gun coming toward her face. He hit her so hard she's gone blind.

"Help!" she bellows, and the word is flat. There is no reverberation, it dies in the thin air. She listens frantically, but the only sound is internal. Her heart, her blood, rushing through the subclavian artery. She can hear its whoosh as clearly as if she has a stethoscope planted against her neck. She moves and her bones creak. Her ears are crackling—the tinnitus she has grown so accustomed to living in the city is like the remnants of a sharp bell pealing again and again.

She is lying down. She sits up and there is still nothing. Nothing but her own body's internal noise. It is cacophonous; she must breathe to allow herself to adjust.

What is happening? Where am I?

"Hello? Help!" Her voice is strange. She doesn't sound at all like herself. Her voice is higher pitched than normal.

She uses her hands to feel around. Whatever she is lying on feels like fine mesh.

She crawls to her left and is met with a sharp triangle of what feels like foam, rows of it, one after the other. To her right, the same. There is not much room to move. She stands up, reaching her arms to what she thinks must be the ceiling, and vertigo swamps her. There is no horizon, nothing to latch on to, nothing to keep her upright. The darkness is so complete, the absence of sound so profound, she has to think this is how the blind and deaf must feel. She collapses back to the mesh. She is now among their ranks. At least with that, she can lie down again.

Her thoughts are jumbled, spinning. Memories of the past week come fast and hard. There is still no light, no sound, no movement. She is buried alive and her senses are gone.

Hysteria seizes her. Tears pour from her eyes. Rational thought is impossible. Her neurons fire, and in the absence of all stimuli and the overwhelming terror of this dark place, something breaks inside her head. She is trapped there, inside her own mind, and can't escape. She has lost her grip on reality. The darkness has eaten her soul.

This is what going insane feels like. She shrieks, wailing, again and again and again, and knows deep inside no one can hear her. The crack inside her sanity is audible to her alone.

She is back in the house she grew up in.
She is six years old.
Her sister is fighting with her mother.
Screaming, crying.
There is a man.
His back is to her.
There is a glint in his hand.
He charges forward.
Her sister screams.
The knife connects.
Her mother falls.
The white carpet, red.
The wail building from deep inside her.
She runs, falls at her mother's side.
Blank eyes, light leaving.
Mouth moving. A harsh whisper.
"Run, Halley Bear. Run."
She runs.
He follows.
Cat cries out.
He ignores the protest.
She knows. She has to die.
He catches her by the foot.
Swings her around.
Her head hits the mantel.
Pain. So much pain.
Red. Red. Red.
Black.
Hands on her shoulders.

"Shh. Thank God. Stay down. Don't move. Make him think you're dead."

I am dead.

I am dead.

I am dead.

Blackness, again.

CHAPTER FORTY

Little by little, she starts coming back to herself.

She is not dead.

She is alive.

I am alive.

And I must live.

It doesn't matter if I have my eyes open or closed, I can sense the smile on the face of the man in the corner.

He is a shadow, and he is talking—talking, talking, incessantly—telling me all the things I always wanted to understand, and much I don't want to know. His voice will not stop. It never has. I can't listen, but I must. I am his confessor, his priest, his savior. His inamorata. I must dole out benediction; he is desperate for it.

"Where am I?" I manage.

"Oh, now you want to talk to me?"

The voice halts. That constant, incessant patter that I've lived with for so long is coming from *outside* my head.

Outside. Which means . . . it's real.

Like I could be dead and still talking to you?

This voice is internal, but the other is external, I'm sure of it. But they are the same. It has lived inside of me for so long hearing it aloud is baffling. Surely I am hallucinating. It wouldn't be the first time. Considering I am in darkness, it's even more likely.

"Yes. Please. Where am I?"

"In Brockville."

Brockville. I remember, barely. The voice was castigating me. I ducked off onto a small trail to clear my head. But before . . . I cast my mind back. I was chatting with a man. He had a sweet smile and kind eyes. He offered to make me dinner.

"Noah? Is that you?"

"Wow, little brother made quite an impression on you. Not bad for a man holding a trout."

Noah is not this man. Not this monster.

Fighting with my own brain is frustrating. Someone followed me into the woods. I ran, crashing through the brush, but he was faster. Stronger. He caught me. He dragged me. I fought, I screamed; he laughed.

"Who are you?"

"Oh, my sweet kitty cat. I can't believe you have to ask me that."

I am filled with horror. This is my nightmare come alive. Every night terror, every bad dream, every sense of fear, of something horrifying scuttling along the baseboards, about to rise up and devour me, is here. Now. In this room. This is no longer a convoluted fantasy. This is real.

"Ian?"

The lights go on, and I am blinded. "Hello, sweetheart. Long time no see."

It takes me a moment to adjust. I am in a charcoal room. Spiky triangles stick out from the walls, ceiling, and floor like hungry maws. It's like being inside a shark's jaws, looking out into the endless sea. My head spins.

"What is this place?"

"This? Dad's anechoic chamber. He likes to come in here and meditate without any sort of sound. Or sensation. Did you know when the door is closed this room registers minus nine-point-four decibels? It is beyond pure silence. It is a void. Drives you a little mad if you're not careful."

"Why am I here? Why are *you* here?"

"You came to see me. I figured I'd repay the favor."

"What are you talking about?"

"Brockville. The writers' retreat? Didn't think I hit you hard enough to remove your memories, darling."

"Don't call me that," I snarl.

I told you not to do it. Do you ever listen to me? No.

I moan, realizing the awful truth. The only voice I've not been able to exorcise is Ian's. It's always been Ian's. Since I met him in that dark forest and he decided I was going to be his, that he would heal me, cure me, love me—and then betrayed me. He's been in my head, mocking me, for years.

Yes, I wanted in to the Brockville Writers' Retreat because I want to be a writer. But the voice knows there was a deeper reason. I needed to be near where we met. I needed to understand why he made me into the creature I am. I needed to understand why I'd listened to him, all those years ago. Why I was so weak. To prove to myself it wasn't just a bad dream. And now, I am going to find out.

I searched for him for so long.

I finally found him. My plan, though, has backfired.

He has found me.

He stands, moving toward me, the smile affixed to his face. The face of a monster.

PART THREE

He who fights with monsters should look
to it that he himself does not become a
monster. And if you gaze long into an
abyss, the abyss also gazes into you.
—Friedrich Nietzsche

CHAPTER FORTY-ONE
THEO

Nashville, Tennessee
One Week Later

Theodore Donovan steers his rental through the entrance of the Donelson Corporate Centre. It doesn't look like much. The Metro Nashville Police brass have quarters here while their new building is being designed and built, and Theo is meeting with the head of the specialized investigative support group, who, as it happens, worked the Susannah Handon murder scene twenty-eight years ago. He counts himself lucky to have found an active employee who was a part of the case. Cops usually burn out after their twenty years on the job. Burn out or get moved up. This guy is the latter.

Theo's gut is twisted with knots. Halley's been on the run for a week now. According to the sheriff in Brockton, she is now the primary suspect in the murder of a woman in Brockville, Tammy Boone, as well as responsible for the near death of the sheriff's brother, with whom she'd been holed up. The sheriff made it clear something was going on between them, and the mere thought makes Theo's blood pressure spike. The primal fury at the idea of his wife with another man is hard to tamp down. But it's his fault, too. He's barely touched her in months. Too busy. Too angry. Too much pressure. She's always been a physical creature. It's his own damn fault she went looking for comfort elsewhere.

Still, he didn't realize she was that far out of the marriage already. Of course, he hasn't wanted to face that things have been over between them for a while now. Guess she needed to make a clean break of it.

But the idea of someone else loving her, fingering that crazy streak of white in her otherwise dark hair, listening to her breathy snores . . . That he's lost her makes him sick. That she's accused of murder and a number of other felonies doesn't help. She doesn't want him, she's made that clear, but he can't let this lie. He has to find her, and he has all the skills and power to do so.

He fumbles an antacid pill into his mouth and dry swallows it. He is low on sleep, low on patience, and high on frustration. Not the best formula for his system.

He hasn't heard from Halley since the text with the photos telling him she was heading to Nashville a week ago. When she didn't answer his texts, he got worried. When the sheriff of Brockville tracked him down and told him Halley had shot his brother Noah, he was in disbelief. When her Jeep showed up in Nashville, but with no trace of her anywhere near it, Theo took a week's personal leave, got Charlie settled at the neighbor's, and got on a plane. None of this makes sense, but he knows his wife. He doesn't think her capable of these crimes. He's worried about her. She might have had a break, yes. That's what the Brockville sheriff wants him to believe. That she was unstable. Upset. Irrational.

But he's inclined to believe something else could be going on.

Which is why he's here. He's going to get to the bottom of this. He's going back to the beginning.

Theo badges the girl at the front desk. "I have an appointment with Sergeant David Lemke."

The woman nods and presses two buttons on her phone. "An ATF agent is here for you. Okay, thanks." Then to Theo, "Have a seat over there. He'll come get you."

He grabs some pine. A door opens a few minutes later, and an older man with graying hair and beard waves him over. "Lemke." He sticks out a hand. "You're Donovan?"

"I am. Thanks for making the time."

He follows Lemke through an institutional labyrinth. The hallways are lined with boxes.

"Temporary digs," he explains. "We've been moving around facilities. Total shit show. They tore down our old place before the new one was built, so we decentralized most of the divisions of HQ, and only the brass and some admins are here."

"Been there. Moving desks is a pain."

Lemke leads him to a generic interior room with glass walls on three sides that looks like something straight out of *The Office*, only with the requisite photos of the chief of police, the governor of Tennessee, and the president of the United States hanging on the one solid wall. An American flag stands sentry in the corner. The desk is clear of detritus, but a thick file sits in its center.

"Have a seat. Your wife's in quite a bit of trouble."

Theo nods. "That she is. But like I said on the phone, I can't see her for this. Attempted murder is not her style."

"But it is her gun, with her prints on it, and on the bullets, according to the forensics. They dug the slug out of Noah Brockton, and the ballistics are solid. No questions there. That's why they put out the warrant for her."

"You've been doing this long enough to know nothing is a fait accompli. I know Halley. She could no sooner shoot an innocent man than she could hurt an animal."

"Then why have the gun in the first place?"

"You know the answer. Protection. Someone was killing people connected to her mother's case, and she wanted to be able to defend herself."

"Then this isn't a stretch at all. What if Noah Brockton isn't so innocent?" Lemke asks. "What if he is the killer? What if he attacked her? She shot him, panicked, and ran?"

"More likely, but I'm still not convinced. We won't know for sure until we find her, or he wakes up. Take a look at this," Theo says. He hands over his phone. "She texted me from Brockton's phone minutes before she went dark. Wanted me to run the faces. Said this was the killer. I got a match to the woman, she was in the juvenile system. That's Catriona Handon. Halley's older half sister. It's the other one, though, I can't land on. He's tied up in this. Halley was convinced that he's the killer, and I'm inclined to agree. I talked with Baird Early in Marchburg, sent him these pics, and he matched this guy up to a video feed he has in Marchburg. That's where two women were killed."

"And let me guess. Noah Brockton was in Brockville the whole time."

"According to one hell of a lot of witnesses, yes. This man, though, wasn't. I'm hoping you can help me ID him."

"That's why you wanted the Handon murder file? It was twenty-eight years ago. We don't have much in the way of visuals. Just a few shots. Lost the video years ago. The floods. All that's really left is up here." He taps his temple.

"Anything could help. I've seen parts of the file—autopsy report, the crime scene stills, but if I could look through the whole thing . . ."

Lemke watches Theo. "You really don't think she did this."

"I don't."

"Okay. Let's play this your way." Lemke sits. "The Handon murder was pretty awful. We don't have a lot of home invasions with women being stabbed here. Especially back in the late eighties. I was new to plain clothes, just moved to violent crimes. Wasn't my first case, but it was close to it. It helped that the daughter copped to the murder. We found her at the bus station three days after, completely fucked up. I'm talking she looked like she'd been run over by a bus. She was meek. Didn't fight, came into custody like she was relieved. That happens, obviously. It's hard to fight the energy of a homicide investigation, and we were on it hard."

"What did she say happened?"

"Mom wanted to send her back to a wilderness camp she'd gone to. She'd had a bad time of it there and didn't want to go. They argued, she got the knife, she stabbed her. Beat her little sister in the head and ran. Public defender managed to get her declared unfit to stand trial because she had some deep psychiatric problems, so she pled out, took a sentence to the juvenile psychiatric facility at Central State." He stops. "That's all in the file. I'm sure you've read it."

"I have. So has Halley. She was told that her mom and sister died in a car accident, and that's where her head injury came from. She was there but didn't remember any of it."

"The kid took a pretty good bang on the head. And the scene was a bloody mess. Disorganized killer, opportunistic crime. All fit with the girl's confession."

Theo senses a *but* coming. He stays quiet and is rewarded.

"There was always something that struck me as off about the whole thing."

"What's that?"

"There was a huge dent in the wood column holding up the mantel, with blood and hair. Hair matched the kid sister. So that was inconsistent with Handon's testimony that she hit her in the head when she was on the ground. And the mom was stabbed by someone right handed. No doubt about it. But Catriona Handon is left handed."

"Opportunistic situation, maybe? She had the knife in her right hand."

"Sure. That's what she said when we questioned her about it. Well, not exactly, she said she didn't remember what hand the knife was in. Hardly enough to make us look twice. She was singing like a songbird. It was open and shut."

"And if it wasn't?"

Lemke raises a brow. "What, you think someone else was there?"

"I don't know, man. This all feels wonky to me. Like you said, it was almost thirty years ago. She did her time, she integrated back into society. Then she disappeared, and according to Baird Early in Marchburg, Virginia, where two of the murders took place, her blood is in CODIS at a bunch of crime scenes. Has she been murdering her way around the country? I don't know. Maybe she is the one who shot Noah Brockton. Maybe she's hurt Halley."

"That's a big maybe, friend. But I'm listening."

Theo pulls out his notebook. "Catriona Handon went missing fifteen years ago after going to Brockville. I did some digging about the town. Another woman who was accepted into the famed writers' retreat went missing, too."

"That's interesting."

"It's an interesting place. Very insular. Run by Miles Brockton, you ever heard of him?"

"Should I have?"

"They made a movie about him years ago, how he went into the wilderness alone for years and came back out this mindfulness guru. Anyway, we're getting too far away from why I'm here. I'd appreciate it if you could run the picture through your databases, and if you could show me the cameras of Halley abandoning the Jeep? I want to see her state of mind for myself."

Lemke frowns. "There were no cameras near where the Jeep was ditched."

"What about traffic cams coming into town? Do you have any toll roads?"

"No tolls. We did a quick look around the area where we found the Jeep but didn't see anything."

"Would you be willing to look again, and expand it? She had to get to the spot—where was the Jeep found?"

"Off of 440, parking lot of Elmington Park. West End. By the school."

"West End School?"

"Yeah."

"Isn't that where Catriona Handon was going to school at the time of the murder?"

Lemke thumbs open the file. "Damn, you're right. She did. How the hell did I miss that?"

"I assume you haven't been poring over this file the way I have."

"Nice of you to say. Shit. Okay. Let me make a call."

He whips his cell from his pocket. Hits a number. "Lincoln Ross, please." To Theo, "Linc's the best computer guy on the force. Works under a specialized group run by Lieutenant Taylor Jackson, but he's always happy to do a favor. Let me turn him loose on this. If there's something to find, he'll get it."

An hour later, a well-dressed man with a gap-toothed smile shows up with a laptop in his hand. Theo feels a pang. He looks like Lenny Kravitz. Halley loves Lenny Kravitz.

They shake hands, and Ross puts the laptop on the desk.

"All right, we got the Jeep coming into town on 40. Picked it up out by the airport heading west. Once I had a date and time, I was able to triangulate its path. Moves off of 40 to 440, takes the West End exit, and then we lose it. But there's a TDOT camera just before that exit, and I was able to get into the system and run it back a week. There is one person in the Jeep. And damn if your instincts aren't right on, sir. Face ID matches it to Catriona Handon."

Theo doesn't know if he's happy about this, or even more upset. Catriona Handon is alive and well.

"All right. So she's driving Halley's car. Where does she go once she ditches it?"

"We've got her in a silver Camry heading back east on 40. In the passenger seat. No idea who's driving, but it's another woman. I'm running her face but nothing's popped yet." Ross pauses. "It is not Halley. I'm sorry."

They all know what this means. Theo forces away the despair that's building. He was right about Halley. She's in serious trouble, or worse. *Stay focused, man. You gotta find her.*

"All right. So her sister drives her car to Nashville and ditches it. Any chance you got plates on the Camry?"

Ross smiles. "I wouldn't be doing my job if I didn't. Got enough to run a comparison. The Camry is registered to a Cathy Esworthy. And guess where she lives?"

"Brockville?" Theo says hopefully.

"Nailed it."

Lemke rubs his jaw. "So Catriona Handon is still in Brockville. Where she went missing fifteen years ago?"

"Catriona Handon *was* in Brockville. At least long enough to get Halley's keys and car. We need a BOLO for Cathy Esworthy, stat. Is she in the system?"

Ross pulls up her driver's license. A pleasant woman stares back at them. "I gotta say the driver is much younger than this woman. She's clean, too. Not even a traffic ticket. Her husband's an upstanding businessman as well, has a bunch of Porsche dealerships all over the South."

"But his wife has a Camry?"

"Third car registered to them at the Brockville address. They also have a 2017 Cayenne and a mint 1987 944. Red. The Camry—maybe it's a kid's car? I wouldn't want my son driving a Porsche until he's off my insurance." Laughs, and Theo's stomach does a strange dance. He won't have a son. He'll never be able to make a joke like that. Especially now that Halley's left him. That was always her dream. A dream he refused to help make come true. A dream he's willing to reconsider if she'd just fucking come home.

He pushes the thought aside.

"I'm calling Sheriff Brockton," he says. "If Esworthy lives there, he'll know about the car."

Lemke's phone rings, and as he listens, he frowns. "All right. I'll come get her." He hangs up. "There's a woman named Donnata Kade in the lobby. Says she has information about the murders in Marchburg."

CHAPTER FORTY-TWO

Donnata Kade is worse for wear. That's an uncharitable thought, Theo knows it, but she looks like she hasn't slept in weeks. There are dark rings under her very large eyes; her short graying hair is unwashed and mussed; there is a stain on her shirt. When he does a quick, discreet search on the name, the first headline is damning. She is former FBI, emphasis on the *former*. Something about that triggers a memory, maybe a piece in the *Washington Post* about her fall from grace, but he doesn't have time to access it before she starts to speak.

Her words are fast and sentences staccato like she's hopped up on caffeine, or cocaine, spilling out so quickly he wonders if she's afraid they will shut her up before she can get them all out.

But he is chilled to the core by her accusations.

"You've probably already looked me up. They all think I'm crazy, but I'm not. I swear to you I'm not. I've been following a killer across multiple states for years. He leaves almost no evidence. The cases are all unsolved. Sometimes there's no body, either; the woman just disappears. He's tied to Brockville, Tennessee. I know he is. I lived there once, and saw all sorts of things. Terrible things. And I spotted him in Marchburg the night Kathryn Star was murdered. He was doing something to Halley James's Jeep."

Lemke interrupts her. "Okay, okay, slow down."

"You don't understand. This is huge, and no one believes me. But now there's proof."

"Proof?" Theo asks. "What sort of proof."

"He took your wife. What more proof do you need?"

"You know this how? Did you witness the crime?"

"No. But how else did her Jeep get to Nashville? He took her and had one of his women drive it here. He collects them. He's a collector. Terrifying psychological profile."

Theo looks over at Lincoln Ross, who is watching Kade with interest. "Where did you get that information? About her Jeep?"

"I'm right, aren't I? This is his MO. The women's cars are always found somewhere else. It took me forever to figure out that he has someone working with him. It's much easier to get away with murder and kidnapping with a helper."

"A woman is helping him?" Theo doesn't offer Catriona's name. Her DNA at the crime scenes has just been explained in the most terrible way.

"Yes."

"I admit, that's a compelling story. I'm curious, though. Why are you here, now?"

"Because I thought you might want to know how to get your wife back."

"So you followed me here?"

She huffs, throwing her arms in the air and her head back. Her actions are overly animated. "I knew you wouldn't believe me. I knew you'd be just like the rest of them. Fine, I'll see myself out. I will find him. I will find Halley. She has to be somewhere close to the head of it all. I've been watching. They think they're so careful, but I know what they're doing."

"Wait," Theo says, trying to keep this on point. The woman is all over the place. "I didn't say I don't believe you. You said she's near the head of it all. The head of what?"

"The cult. Miles Brockton is running a cult."

"A cult. In Brockville?"

"Yes. There are tepees in the woods with all sorts of dark things inside. Witchcraft and devil worship. They burn things in the night and sacrifice their children at his whims. They will do anything he bids them to do. And he has an isolation chamber. You can see the purchase order here." She thrusts papers at them. Her eyes are gleaming with a fervor that Theo recognizes as madness. His last hopes for Halley's safe return are starting to fade away.

"Are you saying it's some sort of religious cult? Preppers? What sort of message is he preaching?" He can't help himself. Theo immediately thinks about Waco and Ruby Ridge. Kade is still talking.

"Not religion. Sex. It's all for sex. They are slaves. There are tunnels. They hide there. They wait for their prey to go mad. He built it, and he puts women in it to torture them. And when they come out they will do anything to avoid being put back in again."

Lemke isn't buying it. "How do you know this? Have you been in the tunnels? Do you know where they originate?"

"No. If I had, I would have already been down there to rescue the women."

"Ma'am—"

"Special Agent Kade," she hisses.

Theo shoots Lemke a look. *Go gently, man,* he thinks. *She's the only lead we have.*

"Agent Kade, will you look at a picture for me?" Theo asks.

"Of course."

He shows her the photo Halley texted. Her reaction is remarkable. She starts to shake, and tears form in her eyes.

"That's him. That's the devil. He's the one I've been following. Where was this taken? That looks like the Farm at Brockville."

"Possibly. Who is he?"

"Miles's eldest son. His name is Ian Brockton."

Saying the name aloud seems to break something in her, and everything becomes unintelligible gibberish. Devils and sacrifices and sex slaves, like she's having a waking fever dream. A full-blown meltdown.

Lemke is trying to talk to Kade, reason with her, but she's rambling now, off on a terrifying tangent of words only she can truly understand. Even if there's a grain of truth in her accusations, they seem internally generated. Fantastical. Lemke finally shrugs and escorts her from the room.

Theo looks at the papers she thrust into his hand. The top page is a sketch of triangles. All four edges of the paper are covered in intricate three-dimensional triangles that reach into a darkened room.

He realizes this space must exist in her head and feels sorry for her. She seems like a very disturbed woman. But it's been his experience that for every ounce of madness consuming a person, there is a tiny bit of the truth. Of reality. And he wants desperately to believe she is right. That Brockville is some sort of crazy cult and Halley is still there. It's a stretch, but he has nothing else to go on.

"Who the hell is this Ian Brockton?" Theo asks Ross, who types like his life depends on it.

"A ghost," Ross says. "Supposedly died back in 1989. Around the same time as the Handon murder, actually. A month or so before. Hey, can I see that?"

Theo holds out the page. Ross frowns at it.

"That looks like an anechoic chamber. They use them to test jet engines to make them less noisy."

"An annie-what?"

"Anechoic. Without echo. The ultimate sensory deprivation." He pulls his laptop over, starts typing. "There aren't a ton of them, they're very expensive to build. There's one at Orfield Laboratories in Minneapolis rated as the world's quietest room. Reporters go to do stories, and there are YouTube videos of them hallucinating in the absence of sound and sensory details. Around here, the music studios all have variations of this. They have to buy specialized foam to line the walls to help absorb sound for recordings. Kade said there was a purchase order?"

Theo flips the page. The paper is soft and old. It is a bill from a place called Newson's Electronics in Waverley, Tennessee, for a load of ferrite tiles to be delivered to Brockville. It is dated November 1980.

Ross reads it and whistles. "Those tiles are military grade. And the company that sold them . . . We had a case recently down in that area, woman who went missing. There's a military supplier down there, and if I remember correctly, Newson's is one of the fronts. Those tiles aren't something you can just waltz into a store and buy."

"What the hell? What would someone in Brockville be doing getting military-grade matériel delivered?"

"Well, it could be they're a private facility and off the radar. Happens a lot, there are places all over the country that are quietly government run, or at least contractors. Could be Brockville is one. It's not terribly far from Oak Ridge, Tennessee, which is a black site."

"I mean, I know that. But a bill of lading from 1980 hardly proves there's some sort of sex trafficking now."

"I agree. She was crazier than a bedbug."

"Look up Brockville and see if they have this anechoic chamber she claims they have."

Ross taps away, his eyes skimming the screen. "Not exactly. Let me just run a quick search . . ." His fingers fly over the keyboard. "Okay, this could be something. Bjorn Lingham, who is tied to Harvard's electroacoustic lab, is on the board of Brockville Township. He has a vacation home there."

"You've lost me."

"He's a scientist. Specializes in cutting-edge acoustics. He worked on the anechoic chamber at Harvard. Then he moved to grid management for Con Ed, working on ways to make the audible electronic exhaust less impactful to the flora and fauna around the plants. Now he's big into clean energy, all that. I can buy him being on the Brockville Township board. According to their website, Brockville is one of the highest-rated biophilic communities in the world."

Theo shakes his head. "Dude, that's not a lot to go on. Nor does it explain Halley's Jeep being dropped here in Nashville, and her text to me with the photo, nor her running and going missing for a week. And Kade is following me around now, wanting me to investigate a cult. I don't get it."

Ross throws Theo a gap-toothed grin. "I agree, it doesn't make a lotta sense. But I can keep digging. There's something here. Kade might be nuts, but she also might be onto something." He taps his lips thoughtfully. "Using sensory deprivation is a pretty effective deterrent. White-room torture, all that."

Lemke comes back into the office, blowing out a breath. "Sorry about that. She left of her own accord. I thought I was going to have to get someone to take her to Vanderbilt's psych unit."

Ross looks up from his screen. "She might not be totally loopy. We did find some sketchy evidence that there might be an anechoic chamber at Brockville. And there are a few influential people on the board."

"I still don't know what that means," Theo says. "Do you actually think Miles Brockton has some sort of weird nonsensory cult hidden away in Brockville?"

"Who knows?" Ross says. "Rich, famous, insular people can get into all sorts of bizarre things. Ask me how I know. You're right, though. It's a rabbit hole. I'll play with it later."

There's a ding from his computer. He taps for a few seconds. "Well, that's interesting. Got a hit on the driver of the Camry."

"Who is it?"

"Name is Heather O'Connor. Five-seven, Caucasian female, brown on brown. Went missing three years ago from San Diego. Shop owner, owned a bookstore and café. Twenty-eight years old. Left a kid and a husband. Well, they're going to be happy to hear she's alive. How the hell did she get from San Diego to Tennessee?"

"Trafficking?" Lemke suggests.

"Maybe. A little old for it, but anything's possible."

"If Kade's right and he's running a cult, maybe she left willingly. Maybe she was following him online and finally decided to join up in person. Who the hell is this Miles Brockton guy anyway?"

Ross reads Brockton's bio from the Brockville website. "So this guy marched off into the wilderness twice? And learned so much about living off the land he made a town that was self-sustaining?"

"And named it after himself," Lemke points out. "Raging ego, if you ask me."

"I admit it's the right sort of mentality for a cult leader, but if this place is so world renowned, why hasn't it come across our radar before now?"

"Darkness hides in unlikely places," Theo says.

They toss around some more ideas. Theo's frustration is rising. None of this is helping him find Halley.

"I have to go back to Brockville. Whatever is happening with Halley, it stems from there. I'm not convinced now that she ever left. And if there's a chance they're trafficking, we have cause to tear that place apart."

"I don't disagree," Lemke says. "We'll keep in touch if there is anything new. Sorry we didn't find her, but we'll keep looking here."

"Hey, you did great helping ID the drivers. Thank you. You should loop in Baird Early in Marchburg. He has some CODIS data that you can plug into your machine there. Maybe you can find some more missing or murdered people with ties to Brockville."

"I'll do that." Ross shakes his hand; Lemke follows suit. "Good to meet you. I'll shoot you more info as we get it."

Theo looks at his watch. "I have a four-and-a-half-hour drive ahead of me. See if you can't find me enough to get my team into Brockville with a search warrant. Anything, okay? Anything at all."

Ross's eyes gleam with the challenge. "You got it."

"What if we can't get anything?" Lemke asks.

Theo shrugs. "Then I'll go in myself."

CHAPTER FORTY-THREE

HALLEY

When Halley was little, her dad used to massage her head when she had a bad headache. She was too young for the heavy-duty painkillers that would help alleviate the migraines, so they went for old-fashioned cures. Cool cloths, dark rooms, gentle massage. It helped; it always did.

She is relieved that he is stroking her hair and running his fingers lightly around her temples now. Her head is in his lap, and her eyes are screwed shut against the pain.

"Relax," her dad says. "You're okay. You're going to be just fine."

His voice is odd and thick. His hands feel bigger than normal. Stronger. They are pressing too hard. She shifts. "That hurts."

The pressure doesn't let up.

"Daddy, stop. You're hurting me."

The pressure releases, and she breathes a huge sigh of relief. "It's a bad one. I can't see anything."

He is running the lock of white hair through his fingers, tugging on it uncomfortably. "Dad, seriously, stop."

"So beautiful." The voice croons to her. "I made this. I got inside you and left my mark on you. I've been with you all this time. And you still don't remember me. I'm wounded."

Not her father.

She tenses, realizing she is tied down. There is nowhere to go. It is dark, pitch black.

Keep your head. Don't panic. Don't freak out.

"Who are you? Why should I know you?"

"Oh, Halley Bear. The most pivotal moment of your life. Think back. Think."

And as he says it, the memories come back.

Ian. Her sister's boyfriend. The boy Cat met at camp. The one their parents fought with her about, over and over. Warning her he was trouble. Forbidding her to see him. Cat was in love, though. She wasn't about to stop seeing the dark and dangerous young man she'd met. Who she talked to constantly. Who followed her home.

Who killed Halley's mother.

"Run, Halley Bear. Run."

"Stay down. Don't move. Make him think you're dead."

The memory speeds up, taking shape, the black darkness shifting, softening, becoming a vapor, the fog of all the years fighting it dispersing to allow Halley a clear view to her past.

She is in Nashville. She is six years old. There is a stranger in the house.

Her sister's boyfriend Ian has come.

Is that fear in Catriona's eyes? Is that laughter Halley hears? They are fighting, arguing. Cat is panicking, pleading, and he just laughs at her. His voice is mocking and sharp.

"You said you wanted to be free of them. Now you will be. We'll wait for your father to get home, and he can join your mother and that brat of a little sister, and you will not be tied to this ridiculous family who hates you anymore."

"You killed her. You killed them both."

"I did you a favor. One you wanted me to do."

"I didn't want them dead, Ian. I just wanted—"

"You said you wished they'd just die. And now they have. Your wish is my command, princess."

"This isn't right. Ian, this is not what I wanted."

His voice, dark and raw. "You most certainly did. You wanted this. You did this, Catriona." The hand holding the knife shifts. It is smaller, more delicate. The nails bitten and painted black. The edge of the knife is red. The rabbit's throat is cut. "If we're caught, you will tell them you did this. Am I clear?"

"But I didn't do it."

A thwack, and a cry of pain, and Halley, who's never been hit or spanked, has no trouble realizing her sister has been punched. She wants to surge up, scream, pummel, rend him limb from limb, but she can't. Cat told her to stay down. To pretend she is dead. So she is dead. Inside her little brain is a small box, and she climbs inside. Pulls the doors closed. And sits in the darkness, waiting for him to leave. A darkness so complete she is safe.

He never left. And now he's here again.

"You killed my mother," Halley says flatly.

"Cat killed your mother. She admitted that."

"Because you threatened her. You hit her. You were the one who did it. Where the hell am I? What day is it? Fucking tell me what's happening!" Halley shrieks this last, and he laughs that awful, empty laugh.

"Let's see if I can help explain. You, much to my delight, finally stuck your lovely nose into your mother's case. My father has a flag on it, naturally, because we can't have people like you digging around in our world. One of his law enforcement pals warned him, and he sent me immediately to deal with things. So convenient that you were mere hours away. So yes, I've simply been removing the . . . impediments as they arise. It's what I do. Someone has to protect us."

Impediments. *Kater. Dr. Chowdhury. Tammy. Me.*

He shifts closer. He is holding her in the dark like a spider about to suck dry an insect that's blundered into its web.

"When I saw you, though . . ." He sighs, and her entire body flinches. "My lucky day."

"I won't tell. Just let me go." She tries to pull away, but he holds her tighter. His voice grows deeper.

"Now, now. You are mine. Time has no meaning for you anymore. It is whatever day, whatever time, whatever month, year, century I say it is. I am your sun, your moon, and your stars. The breath in your lungs. The blood in your veins. I am your sight, your sound, your sensation. I am your universe."

A large hand is traveling up her body, and she is covered in horrid chills.

"You are nothing," he whispers. "You belong to me now."

A sharp prick in her elbow, and the suffocating darkness envelops her again.

Time doesn't exist in the dark.

The absence of senses creates a disequilibrium.

Halley is living inside the blackness that she created. Her defense mechanism to protect herself. All these years, when she's thought of her mother's death, of the accident that shaped her life, all she's been able to muster is darkness. Blackness. Now she realizes that infinite space was protection. It was safety. It was sanity.

Seeing your mother murdered, watching the blood bubble from her lips as she urges you to run, to save yourself and leave her to die, is a mark that can never be erased. A scar so deep its horror becomes sublime beauty. Like the shock of white hair that makes her unique, this awful memory, and her ability to hide herself from it, created her. The mind is an elastic and repairable system. Damaged neurons rewire themselves. Neuroplasticity exists. The mind can protect you from the worst things that happened to you. You can forget. You can block things out. You can find ways to live with your own horrors. Hide from them.

She never thought she would be the one to find this truth for herself, but it was always there. She realizes now that anytime she was scared, or embarrassed, or frightened, or in pain, she retreated into this safe space in her mind.

So she goes there now. The black box inside the black box. The place she's always held within her mind to keep her shielded from the horrors of the world. She climbs inside like she is six years old and covered in blood and pulls the door closed. She will not come out until it is safe again.

And in the absence of sound and sight, in the velvet darkness so rich and tangible, a deprivation of senses that would drive any other person mad, she waits. Something terrible is coming. A monster. An embodiment of fear personified.

She will not let it get her.

CHAPTER FORTY-FOUR

CATRIONA

Darkness is something real. A presence.

I lived in darkness for so long that I still find comfort in it. Being in the light makes me nervous. Uncomfortable. Sounds, too. I'm sensitive to everything, prefer to use my inner sonar to move about.

Of course, I have to exist in the light, because I have to take care of my charges. I am their lifeline to the world. I do what is required of me because not doing so means many will be lost. And I can't let that happen.

I almost escaped once. What he did to me when he dragged me back to the underground warrants description, for it is not what you think. Oh, yes, he did plenty of that. But after a time one can put aside the difficulty of being forced.

No, he did something so much worse.

He gave me a choice.

He's given me many choices over the years, starting when he placed the knife in my hand and explained in no uncertain circumstances that although he struck the fatal blow to my mother's heaving chest, it was me who actually did it.

Me, who would take the blame.

Me, who would, if we were caught, explain in minute detail every step of the process in the how, why, when, and where of my mother's murder.

He spent three days explaining it to me with voice and hand until, I have to admit, I half believed I had done it. I could certainly feel the silken caress of the knife as it split the skin under my palm. I was his surrogate; he created the sensory memories to make it real. Then he beat me, and other things, to make sure I understood the stakes. That if I didn't do as he said, he would find others to hurt, and make it clear that I was behind it.

Honestly, Halley, that choice was easy. I did it to save you.

For years, he thought you were dead. I knew you were alive. I knew you were safe.

I shouldn't have gone to Brockville. It was a mistake, but that's the problem with the kind of illness I have. Being able to stop myself from becoming obsessed with an idea is almost impossible. The voices inside me, you know. They sometimes make me do things I'd rather not.

I was tempting fate. I knew that. I knew there was a chance he would realize I was near, that strange sense he always had about me from the moment we met. Putting myself back in his sphere was illogical on so many levels. But writing quelled the demons, and Brockville was the best chance I had to make my work sing.

And since we're being honest, because there's no reason not to, I really did want to see him again. I know that's wrong. It's sick, and twisted, to love your abuser. Any psychologist would tell you that. Dr. Chowdhury tried, so many times, to help me fall out of love with the monster who made me. Especially when I told her I had to seek him out and end things on my terms.

Without darkness, though, there can be no light.

I am the light to his darkness. I had to be. To save them. To save you. To keep you safe, and off his radar. I did everything I could to hide you from him.

Terrible things. Awful things. Unforgivable things.

He was the spider, yes. But I was the web.

Believe me when I say everything I've done is to keep you—them—us—safe.

I have tried to be their light in the darkness, too. Though I brought the dark with me, I am their only hope.

And now, my dear little sister, I am your light, as well. You came for me, and I will love you for that forever. I was so hard on you. Yes, I was a child. Yes, I was jealous. Yes, I was overwhelmed with the fearsome creatures who lived in my head and screamed. Yes, I reached into the darkness and pulled close the one creature who I thought truly loved me, loved me to my bones, to my very soul.

I was mistaken.

When he started to do to others what he'd done to me, I realized there was no hope for him. No hope for me.

But I loved you. I always loved you. Then, and now.

I am coming for you, sister.

I have the code to the chamber.

And I know how to get you out.

CHAPTER FORTY-FIVE

THEO

Brockville, Tennessee

It's nearing sunset when Theo takes the left-hand turn into the Brockville town limits, grinding his teeth in frustration. Four and a half hours, and there's nothing that Lincoln Ross can find that implicates Miles Brockton or anyone else in this godforsaken town of wrongdoing. They have nothing to go on. No leads. No sightings. The Tennessee Highway Patrol and the Knoxville Police are pulling their traffic cams to see if they can find the Camry, and that's all they've got.

There is nothing he wants to do more than come in guns a-blazing to rescue Halley. Assuming she's here. Assuming she is in danger at all. Assuming she didn't drop her basket and start murdering people.

He can't imagine that from his wife, but they say you never really know someone, right?

Halley's always had a little darkness in her, that he does know. Considering she'd lost her mom so young, he thought he understood why. She always had bad dreams—actual night terrors, saw shadowy figures in the room trying to kill her, that sort of thing. For the next few days, she'd be quiet and withdrawn. He'd try to get her to talk about what she was experiencing, to him, to someone, but she always demurred.

Now, he wonders if she was worse off than he thought all along. If the past week has broken her in some way.

He drives through the town. It is Stepford. It is Mayberry. It is Seahaven. It is a perfect rendition of what a charming small town is supposed to be. Beautifully appointed houses; smiling, waving people; clean and safe and perfect. A cheerful cage for those who want to live a special, unique life.

That's what Miles Brockton sells them, and they eat it up.

What darkness lies beneath this veneer? Because it feels so wrong to him. Everything he thought was engaging and welcoming when he drove in the first time to look for Halley is now strange. Brockville is too pristine, too isolated, too good to be true. It is a movie set for a utopian society; the dystopian world is hidden just below the surface. Scratch deeply enough, and they won't bleed; they will hemorrhage.

He cruises the street and finds himself in the hamlet they call Canter. What the hell is up with these names, anyway? He read that Brockton wanted to re-create the small-English-village feel and used charming British towns for the names, just shortened: Avalon, Canterbury, Glastonbury, and Somerville. He dropped the second halves of the names and gave each quadrant its unique identity.

Presence is vital to a utopian society. He is surprised to realize this perfect haven is now giving him culty vibes. Brockville is an expensive, elegant, sinister place. Maybe Donnata Kade was exactly right. Maybe they do turn people into shells of their former selves. Suck out the marrow and leave only the bones behind. People come to cults to be led, to be sheep, to be told what to do. There is nothing divine about handing over your personal responsibility. To ignore your autonomy. To follow blindly.

He quickly surmises that Canter has nothing to do with horses running through fields, as he'd first imagined, and everything to do with health and wellness. The gym, yoga studios, what seems to be a care home for the elderly, doctors, a clinic, a pharmacy . . . even a small hospital.

When Theo left Brockville, Noah Brockton was in the ICU fighting for his life.

With nothing better to do, he swings his truck into the parking lot and strides inside.

The hospital is quiet and virtually empty except for the few people stationed in the ICU. Theo checks in at the desk and is told to wait. A few minutes later, the nurse returns and points him down the hall. Noah Brockton is pale, hooked to at least four machines, but his eyes are open. He sees Theo through the glass and waves a hand, gesturing for him to come into the room.

"You gonna live?" Theo asks, and Noah smiles weakly.

"So they say. I'm glad you're here. Did you find Halley?"

"Tell me what happened and I'll tell you what I know."

Noah shuts his eyes. "You have to find her. She's in danger."

Theo's adrenaline bumps up a notch. "Are you saying she didn't shoot you?"

He stares at the ceiling, then shakes his head. "No, she didn't."

Relief crashes through him, followed by dread. He knew it. Damn it, he *knew* she didn't do this.

"Who did?"

"You really don't know where she is?"

"She's disappeared. Her Jeep was dropped off in Nashville. But she wasn't the one driving it."

Noah struggles to sit up. "Who? Who drove it?"

"Catriona Handon."

Noah goes limp, staring at the ceiling. "What have I done?"

Theo narrows his eyes at Noah. "What the hell is going on here, man? If it wasn't Halley, who shot you? Was it Cat?"

"No. It was a dead man. My half brother, Ian."

That's the second person who's used a dead man's name. "Do you know a woman named Donnata Kade?"

Noah nods. "Used to live here. She's disturbed. Dad let her stay because he was worried about her. You know what they say."

"Keep your enemies close?"

Noah frowns. "No. Charity starts at home. But she became too volatile, and he had to ask her to leave."

"Oh. Well, I met her, and she said some rather damning things about your brother, and your father, and your family. This town. All of it. Seemed pretty convinced you people are the devil incarnate."

"Not me. But Ian, yes. Though I swear to you, I thought he was dead. He and my dad got into an altercation years ago, and Ian was killed. But apparently that wasn't the truth. Apparently, my father let him go with the caveat that he never return. He unleashed hell into the world to save us. Our town. My family."

"Your dad told you that?"

"He did. He thought that was the best way to protect us. My God, he was so naive. He always has been. Naive and idealistic and easily led."

"Goodness. Those are not exactly the words you want to hear from your youngest son."

Miles Brockton stands in the doorway.

Noah looks at the ceiling again. "Sorry, Dad. But it's true."

"Idealistic, definitely. Naive, maybe. But never confuse compliance with knowing which battles to fight, my boy." He strides to Theo's side, hand out. "Miles. You're Halley's husband."

Noah flinches at this statement, but Theo squares his shoulders and shakes with a modicum of distaste, knowing his only chance here is to appear unthreatening, to make them think he's really the bumbling idiot they believe him to be.

"Yes. You don't have any idea where she is, do you?"

"I don't, no. She certainly did a number on my boy here."

"Dad. I told you. It was Ian."

Miles moves to Noah's side. Pats him hard on the shoulder, making the man wince. "Son. I've told you a hundred times. Ian is dead. You're imagining things."

"He's not. He was in Brooke Cottage, he shot me, and he took Halley."

Miles has Noah's shoulder in a tight grip now.

"You're mistaken. You've had a trauma. You need rest. Mr. Donovan—"

"Agent. Agent Donovan."

A glint in Brockton's eyes. "My apologies. Agent. We need to let my son rest. He's been through a lot."

"You're not going to gaslight me any longer, Dad. This has gone too far."

"Stop now, son. Agent Donovan, after you."

There is no question he's being forced out of this room. But to where? To what end?

"Look at the cottage!" Noah shouts as the glass door slides closed.

Miles approaches the nurse, a woman so young she seems fresh out of school. "Please tend to my son. He is overwhelmed and not himself. I think a sedative is in order."

"Yes, of course, Mr. Brockton. I'll call the doctor right away."

Miles turns to Theo, his face arranged in concern. "I suppose you aren't going to let this go, and I can't say I blame you. If my dearly departed wife got herself into trouble, I would have moved heaven and earth to help her." He guides Theo to the doors and, surprisingly, follows him out. Theo keeps expecting Miles to tell him to leave, but instead he says, "Let's lay all this to rest, shall we? Would you like to follow me to Brooke Cottage? Or ride with me?" He looks pointedly at Theo's huge gas-guzzling truck with distaste, but there's no way in hell Theo is going anywhere with this man without his rolling arsenal.

"I'll follow you."

"Suit yourself. You know they do make electric versions of your vehicle."

"I'm aware," Theo says. There's no way in hell that's happening. He needs a truck he can repair himself if something ever goes wrong. Call him old fashioned.

They drive—slowly—for a few minutes. The lights are turning on all across Brockville, making the streets feel even more welcoming and charming. Miles waves to every person they see. They all wave back enthusiastically. Town founder, mayor, leader, priest, hero—whatever he is to these people, they love him.

Brooke Cottage looks much the same as when Theo drove past on his first trip to Brockville. Miles parks, pulls out a key, and lets them in. Flips on the lights.

The cottage is spotless.

It certainly doesn't look like someone was shot there. Theo's been to plenty of crime scenes. There's no scent of blood, nor disarray. It is a pleasant, empty place, ready for the next excited tenant. The cleaners have been here. They worked quickly. And because of that, there is no trace of his wife. Her indiscretion does not appear before him. Shooting the man she'd taken as a lover . . . It still feels too surreal to imagine.

"Feel free to take a look around," Miles says. "I have no secrets here."

"Do you not have *any* secrets, Mr. Brockton?"

"What do you mean?"

"Do you know a woman named Donnata Kade?"

Miles scowls and tsks sympathetically. "Oh, that poor woman. She had an incredibly hard time of it. Lost herself, lost her job, her marriage, her family, her housing. My friends took pity on her and let her stay in their home here, and for a while I thought Ms. Kade was going to recover. Fit in. But her demons were clearly too much for her. I hated to hear of her death. A true loss to those who cared about her."

Theo jerks upright. "Excuse me? Her death?"

"You didn't hear? Oh, how clumsy of me. My apologies. Ms. Kade passed away last night."

Theo stares at Miles. Something shifts behind the man's eyes. On the surface, Miles Brockton looks benign. Distinguished. He has actor hair and dark-blue eyes, is clearly strong and in shape for a man of his age. He is hale and hearty and beloved. And yet somewhere, deep inside him, lurks a demon that Theo can see as clearly as if he's backlit with fire.

He doesn't believe Donnata Kade died by accident. Not for one second.

"How?" he manages. He wants to step across the room, put his hand around Brockton's throat, and squeeze until the man squeals. He holds himself steady, though. Any false moves and Halley could be lost forever.

"Her car skidded off the road coming over the mountain last night. It was raining. She went right over the edge."

"Last night?"

"Overnight. Yes."

Miles Brockton has just told him a whopper of a lie. Donnata Kade was in Nashville as of five hours ago. There's no way she could have died here last night. And Miles doesn't know it.

"Can I see her body?"

"I'm afraid that's not my decision to make. You can speak to my son, Sheriff Brockton, and make a formal request of him. Because you're law enforcement, he may determine it appropriate. May I ask, was she a friend?"

"You could call her that. I'm certainly shocked to hear this."

"I do offer my deepest condolences. Now, what else can I show you here in our fine village?"

Call him on it? Or get the hell out of there? He opts for the latter. Something is rotten here, and he needs a plan. And firepower. And backup. But before he goes . . .

"One last question. I've heard tell there's an anechoic chamber here in Brockville."

Miles smile widens in delight. "As it happens, yes. I had one built many years ago. I don't know how much you know about my background, Agent Donovan, but as much as I take pride and joy in this little community we've built, I so enjoy silence. As a youth, I spent time in the wilderness, first in Alaska, then in Maine. I was able to be alone, truly alone, just myself and the earth and the sky, and that's not something we can often do in this world. I try to bring that experience to those who live and visit here. There are a wide variety of sensory-deprivation therapies that we use for people who seek to quiet their minds." He leans against the thick slab table, letting his weight sit in his palms. "We are bombarded by sensations. Overwhelmed by them, I would say. The world we find ourselves in now, with computers and phones and the internet, all the dings and bells, it is not a natural state. The way we stare at screens is not something our primordial brains can handle. Oh, we convince ourselves otherwise, let children watch dancing bears and tell ourselves they are being entertained, but the truth of the matter is we are ruining them. Ruined children grow into ruinous adults. Technology has seen to that."

"Interesting theory."

"When you have children, you will understand. You will watch them and realize they are never happier than when they can see the sky. It's incontrovertible. It resolves everything. Beach, a forest, a park, it matters not so long as there is sun and rain and wind at their backs. As for the rest of the time, when we are overwhelmed, there is nothing the brain wants more than to be placed back in its embryonic state. Its biologically appropriate state. That's what my therapies do. Goodness, that's the very mission of Brockville. We help people recalibrate."

"People willingly recalibrate with sensory deprivation? From what I understand, the anechoic chamber can cause serious problems for people."

"Oh, no one is allowed in that chamber but me and a very few investors who are familiar with its effects. I have trained my mind, you see, to be able to withstand the lack of senses. But for a normal person just seeking an escape, the float tanks are our state-of-the-art treatment. Why?" His eyes twinkle; the amiable old man is back. "Do you find yourself needing an escape?"

"I'd like to see it. The chamber."

"I'm afraid that isn't possible. But I'm sure we can get you over to Canter and into one of the less intense sensory tanks right away."

Impasse. Miles Brockton is a cool customer.

"I appreciate the offer. Maybe another time."

"Whenever you're ready. It's ironic, I'd just suggested the same to your wife before she snapped. Her energies were all over the place. She needed to be brought back into equilibrium. Sadly, I was too late to help her. Now, shall we?" Miles gestures toward the door.

"Sure. I've taken up enough of your time. Appreciate it. If you hear anything about Halley, please call me. Think I'll go bend your son's ear for a bit. You say he's in Canter?"

"The sheriff's office is in Somer. You can follow me."

"No, that's fine. I can find it."

Is he going to allow this? Letting the ATF agent with the missing wife and a whole lot of questions wander the town unattended?

"I'll let Cameron know you're on your way."

He holds the cottage door for Theo, who has no choice but to walk through into the Japanese garden. It smells different from when they went in. Instead of cedar and holly, there is a faint scent of char in the air.

Just as his brain registers *Smoke*, Miles gasps. "Oh my God. It's burning."

CHAPTER FORTY-SIX

HALLEY

Halley is startled from her uneasy slumber by a noise.

It is magnified in this soundless space, and she tenses, realizing what's happening.

He has come back.

She opens her eyes. Blackness parades in, and she closes them again. She is safer within her own head than she is in this infinite place; she learned that quickly. Physically, though, she has more challenges. She is still tied down. Her legs and arms have gone past excruciating pain, cramping, itching, tingling—finally going numb with a burning fire that belies the term. She knows she is doomed in this position, weakened and trembling, but now she fights back as best she can, rolling her ankles, curling her fingers, willing blood to her limbs.

Ian has done nothing but talk and stroke her hair and intimate what horrors lie ahead for her, but she knows in her soul that won't last much longer. He likes to talk. Likes to hear his own voice in this deadened space. He is a cat with a mouse already caught in the trap, pinioned to the earth by its tail, waiting for whatever horrors will come before its death.

She realizes the door has opened. Light spills in, blinding her with its intensity. She jams her eyes shut tighter. The brightness is too much to take.

Hands on her now. This person does not smell the same as Ian. The hands are softer and smaller. She risks opening one eye. In the darkness, she sees a murky face, one she knows as intimately as her own but still belongs to a stranger.

"Cat?"

"Shhh." The familiar stranger puts a finger over her lips. "We don't have much time," she whispers.

The fingers are nimble, and Halley is soon freed.

"Can you sit up?" Cat asks quietly.

Halley does and swoons immediately. Nothing works. Her limbs are Jell-O. The sliver of light that comes from the penlight in her sister's lap is excruciating after the days of darkness. A migraine takes hold almost immediately. The world spins.

Cat starts rubbing life into her, and soon enough, the vertigo ceases, and her limbs have feeling again. The pain in her head dulls to a familiar throb.

"How did you know where I was?"

"Later. We have to move. Now."

The urgency in her tone brings Halley's painfully ungovernable mind back into focus. With her sister bolstering her, she manages to stand, then take a few steps. Her head is splitting, and her legs still feel rubbery but now can hold her weight, and the room isn't moving like the deck of a ship at sea. "Okay. I'm okay. Let's go."

They exit the chamber into a long hallway with greenish sconces lining the walls. They disappear around the corner into darkness.

"Where are we?"

"Under town. Fallout shelters. In case there's some sort of major disaster. Oak Ridge is to our west—if it was ever hit or melted down, the winds would come directly over us. It's to save the people of Brockville from the apocalypse."

"Oak Ridge?"

"The nuclear facility. Halley, please, hurry. We can talk about all this later. We don't have much time. We've created a diversion, but the guards will be back soon enough."

"Guards?"

"Later. Please."

She follows her sister into the greenish light, fighting to keep the worst of the headache at bay. "You said *we* created a diversion. Who is *we*?"

"You'll see."

The tunnel forks left, then right, then left again. They walk on for what feels like a mile, moving through this underground warren. At each junction, Cat moves with assurance. Halley's head hurts too much to keep up the line of questioning. Her sister, alive. Her sister, rescuing her. Her sister. With her. *Me* has become *we*.

They hit a steel door. Cat pulls a set of keys from her pocket and turns the lock. The door opens into a cafeteria-style room with long tables, at which are seated several women and children. All heads turn. Everyone is silent. She's never seen such a somber group. These children should be laughing and playing; instead they are pale and stricken. Their mothers—she assumes these are their mothers—rise from the tables.

One, a woman with red hair and a small healing bruise on her left cheekbone, stands. "Is it time?"

Cat nods. "As we planned it. Up and out of the northwest entrance, straight into the labyrinth. Heather is waiting. Hurry now."

They rise as one and move like zombies, all of a piece, together, toward the door. No one will meet her eyes. Cat is counting under her breath.

"Gray. Where is Gray?" she asks sharply, and one of the women turns.

"He went with Heather."

Cat curses under her breath. "All right, move, move. Hurry. We're out of time."

Time. There is no such thing as time. Time doesn't exist in the dark.

But they are moving toward the light. The path they follow angles upward, finally stopping at a set of concrete stairs. The women and children wait, and Cat splits them apart like an arrow as she hurries up the step and unlocks the door. "Stick together. We've marked the path. Look for the small bows in the greenery. Meet me in the graveyard."

"You must lead us, Catriona," the last woman says, and Cat smiles.

"You are leading us now, Gretchen. You're going to be fine. I'm right behind you."

Halley realizes Cat is tugging on her arm. "Come on. You too."

"Are they . . . okay?" she asks. "God, these people seem like they've been brainwashed."

"Again, later. Go."

Halley steps into a world of green so dark it's like midnight. The air is fresher, no longer the stale notes of earth and must that told her she was underground, but something is burning. Her eyes adjust quickly, and she realizes they are in some sort of massive labyrinth. The hedges reach well over her head; the sensation of them touching the night sky is only interrupted by an orangish glow.

The covey of women and children moves quietly. They are used to silent footfalls. Perhaps every sound under the earth is magnified; perhaps they are all simply shell shocked and desperate not to be heard. They move as one in a dance that mimics the underground passages. Left. Right. Left again. Until there is a stoppage. Murmurs.

"Cat," she says, but realizes her sister is no longer behind her.

The woman called Gretchen returns to her side. "It's stopped," she says, panic in her voice. "The hedges. We're blocked. We've taken a wrong turn."

"How were you navigating?" Halley asks.

"There were bows, the girls' hair ties. But the labyrinth path is changed regularly. A deterrent."

Halley has the horrible realization that in addition to being kept locked away underground, this group of women and children is hampered from escaping on foot by this interactive maze. Dear God.

The smell of smoke is getting more acrid and intense. Her headache pulses in response. *Not now,* she commands, and for once, it dims. She turns to the woman behind her.

"What's your name?" Halley asks.

"Summer," the woman supplies.

"I need a few of you to form a pyramid. So I can stand on your backs and see where we are. I might be able to get us back to the right path."

Summer disappears without a word and returns with four women. They quickly assemble like a group of former cheerleaders, and Halley awkwardly climbs up on their backs. The hedges are high, but with this vantage point she can see above them. She rotates her head. She is staring into darkness, and the fire—there's no question now, something is burning heavily—is over her left shoulder. In the distance, behind the billowing smoke and orange glow on the horizon, she can just make out a hill that looks like it is covered in wire. She climbs down. "The fire is coming from behind us. There's a hill, with wires. I don't know what that is."

"The grapevines," Summer says. "That's Glaston. The farm is there. The vineyard. It's the heart of the community. Without it, Brockville is reliant on the outside world."

She says this with pride. "Your idea to burn down the farm?" Halley guesses.

Summer smiles. "I've always wanted to burn this place to the ground. They put too many of us there when they were finished with us."

"Okay. Then if you know where the farm is, do you have any idea how to escape the labyrinth?"

"All I know is there are entrances in all four hamlets. We were under the entrance in Glaston, and the exit we are supposed to find is in Avalon. The graveyard is on the hill by the cliff. About a mile from the labyrinth. It's only one grave, long overgrown. We don't know whose it is. But it has to be one of us, from long ago."

"The city is set on a grid, yes? North, south, east, west?"

"Sacred-geometry principles. The town looks like a grid, but it is really undulating across the Omega."

Halley has exactly zero idea what that means. She thinks for a second, then looks up.

Time is running short. Smoke is filling the air. But the stars are just barely still visible. It is a pattern she knows, loves, and is as intimately familiar with as her own body.

Her headache flees as she stares into the night sky, calculating. Arcturus, and Betelgeuse, and Pollux. Sirius, and Canis Major. Hydra. The Big Dipper.

It is divine luck. With a prayer of thanks to her father for his relentless passion and tutoring, she grabs Summer's hand and turns to the northwest.

"Follow me."

Cat catches up to them as they're backtracking, a small boy in her arms. He is too big to carry, but she is managing, lugging him along, sweat breaking on her brow. Another woman is with her. Halley assumes this is the one Cat called Heather.

"What's wrong? Why are you coming back?"

"Dead end."

"That was quick. They must have changed it this week, once Halley was taken." To Halley Heather says, "Standard operating procedure when a new acolyte is brought in. They change things up until the woman is acclimated."

"We've been planning this for a while," Cat says, shifting the boy to the ground. Halley realizes with a start it's the same child she saw out in the woods. He's older than she thought, but so small, so skinny.

"This is Gray," Cat says. "My son."

"So it was you who put the note in my bag. You disabled my Jeep."

Cat smiles. "You always were so clever. We hoped you would be as stubborn as an adult as I remember you being as a child. And if not, bring someone who was."

She smiles, and Halley smiles back, pushing away the anger. This could have gone so many other ways, and it might still. But they can hash it out later.

"I really do want to know the whole story, but we don't have much time. I think I can get us out of this, but we have to move. The Farm is on fire."

"I know. Summer set the fire."

"Need to bury the ashes of the ones we've lost. Purify them." Heather mumbles this, and Halley shoots her a sharp glance but holds her tongue. She might be saying crazy stuff, too, if she'd been stuck underground any longer.

"We need to move. Avalon is that way." Halley points and looks up again to confirm her direction. Polaris is still visible through the smoke; she uses it to orient herself. She stretches out her right arm. "That way's north. I'm facing west." She moves her head forty-five degrees to the right, points. "That's northwest. Avalon is there. The fire is coming from our south. Let's move."

It's slow going, with a few switchbacks for wrong turns, but each time, Halley is able to align them again, and fifteen minutes later, they break free of the labyrinth and are faced with the woods. They march another hundred yards before Halley realizes where they are. The writers' retreat cabin.

"I assume you know where to go from here?" she asks Cat.

"Yes. Straight through there to the road. We can stay in the woods. We have supplies waiting."

"They're going to come for us."

"I know."

"You can't just live in the woods on the outskirts of this town."

"We can until you bring help. I always knew you would save us, Halley. I believed it in my soul."

Halley impulsively hugs her sister. "Let's go."

They move off, one by one, the women leading their children, Halley's head spinning. She counts fifteen women, and twice as many kids.

"What was this, Cat? Some sort of breeding facility? A cult?"

"It's complicated," Cat says. "Not a cult. None of us are here willingly."

"How do they get here?"

"Me. I bring them. Ian demands it."

Halley is brought up short.

"What did you say?"

But before Cat can answer, a thin mechanical wail cuts through the night, followed by another, and another. Sirens. The volunteer fire department is certainly working the fire already, but these are coming from the northwest.

"The road! Hurry! Fire trucks are coming, they must have called for help. We can flag them down."

"That is simply not going to happen," a dark and brooding voice says.

And Ian Brockton steps from the darkness.

Halley is surprised enough that she freezes, and in that moment Ian lunges for her and captures her arm. He yanks her to his chest and slams a hand over her mouth. He is warm, hot, as if he has a fever. She struggles, but he is incredibly strong. He squeezes her, and she feels one of her ribs give way, cracking, causing so much pain she sees stars.

"Now, now. Don't do that," he says in that silky tone, but it's hoarse now, as if he's been inhaling smoke.

She realizes the women have also stopped fleeing.

"Good girls. You're my good girls," he starts crooning, and Halley feels a strange warmth start to move through her. His sensory deprivation must come with a healthy dose of hypnosis or some other mind control, biofeedback or something to turn his victims into willing participants. That's why he talks so much. He is controlling them with his voice.

Fuck. That.

Ignoring the stabbing pain in her ribs, she goes completely limp. The move surprises him enough that she's able to wriggle free, and then she is fighting, kicking, screaming, and there's more than one of her. Several of the women leap forward, and Ian is stuck trying to fight them all. It is a feral fight. He is subsumed by his victims. The hunter has become the prey.

With an almighty roar, he pushes four of them away. A gunshot rings out, and one of the women falls. The shock of the retort is enough for him to scramble to his feet, but Halley surges forward. She kicks the gun from his hand. It spins wildly in the dirt, toward the fallen woman.

Halley realizes with horror that it is Cat. Cat has been shot. Ian has shot Cat.

The primal scream that comes from her throat is enough to make every woman and child freeze. Not again. Never again. She will not let him hurt her, or anyone else. She will not let him take another person from her. She will not let him take Cat from her.

But as she lunges for the gun, Cat rolls, and in a fluid movement reaches the gun, rises to her knees, and pulls the trigger. Then she collapses.

Red. Red. Everywhere she looks, red.

Ian Brockton goes down.

Screaming. Crying. The chuckling fury of the encroaching fire. The haze descending upon them. Shouts in the distance. It all disappears in the face of the scene before her.

Halley kicks the gun away from Cat's hand and collapses at her side.

"Cat. Oh my God, Cat. Are you okay? Where are you hit?"

It is a stupid question; the blood is spreading across Cat's chest and bubbling on her lips. She looks straight into the night sky, the constellations blotting out with the smoke.

"Leave it to you to find a way out with the stars. Our little comet girl." She coughs, and Halley feels a fine spray of blood on her face. Deep in the woods, with no help, this wound is fatal. Her sister is dying.

Sobs rack her, and the pain in her chest is compounded by the fact that she can't get a breath.

Her sister reaches up, places a soft hand on Halley's cheek.

"Gray. Please take care of him."

"I will. I swear it. But hold on. They're coming."

The sirens are so close. There is a chance. They can save her. Halley finds the wound and puts pressure on it. Cat's hand finds hers. She squeezes, her grip so light. Her strength is waning. She's bleeding out.

Halley has to save her. She has to fix this.

Like she did with her mother, she kneels in blood and holds fast.

"Don't leave me, Cat. Hold on. Please, hold on."

It is not enough. There is no such thing as time in the darkness, no such thing as pleading with a body that is in the throes of death. The beating of a heart is not defeated until the end.

Cat's hand moves to Halley's ear. "Mom's diamonds. She loved them. You wear them still?"

"Always."

"I miss her. I loved her. I'm sorry."

Tears drip down Halley's cheeks, making dark tracks in her sister's hair. "You're going to be okay. You have to be okay, Cat."

She knows that is not to be. Cat is too pale, too still. Her pulse skitters and slows.

Cat's last words are so quiet Halley can barely hear her. It is so like her mother's voice fading as she cried "*Run.*" Except Cat is whispering, "Read. Read. Read the letters. I did it all for you, Halley. To keep you safe. To keep him from seeking you out. Ian was always obsessed with you. Everything he made me do, I did because I loved you. I love you, Halley. You're safe now."

"Cat. Cat, please. You can't die. I just found you. I need to know. Why did you kill our mother? Why would you take her from me. From you?"

Cat's getting paler and paler in the meager moonlight. "It wasn't me, Halley Bear. It was Ian. Read the letters," she says, the light leaving her eyes. "Take care of Gray."

And with a final ragged breath, she goes still. Her hand slips to the ground.

A mournful cry starts up among the women, and Halley joins them. The little boy is brought to her side. Summer is holding him. Heather is stroking Cat's hair.

"Say goodbye to your mother," Summer says. "It is an honor to be by her side as she moves to the heavens."

The little boy looks at Cat with a cry twisting on his lips, but he doesn't let it loose.

Halley is thrown back to the moment she kneeled next to her own mother, bloodied and bruised, the moment before she was yanked by the foot and thrown headfirst into the fireplace mantel. The moment her life changed forever, the moment that set her on this path. She had no time to say goodbye to her mother. She was too young to truly understand what it meant. And now, she's lost her sister, too. The woman she mourned for so long is here, covered in dirt and blood, to be mourned again.

She pulls herself from Cat's side and takes the little boy—her nephew—in her arms.

"Shh," she says, though he is not uttering a sound. She says the words she wishes were a part of her waking memory. The words that will hopefully eventually transform this nightmare into a bad dream. "Shh. It will be okay. You're safe now. You're safe."

CHAPTER FORTY-SEVEN

Death comes for us at the most inconvenient times.

Do not worry.

Dying does not hurt at all.

CHAPTER FORTY-EIGHT

HALLEY

It is dawn before they are found.

The fire draws first responders from all the surrounding areas. Fires anywhere are bad; fires in the Great Smoky Mountains can quickly become conflagrations that take out thousands of acres of property, private and federal. The sirens shriek like lonely seagulls for hours until there is another glow on the horizon, this time from the east.

Ian is dead. The threat is gone.

But Cat is dead with him. An obscene Romeo and Juliet, the two purveyors of hell lie in the dirt above the horrendous world they created.

The women argue a bit about what to do. Summer wants to take the group and keep hiking. Get as far away as possible. Heather wants to go back to Brockville for help. Halley is not about to pull Cat's son away from his mother's body until he is damn good and ready. They tell Halley some of their story. How Ian collected them. How Cat took care of them. They claim Miles didn't know, that Ian hid them from him.

Halley doesn't know if she believes them. She holds her nephew and rocks him, humming, trying, so hard, to keep her own monsters at bay. The darkness has stopped being something protective. It is now full of terror.

In the end, two men appear from the dusty horizon. One is Cameron Brockton. The other is Theo Donovan.

"They're here," Cameron yells.

Halley is relieved to see them both. It must show on her face because his voice cracks when he sees her. He drops to his knees beside her.

"Halley? Baby. Are you hurt?"

"I'm okay. Handle them."

Surely Theo's presence with Cameron means they are safe now. But Halley is never going to feel safe here again. She's been rocking Gray since his mother fell, and the blood is dried on them both. Theo's abject horror at the scene they've stumbled upon is quickly rewritten, his professional facade slamming into place. Training kicks in. He starts gathering women and preserving the scene. Cameron isn't as schooled; he mills about like a lost duckling on the periphery, the truth of his world crashing down upon him. His dead brother was holding a mass of women hostage, and now he is dead again. Lying in the grass alone.

We are all alone in the end.

The crime scene is sorted professionally. Theo knows his job. Halley waits with Gray in her arms. He is fascinated by the blinking blue and white lights. She is glad to see him looking around now, interested. She has no idea what sort of mothering he received, whether he was raised alone with Cat, or as a part of the group. There is so much to learn.

The women and children are taken to a holding area to be reunited with their families, if they have them. Theo comes to Halley's side.

"Hi," she says.

"Did you—are you okay?" He waves a hand; the gesture encompasses the blood, the bodies, the child clasped protectively to her bosom.

"No. Not even close to okay. But God, am I glad to see you."

He blows out a huge breath, and she is happy to see his relief. She's not lying. Their problems seem minute in comparison to what the women of Brockville have experienced.

"This is Gray. My nephew."

"Hey, pal." Theo's voice is shockingly gentle. "Can I help you get changed? We have some cool toys for you to play with."

Gray raises his head and looks Theo directly in the face. He must see something there. Halley is shocked when he detaches himself and clasps his arms around Theo's neck. Theo walks him away from the scene. The boy does not look back at his mother's body.

They are moved to a motel in Bristol, devoid of charm or soul, and allowed to shower and change. Halley has no appetite but forces down a granola bar and banana. There are bruises on her wrists and ankles from the restraints. Her ribs are bound. She feels hollow. Detached from reality.

She is interviewed, again and again. She tells them everything she knows, which is not much. Then they bring Gray to her. He has had a bath and is dressed in Batman pajamas. They've given him a toy truck, and he runs it up and down his leg meditatively.

He is a quiet child. He has no idea who Batman is.

He never asks for his mother. He knows she is gone. And that breaks Halley into a million pieces all over again.

The media is now in Brockville.

While Gray naps, Halley watches the live shots. The town looks utterly surreal. All of Glaston burned. They lost the Farm, the crops, the restaurants. Miles Brockton has been taken into custody—several of the women Cat rescued have levied claims of his involvement in their trafficking. Of the involvement of other men in the Brockville community, the ones who came to them in the darkness. Who hurt them. Who filmed them. Who enjoyed it.

The great utopian experiment, the famed leader of the movement, felled by his basest interests.

Halley speaks with Noah, to make sure he is okay. To thank him for trying to save her.

She speaks with her father and endures his tears and apologies and gives a few of her own. She tells him the story of Cat and the women, what she knows, anyway. He wants her to come back to Marchburg. He is at home doing rehab and has plenty of time to catch up; he and Anne want to meet Gray.

Theo comes to visit every evening. He and Gray have some sort of bond that Halley is heartened to see. One evening, after the kid's passed out in the bedroom, they sit on the motel room's balcony, sharing a beer and talking.

"This is why I never wanted to have kids," Theo says, looking over his shoulder toward the bedroom, where they left Gray sprawled like a starfish on the sheets.

"Because they might be orphaned?"

"No." He takes her hand, and she lets him. "Do you know how many times I've seen that look in a kid's eye? When we roll up on a scene and the shit's hit the fan, and all that's left are these little ones, and they are so shattered. I couldn't imagine ever being in charge of someone's life like that. Not their life, but their soul. I know what it felt like to lose a father, Halley. To watch them lose their people, again and again, knowing how that feels? Broke me."

She sits with that confession. "I wish you'd told me that before."

"I should have. But it's impossible to explain unless you've seen it for yourself. Now you have."

"You know that Gray is mine, now, Theo. Cat left him to me, and I won't give him up. I can't do that to him. He saw his mother die. I know what kind of scars that leaves."

"I understand. I don't want you to. I don't want to, either." He sighs and gives her a rueful grin. "Damn kid's gotten under my skin. To grow up the way he did? And then to see him in your arms, covered in blood . . .

I've never been so happy in my life. I want to re-create that feeling. I want to come home again and again and see you holding him, see him in your arms. A little less blood next time, though."

She smiles. "He's going to outgrow them fast enough."

"Then he'll fit in mine a little longer."

She fights back tears. "I have to tell you something," she says. "And you're never going to forgive me."

"I already know. You're forgiven."

Her mouth drops open. "How?"

"Oh, your pal told me. So did his dad. Charming folks." He sets down the beer. "Listen. I hate that you were with him. But I'm not such an asshole that I can't admit I screwed up. I pushed you away, I forced you to walk. I was scared. And yeah, then you screwed up. But if that was it, that was the only time? Maybe we call it even and try again. Take the kid to McLean. Let him meet Charlie. I bet they'd love each other."

"The only time?"

"Don't make me say it, Halley."

She realizes what he thinks. "I didn't sleep with him, Theo. It was a kiss. That's all."

"What?" The relief cascades out of him. "The asshole didn't say that."

Halley looks out over the parking lot to the misty mountains in the distance. She thinks about Noah, knowing there is absolutely zero chance at a future between them. She does not belong here, and she is not going to stay. The moment she is cleared, she is taking Gray and leaving. She will have to see him again sometime, though. Gray is his nephew, too, after all.

But she knows how she feels about Theo. It's always been Theo. When she saw him emerge from the haze of the fire, the fear on his face, the relief, she knew there was no other person she could ever be with. It might be bumpy. It might not work. But he is the one.

"We can try going home," she says. "But we have to ask Gray what he wants, first."

"Fair enough." Theo drops her hand. "I have something for you."

"What's that?"

"Letters. We found them in the tunnels. They're going to be tied up in evidence for a long while, because we've got a pretty solid idea of the terrors that were going on below Brockville. And she gave us a couple of other tidbits. The farm? Massive graveyard. When Ian finished with his women, he buried them under the fucking crops. They've recovered four bodies so far, matched them to missing persons cases. There are more. The guy was a freaking loon."

Halley thinks about the words Heather spoke in the dark. *"Need to bury the ashes of the ones we've lost. Purify them."*

She wasn't just crazy. She was hoping the fire would set the souls of his victims free.

"What about his dad?"

"Well, that's a good question. Multiple jurisdictions want to talk to him, but surprise surprise, we've been told to lay off and let the man grieve. He's been rocked by this, apparently. His dead son coming back to life, having a coven of women right below his very feet? That his very special anechoic chamber was being used as some medieval torture room?"

Halley shudders. The darkness creeps in when she isn't expecting it. She has to keep looking toward the light so she doesn't slip back in.

"Sorry. Listen, though. The letters? I took some photos. It seems she was telling a story. Writing a pretty disturbing memoir, one of the guys said. She detailed everything, names, places, times. He had her in thrall, but she subverted him whenever she could. She wasn't kidding when she says she did it all for you. You sure you want to read these? They're pretty awful."

"Yes. I need to know."

He hands her his phone. There are pictures of the letters. They tell the story of what Cat went through at the hands of her captor, what he turned her into. How the power he had over her was absolute, because everything she did was to keep Halley safe. He knew Halley had lived through that first attack in Nashville, when he killed their mother, and he used her as a bargaining chip. She became the monster he wanted her to be.

Halley swipes through, reading a sentence here and a paragraph there, her sorrow building with each word. The pictures tell a disjointed tale but are enough to make her understand her sister better, and perhaps allow her heart a step toward healing.

> You cannot possibly understand what has happened, but I want to try and explain. Mom is dead, and it is my fault.
>
> There were too many voices in my head, too many paths I was forced to follow.
>
> I thought I loved him.
>
> He took one look at you and I saw something in his eyes that terrified me. He lost all interest in me. All he wanted was you. He said come here. Come here to me. And you went to him. He cuddled you and said can I see your room? You were so young. So pure. You did not realize what he wanted from you. I did. And I said no. I grabbed your arm and I pulled you away from him. We fought. He hit me. He left and I thought we were safe.
>
> Then Mom came home, and she knew something was wrong. We talked and I told her I was afraid of him. That I was afraid for you. And he came back. This time, he had a knife. He was going to take you by force. Mom stepped in between you, and he stabbed her. I think he was surprised at how quickly she died.

It was like she was there one minute, and the next, poof, she was gone. Her eyes were wide and she fell on the floor.

I screamed, and you screamed, and he laughed. He laughed at us, at our pain. He tried to kill you, and somehow you survived.

Then he said if he could not have you he would take me in your place. I had no choice but to leave with him. He told me if I did not say I killed Mom and make them believe it, he would go back for you.

I know what you've been told, but one day you will want to know who really killed your mother. His name is Ian. Ian Brockton. And I will hunt him down and kill him for what he did to our family. I will keep you safe.

Everything I did, I did for you.

But then, I found myself pregnant. I had to make sure my son wouldn't be marked by the madness of his mother and his father.

There is nothing harder than losing a child.

When my son was taken from me, I had no choice anymore. I had to find a way out. I had to leave. I had to stop him.

You are too young to comprehend how difficult it was for me when you came into our lives. You were

> perfect. You were sunny and smart and joy. I am darkness and rain, a thundercloud. I was always in your shadow, and that was fine.
>
> I hoped I could find him again. As wrong as that was, I needed to try.
>
> I went to Brockville because I hoped he was there. Hoped, because I need revenge. Hoped, because I'd been tracking him for years. And I was right. He was there.
>
> There are so many powerful people involved in this. People who will watch for you to surface. I can't let that happen.
>
> I saved you once, Halley. And I will save you again, even if it kills me.
>
> Six people sit in an anxious circle in a posh, elegant cabin in the woods in a small town called Brockville.

That's enough. She hands the phone back to Theo, wiping her eyes. Looks through the bedroom door at all she has left of her sister, the physical manifestation.

"I don't want him to see. He already knows his mother was a hero in the end. I don't want him to ever know anything otherwise."

"I'll do my best to get them eighty-sixed. But a lot of other families need to know what Cat did for their women."

The thought sickens her. "When can we leave? I want out of here."

"In the morning. We're done here for now. FBI is taking over. I can take you both home."

Home. The word has never been as sweet.

CHAPTER FORTY-NINE

THEO

Halley and Gray are playing in the backyard with Charlie. The dog went crazy for the kid, not a huge surprise. They are fast friends. Charlie makes Gray smile, and when they play, the clouds that loom over the boy dissipate. Somehow, despite the horrors of his young life, they are seeing the possibility of a sunny child.

Theo is in his office, watching them cavort in the grass, when his phone rings. It's Lincoln Ross in Nashville.

"Hey, man. Finally got me that evidence?"

Ross's voice is tight. "Donovan, I gotta tell you something. You're not going to believe it."

"What's that?"

"They brought Ian Brockton's body to Nashville for autopsy at Forensic Medical so TBI could oversee. Somewhere between here and there, he vamoosed."

Theo sits heavily. "What do you mean, he vamoosed? The guy's dead. How does a dead body disappear?"

"They found fresh blood in the bag. Driver stopped to take a leak in Crossville, so the van was unattended for a little bit. They think he maybe wasn't quite as dead as people thought."

"No, no, that's not possible. I saw the guy, Ross. He was dead. And I saw Cameron Brockton take his pulse with my own eyes, then the EMTs loaded him up. You're telling me that many people missed a heartbeat?"

"It's happened before."

"Or someone on the inside lied. That seems to be the Brockville way."

Theo realizes he never confirmed himself that Ian Brockton didn't have a pulse. He believed the bastard's brother when he said the monster was dead.

"Son of a bitch," he says.

EPILOGUE

HALLEY

One Year Later

When you are a child, you don't really understand death. Your tiny brain doesn't have the full capacity to comprehend it. You lose the hamster, the dog, a grandparent, and the people around you, the adults—who *can* conceptualize what this forever abyss means—do their rituals, the things that make them feel better. Then, in an attempt to explain to you—their tiny, previously unblemished by the vagaries of death creature—that there is a darkness into which people and things you love disappear and never come back, they scar you. They don't mean to; they're just trying to help. But to be a child faced with an existential truth? It's impossible to properly comprehend.

There are societal activities to ease you through these incomprehensible tragedies: small Kleenex boxes buried under the rosebushes, a church funeral you're deemed too young to attend, a gravestone to then visit with old flowers wilting in a metal urn. You can understand in some way that you will never see them again, but you are sheltered from the reality. The decay. The decomposition. The embodiment of the biblical concept of ashes to ashes, dust to dust.

Then you get a little older, and someone explains it to you in a way that lands, stomping on your heart, or you see a movie that makes it all click, and suddenly, all you can think about is—death. What must be happening under the dirt? What do they look like? Is the skin falling off the bones? How are skeletons made? Do they stay in one piece? What happens if they come back to life? Would they be the person you remember, intact, or a zombie? Would they sit at the end of your bed and play with your toes, or would they lose that kind of dexterity? How do they eat and drink and dream when they are buried in the dirt? Are they feeling claustrophobic? Is it dark where they are? Do they miss you?

It is these terrors that you dream about night after night until you wake screaming, and the doctors try to drug you to sleep, but that only makes it worse. You can barely remember her, and in truth it is the photographs that give you the story of your life, not your memories, which is a very artificial and fragile state to live in. At one point, some of the pictures are lost, or put away by people who can't handle their own grief anymore, so you have the memories of the pictures only, and that's simply not enough. She fades away, and by the time you're an adult, all you have are snippets. Broken memories, unreliable at best.

Even the photos aren't real. Your favorite is the one of her standing in front of a red door. Her mink-brown hair is curled, and she is laughing. But it's slightly blurry. You don't remember the exact shade of her blue eyes, how tall she was, whether her voice was high pitched or low, because there are no other pictures of her in the house. You know you look like her, but the mirror lies.

She is blood of your blood, but simply a figment of your imagination.

Without a mother, you feel alone in this world. You have no one. No anchor. No knowledge. You envy those people around you who have families and an idea of who they are. Where they come from. You have your foundations, but they are not the same.

Grief lies, too. It will sneak in while you aren't paying attention and lay waste to your heart in the strangest moments. A mother and daughter at the park, playing on the swings. Walking on the beach, a mother chasing her pink-frilled daughter into the water. A commercial, a movie, a television show, a book, a comedy show, a text. You never know when this loss will materialize, a mother-shaped hole that is irrational, as you have no idea what it's like to be mothered, not really.

I don't tell you this for pity. More so you can understand where I'm coming from. I'd already suffered a loss so great none can come close, and yet . . . What happened this year is hard to understand, even for me, who lived through it. Nor is it over, not by a long shot. The repercussions will echo for decades. I hope the worst of it is behind me, think that I am sound, safe, and then, like the grief for my lost mother, it comes roaring back, screaming and vituperative.

Vituperative? Come on, Hal. That's a bit much.

She scratches out the word, replaces it with *abusive*, then continues.

So for the record, I am not doing this for me. It started because my therapist wants me to write it all down. She feels it will be cathartic. I don't know if I agree. Remembering is like touching my hand to a hot stove. It's okay for a fraction of a second, and then your nerves catch up to your brain and you realize how badly it hurts. You whip your hand away and look at the burn, red and blistering, and shake your head. *Why* did you grab that hot pan? You knew it had just come from the oven and is warming on the stove. You knew it would burn you. How could you forget? How could you be so careless?

Writing a book about what's happened . . . I feel my hand approaching the hot pan, and the burn burrowing into my skin. I don't want to remember. I don't want to wonder what things might have been like if I'd had a mother, if she hadn't been taken from me in such a brutal way. If I'd known the truth earlier, would I have been able to process it, and be a normal child? Would I have clung so to my father, to my books, to my isolation? Would I have let the world define me as shy, or introverted, or on the spectrum? Having a mother. Goodness. I can't imagine. I think only someone who's grown up the child of a single parent can understand how hard the one that's left must work to be both mother and father. Comfort and discipline in one sentence.

My dad . . . I will learn how to forgive him for it all, that's what my therapist tells me. We're working on it. Growing up, he gave me everything you can possibly need, from love to companionship to intellectual challenge. He didn't care that I wasn't excited to go out into the world; he understood and homeschooled me until I was. He gave me my intellectual makeup—part English literature, part earth sciences—and where did that take me? To forensics, of course. The one place neither of us could ever imagine me. I caught the true crime bug like half the girls my age and decided I wanted to be a crime scene analyst.

And that's why everything fell apart. I was so focused on the specifics, on the details, that I missed the full picture. It was stupid of me, and it nearly got me killed.

So I will continue writing in this journal, trying to put the pieces together for myself, to understand how I missed the truth when it was staring me in the eye all along. And I will try to forgive myself, because my therapist is right about that: until I give myself a break, until I allow myself to feel again, nothing will ever be right.

Halley James closes the notebook. She's chosen a hardback journal with two hundred thirty-five numbered pages, bought a twelve-pack of blue 0.5-point gel pens, and has set aside one hour every day to sit with her story. She is tackling this like every other situation she's ever been faced with—head on. She might be an introvert, but she's not afraid of a fight. She is compelled to tell the story. To make sure people know the truth. To protect those who survived. Those she saved.

She tries to ignore the fact that when she looks out the window, her throat closes and the panic rises. It has grown dark; she forgets how swiftly the sun sets this late in the day. She never used to be afraid of the dark. Didn't have the sensation of bees coming to life under her skin, didn't feel her breath come short and her heart begin to pound, so intense she can hear it.

Alone in the night is the worst.

She laughs lightly to dispel the silence that's crept into her library office. When the days grow short and the nights long, she's really going to be in trouble. It's hard enough to sleep when there are only eight hours. When it's twelve, fourteen, she's screwed.

But she won't be completely alone. Theo still travels, and she counts the hours until his return.

She chastises herself for the thought. She doesn't need saving. She must get through this herself; delaying the inevitable will mean this fear never really resolves. And we all end up alone in the end . . .

Halley snaps on the lamp next to her desk with a sigh of relief, then begins the ritual of the lights, breath held. She needs to get one of those timers people use when they go out of town that turn on the lamps at specific times. She can put one on every plug, and it will never get fully dark.

You are in control, she reminds herself, moving quickly from room to room, until the house is aglow and she can breathe again.

Timers would work. It would be admitting defeat, but she has to stop thinking that way. She has to allow herself to acknowledge she's been through a terrible, traumatic experience, and it will take months, maybe years, to unwind. That her memories lie. That she is damaged. That the darkness is full of terrors and she is now afraid of the night.

The idea of feeling this level of dread every sunset for years to come is enough to make her square her shoulders. With a deep breath, Halley casts her mind back to that dark place and counts to ten—the only way to dispel the fear is to lean into it, even if only for ten seconds.

Her heart thunders in the darkness. It is alive, velvet in its depth. The absence of light should be a clue to her whereabouts, but she can't think. She's panicking, thrashing. She is buried alive. She is alone in the living dark. And he is coming.

Her eyes fly open, and she swallows the rising gorge in her throat. Her hands are shaking.

There. She did not die. She did not run screaming. She will master this. She will not be a victim. She will be the strong one. She will not let him win.

In the before, she would turn on the nightly news while she made dinner, but now that is completely off limits. The news cycle is, and will continue to be, dining out on this story for months. It is salacious. It is terrifying. There are victims—real victims, not like her—who will never be right again. Many are dead. Too many. The others are permanently scarred. Halley's silly little fears are nothing when faced with what they've been through.

She knows this, and yet . . . the light is not on in the laundry room. Anything could be lurking in that darkness. The door to the backyard, though dead bolted and barricaded, could have been eased open. The glass could have been broken through, the lock turned. He could be waiting for her there, in the dark. Waiting. Breathing.

"Shit," she mutters, hurrying to the laundry room and slapping on the light. The room is empty. The back door is closed, bolted, the glass intact. No one is there.

Her rational brain says "See? Told you!" while her irrational self cowers. She is thirty-five years old, and terrified of being alone in the dark.

When Theo is out of town, she could go home. Should go home. It would be so much easier. Her dad would welcome her without a word, just pull her into his arms and offer to make her dinner. Maybe he wouldn't say anything at all, and she'd be able to revel in the sense of safety she used to feel any time he was near, before she found out how he'd deceived her. She blamed him for what happened; of course she did. If he'd been honest with her from the start, she would never have gotten herself into the mess she did.

She could call Theo and ask him to come home early. He would. He'd drop everything if she asked.

She could ask Noah Brockton to drive north from his home and be by her side.

No. She can't do any of that.

None of that will work until she forgives herself. She created this situation. She made herself into the person she is now.

But all those victims would still be lost and hurt, Halley. What you did was brave. It was good. You saved them.

But I lost myself.

But did you, Halley? What did you lose, and what did you gain?

The boy cries out from his room, and the darkness and fear flee. She hurries to his side.

She is his light now.

Come here. Come with me. Look at the charred remains of my father's legacy.

No, not the farm, not his beloved town, his ruined reputation. His investors fleeing when they realized he was conning them all. The townspeople moving away en masse, unable to stomach the sublime horrors they lived above. They were complicit. The very food their bodies craved was tainted by the blood of the innocent. Imagine that.

Oh, he is so broken. Standing alone, screaming, at the cliffside of the mountain, looking at all he built crumbling at his feet. Cat used to go there, once she was tamed. She cried. She screamed. She pulled her hair. She went mad, then she came back to me. She always came back to me.

No, as much fun as it is to watch that all burn, I'm interested in something else.

Someone else.

Her.

The lights go on one by one, the same every night. She thinks she is so strong, that she has won. That she has beaten me.

Arrogant, traitorous creatures. I gave them both life. And they repay me with death?

Well, they screwed up. They thought they had me.

They were wrong.

I will take back what is mine. Maybe tonight. Maybe tomorrow. Maybe a year from now. Who knows. Just when they think life is perfect, I will strike.

Until then, I will watch.

I like to watch.

Acknowledgments

I owe the deepest debt of gratitude to a number of people—friends, coworkers, family, acquaintances, and strangers:

Thank you to my entire team at Curtis Brown, Amazon Publishing, and Over the River PR. You make this all so much fun!

To the booksellers, librarians, readers, influencers, and everyone in between who make this the best job on earth—I am so humbled by your everlasting support.

Thank you to Heather O'Conner, Tammy Boone, David Lemke, and Cathy and Bruce Esworthy for your exceptionally generous donations to have your names featured as characters in this novel. I hope you love your fictional selves.

Ariel, Laura, Patti, Lisa, Marybeth, Mom, Dad, Jay, Jeff: You all had a hand in getting this one to the finish line. You are the best.

My dearest Jameson, the ghost kitten, who brought this story to me on her last night, is beyond missed. Her sister Jordan has filled the void, and I love you both.

And my darling Randy, the best friend and husband in the world. This one is, as always, for you.

About the Author

Photo © 2023 Kidtee Hello Photography

J.T. Ellison is the *New York Times* and *USA Today* bestselling author of more than thirty psychological thrillers and domestic noir novels, as well as the Emmy Award–winning cohost of *A Word on Words* on Nashville PBS. She also writes contemporary fantasy as Joss Walker, whose titles include the award-winning Jayne Thorne, CIA Librarian series. With millions of books sold across thirty countries, her work has earned critical acclaim, prestigious awards, and multiple TV options.

J.T. lives with her husband and twin kittens—one of whom is a ghost—in Nashville, where she's busy crafting her next suspenseful tale.